PRAISE FOR ARK OF THE APOCALYPSE

I'm absolutely spellbound. This author knows how to put together a good story and his writing is exquisite. It is all too easy to get absorbed into the world he has created.

—Jenny M: "Amazing" -5 Stars

In reading *Ark of the Apocalypse* by Tobin Marks, I find his world building to be masterful.

—JP: "A Must Read" -5 Stars

I read this book cover to cover in one day and will probably do again. I'm excited for the next installment in the series to see what will come next.

—Terry Thibodeau: "Could Not Put It Down" -5 Stars

I couldn't put this book down as the weaving of history, science and dreams kept me turning the pages. I eagerly await the next installment of Tobin Marks' *The Magellan II Chronicles*.

—Vernice Aure (Author): "Mesmerizing" -5 Stars

This is a fast paced , action packed captivating novel. It is nothing short of spectacular. The author's story telling ability is magnificent. His characters are well developed, likable and believable.

—Karen Pessoa (Author): "Spectacular" -5 Stars

I was unable to put it down. This was very well written and the plot was extremely well thought out. If you enjoy Sci Fi, fantasy books this is definitely the one for you.

—Olivia Palloc (Author): "So Intriguing" -5 Stars

There are so many different and vital themes in this book. I find it surprising that someone had the nerve to take them on, especially in one book. Tobin Marks superbly accomplishes this and deserves an award for his recognition of them.

—Monika Martin (Author): "Epic" -5 Stars

Ark of the APOCALYPSE

TOBIN MARKS

THE MAGELLAN II
CHRONICLES

Boyle
&
Dalton

Book Design & Production:
Boyle & Dalton
www.BoyleandDalton.com

Paperback ISBN: 978-1-63337-237-5
E-Book ISBN: 978-1-63337-276-4

Printed in the United States of America
1 3 5 7 9 10 8 6 4 2

FOR THE FIRST PERSON TO BELIEVE THAT
I SHOULD BELIEVE IN MYSELF

RIP C.P.

PROLOGUE

GREEN AMBER
WEKSAL, NORWAY

D ancing across the frigid afternoon sky, the aurora borealis lit up the winter solstice of 1936. On this, the shortest day of the year, daylight lasted a scant four hours in the village of Weksal, Norway, and as its last light faded, the aurora glimmered its dying witchery in the icicles hanging above the front window of the Konrad Knudsen household.

The chief editor of the local paper topped off his cup with steaming tea and set the copper kettle back down on a 100-year-old wood-burning stove. Beneath thick bristled brows his deeply lined eyes constantly watched the road; he peeled the curtain back from the frosted window every few minutes, nervously stroking his greying beard.

As he did every day, Konrad awaited the most anticipated event of the day, and like clockwork, he soon heard the icy clatter of sled runners as they made their way down the poorly lit street. The old mail sled crunched to a halt in front of his house, and within seconds the uneven footfalls of heavy boots came tromping up his shoveled walkway. Normally it was a comforting sound, but today was different. Today his anxiety was rewarded as two sets of boots approached his house, but only one returned to the sled. His throat dry gulped as the mail runner's sled resumed its clattering trek down his frozen street, leaving that second set standing at his front door.

Konrad sucked in a nervous breath when the door chimed. After a moment's hesitation he reached out, turned the latch, and cracked open the door. As soon as he saw the visitor, he exhaled. A genuine smile found his face as he recognized the bundled-up man brushing tiny ice crystals from his heavy coat.

"You gave me a start, Anatoly. What are you doing here?" Konrad asked, looking past his visitor to see if anyone else was there.

"I came to visit an old friend," replied Anatoly Yanbeyev, "and see about that item we discussed the last time we spoke." Anatoly's green eyes were bright, and his full brown beard, dusty with snow, was showing streaks of grey.

"Two years is a long time, and I'm afraid it's as cold here as it is back home. Please come in." Konrad, or Leon Trotsky as he was known back in Russia, opened the door and ushered his old friend inside. "Although, I believe my next home will be much warmer."

"Mexico, I hear," Anatoly mused, pulling the wool cap from his head, "and warm may not describe it. I would say hot."

"Yes, but it's getting hot here too, my friend." Trotsky took Anatoly's coat and hung it on a rack next to the iron stove. "Too hot for me, and I'm sad to say, too hot for anyone who knows me."

Anatoly grimaced. "The wind whispers louder every day, but I pay no attention."

Trotsky's back went rigid. "No attention? Listen to me, Anatoly; the whispers are screams outside of Russia. How can you be so naïve? Almost the entire General Staff has been executed. Tens of thousands of soldiers as well, and anyone even remotely connected to the 'Revolution Betrayal' is in danger." Out of habit, Trotsky pulled the window curtain aside and glanced outside. "You should leave Sevastopol while you still can. The net is being cast wide, and everything caught in it quickly disappears."

"The Yanbeyev family has been in Crimea since Tartars first arrived almost 500 years ago," Anatoly said resolutely, "and we won't disappear anytime soon."

"Are you blind, Anatoly?" Trotsky's features darkened with exasperation. "Ukraine is far from safe. Stalin has starved millions to death. Do you really think that your little jewelry shop will go unnoticed?"

"Metallurgy shop," corrected Anatoly, waving his hand in dismissal. "So, do you have it?"

Trotsky sighed, nodded, and walked over to a bureau near the kitchen door. He returned with something wrapped in a handkerchief. "Of course, I know a Norwegian geologist who owes me, so I saved it for you." He handed over the small item. "What's so special about this green rock that you're willing to risk your life for?"

Anatoly studied the object before answering the question. A satisfied gleam found his eyes. "Leon, this *rock* means everything to me. It's the catalyst for my life's work, and this, my friend, is a perfect specimen of green amber. It feels about twenty grams, and maybe ten centimeters long. I can make two settings from it."

"Although I'm glad to oblige, I don't understand your obsession with this." The curtain lifted a second time in as many minutes. Trotsky stiffened. His face drained of blood as he stepped back from the frosted window. "There're two men standing at the corner across the street." His voice dropped to barely a whisper. "They weren't there when you arrived. Here, take your jacket. Leave out the back alley and stay in the shadows until you're well away from here."

"You've become rather paranoid, Leon," Anatoly said as he shook the other man's hand. He stuffed the handkerchief in his coat pocket, and he slipped out the back door. Before disappearing into the freezing night, he turned and said, "You'll see. We'll be fine. You go get sunburned in Mexico, and I'll keep my little shop to give to my son."

CHAPTER ONE

THE MEDALLIONS
SEVASTOPOL, CRIMEA

M any items were almost impossible to get in the Soviet Union, and it took five more years for Anatoly to finally get the last element he needed: an unusual metal from a meteorite found near Tunguska. During that time he'd also acquired two grams of red amber from the Baltic Sea that he inlayed into the green. Now that he had everything, it was almost finished, just this final setting to mount in place.

Hunched over the sturdy worktable in his austere little shop, Anatoly sat as close as he dared to the heat of the brick kiln. He needed warm nimble fingers to finish his creation, his life's obsession. While his hand reached for the intricately carved setting his memory recalled his friend's long-ago warning, but the NKVD had not visited him. The same couldn't be said for Trotsky. Anatoly was saddened to hear that a Soviet agent had murdered his old friend in Mexico City. Bashed his head in with an ice pick. Subtlety was never their strong point.

The metallurgist had worked for months on two almost identical medallions. Oval shaped, they were ten centimeters long, six wide, and the reddish metal was forged into the outline of two eyes—dragon eyes—a right and a left, one for each branch of the family. The green iris and red pupils were the perfect center point of each.

Looking down at his work, Anatoly decided it was time to complete the process and transform them into far more than simple jewelry. Each medallion fit perfectly as he placed them into his own eye sockets, shoving the amber against his pupils. Ignoring the discomfort, he concentrated on his family's extraordinary preternatural Path. He knew his own ability was limited but felt there was enough to infuse the medallions. They grew warm in seconds, and then hot. Burning pain threatened to overwhelm his senses, and he briefly wondered if the heat would blind him. But the pain soon gave way to something else: visions flooded his mind.

Time disappeared. Anatoly fell into a trance. Images flashed in and out of focus, confusing things. He saw a planet of fire, another of water, and most bewildering of all was a young woman who turned into a dragon. There was something oddly familiar about her, and at first he couldn't place it, but then it hit him: she wore one of the medallions. He watched her for what seemed like centuries, but after an undetermined amount of time the visions disappeared, and the medallions grew cold. He removed them from his eyes and reverently laid them on the worktable.

Rubbing his eyes, Anatoly wondered just what he had created.

He soon shook the odd feeling as he thought about his son and smiled. *Won't little Tadeas be surprised when he gets one of these on his tenth birthday?* He was proud of his son, a seventh-generation male.

The boy was special in many ways.

"Anatoly! Can you tear yourself away for one moment to eat some borscht with your family?" implored his wife, Tatyana. Her tall slim figure filled the rough-hewn doorframe to his shop as she chastised him.

"The children would like to see their father once in a while, and I need my husband to watch the little ones tonight."

"Tanya, what's so important about tonight?" he asked. Suddenly an overwhelming sense of dread swept over him. He quickly put his tools away, tucked the medallions into a small pouch, and hid them under his small foot-pedaled lathe.

Hands on narrow hips, his blond wife tapped her foot as he appeared out of the gloom of his small workshop and shook her head. "You know I have to go back to the hospital tonight for another shift."

"Can't they find another doctor to work twenty hours a day?" he asked, dropping his eyes so as not to see her withering glare. It was a nightly ritual.

"Almost all the doctors have been conscripted into the army," she reminded him, "and the Nazis are closing in, so why do I have to keep reminding you?"

"I know, I know, Hitler's coming one day, but he's not here yet, so can't you just stay home tonight?" The feeling of dread he'd had earlier turned to outright fear as his eyes first darted toward his wife, and then to the front door. Something was coming.

It was the unmistakable sound of marching boots.

"It can't be for us." His assurance sounded weak, even to himself. "We've had nothing to do with the collaborators." The moment he said it, he knew they were in danger.

The boots stopped in front of their home, and orders were barked. The pounding of rifle butts on their front door stopped him in his tracks.

Anatoly waved at the children to go to the back of their modest home. Once they were safely away from the door, he opened it. It took a moment before his eyes adjusted to the darkness, but soon the unmistakable shape of soldiers and the glint of moonlight on gun barrels sent a chill down his spine.

"Anatoly Yanbeyev!" shouted the officer wearing thick shoulder boards, a drab olive uniform, and a scornful look on his whiskered face. "The People's Commissariat for Internal Affairs has charged you with subversion." He motioned for his men to enter the house. They were armed with rifles and clubs. "You have two minutes to gather what few belongings you can carry and come with us."

"But—but, we've done nothing wrong!" protested Anatoly.

A rifle butt clubbed the back of his head, driving him to his knees. "You're a stinking Tat, and that's all that counts," the officer spat at the dazed man, "and you now have less than two minutes. I suggest you get off the dirt and start moving. You wouldn't want your pretty wife to watch you get beaten to a pulp, would you?" he sneered, looking her up and down.

"I'm a doctor at the hospital," she said sharply, "and there's a siege around the city. How can you—" The slap across her mouth ended the protest.

"And now you'll be a doctor somewhere else," his eyes shifted menacingly toward the children, "somewhere far away from here. Consider yourself lucky that your trip isn't a short one."

His soldiers snickered. Everyone knew that executions had targeted the Tartars in recent weeks.

"Quick, children, gather your things." Tatyana began rushing around the little house throwing clothes into the one well-worn suitcase that they owned.

Anatoly groggily stood up and lurched into his workshop. "Stop, you fucking Tat! Stay out of there!" the officer shouted.

But he didn't stop. Couldn't. The fate of future generations depended on what he did in the next few seconds.

Anatoly had just reached the lathe and grabbed the small leather pouch when the shot rang out. The bullet tore through his back and punched out his chest, spinning him around. He was flung across the room where he crashed into sheets of metal stacked against the wall. Tatyana was instantly at his side. "You fool," she cried, trying to stanch the flow of blood pouring out his chest, "What were you thinking?"

He reached up with a bloody hand, grabbed at her high collar, and dropped the blood-stained pouch into her blouse. "Y-you must give one of these to Sasha on his t-tenth birthday," he begged with his last breaths, "S-say you will—" she heard his wheezing plea as he died on the dirt floor of his shop.

"You bastards!" she screamed. "He was a good man, and never once said anything against the state." She was sobbing when a rough hand grabbed her hair and dragged her back into the living area, where the children were now wailing.

"Well, that's one less Tat," chuckled the officer, brutally shoving Tatyana into the dirt. "I suggest that you get a move on if you don't want your kids to become orphans, or worse, this night."

Somehow she managed to stifle any more tears as she raced to grab the few things she could think of. "Come children, now!" With one hand she held the small case that carried all their possessions, and with the other she held the hand of her son, who in turn grabbed the hand of his five-year-old sister. Her swollen green eyes briefly darted to the crumpled form of her husband in the only other room in their home, and then she ran out the door.

They were unceremoniously marched to the waterfront where a dingy trawler waited and thrown below deck amid the stench of an overflowing bilge, and the fear of other Tartar families. Tatyana had no idea where they were going as she held her two frightened children close.

CHAPTER TWO

ENEMY OF THE STATE
TASHKENT, UZBEKISTAN

The devastated family was exiled from the besieged city of Sevastopol, and though the invading Nazi Luftwaffe sank many of the fleeing ships, their little boat escaped. Along with thousands of other forced immigrants they were eventually dumped into the port city of Sochi, Russia, where they could hear the weapons of war thundering in the distance.

Like cattle they were herded into filthy boxcars and headed east. No one knew their destination, but the crowded train cars were rife with rumors—Uzbekistan. They eventually reached the Caspian Sea, where they were loaded onto a stinking fishing boat, sailed across the sea, and put on another rickety train. After traveling several more days they arrived at Tashkent. It was here that they were dumped into an internment camp that became their home for the next five years.

While they took up residence, first in a ramshackle hut, and later in a communal apartment, the war raged on in Europe. On June 21st, the year Nazi Germany fell, Tadeas turned ten years old, and Tatyana, honoring her husband's dying wish, gave her son one of the dragon eye medallions.

After the war Tatyana had hoped that they would be allowed to return to Crimea, but it was not to be. She was ethnic Russian, and guilty of marrying a Tartar and having his children. That it had been an arranged marriage meant nothing. Both Tadeas and his younger sister, Irina, grew tall like their mother, towering over the local kids. They also spoke with a strong accent, and for this crime they were shunned and bullied by the local kids. Even the Tartars who'd arrived with them kept their distance. It was a bad time to be a Russian refugee in Uzbekistan.

Tatyana Yanbeyeva eventually got a job at the Tashkent hospital, but not as a doctor. She spent the next two years scrubbing floors and cleaning bedpans.

The Soviet attitude toward the Tartars eased after the war, and along with this new attitude came a new director of the hospital. Tatyana eventually got an interview with him and explained that she had been a doctor before the war but had no proof of it. Her diploma had been left the night her husband was killed, and without proof, she was nothing more than a floor scrubber.

Soon after the interview the new director sent away to Moscow to try to get her records from the university. After six months, they finally arrived, and he called her into his office. She walked in and froze when she saw what was sitting on his desk.

"Tanya, I have good news for you." He gestured that she take a seat in one of the office chairs. It was the first time she had ever been invited to sit while talking to an administrator. "These are your transcripts from Moscow."

"And they prove that I really am a doctor?" she timidly asked.

"Yes," he patted them, "they do."

"Then, I can begin to practice?" Her hopes were rising fast. "Here?"

"No, unfortunately, you would never be allowed to practice here. You're a Christian woman, and this is a Muslim culture." He saw her crestfallen face and quickly added, "But there's another place, in Russia, that has a pressing need for a doctor."

Her face lit up again. "I'll take it, Director!"

He gave her an indulgent look. "I was hoping you'd say that, but you must be aware that this village is remote, in a rather primitive part of eastern Siberia."

"Eastern Siberia! That's the end of the world," she blurted out, and then clamped her hand over her mouth.

"I'm afraid that's the best I could do," he said. "This is still the Soviet Union, and you *were* ejected from Crimea for sedition."

"But we did nothing," she protested. "My husband was innocent, and he—"

"Was an enemy of the state!" snapped the director. She jerked back as if struck and stifled her growing panic, but his voice soon lost its harshness. She was a doctor, after all. His next words were softer. "Yes, I know all about it, and though it isn't fair," he conceded, "guilt or innocence never had anything to do with it."

She sat there with her hands folded tightly in her lap and kept quiet.

"So, Dr. Yanbeyeva, if you accept, then you should go home and pack right away." He stood up, indicating that the meeting was now over. "I'll arrange for you and your children to leave on tomorrow's train, and accommodations for when you arrive."

She couldn't believe her ears, and wanted to cry for joy, but instead quietly said, "Thank you, Director. If I may ask, where are we going?"

"Somewhere on the Kamchatka Peninsula." A slight wrinkle creased his brow. "What's that name again?" he wondered out loud while tracing the form with his finger. "Oh yes, here it is. It's called Koryak."

———————————————

Two hundred miles above the Arctic Circle sits the frozen city of Norilsk, where the sun disappears for two months a year, and winter temperatures never rise above 30 degrees below zero. Each year in this frigid world of forgotten souls thousands of inmates perished working the mines at the gulag known as Stalin's Siberian Hell. They were mostly political prisoners from Ukraine and lived in squalid conditions. Internment at this corrective labor camp was usually a death sentence; few prisoners ever left alive.

In the spring of 1950, a rare event was about to take place at Norilsk. "Andrei Yanbeyev!" the guard yelled across the ice-covered prison yard. A filthy denizen dressed in rags stood out from the other prisoners. They'd shuffled away from him. It was never a good idea to be close to someone the guards wanted.

He'd known for years that this day was coming.

"Yes, I am Andrei Yanbeyev," said the shivering inmate. He resembled a wild beast more than a man. "How can I be of service, comrade?"

The guard looked disdainfully at this smelly sack of skin and bones and said, "You are to report to the infirmary right away. Follow me." He marched away. Hobbling as fast as he could, the prisoner barely kept up as he was led out of the yard, down a path lined with ice-encrusted barbed wire to a set of unpainted brick buildings, and finally into a drab waiting room. It was the warmest Andrei had been in years.

It took an hour, but Andrei was finally ushered into a large cot-filled room that smelled of decay and disinfectant. The prison doctor took one look at the miserable apparition smelling up his infirmary and demanded, "Who the hell are you, and what are you doing here?"

"I was sent for, comrade Doctor," the creature whispered through unkempt whiskers, "and I don't know why I'm here," he lied.

The doctor looked down at his chart and scrunched his face in confusion. "*You* are Dr. Andrei Yanbeyev?" Then he added with distaste, "Surely not?"

"I-I was," Andrei stammered as he thought about his distant past, "before the war, you see, before I-I was sent h-here."

"Well, now you're being sent somewhere else," the doctor said scornfully, and turned his back on the newly freed man. "Far from here."

The next day the prisoner was free for the first time in almost a decade. Upon release he was given cheap shoes and a blanket and put on a train.

Andrei's life work was here at last. The gathering of the family was about to begin, and they needed a guide on their Path. The train headed east.

CHAPTER THREE

TERROR IN THE NIGHT
FUKUOKA, JAPAN

S tanding over a grimy workbench inside an inconspicuous two-story wooden building, the two men couldn't have presented a starker contrast in appearance. The small elderly Japanese man was balding and slightly stooped but had an efficient energy about him. He wore a stained lab coat and bamboo sandals. Towering over him, his much younger companion's starched demeanor seemed to belie the civilian clothes he wore. "Dr. Mizushima-san," said the tall German officer, "I'm afraid our operation must now be terminated."

"But, I have a working model," protested the scientist. "All I need is more electricity to make a larger device." He pointed at the bowl-shaped object on his lab table. "With a bigger device we could disrupt and even destroy these B-29 fire raids." He looked back at the man he only knew as Herr Müller. The German just shook his blond head, a dejected look on his chiseled features. "You can take the design back to Germany and stop the Americans there as well."

"There is no Germany to go back to," Müller muttered bitterly. "Hitler is dead, and in a few days we will fall to either the Russians or the Americans. Probably both." He took a deep breath and looked down at the object on the table. "So, this is Tesla's design, and you say it actually works?"

"Yes, Herr Müller, all I need is more power. It requires a tremendous amount of electricity, and, alas, I can only provide a small amount." He pointed to a small diesel generator in the corner of the lab.

"The generator was the size you asked for, Mizushima-san."

"You misunderstand," the doctor said, "the generator is not the issue." Seeing the German frown, the doctor explained his problem, his country's problem. "I don't have enough fuel to run it for very long."

"Do you have any fuel left?"

"Only enough for a few seconds."

"May I see it run?" asked Müller. "If it works, then maybe after the war," he shrugged, "who knows?" He glanced around the room as if he could be overheard. "It's being whispered in Germany that many scientists have already fled for America. Maybe the Americans will use it against the Russians, and all this will not have been in vain."

"Yes, why not?" Dr. Mizushima moved closer to the device and called over his shoulder to a grease-smudged little boy, "Aito, start the generator, and stand by the magnetic transfer switch." The boy scampered over to do his grandfather's bidding.

"You have a child for an assistant?" the German asked incredulously.

"I'm afraid it's only the elderly and the children who are left." The old man's voice quaked as he explained. "An entire generation of our young men are gone—dead, or soon will be." He connected two rubber-coated copper cables to their transmission posts and called to the boy, "Okay, Aito, start the generator."

The lab filled with sound as the diesel generator roared to life. "Now, Aito, engage the transfer switch." The boy flipped a wooden handle, and the bowl-shaped device began emitting an electronic humming sound. The doctor turned three knobs, and the hum became a piercing whine.

The device lifted off the table amid arcs of electricity and hovered steadily two meters in the air. The doctor adjusted more knobs, and the device moved in a circular pattern around the lab. The generator soon sputtered and went silent. As it died, the device crashed and broke into several pieces.

In spite of its brief flight and untimely demise, Dr. Mizushima looked down at it with pride. He glanced over at the German who was standing with his mouth agape.

"It works!" said the excited German. "It really works."

Dr. Mizushima gave a slight bow. "If only we had more time and more fuel, we might have won the war. But now," he said grimly, "the Americans have both the fuel and the resources to complete my," he paused and awkwardly bowed again, "our work here." He briefly closed his eyes. "It seems ironic, doesn't it, Herr Müller?"

"What's that?"

The doctor closely inspected a damaged piece of coil as he explained to Müller. "We're going to give this to the country that has destroyed both our own."

"Not give, Mizushima-san; sell it to them." A small smile crossed the German's face. "And better them than the Soviets."

Early summer in the Mariana Islands is miserably hot. There's little rain, and the humidity is stifling. In January of 1945, the U.S. Army Air Corps had given overall command of the 21st Bomber Command to an officer whose edgy temper was legendary, and by June, General Curtis LeMay was ready to ignite.

The civilian sweated profusely under his Hawaiian shirt as he sat in the general's office fanning himself. In spite of the heat he sat calmly across from the khaki-clad officer, the man expected an outburst at any time, but if LeMay intimidated him, it didn't show.

The general eyed him warily, and asked, "Just what is it that you want, Mr. Smith?"

Mr. Smith placed a manila envelope on the desk, with TOP SECRET stamped in red, and slid it toward LeMay. "You'll want to read this right away, General."

The general bit down hard on his smoldering cigar and grumbled, "Doesn't Washington think I have better things to do?"

"No, they don't," said an expressionless Mr. Smith.

"I'm winning this goddamned war without their interference," LeMay fumed as his face darkened, "and I don't need more political target requests, I need more goddamned B-29s!"

Smith's emotionless eyes blinked once.

"All right, I'll look at it when I get the goddamned time," the general growled in dismissal.

"Sir, my orders are to remain in your presence until you've read it." Smith looked the general straight in the eye. "So we can discuss any questions you might have."

"That so?" said the general and shifted his cigar from one side of his mouth to the other. He grunted disapproval, and then picked up the envelope and ripped it open. After a few seconds of reading it his eyebrows rose, and Curtis LeMay was rarely surprised. "You mean to tell me that the old man actually signed this?" he demanded.

"And handed it to me personally."

LeMay's head barely moved as he squinted at the orders from top to bottom. After a minute his eyes flashed up, and he shook his head. "Our new President wants me to divert my war-winning assets to fire-bomb a goddamned city that has zero military value?" Nothing pissed off LeMay like interference from Washington, and this latest set of orders was the most intrusive so far. "Doesn't Truman know that there's a POW camp there?"

"The President has been advised about Omuta 17, sir, but as you can see, there are extenuating circumstances."

"Extenuating! And did this *advice* tell him that they're asking me to bomb my own captured aircrews?"

"Sir, as you can see, the POW camp is almost thirty miles away from the target area."

"This mission statement says this is to be a nighttime raid." LeMay was building up to a full lather. "Do you have any idea how easy and often it is for a bomber to stray thirty miles on a night raid?"

The man in the Hawaiian shirt was unmoved. "Sir, this could affect the outcome of the war."

"By bombing civilians nowhere close to any military target?"

"We have reliable evidence that a secret Japanese-German weapons program is almost ready for introduction," he told the disbelieving general, "and it could be a game changer, sir."

"A game changer? Goddammit! Has the White House lost its mind? Germany surrendered eight weeks ago, and Japan is teetering on the brink of collapse now. The game *is* all but over, Mr. Smith."

"With all due respect, sir, the White House wants this weapons program taken out, and taken out now."

"What's the big rush? Can't Washington wait until more of the Japanese military infrastructure has been destroyed?" LeMay turned to his main point. "We're looking at a probable invasion here, Mr. Smith, one that could cost a million U.S. dead. It's my job to reduce that number by taking out military targets, not defenseless pockets of civilians."

Mr. Smith locked eyes with the obstinate general, lowered his voice, and said, "The Soviets are also aware of this weapons system."

"How?"

"They captured a huge cache of German documentation recently, and this project was the most clandestine in the German-Japanese cooperation network." He stood up and leaned on the general's desk. "Japan will be a chaotic mess after the war, and there's no way to definitively eliminate this weapon unless we bomb it now." He bent over the desk to press his point. "Are you starting to see the big picture now, General?"

"Fine, fucking fine. If they want yet another defenseless Japanese city firebombed, then I'll send my boys in to do it." Still holding the cigar, he stabbed at the orders with his index finger, dropping hot ash onto the paper. "And wipe Fukuoka off the map."

In the evening of June 19th, 1945, 136 B-29 bombers took off for three different Japanese cities. An hour before midnight one of the flights unleashed their incendiary bombs on the sleepy seaside town of Fukuoka, and less than thirty minutes later half its paper and bamboo buildings were a raging inferno.

Terror had come in the night.

"Papa-san!" cried little Aito, "I hear thunder. Is a storm coming?"

Dr. Mizushima's head jerked up, panic gripped him, and he raced to his lab yelling at his wife to go to the nearest air raid station. "Take Aito and go! There's no time to lose. We may have only a minute before they get here."

"Husband, you must come too!" she implored him. "This is madness. You're just trying to protect one of your crazy inventions."

The old man squeezed his eyes shut and hesitated for a split second, but desperation drove his next move. Gripping both sides of his head, he yelled, "I'll be along soon, but you must go now!" The moment his little family fled to the bomb shelter, he ran to the workshop and began tearing at its floorboards.

The small house jumped when a bomb exploded across the street, followed by a horrific boom. The walls in his workshop blew apart, piercing him with slivers of bamboo. He wiped away the blood, now streaming down his face, and frantically pulled aside the last floorboard until the meter-wide steel door lay exposed. He grabbed for the handle just as another bomb blew away the rest of his house, spreading burning napalm everywhere.

The stench of his own flaming skin gagged him, and he screamed in agony, but his resolve was single-minded. Mizushima threw the anti-gravity device along with his notebook down the metal shaft. He grabbed the heavy metal handle, cooking his palm on the red-hot steel, and slammed it down just as another bomb exploded. Fire devoured him as the shock wave blew his blazing body a dozen meters, breaking his neck against a neighbor's stone wall.

On that night of terror only two people made it to the neighborhood bomb shelter. Seven weeks later, those two were picking through the charred rubble where their village once stood. They found nothing. No building, no person remained. All had been consumed. Aito and his grandmother had survived the raid, but surviving the aftermath was not assured. There was almost nothing for them to eat, but Aito's tiny grey-headed grandmother made sure the boy had something to eat each day, even if it meant going without herself. The old lady's world was gone—she wanted to die, and the only thing that kept her from ending the pain was her commitment to the boy.

One day an hour before noon they sat in the shade of a scorched stone wall, and as Aito prepared to eat that day's meager meal, a bright flash suddenly lit up the sky. "Obaasan, what was that?" asked the little boy, pointing in the direction of the flash.

"I'm not sure, little one, but it came from the direction of Nagasaki."

CHAPTER FOUR

HOLES IN THE GROUND
KORYAK, RUSSIA

Tatyana slammed back into her body, gasping for breath. Hesitating a moment before daring to open her eyes, she gripped the armrests of the chair and stood up. The widow had been out on her daily astral projection when she'd spotted a man walking only a few kilometers away. He was bedraggled, used a threadbare blanket as a coat, and looked almost exactly like her dead husband.

It was like seeing a ghost.

She ran out to the porch and watched the village's deep-rutted dirt road for any sign of his approach. Tatyana wasn't sure how she felt about his unannounced visit. It had been over a decade since she'd last laid eyes on him, and then, only the one time. It was the day she'd married his twin brother.

Despite her qualms, the moment Tatyana saw him trudging up the road she hurried back into their rough-hewn wooden house that also served as the clinic. "Children," she called out near the door of the rustic building, "come meet your father's brother, Uncle Andrei."

Not knowing how to feel about his unannounced arrival trepidation gripped her. What is he doing here? So it was with some relief when she noted his obvious embarrassment at his scruffy appearance. She watched him stop short and hang his head. His dirty brown hair hung limp across his face. After a moment he pulled the tattered cap from his head, pushed his filthy hair aside, and approached. Standing next to her the children watched him with distrust written on their faces.

Like a supplicant he held his cap to his chest with both hands, cleared his throat, and said, "Hello, Tanya. It's been too long, and who are these two handsome kids?"

"This is Tadeas and Irina." She gently pushed them forward so he could get a better look at his brother's children, the only family he had left.

The family he had come to guide, especially the boy.

"You can call me dyadya Andrei," said the gaunt man. He dropped his patched travel bag to the ground and squatted down to look his niece and nephew in the eye.

"You look like my dada," the blue-eyed little girl shyly said as she scooted back behind her mother.

"Why are you dressed like that?" the boy boldly demanded. His eyes flashed green ferocity as he stepped protectively in front of his mom and sister. "And why are you here?"

"Tadeas!" scolded his mother. "You treat your uncle with respect."

"I-I've been—" Andrei dropped his eyes, "going through a rough patch."

"Never mind the boy," Tatyana offered, glaring at her son. "Come into the house and eat some dinner. You look like you haven't eaten in days."

"True enough," he answered gratefully.

Tatyana led them into the small one-room house and set the table with bread, borscht, and fresh cucumbers. "This is all we have, Andrei, but you're welcome to it."

The starving man sat at the table shaking with hunger. He'd barely eaten since leaving prison, and not every day. "Thank you, Tanya. I didn't know how you'd feel about me showing up here like this."

"Nonsense, Andrei, you're family." She spoke the right words, but her expression hardened when she looked him straight in the eye. "But

I really do want to know what's happened to you, and why you're here."

Andrei set down his wooden spoon and went still. He finally braved a glance, but couldn't meet the vigor of her green eyes, so much like her son's. Andrei looked back at the table. "Prison, Tanya. I spent the last six years in a gulag, and I only found out you were here when they released me. They sent me here, but to be truthful—it's where I'm meant to be."

"Why were you in prison?" she pressed.

"For the same reason they murdered Anatoly, and sent you away: because we're Tartars." He finally glanced up, meeting her eyes with a hint of defiance. "As for why I'm here—the same reason you are. We're both doctors, and the Soviets need us in this remote region. What better way to exile us Tats than to send us to the end of the world and use our skills at the same time." He spread his thin arms out, then decided it was time for the whole truth. "But there's another reason."

"There always is."

"This is where we, the family, will grow strong. Far from prying eyes." His own swept the table, locking onto the boy. "And prepare the Path for our progeny."

"I see," she said. "But what I don't get is why, all of a sudden, the Soviets want medical services in a region they've ignored until now?"

"Gold," he said, shifting the focus away from the family. He reached for another slice of bread. "And platinum. Mines, dearest sister." She smiled at his use of the endearing term. Andrei flushed and looked away before continuing. "And the miners who'll soon come to dig those deep holes in the ground. They'll need medical attention, and that, Dr. Yanbeyeva, is why we're here."

"But this small hut is all there is, Andrei. It's both the clinic and our home."

Andrei looked around the meager dwelling. "Tanya, this little shack is just the beginning. Together we'll build a medical community second to none, and those two," he beamed at the two wide-eyed children, "we'll send to the university in Vladivostok, where they too will become doctors, and return to help build a family legacy that will last for more than a millennium."

She got up and began cleaning up after the meal, then suddenly stopped as a frown found her face. "Andrei, there is no medical university in Vladivostok."

"Oh you of little faith. By the time these two are of college age there will be."

"How can you be so sure?" demanded Tadeas.

"A little bird told me, young man." Uncle Andrei's eyes twinkled.

"A bird with a *vision*, Andrei?" teased Tanya.

The family's newest member just laughed.

Uncle Andrei's words proved accurate. Within twenty years Koryak had become an important mining district. Thousands were sent to work the mines, and with them came the machines needed to dig deep into the rocky formations. Tatyana's little hut was eventually replaced with a much larger hospital, and once Tadeas graduated from the newly established medical university at Vladivostok, he returned home to join the medical staff. He eventually married someone Andrei chose for him and eventually had five kids. After graduation Irina stayed and joined a clinic in Vladivostok, where she married a man of her choosing and raised a family. Though Irina's abilities were weaker than her brother's, what she did have was passed on to her own children, many of whom became doctors, and relocated to the small village in the woods.

The preternatural legacy of Koryak had begun.

CHAPTER FIVE

THE BOX
FUKUOKA, JAPAN

L ittle Aito and his grandmother lived in the rubble that was once their home for almost a year before dwellings were finally provided. Reconstruction was slow to come, but the Nagasaki prefecture gradually rebuilt, and replaced the wartime weapons manufacturing industry with one focused on foreign trade. Almost all of the neighbors who lived near the Mizushima house were killed the same night as Aito's grandfather, and much of the land where their homes once stood now lay unclaimed.

There was only one thing of value that had survived the firebombing. No adult even knew it existed, because the doctor had never said a word about it. Not even to his wife; but the boy remembered. One day he was rummaging through the rubble when he uncovered the scorched metal cover buried where his grandfather's lab once stood.

"Obaasan!" he called out to his grandmother. "Come see what I've found." She ambled over to where the boy was pulling at the lid. "It's too heavy for me, Obaasan, help me lift it."

Although she was never allowed to know its contents, she instinctively knew that this was what her husband had died trying to protect. Pulling her tattered black obi tight, she ordered the boy, "Come away from there, Aito. This is a place of death."

"But, Obaasan," the boy protested, "there might be something of value, something we can sell." He'd seen it many times.

She saw the logic of this but was still reluctant and tried to pull the boy away. Aito squirmed free, ran back to the metal lid, and tried to pull it open by himself. She soon gave in and joined him. "We shouldn't do this, Aito, but maybe there is something we can sell." She grabbed the metal handle, and the two of them began to pull. It took a few hard pulls, but finally, screeching in protest, the lid revealed its secrets. Revulsion engulfed her as she gazed inside. This was what made her a widow.

Aito grew more excited by the moment. He reached down and pulled out the device he had last seen over a year ago, but his grandmother forbade him to keep it. Before obediently placing it back inside, he saw another object. A wooden box sat at the bottom. It was scorched, and the iron lock had corroded to the point of never working again. He'd never seen this box before and begged his grandmother to allow him to look at it. "Just to see what it is, Obaasan, please."

Her husband had been the last person to see inside it, and despite her misgivings, curiosity got the better of her. Both she and the boy reached down and were barely able to lift the fifty-centimeter box. Once they got it to the surface, she took a rock and smashed open the brittle wood. Inside was a leather bag full of metal, and it was heavy. She opened the bag and gasped. It held coins with Nazi swastikas engraved on them.

It was pure gold.

"What is it, Obaasan?" asked the boy when he saw the shock on her face.

"It's the future, Aito," she cried softly. "It's your future."

Within a month she'd bought all the property that surrounded their home. Everything was rubble, and what landowners she could find were eager to sell. She now owned over ten hectares of land and had spent less than half the gold to secure it. The rest was saved for her grandson's education. She owned wasteland now, but knew that one day this land, bought by the gold that had cost her husband's life, would create a future for her family for generations to come.

What she didn't know, what she would never know, was what she left lying beneath that scorched iron lid would help create the future for all of mankind.

Ten years later a large warehouse stood in what had once been a quiet residential neighborhood. At first it was only used to store export goods for the growing foreign trade market. Ten years after that Aito was a man with ambitions, but he knew the warehouse wasn't the most efficient use of this land. When his grandmother had died six years before, she'd willed him everything.

Although small in stature like his grandfather, Aito had boundless energy, and was driven to do more than just store the goods that other companies made. When he turned twenty-six he changed the warehouse from storage to manufacturing. It was the start of the family fortune.

At first, he built cheap toys that America couldn't get enough of. Later he began making small electronic goods that the Americans were even more eager to buy. From small radios and record turntables he eventually graduated to making components for a giant television manufacturer. His little factory couldn't keep up with the demand, so he bought even more land all over the Nagasaki prefecture. By the time he reached fifty he was one of the biggest barons of the revived Japanese economy and ruled over the manufacturing empire of the Mizushima Corporation.

Even though Aito built bigger and more modern factories, he always kept his personal office at the original site where he had lived as a little boy. The site where his grandfather died trying to protect a secret. A secret Aito Mizushima was the only living soul to have personally witnessed, and he knew exactly where it lay buried.

Once, he'd tried to interest his son, but the young man was too wrapped up in the modern world to be interested. Their family business was helping propel Japan into one of the largest economies the world had ever seen, and Aito's son couldn't be bothered with his father's ramblings about some long-lost magical device.

By the time Aito reached seventy years old he knew his time was coming to an end. He'd long since been removed from the workings of the empire he'd created. Often there wasn't anyone for him to talk to but servants, and sometimes, to his great pleasure, his grandson.

Hikaru Mizushima was an extraordinarily bright boy, and loved the tales his doting grandfather told him, especially the one about a flying machine buried underneath the old factory. When Aito died he willed half his assets to Hikaru, including the old factory. But the most valuable thing he willed to his grandson was a dream.

A dream to reach the stars.

As stipulated in the old man's will, until Hikaru graduated from college, his parents would control his inheritance—they'd gotten their share too—but the one thing that Hikaru always kept to himself was a map. The treasure map, his grandfather had called it. It had been their secret.

Instead of fading from his memory, the older Hikaru got, the more vivid those stories became. Finally, when he reached college age he picked the exact subject his grandfather had written down on the map. He remembered the day his grandfather wrote it. When he finished writing Aito told the boy, "This map is the key to the treasure, little one. It will unlock what has been hidden for so long."

"Why didn't you unlock the treasure, Ojiisan?" asked Hikaru.

"Because, mago-musuko, I didn't have the right key." He tapped the words that he had just written on the old map and whispered so only the two of them could hear, "But you will."

When Hikaru first enrolled at the Massachusetts Institute of Technology his mother was indignant. "Why America, Hikaru? MIT is too far away. You should find a university here in Japan," she practically ordered him.

"No, Mama, MIT has the best astrophysics program in the world."

"Old Aito's crazy stories of magic flying ships," she carped bitterly, and slapped the back of her hand into her other palm. "So, manufacturing televisions isn't good enough for you. You want to build rocket ships."

"Rocket ships first, but later I want to build something else, something better."

She hissed, "How can you still believe in those fairytale stories that foolish jijii told you when you were just a child?"

Hikaru's back stiffened. "He believed in those stories, and he believed in me."

A week later the eighteen-year-old left and spent the next ten years in America.

CHAPTER SIX

THE LAST WHALE
SAN FELIPE, MEXICO

"Looks like today's gonna be another scorcher," groused Ringo, wagging two fingers above his sweat-stained ball cap. "We can't even beat the heat here in the shade. Uno mas!" he yelled across the bar.

"Why should today be any different?" answered his drinking buddy. It had become the standard answer for the past several years. Both old-timers wore grimy T-shirts, cargo shorts, and plastic flip-flops. They called it their twelve-year-old uniform, and both snickered morosely as two shots of tequila arrived at their table.

"Yeah, another day over 120 degrees," Ringo said as his empty shot glass hit the table. "What's it been now, like, three years since we had a cool day? You know, a nice pleasant 110."

"What, are you drunk?"

"Get'n there," belched Ringo.

"Hasn't been below 115 since 2027. I think all this agave juice is affecting your short-term memory," said Grundy, and took his turn waving two fingers. "At least there's plenty of tequila to take our minds off it."

"Tequila yes, water no. I jest can't afford them prices they wanna charge for that desalted seawater," Ringo complained. "And they just raised the price to 500 pesos a gallon! Shit, man, a shower costs me almost 1,000 pesos."

"That explains the smell, I reckon."

"Fuck a wildman, Grundy. You ain't no better."

"Aw hell, I just go take a dip in the sea when it gets too bad."

"What? Are you effing loco, man?" Ringo grimaced at his friend. "You can't get in that water. Since the sea come up and submerged downtown, all that water is full of shit and stuff." He knocked back his shot and stuffed a lemon wedge in his mouth. "Nothing can live in that crap."

"Yeah, I know," mumbled Grundy as he scratched his sweat-slicked hairline, "but sometimes I just gotta wash off all that dirt that never seems to stop blowing." He gulped down his shot. "Hell, Ringo, I can't even afford to make a pot of coffee, much less take a shower, and I don't even wanna tell you how shitty it is to take a dump."

They both chuckled as a white van pulled up and parked across the street. "Looks like them college kids are back to study what sea life ain't here no more." Ringo squinted into the glare of the morning sun. "Where's UCSD anyway?"

"That big university in San Diego," answered Grundy. "Just more city folks come to drive up the price of tequila."

"They should stay home and study their own city. Hell, I heard downtown San Diego's underwater now too," groused Ringo as he tried to dig out a lemon seed stuck in his yellow teeth.

"It's not just them. Most of them big California sea view cities lost their beaches."

"Yeah," said Ringo, flicking the offending seed off his finger. "East Coast cities too. I guess all them tourists gotta go to Arizona to find a beach to get sunburned on nowadays."

Grundy just shook his head and yelled at the bar, "Uno mas, por favor!" Then he turned back around to watch the college girls get out of the van.

The van's door slid open as four people—three young women and a young man—got out, grimacing at the intense heat. They all wore sun hats, sunscreen, and unhappy faces. The air conditioner had been running full blast since they left the cooler Pacific side of Baja, but here it was a shock to their systems.

"Jesus, Dr. Martin, couldn't we have waited for a cooler day?" complained a pimpled, gangly young marine biologist wearing a faded blue T-shirt sporting a cartoon killer whale that said, *I'm So Orcward.*

"I did, Randall," replied their team leader, whose dark tan and deep facial wrinkles suggested a life spent on or near the ocean, "and this is as cool as it gets here. You know that. So quit bitching and unload the vans while I go find that charter boat captain." Just before disappearing around a corner she yelled back, "Make sure you stack all the stuff in the shade, and do not for any reason leave it unattended."

The rest of the team began unloading the test equipment from the two vans. It was the third time in the past year that they'd made this trip, and the results weren't encouraging. The rising ocean levels had not only devastated coastal cities around the world, but now they were turning once-thriving marine ecosystems, like the Sea of Cortez, into dead zones.

After they stacked the last of the gear on the shady side of the street next to a closed business, they sat down and waited for Dr. Martin to return.

Wiping sweat from her brow, one of the grad students, a surfer girl with tribal tattoos emblazoned everywhere skin showed, griped to the others, "It's almost as hot in the shade as it is in the sun."

"And it's not going to get any better out on the water," said the other young woman, a tall African American bespeckled with a birthmark starting on one side of her neck and running halfway down her left arm. "I for one am hoping she doesn't want to spend all day out there this time."

"Look, guys, I don't like it any more than you do, but it's gonna take as long as it takes," chastised Randall Burt. The young man's bare hint of facial hair was a shade darker than his shoulder-length ponytail. "We need this data, and we need to record the trends. The only way to do that is hands on."

"Yeah, I get it, Ranz," said the surfer girl, "but we already know that the krill disappeared seven years ago, and the last whale was sighted more than four years ago. Our constantly checking for any change is getting really depressing, especially in this heat. Let's face it, this is a dying sea."

"Dead," cut in the other young woman, "and we're the postmortem team."

Burt frowned under his glasses. "There's a bigger picture here, and we're on the front lines to try to find out if any solution is possible. The rising sea levels are threatening to connect California's Salton Sea with the Sea of Cortez. If that happens then a major agricultural region disappears forever. There's been zero snow pack in the Sierras for ten years, and none in the Rockies for the last three. The Colorado has dried up, as have all the rivers that feed California's Central Valley. San Francisco Bay has flooded into the delta, and the rising water is now threatening Sacramento."

"Cool," mused surfer girl. "I always wanted to surf Sackatomatos."

CHAPTER SEVEN

REGRETTABLE
MOSCOW, RUSSIA

Wearing a grey pinstriped suit, a loose red tie, and a tight frown, Russian President Yuri Volkov sat at his large desk looking down at the damage report. Volkov knew an American response was coming and knew there wasn't much he could do about it, no matter how much he wanted to. "Those damned Iranians," he muttered to himself, "just where the hell did they think this was going to lead?" He slammed his fist down on the report just as a tap sounded on his door. "Da, Borya, what is it?"

His personal advisor walked into the office donning an impeccably tailored suit and his usual scowl. He was a big man with perfectly styled jet-black hair and was the President's oldest friend. "Yuri, the American President is going to be calling you in seven minutes, and we need a prepared response."

"To this?" Volkov jabbed at the report on his desk.

"Of course. What else?"

Volkov stood up. He wore his retreating grey hair slightly long, and even though he wasn't as tall as Borya's two meters, he wasn't considered short. The Russian President went over to the bar and poured two shots of vodka and handed one to Borya. The two drank a toast. "To allies, and other enemies!" Borya said. "So, what are you going to say when the Americans threaten retaliation?"

Volkov returned to his desk, slumped back in his deeply cushioned chair, and shrugged. "The usual." They both knew it wouldn't be enough.

A buzzer sounded. Borya picked it up, nodded at Volkov, uttered one word, "Slushyt," and pointed at the video monitor.

Volkov grunted, pushed the visual button, and put his elbows on the desk. "Good afternoon, Madam President," he said in perfect English. "To what do I owe this pleasure today?"

At sixty-one years old, Abigail Moore looked exactly like the plump brown-eyed white-haired grandmother she was. But no one in the world confused her for a sweet little old lady. "Let's cut the bullshit, Yuri," said the American President. "You know exactly why I'm calling and believe me when I say this is just a courtesy call." For twenty-four years prior to the presidency she'd been a take-no-prisoner senator from Wisconsin's First Congressional District. She had zero intention of taking any today.

"Then let's be courteous to each other, Abby. I know why you are calling, and I was literally just now looking at the report."

"Good, then that'll save us a cock and bull session, and I can get straight to the point. This attack requires a response, and that is exactly what I've ordered."

"Without even discussing it with me?" Volkov's voice rose. "You know I can't allow any military action against Iran. We have a defense pact."

"Like I told you, this is strictly a courtesy call. You have forty-eight hours to get your people in Tehran to safety. After that their lives are on your head." The screen went dark.

"Damn it!" swore Volkov, shoving his chair away from the desk. He turned to Borya. "Call Neely and tell him to get his ass over here right now. We need to keep a channel open, or this thing will escalate beyond our control."

An hour later the American ambassador sat in Volkov's office. A former football player, Neely still had a linebacker's physique that his Savile Row burnt charcoal suit did little to mask. "I've just had what I believe to be a very similar conversation to the one that you did, Mr. President." Neely's usual affable presence was not in play for this meeting. Speaking in a clipped tone, he told the Russian President, "And she's in no mood to negotiate over this." He placed his glass of sparkling water on the expensive teak coffee table, leaned forward, and said, "There's going to be a response. Now, we can sit here and debate this all day, but you know as well as I do that an attack of this magnitude on Israel will always garner a response."

"But your anti-missile defense system, illegal I might add, destroyed all the Iranian missiles aimed at Israel." Volkov threw his hands in the air. "No one was hurt!"

Neely frowned at this cheap tactic. "No one was hurt?" He harshly repeated the words. "There were 117 American and 362 British nationals on those oil platforms killed by this sneak attack."

"Expats who earn twenty times what the locals do," Borya interjected.

"Yeah, well, those high wage earners produced over a million barrels a day," Neely spat out. "I wonder who benefits from that being removed off the world market?"

Volkov smacked his open palm on his desk. It made a loud sound, and his voice rose to match it. "While regrettable, Azerbaijan is not in an American sphere of influence, Mr. Ambassador."

"Regrettable, Mr. President?" Neely was diving into uncharted territory for a career diplomat—losing self-control. "Those were unarmed civilians murdered by your ally! An ally who, I might add, launched this attack at the exact same moment that they did at Israel." He stood up, clenching his fists. Borya slipped his hand into his breast pocket.

"This coordinated attack was carried out to do exactly what is happening now: drive a wedge between Russia and America."

"Perhaps regrettable was a poor choice of words, Mr. Neely." Using a calmer tone, Volkov added, "But nothing is irreversible. Especially if we keep channels open."

Neely walked over to the door, stopped, and turned at these last words. "Let's hope that we can have a similar *'irreversible'* conversation two days hence, Mr. President."

Volkov's voice remained calm, but his meaning didn't. "While I hope that this is the truth of things, if a nuclear weapon is used, then I don't see how it will be possible. Good day, Mr. Ambassador."

As soon as his door closed, Volkov glanced at Borya. "Now what?"

It was a rhetorical question, but Borya answered it anyway. "We watch as the Iranians strangle on the noose they've so insanely placed around their own necks."

"So, we allow our ally, who buys billions of rubles worth of weapons from us every year, to commit suicide?"

"Tochno, Yuri." *Exactly.*

"And if the Americans use nukes?"

Borya brushed it off. "They don't need nukes to turn Tehran into a smoldering pile of rubble." Ever the strategist, he continued, "Look on the bright side."

"What bright side could there possibly be?" Volkov blurted out.

"We get a front row seat watching the Americans' new space-guns in action."

They weren't disappointed. Two days later, as promised, retaliation against Iran was launched. Deep within Cheyenne Mountain, the reactivated NORAD command center was readying America's newest space-based weapons system. The Theater High Orbital Rover, or THOR, now had an orbital path directly over the Persian nation.

A direct line was open between the underground command center and the White House war room. "Madam President," said the commanding Space Force general, "THOR is now fully charged and almost position ready."

"Good to hear, General Braniff," responded his commander in chief. "How long until all 312 shots have complete target acquisition?"

"Sixty-seven percent are presently locked on, and we'll have the remainder in less than five minutes, Madam President."

"And that gives you what—a fourteen-minute window until your orbit is off station?"

"Yes, ma'am, that's correct."

"Stand by." Abigail Moore then spoke with the commander of the second arm of the attack trident. "Admiral Martinez, we need to launch in less than five minutes. Are the Konas on station?"

The answer came from less than ten meters below the Persian Gulf. "Yes, ma'am, we're in firing position now. Once launch is ordered half our SMITE missiles will be underway. They'll take three minutes to reach the target theater."

She turned to the USAF general from the Joint Chiefs staff standing next to her. "General Reed, your B-4 bombers will start this show. Are you ready to commence operations?"

"That's a roger, Madam President," came the formal response. "Our squadron is now in a thermospheric holding pattern and have target acquisition. We await the command."

"In that case, gentlemen," said Moore, "you have a go. Begin Operation Thorn Purge."

Reed touched his com-link, instantly transmitting the strike order to a squadron of America's newest bomber, a space plane capable of hypersonic speeds in low Earth orbit. Each B-4 carried ten Mjölnir bunker buster missiles, which could penetrate any known missile silo, and on this sortie they targeted every underground Iranian military installation. They would reach their targets thirty-four seconds after launch.

Each crew inside the orbiting bombers could easily see the raging fires from the twenty-four oil platforms on the Caspian Sea. The greasy smoke shrouded much of central Asia, including Iran, but the heavy pall had no effect on the B-4 targeting systems.

Three of the latest Kona class attack submarines prepared to launch the newest cruise missile in the American arsenal—the hypersonic SMITE missiles, capable of reaching speeds of up to Mach six. The seventy-seven missiles targeted the Iranian military network, from their naval headquarters at Bandar-e Abbas to the Payambar-e A'zam command and control center.

As sophisticated as these high-tech systems were, nothing surpassed America's newest, the unstoppable THOR system orbiting Earth at an altitude of 4,000 miles. The six unmanned platforms used a combination of a small nuclear generator and an array of solar panels to charge up their powerful particle beam cannons. These precision-targeted weapons could hit targets at close to the speed of light and could destroy entire buildings with a five-second blast.

Operation Thorn Purge commenced with the launching of the SMITE missiles. Bursting out of the gulf's warm water, the almost four score cruise missiles engaged their ramjets and raced toward the eastern side of the Persian Gulf at an altitude of 400 meters before making their attack drop. When the cruise missiles were thirty-five seconds from impact, the B-4s launched their Mjölnir silo killers from an altitude of

253 nautical miles. The heat-protected missiles swarmed down on the hardened bunkers from practically a vertical trajectory. There was no defense against either system, and they struck within seconds of each other, destroying almost the entire Iranian military complex from one end of the country to the other.

Once THOR detected the explosive flashes, a series of high-energy particle beams blasted down from the heavens. The first ten shots hit the pyramid-shaped Islamic Consultative Assembly housing the Iranian parliament. Within seconds the building collapsed. The next five hit the former American embassy compound that was now the headquarters for Quds Force, the main tactical arm of the Revolutionary Guards. It too was reduced to rubble. At the same instant, the golden-domed Iman Reza mosque was pulverized into small fragments, and the blasts weren't even close to being finished. A few more government buildings met the same fate as their parliament building, but halfway through THOR's expendable firepower, the target profiles changed. Now, personal homes of Iranian government and military leaders were hit without mercy. This included the Prime ruler, Ayatollah Mohammad Ka'bi.

The entire Iranian government and military infrastructure were devastated. Within four minutes of the first strike, the Iranian war was over. President Abigail Moore wanted to send a message, and that message was personal.

Smoke from the hundreds of fires raging throughout Tehran mixed with the oily pall still darkening the sky as it drifted in from Baku, 550 kilometers north.

The Iranian capability to deliver nuclear warheads was now almost completely destroyed.

Almost.

One mobile missile launcher, near Rasht, was intact, and thirty minutes after the American attack, it launched. The target was Israel, but immediately after launch the old Shabab-4 targeting system failed. It began to wobble, and its trajectory changed.

With corrupted avionics the medium-range missile became mankind's worst nightmare, a nuclear weapon with an undetermined destination. Carrying a forty-four kiloton warhead, the aging rocket flew north instead of south, and regrettably exploded over the wrong target—Samara, Russia.

CHAPTER EIGHT

THE DISEASE
KORYAK, RUSSIA

In five generations Koryak's once-primitive hospital had grown to seven doctors, and gradually acquired state-of-the-art equipment. Its reputation had reached national prominence, and even the jaded media in Moscow hailed it as eastern Russia's "finest medical community." Not only did the local miners benefit from the extraordinary level of health care, but patients came from all over Kamchatka, and even European Russia for treatment. Word slowly spread that the rate of recovery was remarkable in this remote corner of Siberia. Some even called its healing proficiency magical. Its staff was exclusively members from the Yanbeyev family.

It was a far cry from the ramshackle wooden hut began by the exiled family who wasn't allowed to practice anywhere else. With the fall of communism and the advent of new freedoms in Russia, the state-enforced restraints that had once kept the Yanbeyev family cloistered in this remote part of the world were no longer in place, but the family had no intention of ever leaving.

Their legacy of healing grew with each passing generation.

But something else grew there as well. It was akin to the healing arts, but not taught at any university. The family called it the Path, and only their bloodline possessed it. It was never talked about outside family gatherings, and then only by senior family members. Like a rare flower this gene pool was closely guarded and carefully propagated.

Old Andrei spent the rest of his life cultivating the Path in young Tadeas. As a seventh-generation male, Tadeas was a huge evolutionary leap for the family, and his uncle made sure the boy understood the importance of his legacy. The day the old man died Tadeas took his place as the family patriarch. Under Tadeas's leadership there was no deviation from the Path, and he ardently followed Andrei's vision of a healthy world.

It was a vision to eradicate disease from planet Earth.

Rising global temperatures and associated sea levels had no ill effect in this corner of Siberia. As time wore on the climate in the region became less frozen in the winter, with wetter springs and temperate summers. Fifty years after Tatyana opened that first rustic clinic, the small woods that once surrounded the tiny village had become a thriving forest. Woodland had replaced the tundra that once dominated this barren land. The forest continued to spread out for hundreds of kilometers in every direction. It wasn't just the people who were healthy in Koryak, but the land itself.

Meanwhile the mines that had first driven the authorities to supply health care to the region continued to produce wealth. The precious metals they extracted enriched the companies that ran them, and the workers who mined them. As Koryak became more affluent, more people arrived, and what once was a town of a few dozen herders became a small thriving city with thousands.

And the mines grew ever deeper.

The tragedy that struck Samara was felt throughout Russia. Panic seized the country, and calls for retribution grew louder with each passing day. Because of its reputation, the Northern Kamchatka Medical Center received dozens of patients with radiation burns, but there were no calls for retaliation coming from Koryak. There was only overt silence, and covert planning.

Late night on the summer solstice of A.D. 2035, while the sun still shone on the tranquility of Koryak, something dark lurked in the shadows of the midnight sun.

A family meeting was about to take place in the parlor of the eldest member of the Yanbeyev family. Even at 100 years old, Tadeas was still tall, with a full shock of thick white hair, and proudly wore the dragon eye medallion his mother had given him ninety years before. He never took it off. There were three other family members present, all women. His grey-haired daughter and redheaded granddaughter sat together on a plush divan in the center of the room. Sitting in a window seat as far from the adults as she could possibly get sat his headstrong but preternaturally powerful seventeen-year-old great-granddaughter.

"Good evening, ladies," Tadeas greeted them. "It's nice to see all of you here at this late hour. I apologize for the inconvenience, and I hope you all wore your sunscreen." A small titter rippled through the room as the women indulged the old man's small jokes. "It's time we discussed Samara."

"Yes, we should," sulked the pretty blond teenager. "Why did it have to be a Russian city? Couldn't you have picked another target? Another country?"

The old man stood up with the help of his cane and, with some difficulty, walked over to the cold brick hearth, where he gazed up at the family portrait painted shortly after they had arrived from Crimea. He studied the face of his long-dead dyadya Andrei, the most influential man in his life, and spoke as if talking to the painting. "You knew our family had always been victimized by these political cycles of good and evil. Now, that persecution is coming to an end." Keeping his back toward the group, Tadeas continued to stare at the old painting. "It was the most opportune moment we've had, Olga, and I'll not hesitate to use the next opportunity either." He turned around and glared at her. "You know our plan, and all of you have helped bring this to fruition. Why are you having second thoughts now?"

"Because those were our countrymen who died. Thousands, Dedushka." Olga circled a dainty finger around the thin edge of the porcelain teacup and considered its wisp of steam. "And now our burn wards are full of the misery we've caused."

"Billions more will die like this before it's over," Tadeas snapped. "You all knew this as well." His voice softened as he sensed their resolve weakening. "The die is cast, and the beginning of the end of this sick and dying planet has begun. We're simply accelerating the process."

"Can you see no other way?" asked his daughter, the eldest of the women. She took a sip of tea and sat back holding the cup. "It's all we're asking."

"No, Alyona!" He banged the mantel with his fist as his tone grew hard again. "Our planet is terminal, and the disease is mankind. We can't heal Earth until we expunge its ailment." He shook his head as he stared down each of the women. "You must be able to stomach what is yet to come, because believe me, it's coming. In three generations our blue planet will become unfit for life, and if there's any hope for mankind, then something drastic has to change." His tone became more conciliatory as he continued, "I didn't cause the Iranian missile attack, but I did take advantage of it."

"But, Dedushka," asked his granddaughter, who'd remained silent until now, "what if Russia and America go to war over this? We're not ready yet, and it would destroy everything, including our plans. Even our abilities can't control that."

"Ah, Luda." He smiled indulgently at her chubby face. "With all of your help, I can control it."

"How?" demanded Olga, glowering at him from the window seat.

He met her fiery green eyes with much less intensity than he'd shown earlier. She was his favorite, after all. For a brief moment he seemed like the old man he really was, but only for a moment. "Because, dear child, there's another storm coming, and one that we can manipulate. One that will actually ally Russia with America."

"How is this thing possible?" scoffed Olga. "We are at each others' throats."

"Patience and perseverance, my child, and a little help from Mother Nature."

CHAPTER NINE

CONSEQUENCES
WASHINGTON, D.C.

Hovering near the Resolute Desk, President Moore's cabinet waited for the call they knew was coming. The President had discussed her stance, and with the exception of the Secretary of Defense, Hugo Fournier, a gloomy man who wanted no part of her plan, the rest were in agreement. Fournier stood alone and stared up at the portrait of George Washington. He'd said his piece and had run up against a brick wall.

A light finally lit up on her desk. Dan Belcher, the rotund National Security Advisor, picked it up, listened for a moment, and then turned to the boss. "Abigail, President Volkov is on the video line, and he's pissing vinegar." A grin twitched on his round face as his finger wavered over the button. "Do you want me to hold him off?"

"No need, Dan," said the POTUS, "and no time like the present. Put him on."

Belcher opened the line and stood back to watch the fireworks. It didn't take long. As the screen flickered to life Volkov's face was a mask of rage. "What the fuck happened, Madam President?" Volkov demanded.

"That wasn't our missile that hit Samara," retorted Moore. "It was your own ally who fired that weapon." She could see Volkov's advisor hovering in the background.

"It was your goddamned attack that pre-empted their launch, and you fucking well know it," growled Volkov.

"What I fucking well know," she said, staring down his digital image, "is that missile and its warhead were built using technology that Russia sold them, that *you* sold them, Yuri. Technology that's illegal in any number of anti-proliferation treaties."

"Tell that to the 22,000 dead in Samara!" Volkov shouted. "Do you really think they give a rat's ass where that fucking missile was designed?" He hissed the question through clenched jaws. "All they know is what the rest of the world knows: America's attack on Iran caused the first city to be destroyed by a nuclear weapon since America destroyed the last one over ninety years ago."

"Don't you dare go there." She wagged a finger at the screen. "We removed a huge thorn from the entire world's side. Including your own."

"Our foreign policy is not a matter for debate, Madam President, and there will be consequences. You can count on that!"

She was ready for this, and already had her stance worked out. "What consequences?" She'd removed her finger from his face and regained her composure. "Do you mean war with America? Because it seems to me that you have bigger problems. Problems massing on your border as we speak."

"Did I not make it clear that our foreign policy, our borders, are not your concern?" he shot back. "We can handle the Chinese."

"Actually, Yuri, you can't. As I'm sure you'll recall, China abandoned you and your collapsed economy after your predecessor's debacle in Ukraine. And except for those crazy Mullahs in Iran, Russia was friendless. Nobody, and I mean nobody would give Russia the time of day for more than a decade. Then you made it worse with your unabashed support for Iran, and their subsequent cozying up with Pakistan. Hell, Yuri, you've been digging your own grave this whole damn century, and frankly, all our warnings to the contrary have fallen on deaf ears at the Kremlin."

She noted the furtive glance Volkov cast at Borya, who was barely visible on her screen. "Where the hell are you going with this, Abigail?"

"I'll make this as plain as possible." She raised a hand so that it wasn't in the camera shot and flashed a thumbs-up at Belcher. "As you well know, your ally, the former Iranian regime, funded Islamic terrorism, and had emboldened Pakistan to launch terrorist attacks against India. Unfortunately, the previous American administration did nothing but hand-wringing, and India turned to the only regional superpower they could: China."

"I don't need a history lesson from you." Yuri glanced at Borya, who wagged a cautionary finger. "This is not about the past."

Moore took note of Volkov's interaction with his advisor. "Fine, then let's talk about the future, shall we?" She scribbled three words on a note pad, tapped on it to get Belcher's attention, and pushed it toward him. *Borya. Watch him.*

Belcher sat down out of camera range and studied the screen.

Still fuming, Volkov went on. "I smell American meddling, and I won't have it."

As if she hadn't heard a word he'd said, she continued along in the same vein. "Shit rolls downhill, and the Sino-Indu defense pact has allied two resource-desperate countries with half the world's population between them sitting at the bottom holding a wheelbarrow."

Belcher watched Borya's reactions like a hawk, taking note of the big Russian nodding at Moore's statement. Volkov saw it too, and he relented ever so slightly. "And your point, Abigail?"

"I'm glad to see you're willing to hear me out, Yuri."

"Hearing is not listening. Please get to your point."

"Fine, then hear this: both India and China are practically out of water, their populations are literally baking to death, and if their governments don't do something soon, there'll be civil war. Hell, they don't have a tenth of the oil they need to keep the lights on, much less run their economies. Are you following me?"

"I heard what you said."

She ratcheted up her pitch. "Russia, on the other hand, has plenty of both. Just where do you think their eyes are turning as we speak? That's a combined six billion people, both of whom have nuclear arsenals and can field armed forces larger than Russia's entire population. Are you still with me?"

With hands clasped behind his back Volkov started pacing. "Just drop the other shoe already. Will you?"

"I wear pumps." She smiled at him. "I thought you knew that?"

"Abigail," he snorted, "this cat-and-mouse act is getting old fast."

"All right," she said, "here's my offer. We'll place a few more THOR platforms into orbit within months. The next generation."

"How many?"

Moore gave him a sympathetic look. "Nice try, Yuri. Let's just say—enough."

Volkov stopped pacing, glanced at Borya, and threw both hands in the air. Borya shrugged back. "Are you suggesting a Russian-American alliance, after Samara? Seriously? That would be political suicide for me. You know that." The pacing started again.

"Then let's just call it cooperation. I've got no doubt that in a few weeks' time you can spin something about Samara that'll placate your people. Without our help, you could well be the last Russian President for a very long time."

"Is that some kind of veiled threat, Abigail, because if you think—"

"As I said, those aren't our troops massing at your borders, but we can help each other if things go pear-shaped." Her voice dropped down to an almost-whisper. "Frankly, the survival of both our countries are linked in this."

"What's that supposed to mean?"

The other pump hit the floor. "Because if the Sino-Indu alliance succeeds in taking your water, who do you think is next?"

Volkov stopped pacing, walked over to his desk placing a hand on each side of the camera, and stared down at it. "Just what are you suggesting?"

She glanced at the others who were absorbed by what was possibly the most important foreign policy conversation of the century. "What I'm suggesting is that we tone down our rhetoric and start sending signals that no escalation is forthcoming."

Volkov shook his head, but Belcher saw Borya point at his ears. *Keep listening.* "I'll get strung up in Red Square if I'm seen cozying up to a lame duck American President," he growled. "Samara is still smoldering."

"*Cozy* doesn't work for this plan," Moore said, "but what does work is for you to continue your ridiculously close fly-bys toward our carrier battle groups, and for us to keep pretending to chase you off."

Standing aloof and alone, Fourier grunted in derision, but was still ignored.

"And then what?" Volkov asked.

"Then we wait to see what Chairman Bojing Xu does," she said, "and if it degenerates into an invasion, then we'll stand by you."

Volkov's eyes narrowed suspiciously. "Have you spoken to NATO or ANZUS about this yet?

"No one is comfortable with the Chinese situation right now. Let's just say that Brussels and Canberra have no objections." She hesitated for a brief moment. "Do you?"

"Do I really have a choice, Abigail?"

"There's always a choice. Just not always a convenient one."

Volkov used both hands to nervously rake back his thinning grey hair. He took a deep breath and glanced at Borya, desperation etched in his face. The big man gave his opinion with a raised brow. Volkov finally exhaled, saying, "Get Ambassador Neely up to speed, and have him come see me."

"Then is that a yes?" Moore pressed.

"That is a let's talk, then we'll see," Volkov replied.

"Fine. I'll send over Neely, and then—we'll see."

"Your successor will have some very big shoes to fill, Abigail."

"Pumps, Yuri."

The instant the video feed went dead Belcher turned to his president. "Those two seem attached at the hip, Abigail."

"But did you see enough?" Moore asked.

"Yeah, and not only does Borya seem the more level-headed of the two, but I noticed Volkov looks to him for every decision."

"That's an avenue we might want to explore, Dan," Moore suggested.

"I'll look into it." He rose to leave but stopped abruptly and added, "God help us all if anything ever happens to Borya."

CHAPTER TEN

GOING UP IN FLAMES
LOS ANGELES, CALIFORNIA

The International Convention on Climate Control convened under a pall of dark smoke shrouding the entire western United States. Ash was a constant irritant, clogging up air filters and the dust masks that at least half the American populace was forced to wear. And there was no end in sight.

A small Asian woman wearing an aspen green dress and sensible shoes walked out on the stage. She motioned for everyone to take their seats. "I'd like to welcome everyone to the UCLA Meyer and Renee Luskin Center. Before I introduce our keynote speaker, I'd like you to record what you hear here. This may be our last chance to have an impact on the world's deteriorating climate." There was a murmuring of agreement that swept through the hall as she held her hands up for quiet. "So, with no further ado, it's my pleasure to introduce one of the world's foremost authorities on climatology, Dr. Randall Burt." A smattering of applause met the lanky acne-scarred young man dressed in brown slacks and a white tieless shirt as he walked out on stage.

"Thank you, Dr. Park, and thank you all for coming to this last-ditch effort of trying to influence the world's governments to enact policies that are, frankly, already too late." A wave of groans rippled from the audience. Burt raised his hands to quiet the crowd.

"The warming of the planet is accelerating." There was more grumbling from the audience; this was old news. They wanted answers, not a status report. Burt's hands went up again, and he continued once he had their attention. "The average human requires about 1,600 calories and needs to drink almost two liters of clean water each day to maintain balanced health. Present conditions worldwide dictate the average available caloric intake is little more than half that, and the amount of clean water is measured in grams, not liters. Those numbers drop every year." An impatient murmur rolled throughout the crowd.

"So, here's the deal: Earth can no longer produce enough food to maintain its burgeoning population. In the next twenty years we'll surpass twelve billion, but the lack of water means we can only adequately feed 20 percent of that number." He moved to the side of the podium, allowing access to a giant screen, and clicked a remote. A graph appeared on the screen. "As you can see, the lines depicting the world's population and the ability to provide sufficient nutrition crossed about ten years ago. We are now in the red, folks, and the spread is accelerating." With a grim look he gauged the audience, and asked, "Why?"

His question was answered with more groans.

"Water," Burt answered, and let the word linger a moment before continuing. "Ten years ago I got my first doctorate in marine biology from UC San Diego and studied the dying seas around the world. We focused on the Sea of Cortez. It was practically dead by the time I first joined the team as a graduate student. It is now completely devoid of life and is only one of many around the world." He pushed away from the podium and moved to the edge of the stage.

"Once I realized the full impact that climate was having on the oceans, I changed my focus to climatology, and what I've found is disturbing in the extreme. The complete lack of precipitation in most of both the eastern and western hemispheres has created a dire situation in a whole list of categories." He walked back to the podium, picked up a glass of water, took a drink, and held the glass out to the crowd. "This is now the world's most precious commodity—fresh water. Make no mistake our glass is half empty.

"Not only has there been zero snow pack in the Sierras, Rockies, and Andes for almost two decades, now the Alps, the Himalayas, and Tanggulas are experiencing the same thing. Once-arable regions have turned into parched deserts, dust bowls on a continental scale. Food production has deteriorated to the point that hundreds of thousands starve to death every year.

"The Indus, Yangtze, and Yellow rivers are now just a trickle, putting billions of people in India and China at risk of famine on a cataclysmic scale. And yet they keep having babies, and their factories keep belching out coal exhaust, adding to the world's heat index. But they're not solely to blame. Oh no, here in North America we continue to drive our 378 million passenger cars, all while forest fires rage across the globe. These fires create planet-killing levels of carbon dioxide, intensifying the worldwide drought. We are literally going up in flames.

"The rising, and accelerating I might add, sea levels have inundated most seaside cities, where fully 40 percent of the world's population still attempt to live. Typhoons and hurricanes used to have their own season. No more. They are now a year-round threat and keep getting stronger. The type of super cell that recently obliterated Jakarta is now destroying other cities once thought to be immune. Last year the biggest hurricane in history had enough energy to devastate Paris. Nowhere, it seems, is safe.

"Here in North America we still have the largest bodies of fresh water in the world, the Great Lakes. Unfortunately, the tributaries that once fed them are now dry riverbeds, and the lakes themselves are rapidly shrinking as we use the water to feed our people and hope that it starts raining again. Have no illusions about this hope. It's a fool's errand. This is not to say that the entire world is dying. Rising temperatures are making once-cold and barren regions more habitable. Frozen tundra once covered wide swaths of Northeast Siberia, Canada, and Alaska." As if to reinforce his point, he took a long drink of water. "That tundra is being replaced by temperate forests." He held up the almost empty glass, looking through it at the audience. "They are now experiencing climate change in a positive way. They're the beneficiaries of our misery. These regions not only have no drought, they have a higher than normal precipitation, and less cold. This has made them comfortable, and out of the crisis corridor. But they are a tiny fraction of the world's population.

"Now, we find ourselves in a very dangerous geopolitical crisis. The worldwide drought has pitted the world's few water-have countries against the vast majority of have-nots. The potential for conflict is now greater than it's ever been. Even the oil wars at the turn of the twenty-first century didn't have the far-reaching impact that the water wars could very well have now. If this crisis explodes, it'll likely turn nuclear. If that happens, then the heat index will go right off the scale.

"So, in closing, I just want to send you all back to your respective countries with the same message that we've been trying to get through their heads since Kyoto: we simply cannot continue down this road. The Earth has had enough. Frankly, I believe that we're already twenty years too late, but all we as scientists can do is keep trying to find an answer no matter what the odds against us are. And believe me, ladies, gentlemen, to me it seems as though all bets are almost off the table. The end is most definitely nigh.

"I apologize for this dark message, but there's just no way to put a positive spin on our future. Please don't forget to put on your dust masks before you go outside. Apparently the Sierra Nevadas still have trees left to burn."

As Dr. Burt left the stage, he was confronted by Dr. Park. "Well, that was really uplifting, Randy," she snapped. "I bet half of them will go home and slit their wrists."

"That only means it's 40 percent too few," he shot back and watched her face turn red. "Did you really want a message of hope where there is none, so they can fly home, take mass transit to their favorite watering holes, recycle their purified water bottles, and tell themselves that they're doing their part?" His tone turned caustic. "And then run their air conditioners to get away from the heat thinking we have a snowball's chance in hell? No, I just couldn't do it."

"Couldn't you have told them something that wasn't so bleak?"

"It is bleak, Chen," he declared. "Our planet's in a meltdown."

"But the truth is that there are pockets of hope. Couldn't you have exemplified that?"

He gave her a hard look. "Be thankful I didn't tell them the only hope we really have."

"And just what 'hope' is that?"

"That we need to eliminate 90 percent of the population or go find another planet to live on."

CHAPTER ELEVEN

TREASURE MAP
FUKUOKA, JAPAN

Twenty-eight-year-old Hikaru Mizushima returned home with two doctorates: a Ph.D. in astrophysics and another in theoretical physics. Standing at 170 centimeters with a shock of fine black hair and intense brown eyes, he was young, slim, educated, and had all the influence that came with running a corporate empire. His factories were producing at an unprecedented rate: high tech televisions and air conditioners that the first world bought as fast as his companies could manufacture them.

But he was troubled.

For one of the few times ever, Hikaru sat at the large cherry wood desk in the spacious corner office that had belonged to the previous CEO, his father. Now it was his, and it was the last place he wanted to be. Since returning to Japan he'd been ducking his duties as the new CEO, and lately, he'd been avoiding the dragon lady as well. But hiding in this thirty-fifth-floor office did him little good; her vice president's office was just down the hall.

And the dragon knew exactly where to find him. Wearing a tailored blue silk dress, Jimmy Choo heels, and a disapproving lour, she glided in unannounced. "I just got a call from security; it seems they're wondering who you are."

Hikaru rolled his eyes. "This," he pointed at the expensive desk, "isn't what I went to school for."

Kōshitsu Mizushima walked stiffly to the window and stared out at the view. "I don't understand you." His mother swept a heavily jeweled hand toward the modern splendor of Nagasaki Bay. "What more do you want?"

"I didn't spend a decade in America to learn how to make the rich more comfortable, Okaasan. I want to do something worthwhile."

"The *rich!*" She spat his word back at him and spun around. "Take a good look, you ungrateful botchan," she sneered at his faded jeans, "and then tell me about all these so-called rich. Your father killed himself building this extremely successful company." Her voice cracked; twisting a heavy gold bangle on her wrist, she barely whispered, "For you."

It was her most coercive rebuke to date, but using his father's death was just the type of cheap tactic that he'd become inured to. "This *boy* is going to pursue his own dreams."

"I had hoped that MIT would have erased that foolish old man's influence."

Hikaru bristled but fought not to let it show. "I'm going to build spacecraft."

"Why?" she demanded through clenched jaws. "America is better suited do that."

"No, Okaasan, they're not." He joined her at the window. "NASA's been sending manned missions to Mars for over twenty years, and in all that time less than 40 human beings have ever set foot on it. I want to change that. The cost of sending humans to Mars is too expensive, even for a country like America."

"And you think your grandfather's fantasy will make a difference?" she said sharply.

Hikaru sighed and placed his hands on her shoulders. "I need my mother to believe in me." His voice turned supplicating. "The way he did."

"Then convince me, son." Her dark eyes had lost some of their fire and the tight edge in her tone softened. "Explain to me how Aito's pie in the sky could be more important than running our rather profitable family business."

"I will run Mizushima, Okaasan. My way." He placed a finger across her lips when she started to protest. "Because I believe the key to space exploration is the elimination of propellant-fueled spacecraft. Rockets are too slow, and most important for Mizushima," a suspicious squint wrinkled the corners of her painted eyes as she listened to her son, "the return on investment is almost nil."

"Investment." This time repeating his word brought a faint smile to her lips. "You'll have to succeed first."

"I will, Okaasan."

"Then go, Musuko," she ordered, "and succeed."

In spite of his bravado there were times when Hikaru wondered if his boyhood dream of building magic flying machines was just what his mother had called it, a fantasy. But it was one that refused to go away. Many nights he'd go to bed convinced of its fallacy, only to wake up the next morning with renewed enthusiasm. He was torn between two worlds: the fantastical and the pragmatic.

And the pragmatic world was dying.

In the weeks after the talk with his mother, Hikaru became morose about the path that his multi-billion-dollar company was on. It was also apparent that the old factory in Fukuoka needed to be replaced with something far more modern.

For weeks he'd studied different designs for the new building, and the more he tried to decide, the more obsessed he became with the old map he'd had since he was a boy.

The day the old factory was demolished, Hikaru showed up at the job site. He wouldn't allow it to be razed in the usual manner. It had to be carefully taken apart as if it was a precious family heirloom. Once the walls were down an excavation team started at the edge of the building pad and carefully worked their way in. When they got to the exact spot on the old map, grinders were used to remove the concrete slab. Slowly but surely, they ground down until one of the workers hit something metallic. Sparks flew for a moment until Hikaru raced up and made them stop. He brushed off the bare spot and continued with nothing more than a small chipping hammer. Finally an old piece of metal appeared exactly where the map said it would.

A tent was erected over the spot, and the careful excavation continued. Soon the metal was exposed for what it really was: the lid of a chamber that sunk much further into the ground. The old lid was badly corroded, and it took a small blowtorch to finally free it from its hinges. A pry bar was used to wrench up the cover, and as soon as it was opened Hikaru made everyone leave the tent. Alone, he held his breath, and stood shining a flashlight into the chamber's darkness.

What he saw didn't look impressive. He reached down and pulled out some sort of badly corroded bowl-shaped device wrapped in copper wire. Then his flashlight shone on something else. Something wrapped in an oilcloth. He took it out, and carefully removed the cloth. Inside was a journal. He swallowed the lump in his throat as he realized just what this journal was—the key to the treasure. Almost hyperventilating, he trembled as the book was held for the first time in almost a century. Hikaru knew that if this thing really worked, the journal would tell him how. He wrapped it back up and took both items to a small lab he had at his home—a lab that was soon to become the birthplace of a new technology. The old man's stories were real after all.

Except for the six red wa-rosoku candles flickering beneath his most prized possession, the only other light in Hikaru's private study was a small brass reading lamp casting white light on the ancient journal sitting on his desk like an unopened tomb.

The key to the stars lay in front of him, and though he'd waited for this moment his entire life, now that it was here, Hikaru found it almost a desecration to exhume its contents. Sitting at his desk wearing a black silk kimono, the young physicist's hand hovered over the cracked leather, lacking the courage to disinter what had been buried for so long. His lifelong anticipation had been replaced by fear.

What if it didn't work?

The metallic glint of candlelight on the far wall suddenly caught his attention. For several moments Hikaru stared at the sword made from a star. As if to mock his fear, the lore of its tragic history flooded back into his memory.

The 500-year-old legend said that the swordsmith died making that sword.

Dedication to die for.

Hikaru opened the journal and began reading. He read all night and well into the next morning. He read all day, every day, and still it took him weeks of intense study before he gleaned even the most basic concept. The antiquated script was barely discernable, and much of it was written in a foreign language. Now he understood why his grandfather had insisted he take German at MIT. Adding to the burden of translation was the absence of any type of codex explaining how it all fit together.

It was like deciphering an Ishikawa puzzle box.

As with the legend of the swordsmith, Hikaru drove himself to the point of collapse, but refused to give up. Eventually he retired to his lab and began to reverse engineer the old device. Its pieces lay scattered across his workbench. He'd obtained new materials early on in the process but had not yet attempted to actually construct a new device.

It took another few weeks before he finally got something that worked. It looked different than the old bowl-shaped device, but ultimately lifted off its cradle and hovered exactly like Aito said it would. The key was the temperature and magnetism of both the craft and the cradle it launched from. At absolute zero the applicable magnetic energy could be intensified almost infinitely.

The next day Hikaru created a new department. It was miniscule by comparison to the other divisions, but as time wore on he surrounded himself with the best engineers and physicists he could find. The department grew, and the new building, built where the old warehouse once stood, was solely devoted to its research and development. Within two years the department became a company all of its own. He called it Interstellar Mizushima Incorporated, and its focus was the Enhanced Magnetic Drive.

CHAPTER TWELVE

THE RIGHT HANDS
KORYAK, RUSSIA

Adorned in warm earth tones, attractive silk plants, and with a large curtained window overlooking the lush forest just outside, the charm of the hospice was as antithetical to its present occupant as it was to his single guest. Tadeas's shriveled hand barely had the strength to place the family medallion into his great-granddaughter's soft palm. After her slender fingers wrapped around it, he grabbed her wrist. "It's now up to you to make sure this is passed on to the next head of the family." His voice was raspy, but his grip remained strong. "You must promise me this and stay true to the Path. Promise me!" He tried to draw her closer.

Gently nudging him away, Olga told him, "I promise, Dedushka. It will be as you ask." Wearing a low-cut high-hemmed white dress, matching heels, and the latest eau de parfum, she smelled death on him, and it sickened her.

"Good, child, good. It must be you," he said, loosening his grip, "because the Path is stronger in you than anyone ever before. Stronger than even mine."

Knowing that this distasteful conversation wouldn't last long, Olga decided to allow him to die with the knowledge he so desperately wanted. "I know, Dedushka, and events are quickly unfolding," she informed him while prying his fingers off her arm. She stood up, casually pushed a long blond tress behind an ear, walked over to the heart monitor, and stared languidly at the machine as its beep slowly weakened.

"Tell me what you know." His head sank deep into the soft pillow. It seemed that he'd slipped closer to death in the last few seconds. It was only a matter of minutes now. "I need to die in peace, and only your knowledge will give me that."

A bored sigh escaped her bright red lips as she glanced at her matching nails and then back at the old man. "I've observed both the Chinese and Indian leaders." She noted satisfaction work across his sallow face. "They're in the final stages of planning their attack."

"And the Americans?" He could barely speak. "What of them?"

"They're aware," she said, her voice dripping with tedium. "Their spy satellites and listening devices have kept them completely in the loop, not to mention a few accurate intelligence reports from an unnamed source." She found the dry wrinkles of his smile somehow repugnant and turned to look out the third-story window at the serenity of the surrounding woods. "Moore's aides have been in continual contact with the Kremlin, and both countries act as if nothing is amiss." She walked back and sat on the edge of his bed, smoothed out her short dress, and crossed her slender legs. "By acting ignorant they've laid a trap luring the Sino-Indu allies into thinking Russia is friendless and vulnerable."

Tadeas's death rattle quickened. "A-are the Chinese overconfident?"

"Yes, Dedushka, they have no idea America will side with Russia, and the new THOR systems recently placed into orbit are on a trajectory that places at least three of them over the Russian-Chinese border at all times."

"Then the time to strike is n-now," he coughed, sinking deeper into his bed, "while the iron is h-hot."

He had only moments left, and she didn't want him to die without hearing everything. Almost everything. "While I can observe them, my ability to control their thoughts is somewhat limited. But, from what I've heard, I believe that the Sino-Indu attack will happen in a matter of weeks."

"Then this is w-what I want you to do—"

For the first time in her life she interrupted him. "No, Dedushka, your days of dictating are over. I've waited for this long enough." She twirled the medallion. "I now control this family." She smiled for the first time that day. "And our Path. So, here's what I want you to do." She stood, walked over to the cardiovascular support system, and turned it off. "I want you to die knowing that you left the family in the right hands, but most of all, I just want you to die."

His eyes flared with shock; then, just as quick, a small expression of contentment crossed his wrinkled face. She'd expected his final words to be condemnation, but instead he gave her a weak smile and in an almost inaudible voice gasped, "I chose my s-successor well." The heart monitor flatlined.

Exactly twelve hours after his death, in a room lit by hundreds of candles, Tadeas's corpse was prepared for the grave. After embalming, the body was wrapped in a richly embroidered shroud, placed on a pallet, and hoisted atop a droska. Four young men stood at each corner holding a three-meter wooden pole. Once the body was secure they hoisted up the platform, steadied it, and ran to the family cemetery as fast as their cumbersome burden allowed.

A gentle rain fell as the Yanbeyev family followed the droska through the lush woods toward their patriarch's final resting place. He'd wanted to be buried next to his mother and uncle. His first wife, who'd died in childbirth almost eighty years before, had been cremated, as were his second and third wives. Tadeas had outlived them all.

The two sides of the ever-expanding family surrounded the open grave as he was lowered in. Olga, wearing a suitable but stylish black full-length dress, threw the first handful of dirt into the grave. She stood back as the rest of the family did the same. Old Tadeas's sons and grandsons stayed after the service to fill in the rest, and then made their way to the old man's home for a family meeting.

The house now belonged to Mother Olga.

Tadeas's youngest great-grandson removed his hat, loosened his black mourning tie, and dutifully approached his cousin to pay homage to the new matriarch. "My condolences, Mother Olga," he told her reservedly. "So, what happens now?"

"Now, Yevgeni?" She studied her handsome, athletically built cousin with a cold stare. "Now we stay true to the Path that Dedushka Tadeas set for us. Why do you feel a need to ask? I sense reluctance here. Are you still with us?"

Yevgeni's long brown bangs fell across his green eyes as he jammed his hands in his pockets and shook his head. A hard frown flashed across his face as frustration found its voice. "No, Olga, I'm not." He caught the fire in her eyes but knew this had to be said here and now. "My wife and I are about to have our first child, a little girl, and—"

"Yes, I know," interrupted Olga, and with a sweet voice she gave him a small example of her power, "and you've already picked the name Nadezhda. I love it. Every family should have its Hope. Don't you agree?" His anger was instantly replaced with shock; she went on to astonish him further. "And what's more, little Nadya will become the most influential Yanbeyeva ever. More so than even me."

"Yes, that's the name we've decided on," he stammered, and took a step back. "Why am I not surprised that you already know that?" The new matriarch shrugged. "But know this, Olga, we'll not let her fall under your spell, and we won't be party to this—this diabolical plan." He stepped back even farther. "This is insane, can't you see that?"

Olga's mother backed against a wall, stared at the two cousins, and chewed her nails.

"What I see," said Olga, "is what Dedushka always taught us: insanity has already gripped our world and is leading it to destruction. We're simply speeding up the process." Yevgeni recoiled and turned to leave, but she stopped him with her next words. "All those who're with us will not only survive but thrive."

He started walking away again.

"And this family will eventually rule the world," she yelled at his retreating back, "and rule as it should be ruled! Think about *that* as you bring another Yanbeyeva into the world, cousin. Think about that!"

Tension gripped the silent room. After a moment Luda ceased biting her nails, dropped the offending hand, and approached her headstrong daughter the moment Yevgeni slammed the door. "That man is trouble. He never would've challenged Dedushka like that."

"A small matter." Olga waved a hand in dismissal. "Just a slight tear of the ranks, and of little consequence." She narrowed her eyes and hissed a warning to her mother. "There will be no hand raised against him, or his wife. Do I make myself clear, Mama?"

Luda flinched. "I understand your words but not your reasoning. Why?"

"Because, Mother, their unborn baby will be the most powerful Yanbeyeva ever."

"B-but Dedushka chose you," spluttered Luda.

Olga looked around the room. "Only for the interim," she confided, "and just until little Nadya comes of age. Her visions will guide the Path for 1,000 years."

CHAPTER THIRTEEN

A MOLE
BEIJING, CHINA

O n the eastern edge of Tiananmen Square sits the rectangular behemoth known as the Great Hall of the People. It was purportedly built to house the voice of the communist party. In practice that voice was the sole mouthpiece for the party's General Secretary, President Bojing Xu.

Inside the Great Hall, Xu and his advisors were presently hosting a high-powered delegation attended by their strongest ally, Indian President Sahil Patel. Also attending the meeting, and fully supportive of the agenda, was the impoverished but militarily advanced state of Democratic People's Republic of North Korea, represented by their Prime leader, Kong Jung Ghim.

Sitting in plush armchairs, the delegates met in an opulent conference room topped by an intricately woven porcelain parquet ceiling. Its pillared walls were festooned with art characterizing traditional Chinese life. Covering an entire wall was an idyllic mural depicting a charming rural village resting beside a lush rice paddy. In the distance a sparkling waterfall cascaded down from forest-laden mountains. It was a scene that no longer existed in China.

They were discussing the final preparations for a lightning-quick invasion of Russia, an invasion that would cut off the resource-rich east from the militarily powerful west. The plan dictated that the 109 Indian divisions already stationed in northeast China would drive a wedge through the narrow corridor between Kazakhstan and Mongolia, cutting off any help from western Russia. Simultaneously, 263 divisions from the People's Liberation Army would tear through the sparsely populated east and drive straight for northeast Siberia. North Korea's fifty-two divisions were to swarm their common border at Khasan and make a lightning-fast air assault on the crucial Pacific port of Vladivostok.

These meetings were held in the strictest of secrecy. All attendees, including the respective Presidents, were closely monitored. But there was one attendee who was never invited, never screened, and never noticed. A green-eyed beauty routinely sat in and listened to the plans that she'd helped cultivate. No one could see her astrally projected form, and no one suspected that a mole knew every detail of their plan.

"I'm worried about the Americans," insisted Patel, sitting opposite Bojing. "Their THOR systems are always in an orbital path on or near your border with Russia. These could present a problem should they decide to intervene."

"We need to launch a nuclear strike against the American Pacific fleet and destroy it as soon as the liberation of Manchuria begins," cut in Jung Ghim.

Bojing pushed away these concerns. "Don't worry about the Americans," he said confidently. "Their relationship with Russia has badly deteriorated since Samara. Our intelligence has ruled out any American intervention. Volkov is too proud to ask for their help and, as we've all seen, he's a weak leader." His voice grew mocking. "Other than a few meaningless air space incursions over their carrier battle groups, he's done nothing but make damning speeches about President Moore. I dare say if that woman were leading Russia, then we might have to rethink this invasion, but she won't lift a finger to help him. Russia is broke, vulnerable, and quite alone.

"In addition, it won't take more than a week for our forces to destroy any Russian opposition in the field, and once we have Siberia, then the Americans can do nothing but complain, which they seem to be experts at." A few listless chuckles followed this remark. "And lest we forget, this is an all-or-nothing operation. We are out of resources, which means we're out of time." Adopting a serious demeanor, he let his eyes sweep the other delegates. "This is a matter of survival for all our countries. Without Siberian oil and water we wither and die. So, let us save any recriminations until after we have secured survival for our people."

"So, we're still set for ten days from now?" asked Patel.

Xu nodded across the table. "Yes, my friend. We'll continue our joint military exercises near the two invasion points, and then on the prescribed date we launch Operation Feng Shui. That will be the beginning of the end of our people's misery."

The mole had seen enough and returned to her body in Koryak.

Squinting over the top of her glasses, President Moore was sitting at her computer reading reports when her security advisor, not waiting for his knock to be answered, walked into the Oval Office. "Those work better if you actually look through them, Abigail."

"Tell me something I don't know."

"Fair enough. The NSA has gotten another of those strange messages about the Sino-Indu invasion plans."

Her head swung in his direction. "Do they have any idea of their validity, Dan, or who's even sending them?" Moore pushed her glasses up to the bridge of her nose and clicked on the file that held all the data collected from this mysterious source. "If this turns out to be some kind of elaborate ruse, we're all going to look like damned idiots."

"All the NSA knows for sure is that somehow someone has hacked into our most secure communication network, and has been sending them via our own satellites," explained Belcher. "As for their validity, so far all of them have proved 100 percent accurate."

"So much for our un-hackable Comsat, huh?" She closed the file and rubbed her sore eyes. "Well, what does this one say? That's why you came in here in the first place, isn't it?"

Belcher sat down, placed his tablet on the President's antique desk, and tapped a folder. "The invasion is set for nine days from now, and it's going to involve the full weight of all three countries. They've been conducting constant war games near the Russian border for weeks now." He pointed at one line in particular. "The Indian army will invade through the narrow corridor of the Altai Mountains and into the Kemerovo Oblast. Then they'll turn northeast and take Lake Bakal."

"Why the hell would they want to take that place?"

"Water, ma'am. They're desperate, and the lake is almost full."

"Got it, but then what?"

"Then the Indian army sets up their headquarters, an aerodrome, and spreads out to act as a picket against any advancing Russian counter-strikes. Meanwhile, the two massive Chinese armies will pour across the border at the Chitinskaya and Amurskaya Oblasts, and head straight for northeast Siberia where they'll secure the world's richest fresh water district, not to mention oil and gas."

"What's the latest on North Korea?"

"Haven't you read the latest National Intelligence Estimate?"

She blew an irritated sigh his way. "Just fill me in, would you?"

"Right. Well, last week they received two battalions of Hóng Fēng, the newest Chinese VTOL. They're now conducting trials around Chonjin."

"Hóng Fēng?"

"Red Wind."

"So, what're we talking, 300 birds?" she asked. "Doesn't seem like a lot."

"That's 316 fast air cav units capable of moving 4,000 shock troops 300 kilometers in less than thirty minutes."

"And?"

"And Vladivostok is only 227 kilometers from Chonjin." Dan used the map on his tablet to illustrate his point. "Abby, that's what the this strange intel has told us, and not only that, but it's an obvious objective, and if they take it, then Russia's main Pacific port will be removed as a supply depot. Strategically, this is a game changer if we can't stop the invasion in the first week."

"So." She pushed her chair back and glanced up at the Greta Kempton portrait of Bess Truman. "What are you proposing?"

"We lie in wait for the Hóng Fēng task force, and make our first move there."

President Moore nodded and turned back to her advisor. "So, we slap Jung Ghim down hard. It's a good start." She tapped her screen. "Well, I guess we better get Yuri on the line and give him the news. It's gonna be American air power and Russian boots who fight this war." She looked up at Belcher. "But will it be enough?"

"Believe me, Abigail," Dan told her as he switched off his tablet, "between NATO, THOR, five wings of B-4 bombers, and the three carrier battle groups stationed around the Sea of Japan, the Chinese won't know what hit them. Not to mention that if they or that lunatic in North Korea react with nukes, then THOR and our chemically laser-armed F-45s will take their missiles down over their own terri-tory." He stood up, straightened his tie, and gave her a confident grin. "Yeah, we have enough, and frankly, the Russians will be fighting for their motherland. The last two times they were forced to do that, nei-ther Napoleon nor Hitler survived the ass-kicking they got. Bojing and Patel will fare no better."

CHAPTER FOURTEEN

KEY TO THE STARS
FUKUOKA, JAPAN

Years of punishing work finally produced the first test vehicle outside of the lab. Because the old journal hadn't been recorded in sequence, it was difficult to decipher. It had been documented as per discovery at a time when data storage meant the written word, and the human brain.

Frustration mounted each time Hikaru hit a dead end forcing him to backtrack to discover his error. Many times he felt like defying the old legend and giving up, but one glance at the Hoshi Katana and he'd return to hammer out the answer from some scrawled formula or notation, often scores of pages back. Then, early one morning after yet another all-night session of trying to connect the dots, something happened.

It all made perfect sense.

A small island in the Genkainada Sea was used for their live test. The first craft was two meters wide and, just like the original, shaped like a bowl. It took months of prep before the first test flight was finally made. On a clear hot day, within sight of the sea, a small group of scientists were gathered inside the control van as sunlight gleamed off the shiny steel alloy craft. The vehicle, named IMI-1 but nicknamed the *Ryūjin*, or father of dragons, sat atop a ten-by-ten-meter magnetic accelerator.

At T-minus seventy-two minutes the accelerator's refrigeration system was activated to half power with four giant diesel generators charging up the massive battery that was at the heart of the accelerator. A much smaller accelerator was aboard the craft, and at T-minus twenty-five minutes this too was activated, and the battery charged to full capacity.

At T-minus one minute both refrigeration systems had reached absolute zero, the batteries were fully charged, and the diesels cut back to an idle. At T-minus ten seconds the chief launch technician began a verbal countdown. Everyone held their breath as the countdown reached zero.

Liftoff went beyond Hikaru's wildest dreams. A bright flash accompanied by an electronic whoosh and the *Ryūjin* not only launched but was out of sight in an instant. It had simply disappeared.

At first uncertainty gripped the launch team. Several of the crew rushed to the accelerator, thinking that something had gone wrong. Their fear was that the vehicle had somehow been destroyed in the bright flash, but when they got there, the launch cradle was undamaged. It was also empty.

Suddenly, a voice from the van began yelling at them, "I've got control of *Ryūjin*. It's already in the stratosphere, and still accelerating." The group ran back into the van and watched the monitors from the onboard cameras.

Hikaru couldn't believe his eyes. It worked! And not only that, but it was working far beyond expectations. "Stop its lift and move it horizontally." The man working the joysticks made a couple adjustments on his control panel. The craft stopped rising and began to move in the direction that the pilot directed it and going very fast. Through the onboard cameras Earth's curvature was not only visible, but most of the planet could be seen. "What's its altitude now?" he asked anxiously.

"It's 4,325 kilometers, and it only took twenty-one seconds," reported the pilot. "It's now moving horizontally at 20,000 kilometers an hour."

"Is that maximum speed?"

"No, bosu," said the pilot, his eyes glued to his flight console, "I've only got it at a fraction of potential speed." He looked up expectantly. "Do you want to go faster?"

"Of course," replied Hikaru, "but not today. Bring it back and land it."

"Hai, bosu." Within six minutes *Ryūjin* hovered three meters above its cradle. The pilot reduced power and the craft touched down exactly where it had launched.

Later, back at Fukuoka, Hikaru and his chief scientist, Riku Sumida, a short, prematurely balding young engineer, pored over every aspect of the flight data. "It performed better than expected, Hikaru. With a few more flights *Ryūjin* can reach its full potential."

"True, Riku, but this technology's full capability can't be reached with this vehicle." His eyes grew bright with anticipation. "We need to build a craft that'll carry men into space. Only then will we approach full potential."

"I agree, Hikaru, but it'll take decades before we can design a vehicle that'll carry anything but electronics. The acceleration alone will kill anything inside it."

Hikaru walked slowly around the craft, running his hands over its smooth outer skin, and pondered the possibilities. "I understand, Riku, but time is a luxury we don't have."

The other scientist nodded. "What do you have in mind, bosu?"

"Bigger, faster," Hikaru grinned mischievously, "and safer."

"Yes!" Riku exclaimed. "All we need is a bigger lab, bigger launch facility, and a bigger bank account," he said unabashedly. "A hell of lot bigger, because this, tomodachi, is going to be really expensive."

"Even so, we have the right technology, Riku," Hikaru insisted, "but we need to be able to refine, enlarge, and create a craft that can accelerate like this and not kill its occupants. We also need to build one that can use a planet's electromagnetic field as its source accelerator. Once we do that, everything will be within reach."

"Then we better get started as soon as possible, bosu."

"I already have," Hikaru said, looking up as though seeing the stars. "We'll be moving this facility to a much larger facility and will contact NASA within the month."

"NASA?" Riku's eyes widened. "Why do you want to let them get their hands on this so soon after our first launch, and do you think that they'll even want to invest in *our* breakthrough?"

Hikaru whispered as if someone else was in the room. "Of course they will. They must, because what I have in mind will take resources far beyond what our company can afford. Once they see that this technology will give access to the far reaches of space, they'll jump at it." Looking fondly at his friend, he said, "This is bigger than us, Riku. It needs to be shared, and it needs to be accelerated much faster than what we're able to." He stood up and walked over to the data screen still up on the computer. "So, we need to get back to the drawing board."

"Drawing board, bosu?" Riku was confused. "I thought this was it, and that NASA would leap into our laps once you show them these plans?"

Without taking his eyes off the screen, Hikaru said, "Oh, they'll jump, all right, but first we need bigger plans, something that'll take their breath away." He looked back at Riku. "Not this toy that they should have figured out decades ago. No, we need to shock them with better plans, and prove that the sky's not the limit."

The breakthrough came two years later. Riku ran into Hikaru's office waving a printout. Without saying a word, Riku placed the paper on Hikaru's desk and stood back to watch his reaction. "What have you brought me, tomodachi?" The engineer grinned but kept his mouth shut. Hikaru took the hint and sat down to study the paper. After several minutes he slapped the desk and shouted, "Hai! This could really work."

They spent the next year designing and building a larger craft. Size wasn't an issue, not for the crew they had in mind. Finally came the day when they had to decide—what crew?

"What's the big deal, bosu?" asked Riku. "We'll just use a rat."

"No," insisted Hikaru, "we need something more noble than a rat. Think of something else."

"My son, Isami, has a small Komodo dragon," Riku suggested. "It's still young, but this is the *Ryūjin II*, after all."

"That's perfect, but will your son be willing to sacrifice it?"

"It's no sacrifice, bosu," Riku asserted. "It'll survive. I bet a dragon's life on it."

A year later, after sending *Ryūjin II* around the moon and back in less than twelve minutes, the launch crew anxiously waited to view the payload. Upon opening the small hatch, a chorus of human cheers drowned out the angry screeching coming from inside the cockpit. Isami's pet leapt from the still-humming craft and escaped into some nearby rocks.

At long last, the dragon was free.

CHAPTER FIFTEEN

WORLD WAR THREE
MOSCOW, RUSSIA

For over a century the machinations of mankind had successfully prevented this day. But that was then. Now, there was no more compelling impetus for going to war than dying of thirst on a national scale.

It started with the combined armies of China, India, and North Korea simultaneously attacking over a 2800-kilometer front. The three-pronged attack involved 16 million soldiers, over 11,000 tanks, and the full throw weight of their combined air forces. All three armies smashed across Russia's southern border just after midnight China Standard Time.

Borya put the call in to the White House less than a minute later. When President Moore's face came into focus, he noted Dan Belcher lurking in the background.

Without saying hello, Volkov snapped, "It's started."

"I know," Moore told him. "We're watching it now."

President Volkov paced back and forth in the Kremlin war room. All his spy satellites, ground-based radar, and listening stations had been prepared for this moment. "I'm about to send in the few ground troops we have in the area, as per our agreed-to diversionary tactic, and while they're being slaughtered trying to slow down the Chinese juggernaut, your remote THOR crews can do their magic while safely out of harm's way."

"As you said, Yuri, it's the agreed-to tactic."

"Of course it is," grumbled Volkov. "What's happening right now?"

"Now? We're finalizing the systems check," she assured him. "We need to wait until the bulk of the Chinese armored forces are in the open plains of Amurskaya before we launch countermeasures with either THOR or the B-4 bombers."

Volkov had never liked this part of the plan, and once again let her know his misgivings. "Madam President, if you wait that long, there'll be millions of invading troops on Russian soil, not to mention multiple divisions of armor. I implore you to adjust your plan and attack them sooner."

"We've already discussed this, Yuri," she patiently explained. "However, let's visit this again. Because THOR is a line-of-sight weapon system, we need them in open territory. If the target, take tanks for instance, are in the mountains, then that can reduce target acquisition by as much as 50 percent if the firing platform is not in a 22 degree perigee. Therefore, we need the leading edge, those damn tanks again, in an open plain, so we can hit them from horizon to horizon."

Volkov wasn't happy with allowing thousands of tanks onto his motherland before the first attempts to take them out were made, but he knew she was right, and only the THOR could remove hundreds of tanks in seconds. "Have it your way, Abigail. I just hope that your systems will work as good as advertised, because if they don't then I've lost half my country."

The POTUS took a deep breath. "Relax, Yuri. When we finally launch our counter-attack, their armor will disappear within minutes, not to mention their air forces will be fully engaged by several flights of NATO, Australian, and Japanese squadrons of F-45 Mirror Stealth fighters."

"How many squadrons, Abigail?"

"Many, Yuri," she dryly answered. "You know the rules, and I won't discuss numbers with you. All we'll discuss are results, and speaking of which, thank you for placing your attack submarines in the designated blinds."

"How do you know that we have?"

Moore blinked once at the screen. "I read the report."

"Why can't you even tell me that?" Volkov blustered.

"You do remember the last five or six conversations we've had, don't you?"

"Da, I remember." He muted his line and grumbled to Borya, "She reminds me every time we talk," then turned his mic back on. "So, when will we discuss *results*? I've got the entire Russian government breathing down my neck."

"Then just create a new government like you did after Samara." She grinned when Dan rolled his eyes. "And your problem is solved."

"Please call me when you have confirmed kill numbers, and I'll pass it along to the Russian government at that time." The screen with Volkov's face went dark.

Within twelve hours of the initial border incursions there were thousands of Chinese, Indian, and North Korean armored units in Russian territory, covered by an overwhelming umbrella of air cover. As planned, the Russians offered a spirited but futile resistance, and were quickly brushed aside. The three huge armies of the Sino-Indu alliance poured through the invasion points practically unhindered. After enjoying tremendous success in the first few hours, Bojing was now confident that the Americans would do nothing.

That confidence soon evaporated.

American satellites watched the heat signature in Chonjin spike as the North Korean Hóng Fēng task force lifted off. The VTOL battle group carried five battalions, 3,600 soldiers and all the equipment needed to take and hold a major airfield. Supported by three squadrons of the Chinese-built Chengdu J-30 sixth generation strike fighters, the invaders flew north.

The first NATO response of World War Three came when a wing of space-borne B-4 bombers fired two dozen high-intensity electromagnetic pulse weapons directly into the North Korean task force already in Russian airspace.

The commanding officer of the North Koreans personally piloted the leading Hóng Fēng VTOL. Since leaving Chonjin, the flight had been uneventful; that suddenly ended when an intense flash detonated 200 meters away. The North Korean commander instinctively covered his eyes and then felt his VTOL shudder. The Hóng Fēng was powered by four tilting jet engines, one at each tip of its two sets of wings. When the commander banked away from the blast, the two port engines sparked, caught fire, and exploded. The aerial troop carrier began a spiraling plunge toward the icy waters of Ekspeditsii Bay. Just before impact the terrified commander caught a glimpse outside the cockpit window.

His entire task force was falling out of the sky.

Most Chinese fighters had been built to withstand low-intensity EMP, but not what hit them. Almost immediately the disruption of their avionics proved more than their systems were designed for, and many spun out of control and crashed. The North Korean task force was only the first. Soon, the entire Sino-Indu air umbrella was riddled with holes as whole squadrons were forced out of the fight.

It was now time to take on the armored spearhead rolling into Russia.

With the unbroken steppe west of Novsilbrisk stretched out before them, the twenty-one strike corps of the Indian First Army saw almost no opposition. Three thousand main battle tanks and twice as many mechanized infantry units roared onto the dusty plain without firing a shot. The Russians, it seemed, had been caught napping.

Once covered by an endless sea of grass, the steppe that the Indian army rolled onto was nothing but parched dirt. The dense brown cloud thrown up by thousands of tracked vehicles created a choking veil hundreds of meters high. With approximately twenty meters' spacing between vehicles, the tank commanders could barely see the units next to them. But the dust was no hindrance to THOR, and once the bulk of the enemy armor was exposed, THOR's target acquisition sensors locked onto individual units and fired the first volley. On the ground the first hint of an attack was an electronic sizzling sound that seemed to come from everywhere at once. Obscured by dirt fog, the tank crews never saw what happened to those units beside them before they too died in a flash of intense heat. The short-burst particle beams burned with such intensity that each hit sliced through the heavy armor, instantly cooking the crew in a broiling cauldron of microwaves.

It took seven seconds for the first array of THOR units to deliver 936 shots.

And they were just getting started.

The leading edge of the Indian invasion force was eviscerated in less than five minutes, and what was left ground to a halt. Their fighter cover buzzed over their burning army like a swarm of angry bees, but there were no targets to engage.

That soon changed.

Squadrons of F-45 Mirror Stealth fighters launched from bases all over Europe, refueled midair, and entered the theater within three minutes of the first THOR attack. NATO was coming to rescue the country it had been designed to destroy.

Stealth technology had been compromised the generation before, but the new Mirror Stealth had once again given the edge back to the fighter. While having a similarly tiny radar signature as the old stealth, the new Mirror Stealth could project that image up to 200 kilometers away from the actual aircraft. Any counter-fire aimed at the F-45 would be shooting at a phantom, while the real fighter snuck in at hyper speed and delivered its payload.

NATO's Mirror Stealth fighters closed in on the Chinese-built Indian air force unseen and fired their high-powered lasers. Within seconds more enemy squadrons dropped from the sky. The F-45s then turned their attention to ground support VTOLs that had managed to escape the higher altitude EMP blasts. These too soon met the same fate as the fighters. Within twenty minutes, the entire Indian front was in full retreat and fighting a losing rearguard action.

To the soldiers on the ground, it quickly became obvious that retreating inside a tank was just as dangerous as advancing in it, and the Indian army soon abandoned their mechanized units en masse. They began streaming back into China trying to escape the inferno that had so recently been their army. Millions of fleeing soldiers were on foot and vulnerable to the bulk of the Russian army that been latent until now.

With little air cover to oppose them, the Russian army showed no compunction about slaughtering the almost defenseless retreating soldiers. Tens of thousands of Indian troops were cut down by clustered anti-personnel weapons, turning the plain of Novsilbrisk into a meat-grinding charnel house.

As each THOR system fired its payload at the wreckage of the Indian army, it recharged just in time for its pass over the two Chinese armies striking northward in a pincer movement toward their main objective of Yakutsk. Once the Chinese rumbled onto the open plains of Amurskaya, they became easy targets for the space-borne weapons system, whose orbits were just now popping up on the horizon. Repeating its earlier success, the THOR units took out scores of the leading armored battalions with each pass.

Dozens of satellite-killing missiles were fired at THOR, but roaming squadrons of high altitude F-45s shot them down with laser precision, and the bastion of American firepower remained unscathed.

As the Chinese armies ground to a halt, two squadrons of B-4 space bombers began firing their rail guns from an altitude of 75,000 meters at the trailing edge of the advancing armies. They were firing into China itself and turning the Chinese rear into a smoking ruin, clogging the avenues of retreat.

A target-rich killing ground was now exposed with nowhere to run. More Russian ground forces smashed into the fray with their own armored units. The Russians sliced through the now-decimated leading edge of the invading army. Few Chinese units were still active, and contrary to the agreement that Volkov had made with Moore, the Russians didn't stop once they had reached the border but swarmed into China with a vengeance.

The North Korean advance, which had been expecting light Russian resistance, ran into a buzz saw. Pre-positioned Russian rail guns set far back from the DRPK advance opened fire with extremely accurate light-armor-killing shellfire. One pass of a single THOR system, coupled with the rail guns, and the North Koreans met the same fate as the other two invading armies.

Once it became obvious that their invasion had failed and that the American-allied Russians were now invading China proper, Bojing called Patel and ordered him to fire his nuclear missiles at the NATO meddlers. China would fire her nukes at Russia, and this war could still be saved.

But Patel refused. He'd seen enough and wanted to save as much of his army and his country as he could.

North Korea had no such reservations and was more than willing to launch nukes.

Bojing slammed the phone down and screamed at his advisors. "I knew I couldn't count on that so called democratically elected charlatan to do what is necessary. Prepare to launch Operation Huŏlóng!"

"President Bojing," reported his chief military liaison, "our anti-satellite missiles have already proved vulnerable to NATO's F-45, and if we don't take out THOR, then most of our ICBMs will be destroyed in our own airspace."

"Then swarm them, General," Bojing ordered, "and eliminate the threat."

Both the entire Chinese and North Korean missile forces suddenly came into play. What began as a conventional war, with massive set piece armies, was about to become a planet-killing cataclysm.

Fired from below the surface of the world's oceans and deep within China and North Korea, hundreds of anti-satellite missiles were fired at the THOR units. Seven minutes after launch, the chief of staff hung up the phone and turned to Bojing. "Mr. President." He bowed, not once looking at his boss. "The F-45s have compromised our attack on the THOR system."

"How many got through, General?"

"None, Mr. President."

"So be it," muttered Bojing, unable to mask his fury, "but if China loses the day, we'll make sure we are not alone. Launch everything."

The cat-and-mouse game that had played out under the surface of the world's oceans for over a century suddenly became deep-water death on a massive scale. Within minutes of each other, every NATO and Russian hunter-killer submarine that had been shadowing a Chinese boomer destroyed their quarry.

As soon as THOR detected the heat signature from a Chinese missile it was cut to ribbons. Not a single ICBM made it past the first fifty kilometers. Unfortunately for the Chinese and their North Korean allies, 11 percent of their missiles detonated over their own territory with their full nuclear yield. The rest fizzled or failed completely.

But, it was enough.

One hundred twenty-six missiles averaging fifty-kiloton warheads apiece exploded on or near some of the most populated areas of China and North Korea. The nuclear catastrophe visited on these two countries by their own missiles eliminated them as a threat. It also created the largest refugee crisis in the history of the world. Nine hundred million Chinese and 163 million North Koreans died instantly. Another 200 million more would die in the radioactive hot zones within the next week.

The whole of the Chinese and North Korean governments ceased to exist, and with their demise their countries' infrastructures disintegrated, leaving hundreds of millions without access to power, water, or food.

The collapse of these civilizations exposed the vulnerabilities of the modern human condition. The worst dystopian scenarios imaginable became commonplace as millions of survivors turned on each other in order to survive. In the remnants of Xi'an cannibalism quickly spread, targeting the weakest and least able to protect themselves. Children and the elderly in the region all but disappeared. The urban area surrounding Guangzhou completely depopulated as disease quickly swept away what little life had survived radiation poisoning.

Only the vermin survived.

Making this nightmare even worse was the fact that there would be little help from the outside world. No one was willing to risk sending aid into nuclear hot zones.

World War Three lasted less than twenty hours and irreversibly changed the geopolitical face of the planet. India survived but became a beggar state. China and North Korea ceased to exist as national entities.

President Volkov didn't need to create a new government after all. He now led one of the only two superpowers left on the sick planet.

A planet whose fever just rose by 5.3 degrees.

CHAPTER SIXTEEN

LIFE AS WE KNOW IT
MÜNCHEN, GERMANY

"Ten years ago I spoke in Los Angeles," a subdued Dr. Burt told the International Convention on Climate Control, "and wasn't very well received." Murmurs of agreement rippled through the audience. "I told the truth, and was ridiculed, ostracized, and pushed to the side for my views." His fist hit the podium next to the mic so hard that the audience jumped when the sound system reverberated the impact. "Don't look now, folks, but the truth has come home to roost. Everything that I said in Los Angeles, I'm reiterating here." A morbid grin split his face. "The last time I gave the world no hope of survival," he said, then closed his eyes in silent reflection. "But now I have an addendum to my last diagnosis—the world deserves its fate."

The reaction from the audience was instantaneous. At first there were only a few angry shouts, but these were soon joined by several more. Someone threw a half-empty water bottle at the stage that ruptured and soaked Burt's shoes in precious water. A white-headed old lady made her way to the aisle, gave him the finger, and left the building.

In the front row a man jumped to his feet and howled at Burt, "Where do you get off telling us that we *'deserve'* what's happened?"

Several others shouted their support and the man kept up his verbal assault. "Every ICC convention has taken hard data, dire predictions, and stark warnings back to the governments of the world, and have, for the most part, been rebuffed for our efforts."

"Well, it wasn't good enough, was it?" retorted Burt.

"Yeah well, since you're so quick to condemn, tell us, what else could we have done? What the hell did you do, Mr. Speaker?" The man sat back down wearing an angry smirk.

"When I condemn mankind for our deserved fate, I'm not pointing fingers at any one group." Burt paused for a moment as if in deep thought. "No, I'm pointing fingers at every group. Including myself. Everyone is guilty."

A young woman angrily pushed her way through the throng of people leaving the auditorium and stalked to the edge of the stage. She took a shoe off and banged it on the wooden dais. When Burt finally noticed her she yelled at him, "You say everyone, but that's total bullshit! I want to know exactly who you're really blaming."

"When I say everyone," explained Burt, "I *mean* everyone: the governments who ignore us, the corporations who demand exemptions in the name of profit, the religious institutions who preach procreation when thousands starve to death every day."

By now scores had left the auditorium, and many more were on their way out. But those who remained shouted insults, booed, or sat with their arms folded glaring at the speaker. Someone grabbed a stack of event programs and walked up and down the aisles throwing handfuls into the air.

Burt hadn't expected a riot, especially from academics, but he didn't care. He went on to spread the guilt, but the booing practically drowned him out. "I blame individuals who vote for those governments," he shouted above the cacophony, "buy shares in those companies, use their products, and abide by religions that use God to push their own agenda." The defiance in Burt's eyes lost some of its fervor. "And I blame myself for living a modern life and enjoying all the luxuries that are powered by Earth-killing heat. Our home planet is literally burning to death." He slumped his head in resignation. "Yes, I too am to blame."

"Yeah, that's right, asshole," someone yelled out, "you're a fucking hypocrite!"

Burt looked around at the pandemonium he'd instigated, nodded, and gave a tight-lipped smile. "That's right! I'm a hypocrite, you're a hypocrite, everyone is a hypocrite when it comes to what we've done to our planet."

The woman at the stage had quit beating it with her shoe but hadn't finished yelling at Burt. "You've given us nothing. Everyone here knows the statistics. Everyone here knows the failings of modern civilization, but what we really need to know is what to do about it, not listen to your bullshit."

Burt nodded again, remorse written across his tired features. "Yes, yes, I understand how you must feel, because you came here expecting words of hope, words that might offer a sanctuary in a world gone mad, but I just don't have any."

More slurs from the crowd. "That's just terrific, you jerkwad!"

"Why are you even here, then?"

"I flew thousands of miles for this crap?"

Burt let the derogatory remarks slide by and pushed on with his speech. "The last time I spoke to the ICC I talked about how the world had turned on us. How we're out of water, out of food, and out of time. I said that our home, the only one we have, was about to place mankind on its endangered species list." He spread his arms out wide to encompass the entire room. "All still true." He pointed accusingly at the audience. "But this time we willingly accelerated our own demise." His hands dropped limply to his sides. "Six years ago we used but a fraction of the atomic destruction available to our species." He dropped his voice as well. "We *only* used 3,300 kilotons out of the tens of thousands available to the arsenals of mankind!" A small tear appeared in his eyes. "A billion people died within days of that horrific war, and a billion more have starved to death since then, and yet—" Burt stopped mid-sentence, placed a hand on the microphone to steady his emotions, and shook his head. "Have we learned nothing? Life as we know it will kill us all."

———————————

Burt left the convention center a beaten man, flew from Munich to Denver, and took the municipal train to his home in Boulder. He opened a bottle of wine the moment he walked through the door, took it to his back porch, and stared up at the flatirons on Green Mountain. It was no longer green. The forest that had once shrouded the giant slabs of rock was long gone. It had succumbed to a variety of destruction, but heat and the lack of precipitation was the main killer. The Rocky Mountains had burned out two decades before. Now, there were just eroded rockslides on scorched, lifeless mountains.

The self-recrimination that he had cloaked himself in long before the convention was all-consuming. *They were right,* he thought, *I am an asshole.* He blamed everyone, including himself, for the plight of the planet, and well into his second bottle he decided to do something about it. *I really am a fucking hypocrite and deserve what I've got waiting for me—a hypocrite's fate.*

Filling what he thought would be his final glass of wine, he morbidly thought, *No sense in wasting the last good vintage to ever have a cork stuffed in it.* He staggered into his modern bathroom to make use of the sleeping pills that had been waiting for this moment. Gripping the wine glass with a trembling hand, Burt turned toward the medicine cabinet, his mind made up. Only death would give him solace.

Stunned, he stood stock-still and stared at the words etched in his bathroom mirror. *"Live, Dr. Burt. Humanity will soon need your influence to save itself."*

The wine glass shattered when it hit the floor.

CHAPTER SEVENTEEN

THE CHILD FOR THE AGES
KORYAK, RUSSIA

"**M**ama, Papa!" cried eight-year-old Leka, running out of the woods. Her light brown ponytail bounced in rhythm with each footfall. "Nadya fell down again!" The little girl raced past the white picket fence, up the front steps, and into her mother arms. "She's sleeping. Just like before."

Lena had just finished a shift at the hospital and still wore her greens. A few loose strands of hair, the same shade as her youngest daughter's, escaped from under her surgical cap. She exchanged a concerned look with her husband, Yevgeni, who was getting ready for his shift. They both dropped what they were doing and followed Leka into the woods. It had rained the day before and everything smelled fresh and alive. Spring had come to northern Kamchatka. The larch trees were budding, and the new leaves gave the forest a sense of rebirth. The anxious parents arrived at a meadow carpeted with wildflowers and found their eldest daughter, twelve-year-old Nadezhda, laying on her back next to a babbling brook. Just like Leka had said, she was fast asleep.

It had happened again.

"What's wrong with her, Yevgeni?" asked Lena as she reached down to pick up their sleeping daughter. "This isn't natural."

"Don't!" Yevgeni stopped his wife from touching the girl. "Nothing about this family is natural," he reminded her. "We've got to let her wake on her own. You know that."

"What I *know* is I don't like this," Lena complained to her husband. "What if she's hit her head?" The two parents had been down this road before. After hearing a soft moan, their argument was instantly forgotten. They looked down at their daughter, who was now wide awake and staring at them with vibrant green eyes that matched her father's.

Lena kneeled beside her daughter and laid the girl's blond head in her lap. "Are you all right, Lubimaya?" She stroked the girl's brow.

"Y-yes, Mama," Nadya answered, and glanced at her father. "It happened again, Papa."

Yevgeni knew what she meant. With both fear and pride in his voice, he knelt beside his wife and asked, "What did you see this time, Nadushka?"

Nadya's eyes focused on the green lushness of the woods surrounding the meadow. "Fire," she whispered, "and water."

"Hush now." Lena kissed Nadya's forehead and raised her to a sitting position. "We'll talk about this once we get you home." Lena's eyes turned sharp as they shifted to her husband, a silent warning. He nodded and picked his daughter off the grass.

"I can walk, Papa," Nadya said. "I'm fine, really."

"Okay," he said, setting her down, "but hold my hand while we walk."

They slowly made their way back to their modest two-story red brick home at the edge of the forest. As soon as they walked in the house Lena smelled something out of place. "Were you making chai before we left?" she asked her husband.

Before he could answer, a woman's lilting voice called out from the dining room. "No, dear, I brewed a cup while waiting to see if Nadya was all right."

Lena bristled at the handsome blond woman who walked into the living room blowing steam off a teacup. "Why are *you* here?" demanded the girl's mother.

Paying no attention to Lena, much less her demand, the most powerful person in Koryak walked past the two uneasy parents and knelt in front of the girl. "How are you feeling, my child?" she asked tenderly.

"She's not your child," flared Lena.

"Every Yanbeyeva is my child," Olga said sweetly without turning to Lena. "You know that, so please don't try to shield my concern."

Lena gave Yevgeni an exasperated look, but he just shook his head. *Don't say anything more.*

Olga turned her complete attention to the girl. "So, you have no ill effects this time, little one?"

Nadya stared at her feet, and shyly answered, "No, ma'am."

"Good, that's good." Olga rose, holding Nadya's hand, and gently guided the child to the sofa where the matriarch gracefully sat down. "Now, tell me please, what did you see exactly?"

Nadya glanced anxiously at her parents, and saw her father nod his approval for her to answer Mother Olga. Lena fumed in silence. "I saw fire, ma'am, and water."

"Tell me more about this fire, please."

Nadya stifled a sob as she recalled the vision. "Everything was burning—cities, land, mountains." She closed her eyes. "And people too. Even the sky was on fire. It was all bad, so bad."

"I see that distresses you," Olga said with her voice full of concern, "so let's talk about the water. Did you see any bad things in the water?"

"No, ma'am," Nadya replied. "I saw—I saw water everywhere, but there was land too, green, and full of life, and very tall snow-capped mountains."

"Tell me more about these snow-capped mountains."

Nadya scrunched her brow as she recalled mountains that no longer existed on Earth. "Well, they were tall, with snow, but they were strange."

"How so?"

"Below the snow I could see that they were made out of a strange kind of rock." She closed her eyes and tried to describe the memory. "They looked like giant crystals, but that couldn't be, could it, Mother Olga?"

"Perhaps, child," came the gentle response, "and were people the life you saw?"

"No, ma'am," more confusion, "I saw big creatures, like—"

"Yes, *like* what?"

"Like the dinosaurs I've read about in school, but different."

Olga placed her hand under Nadya's chin and raised it up so they were looking eye to eye. "Interesting. How were they different?"

Unaware that she couldn't break the eye contact even if she wanted to, Nadya suddenly felt like telling this woman everything. "There were giant reptiles, like dinosaurs, but not like any I've ever seen in any book." Her eyes lost focus as she came to a part of her memory that she'd suppressed until this moment. "There was another. A giant flying reptile."

"You mean, like a pterodactyl?" Olga leaned in closer.

"No, ma'am, it was—was—"

"Was what, child? Please go on."

Nadya opened her eyes. They were clear and focused. "It was a dragon, ma'am." Now it was the matriarch who couldn't tear her eyes away. "And there was something fantastical about it too."

"Do tell, child," said Olga, completely captivated. "Tell me of this fantastical thing you saw."

"I was the dragon."

When Mother Olga left the stunned family, Lena stalked after her into the front yard. "I want you to leave my daughter out of your evil plans and schemes. She's not yours to manipulate, do you understand me?"

"Oh, I hear you, Lena," replied Olga, "but you need to hear and understand me. Your daughter is *the* child for the ages," she took a step closer, "and will one day succeed me as the family matriarch."

Lena gasped and took an involuntary step back as she whispered, "Never."

Olga stood stock-still and, as if confiding to an old friend, told the girl's mother, "When Nadezhda comes of age she will be the most powerful Yanbeyeva ever."

The other woman shook her head back and forth. "Noo—"

"Yes, Lena," she continued, "you heard what she said in there. She has powerful visions—"

"The imagination of a child!" insisted her mother.

"Hardly. They're the visions of a leader who will one day lead mankind beyond the cataclysm."

"A cataclysm you created by detonating those missiles and murdering billions in that awful war," Lena said, going on the offensive. "I don't want you involving my daughter. Can't you get that through your—your perfectly coiffured head?"

Olga narrowed her eyes. "Missiles, which they fired against Russia, your homeland!" She took a deep breath. "There is worse yet to come, Lena," she reminded the other woman. "Don't be a fool or try to hold her back, because, my dear, no one can. Not you, not me, not ever." The Yanbeyeva matriarch turned on her high heels and left the other woman defeated in her own front yard.

"What if she isn't the one you think she is?" Lena yelled after her.

Olga reached the gate, paused, and turned to face the other woman. "You heard her vision, Lena, and you can't discount it." She undid the top button of her blouse and pulled out the medallion. "When the time comes our little Nadya *will* wear this, and when that happens she'll become that dragon who guides our family through mankind's darkest hour."

CHAPTER EIGHTEEN

ARK SHIP
HOUSTON, TEXAS

They met in mid-August at the NASA National Space Center, Houston. The outside temperature had hit 128 degrees and the humidity from the ever-encroaching Gulf of Mexico was stifling. The guests hurried from their cars through the penetrating heat and into the air-conditioned confines of the center. Each was met by an Air Force officer and escorted deep inside the huge complex.

Under a cloak of secrecy the largest players in the space industry had gathered to discuss the most ambitious construction project ever conceived.

Once everyone was seated in the small raked auditorium, the twenty-first director of NASA took the podium. He was a tall African American whose dark blue uniform cut an imposing figure. "Welcome to Houston, ladies and gentlemen. My name is General Cleavon Manuel, and I'll be the facilitator of this meeting, but by no means the focal point. The reason why we are here and the objective we wish to attain is that focal point. Some of you are already aware of why you were asked here today, and some of you are not. This meeting will clear that up." His eyes darted to a set of double doors at the top of the center aisle as someone entered. "Allow me to introduce NASA's top astro-physicist, or as we like to call her, our very own mad rocket scientist."

A few smiles greeted this loose introduction as he continued, "Dr. Bayla Chait. Please follow closely while she explains the general outlines of our goals in this initial meeting."

He moved aside, allowing a short middle-aged woman to step up to the podium. She had spiked white hair, a blue tattoo of a shooting star on her throat and wore a white lab coat over jeans. With an Israeli accent, she said, "Thanks a lot, General."

Turning to the group, she wasted no time with pleasantries. "We now have the technology to reach well beyond our own solar system. For the first time in history we can explore interstellar space," a few gasps filtered back from the group, "and do it well within a human life-time." Some of the gasps turned to outright shock. "Which is why we're all here today. NASA, along with our Russian friends and colleagues from Roscosmos, are going to build mankind's first interstellar starship, and we need all of you to help do it."

Her last words were met with a smattering of applause. Chait held up a hand for quiet. "I quite understand your feelings, but please, keep a lid on any more emotional displays. They'll only slow down the process, and as you'll soon find out, time is not on our side." The room went quiet.

"Everyone has a microphone in front of you. If you need to speak, push the green button next to it." She paused a moment while several attendees fiddled with their mics. "Among us is the esteemed clima-tologist from the University of Colorado, Dr. Randall Burt. His dire predictions over the past two generations about the state of our planet have proved eerily accurate, which is why I've asked him to speak here today." She nodded in his direction. "Doctor, in your estimation, how much time does Earth have before human life is no longer possible?"

With a steady hand Burt leaned forward and pressed the green button. "It's my belief that if precipitation rates remain at cataclysmic drought levels, coupled with the increasing global temperatures, then the end of the Earth's sustainability is no more than a few decades. Thirty, maybe forty years at most."

"And what happens after that, Doctor?" asked Chait.

"The most essential resource for life, fresh water, will vanish." He paused for a moment, but Chait's nod prompted him to continue. "It's an extinction-level event that mankind will not survive."

"Thank you, Doctor," she said as Burt leaned back in his chair. "So, as you can see we have very little time to accomplish what is now within our grasp to do." Her eyes swept the room, and she noticed several confused faces. "And what is that exactly, you might ask?" She pointed over at the two Japanese men seated near the front. "Thanks to the invention by Dr. Mizushima and Interstellar Mizushima Incorporated, we can now travel hundreds of light years in only a handful of solar years. Gentlemen, the human race owes you a debt of thanks." Both men made a small bow with their heads. "As I was saying, utilizing this new drive system, called the Enhanced Magnetic Drive or EMD, we are going to build an ark ship."

In spite of her earlier request that everyone remain quiet someone in the back asked, "What do you mean by 'an ark ship', and where are we going to go?"

Without directly answering his question, Chait tapped a remote, and several large panoramic screens lit up on the wall behind her. "Ladies and gentlemen, the screen on the left is a rendering of the ark ship, called the *Magellan II.*"

"It's huge," several members remarked simultaneously.

"Can we actually build that?" asked another.

The middle screen was a low-resolution image of a blue planet. Dr. Chait used a laser pointer as she described the image. "This shot was taken by the most powerful deep space telescope ever built, the *Spitzer*

IV. Last year it was sent beyond the Oort cloud via EMD in search of an M-class planet, and within three months, it confirmed that Kepler 3211a, the planet on the screen, is environmentally compatible with Earth."

"It's so blue—" someone blurted out.

"But, will it support life—our biology?" came a direct question.

Dr. Chait pushed another remote button, and a second depiction of the planet came up on screen. "The planet, Kepler 3211a, is 1,187 light years from Earth. It's in a red dwarf system in the Draco Constellation. Using an astronomical spectroscopy, the *Spitzer IV* analyzed this candidate planet, as it has several others." She brought another image of the planet to the third screen. "The spectroscopy revealed that Kepler 3211a is an Earth-size rock with an ocean of liquid water. As in H2O, folks, and its atmosphere is 21.2 percent oxygen. By comparison, the Earth has 21 percent oxygen." She turned and smiled for the first time during the presentation. "This planet can sustain life as we know it. Human life."

"But what if it's already inhabited by intelligent life?" a woman asked.

"Analysis has not shown an abundance of greenhouse gases, so we're assuming that there's no species capable of advanced industry."

"That only means that any sentient species that may exist there isn't in the same technological window as us," said the same woman.

Conceding the point, Chait nodded. "We're aware that it's a gamble, but we really have no other choice."

Everyone went silent, and Chait continued. "We're going to build the *Magellan II*, place 10,000 colonists on board, put them to sleep for the duration of the voyage, about ten years, and send them to Kepler 3211a where they will create a colony."

Burt leaned forward and pushed his green button. "What about the rest of humanity left on Earth, Dr. Chait? What happens to them?"

Chait pursed her lips in a slight grimace. "A good question, Dr. Burt, but difficult to answer."

"It's not that difficult a question," countered Burt.

She closed her eyes as she formulated a response. When she opened them again her eyes were hard and calculated. "Correct, it's not a difficult question to answer, it's just that the answer is difficult to say." She moved to the podium and gripped both edges. "As you've stated, Dr. Burt, Earth only has a few decades left. Our colonization plan is to save our species from extinction, but we can only save a tiny fraction." She glanced over at General Manuel, who nodded his assent. She turned her attention back to the group and explained, "We had to make some hard choices."

"Care to enlighten us on your choices?" Burt asked.

"We've adopted the triage concept," replied Chait, "which means that these 10,000 colonists, and hopefully any follow-up missions, will be the seeds that humanity needs to re-establish itself, and ultimately survive."

"You still haven't answered my question."

Chait sighed heavily. "If your prognosis about Earth holds true, then whoever is left will perish with it." Everyone started talking at once and she again held up her hand for silence. "Due to the advantages provided by the EMD, we can now quickly transit to Mars, where we are presently creating a colony." The room fell quiet again. "But Mars is a hostile environment, and can only support a few dozen people at first. Our eventual goal is to terraform Mars. However, this will take hundreds of years, and Earth will be long dead by the time it's ready to support life. This means that Kepler 3211a is our best chance for our survival as a species."

"Are you going public with this?" asked Burt.

Chait again glanced at General Manuel who made a slight shake of his head. "Dr. Burt, I don't really know what the policy is."

"Well, take it from me," said Burt, looking like he was staring into oblivion, "people don't want to know the truth." His focus turned back to Chait. "Because, if your 'triage concept' gets out, everything associated with this project, including us will be demonized."

"We know, Dr. Burt, and appreciate the ramifications of full public disclosure. We also appreciate that this is an extremely unpalatable concept, choosing who lives and who remains to die." Chait paused momentarily while her steely blue eyes swept everyone in the room. "But what other choice do we have?"

CHAPTER NINETEEN

CONDOLENCES
MOSCOW, RUSSIA

D riven by gale force winds, the torrent pounded Volkov's office window like a pluvial hammer. Explosive thunder closely chased flashes of lightning exposing the dark day. The newly reelected president was in an equally foul mood. Borya had been far more than a personal advisor. He'd been the driving force behind presidential policy, and the real reason Volkov had remained in power for so long. Now he was gone.

But he'd left a legacy.

Four hours after Borya died, a private courier delivered his handwritten note to Volkov. An hour later, the President, still clutching the note, stared limply at the Russian flag violently whipping at half-mast. The note's words were like a gunshot to his head: *Yuri, I'm sorry to tell you like this, but you must name my nephew, Viktor Petrov, as my successor. He knows everything about us, and his knowledge could destroy you. Please forgive me. I have no idea how he found out. B.*

But Olga knew how. Having seen enough, she returned to her body after the heartbroken man burned the note.

"Petrov!" Volkov yelled at his new aide, "get that mouse on the phone, and I don't give a rat's ass what time it is in Washington!"

The diminutive thirty-two-year-old aide had small grey eyes set too close together and a nasal voice. "Right away, Mr. President," he said, hurrying into the outer office to put in the call. Petrov returned a few minutes later and stood stiffly in front of Volkov's big desk. "He's on the line now, sir."

"Took long enough," Volkov said sourly. "Now stand there and try to learn how a real leader handles these temporary occupants of that fucking round office."

"Oval Office, sir."

"Shut the fuck up, Petrov," Volkov swore. "Sometimes you're just a waste of air."

Volkov picked up the phone, heard an electronic click, and knew the encryption system was now filtering the call. "Good morning, President Puentes."

"It's eleven thirty at night here, President Volkov," came the cordial but swift response. "What can I do for you?"

Volkov leaned back and put his hands behind his head. "I just called to congratulate you on your reelection yesterday."

"Why, thank you, Yuri," yawned Mario Puentes, "and my congratulations on your reelection last month, and with an amazing 94 percent of the vote." Puentes's sarcasm had no effect. "I also wanted to say how sorry we are to hear about Borya's passing, and the same day as the election if I'm not mistaken. He was eighty-three, was he not?"

"He was old," Volkov carped bitterly, "and it was his time."

"Nevertheless, my condolences." Puentes was ever the consummate politician. "I know he was a lifelong friend." Puentes waited a polite moment before rephrasing his earlier question. "So, Yuri, what is it exactly that you wanted to talk about?"

"I too wanted to give my condolences about the untimely death of your predecessor. She was a remarkable lady."

"And a formidable opponent in the legislature," remarked Puentes, "who I was never able to pin down on any important bill." After a moment of reflection Puentes pressed his point again. "Now that we have that out of the way," he said, his voice dropping some of the pretentious politeness, "what did you really want to talk about?"

Petrov coughed mildly and got a withering glare from his boss.

Volkov hesitated a moment. "Well, there is one matter of some urgency, Mr. President." There was a moment of silence on the line. "It seems we need to temporarily reduce our contribution to the *Magellan II* project."

"But Yuri, Russia only pays one-third of the cost now, and yet you still have almost half the crew complement. We're supposed to be equal partners in this. This doesn't have anything to do with your launching of those ten proton space cannons, does it?"

Volkov was more than ready for this showdown. "If you mean the anti-missile defensive platforms, then yes," he admitted. "We now have ten VOLK systems to your thirty-two THOR platforms."

"VOLK. How subtle," said Puentes, "and yes, I'm talking about those. You do realize that we've dismantled four of our units, as per our *Magellan II* agreements?"

"Older units that were at the end of their effective lifespan, and yet, still somehow you manage to have twelve units over Russia at all times, which is, I believe, counter to our *Magellan II* agreement."

"I'll have to check on that," Puentes said, "but in the meantime we still need your cash infusions to finish *Magellan II* on time."

"I understand, Mr. President, but we have another matter of some urgency. A security matter, to be precise."

"You mean the terrorist bombing in St. Petersburg." Puentes slipped back to the ever-patient politician. "You have my condolences on this as well. It's a global concern."

"Thank you for your sincere sympathy in this matter, and just to let you know, we caught one of the terrorists. Alive."

"Well, you do have excellent investigators."

"Yes, we do," agreed Volkov, "and a most interesting thing occurred during the interrogation of the prisoner."

"And is this 'interesting thing' the reason why you can't fulfill your fiscal obligations to the *Magellan II* project?"

"I'll let you decide," Volkov replied. "You see we picked up the suspect in Tbilisi."

"Yuri, we have zero interest in Georgia." Puentes saw where this was going and tried to head off what he knew was coming. "Their separatist movement is not our concern."

"Of course not, but the strange thing is that the suspect confessed to a most disturbing business." Puentes said nothing. "He said that financing for the bombing came from the CIA."

"Was that before or after you broke his legs?"

Other than one of Volkov's eyes slightly twitching, the Russian President maintained his composure. "Please, Mario, you know we don't use such barbaric tactics as these." A long moment passed during which Puentes remained silent. "Okay, it was after, but nonetheless, he signed a confession, and it clearly implicates the CIA."

"I assure you that we had nothing to do with this act of terrorism, but I'll look into the matter. In order to properly conduct our own investigation, we'll need to see that confession. Perhaps you could send it to us?" His voice became uncharacteristically hard. "And it would be best if there weren't any bloodstains obscuring the writing."

Volkov feigned shock. "You do us an injustice with this allegation, President Puentes. We'll handle this internal matter ourselves. I'm sure you understand."

"We can't conduct a proper investigation without evidence, Yuri."

"I understand, but you must understand my delicate position, and of course, considering your own delicate position—you have my sincere condolences. Good morning, Mr. President." He hung up and looked over at Petrov standing blank-faced by the door. "And that is how a leader deals with inferiors."

Petrov looked thoughtful for a moment before musing, "Maybe the Americans really didn't have anything to do with the bombing, sir."

"Don't you have some typist to go fondle in a broom closet?"

CHAPTER TWENTY

A SMALL SEED
KORYAK, RUSSIA

Buffeted by the storm, tree limbs heavy with wet leaves banged against the wood shingles of the large house. Several in the group jumped at the impact. They were gathered in the parlor facing the catatonic woman sitting in the Mother's chair.

Her eyes snapped back to life just as thunder and lightning exploded together. "I'm glad to see you're all still here," she told them. "Sorry about the extended away period. Their phone call lasted longer than expected, and I needed to check the status in Baku."

"I don't like this Path we're on, Mother Olga."

"You never do, Yevgeni," sneered one of his red-haired cousins.

"Because it's risky," he asserted, "and some might even say, evil."

Mother Olga scanned the group, reading each one perfectly. "While this may seem 'risky', it is, in fact, rather calculated."

Yevgeni sounded indignant at her choice of words. "I guess you could call all terrorism 'calculated', but I call it mass murder." His knuckles turned white as he tightly clenched his fists. "Why kill innocents, or foment dissention between Russia and America?"

Mother Olga was still a handsome woman, and though there were streaks of white in her long blond hair, her beautiful face remained as unblemished as it was when she was twenty-five years old. Always dressing impeccably, she handled every matter with complete aplomb. "We've discussed this before, Yevgeni," she said calmly, "and the family voted to continue with our goal."

"If you recall, I voted against terrorism," he reminded her.

"You always do," the redhead needled him again.

"It was a means to an end, Yevgeni," Olga broke in, folding her gloved hands in her lap, "and was but a small seed."

Pointing at the matriarch, Yevgeni jumped to his feet. "Which will bear poison fruit, and the world will suffer for it." He sat back down, tightly gripping the armrests of his chair.

"That is the plan. You know this too." Though she kept her voice unemotional, her eyes narrowed as they bored into him. "We must wipe the slate clean before we can rebuild."

"How can you rebuild a destroyed planet?" he asked. "And what gives us the right to play God?"

"The planet," she said, ignoring his allegation, "is on life support now, and we're simply performing euthanasia. An act of mercy really."

"Mercy? You call global genocide 'mercy'? Not to mention that 'seed' you've sown involves the only two countries capable of building the *Magellan II*."

Mother Olga let out a dainty laugh. "Oh, Yevgeni, sometimes you do amuse me. The *Magellan II* will be completed, a little late perhaps, but it will launch." These words were airily light, but her next were whispered as if confiding a deep secret. "And your daughter, Nadya, will be on board."

"What! How could you involve her in your insane plans?" he sputtered, barely able to speak. "Why, Olga?"

Mother Olga stood up and walked over to where her recalcitrant council member sat fuming. "I told you years ago that Nadya will be the most powerful Yanbeyeva ever born." She gazed down at him. "She will be on board the *Magellan II* because mankind needs her, cousin."

"I need her too," Yevgeni murmured. "She's my daughter,"

Olga's eyes lost their fire as she looked at the deflated man. "I understand. Really I do, but if she stays here, then she'll live the rest of her life in that old mine shaft. Do you want that for her?"

"No," he said forlornly, "but still, I lose my daughter."

"You have another daughter. One who will soon be entering her internship, which reminds me, I must go see Nadya and congratulate her on ending her residency." She turned on a heel, grabbed her coat, and strode out the front door. "This meeting is now adjourned," she called over her shoulder just as lightning briefly lit her silhouette against the darkness of the storm.

Mother Olga buttoned her expensive jacket as she walked the short distance to the large hospital, nodding pleasantly at the reception desk when she entered without signing in.

She was free to come and go as she pleased.

Her knee-length sable coat shed itself of rain and left a trail of water deep into the hospital. Once Olga reached the doctors' change room, she walked in without knocking just as Nadya finished putting on her scrubs.

If Nadya was surprised to see the matriarch dripping onto the tiled floor, she gave no indication of it. "Mother Olga, how nice to see you again. It's been what, a day?"

"Nadezhda, it's always a genuine pleasure to see you." It was easy for Olga to say, because it was true. "I have some news for you that I think you'll be happy to hear. I'm excited just telling you."

"Really?" Nadya was always slightly suspicious of Mother Olga's motives. "What news is that?"

"You're going to London, my dear."

"London! That's wonderful." Suspicion crept back into her voice. "But whatever for?"

"Well, Cambridge actually. You'll be staying there, but I'm sure you'll have a chance to see all the sights in Piccadilly, and maybe even meet the Queen." Olga was almost giddy at Nadya's opportunity. It fit perfectly into her plans.

"Why Cambridge, Mother Olga?" Nadya asked warily. "What's there for me?"

Olga placed a gloved hand under the Nadya's chin as she smiled maternally at the young doctor. "Cambridge University, of course, silly girl; or rather, the School of Biological Sciences, to be specific."

Nadya tried and failed to keep her grin guarded. "But why me? I've just now started my practice."

"Nadya, dear, you can't swing a dead cat in this hospital without hitting a doctor named Yanbeyev, and we need to expand the scope of our knowledge. We need more than a doctor. We need a scientist, or more precisely, a geneticist. A world-class geneticist, and there's no one better qualified to fulfill that role than you."

"I don't know what to say," Nadya stammered.

"Say that you'll get good grades," said Olga, "of which I have no doubt, and then come back and fulfill the role you've always been destined to play."

"What role is that, Mother Olga?"

Olga sat on the change room bench and patted the seat next to her. "Before we get into that, come tell me more about your latest visions." She took note as Nadya sucked in a shallow breath. "The one with the golden dragon, and a red star."

CHAPTER TWENTY-ONE

ICARUS DOWN
MARS ORBIT

The *Magellan II* was assembled in low Earth orbit piece by piece. At the outset everything required to build the ark ship had to be blasted out of Earth's gravitational pull using rocket technology. This proved completely inadequate. Their payloads were too small and too expensive to make the massive project cost and time-effective. A new propulsion system was needed, and the EMD was the best candidate for the job.

It was the only candidate.

Newly equipped with the EMD, a fleet of shuttles now made almost daily flights, with both equipment and workers to and from orbit at a fraction of the cost. The shuttles were designed and built by the project's main subcontractor, Interstellar Mizushima Incorporated. IMI used their own fission reactor design to drive the power-hungry EMD, and they worked flawlessly.

But NASA had a second agenda.

Even with the huge cost of building the *Magellan II*, NASA had enough override funds hidden in the budget to continue the Mars project, and they wanted this to be exclusively American. While the ark ship was deemed the nation's top priority, there were strong congressional interests that insisted on an alternative plan, and an American colony on Mars was deemed the only option.

Allocations for the *Magellan II* project allowed for two extra shuttles to be built solely as backup, but without consulting any of their partners, NASA reassigned them to their Mars mission. They called this new program Pytheas, and the shuttles assigned to it were engineered differently than those used in the ark ship construction. As per the Pytheas tender, the new EMD design wouldn't be built in Fukuoka, but in Pasadena by an American subcontractor, and this company replaced fission with the next generation power source: fusion.

At first the Pytheas program worked without issue, and within ten months a permanent Martian base was established at Olympus Mons. The base soon grew from a handful of astronauts to hundreds, and NASA's vision of a second human asylum seemed destined to succeed.

It was during the eleventh month that the first hint of a problem exploded on the scene. With a crew onboard it was essential that the power output be perfectly balanced with the EMD consumption. Any imbalance caused unstable power fluctuations to the drive system, and instability during acceleration or braking could be catastrophic and end up turning humans into blood splats on the opposite wall.

And dead crews were bad for business.

The inbound *USS Icarus* carried a water purifier and was on course to make orbit around Mars in less than an hour. At 200,000 kilometers the pilot, Commander Kate Zuniga, began the braking procedure.

The Martian magnetic field is much less than Earth's, and what little it did have was localized in mini-magnetospheres which fluctuated at unexpected intervals. All this was known, and the automatic magnetic pulse bearings on the EMD were programmed to sync with any fluctuations.

Commander Zuniga called back to her three-man crew as she prepared to enter the braking envelope. "Make ready for deceleration," she told them in her unflappable commander's voice, "and Lieutenant McConnell, keep an eye on the gravitational balance. I want an uneventful drop."

Even from this distance the EMD computer was able to lock onto Mars's weak magnetic field, automatically adjust its power setting, and begin a smooth braking procedure. "Everything's looking good from this end, Commander," reported the drive system officer.

That all changed the moment *Icarus* got within the Martian gravitational range. The fusion reactor began oscillating. The first fluctuations were infinitesimal; they were barely picked up by the computer and went completely unnoticed by McConnell.

Nothing seemed amiss until the decelerating *Icarus* began to vibrate. Zuniga immediately assessed the problem and yelled into her mic, "What the hell's happening back there, Lieutenant?"

McConnell instantly began a diagnostic. He scrolled through each system parameter, reading it, and moving onto the next one. Just as he got to the balance indicator an alarm sounded. The crew compartment had fallen out of sync with the ship's deceleration rate.

The instant Commander Zuniga felt the imbalance she keyed her mic. "Do something quick, McConnell," she ordered. "We're coming apart."

When the vibration turned violent, Zuniga hit the space comm and yelled, "*Icarus* down, *Icar—*" It was all she could say before her ears ruptured and she started screaming. At that moment the massive g-forces ended all rational thought as pain overcame every other sense. The screaming crew felt an excruciating stress on their flight harnesses just as their internal organs burst through every bodily orifice, and the screaming stopped. An instant later their bodies disintegrated into microscopic specks of blood.

Zuniga's mic was left open, and four minutes after the death of *Icarus*, Bayla Chait sat in her office listening to the gruesome transmission. An hour later she stood in front of Cleavon Manuel's desk, tapping a foot with barely contained emotion. "Hikaru warned us about these fusion reactors."

"He's just upset we used another contractor to build the new shuttles," said Manuel.

"Maybe," Bayla allowed, "but if he's right, then losing Pytheas is the least of our problems."

CHAPTER TWENTY-TWO

THE CLOCK IS TICKING
FUKUOKA, JAPAN

D r. Riku hurried into the lab and bowed to his old friend, now confined to a wheelchair. Hikaru was almost ninety-two years old, slightly stooped, but his mind was still razor-sharp and he didn't miss a thing. "Riku, what did Dr. Chait have to say?"

Riku shook his hairless head. "She said that another shuttle craft malfunctioned on approach to the *Magellan II*." Riku grimaced. "Another crew died."

"During the braking sequence again," Hikaru said matter-of-factly. "Did she say what happened?"

Riku gave Hikaru his first mild surprise in many years. "Yes, and she wants to talk to you personally, bosu."

"About time," muttered Hikaru.

"And as soon as possible," Riku said. "She said the whole *Magellan II* project is in jeopardy if these instability issues can't be resolved."

"I told her six months ago what the issue was," griped Mizushima, "and she didn't want to hear it. Couldn't get off the phone fast enough and hasn't talked to me since."

"I know, bosu," said Riku, "but I believe this time she'll listen."

"What makes you so sure?"

"Because she's on hold now," chuckled Riku. "Just touch the face-link button."

Hikaru squinted at his old friend and mumbled, "You old eel." He hit the face-link and a high-resolution image of Bayla Chait's troubled face appeared on his screen. "Dr. Chait, how good of you to call this decrepit old man. I was just about to have my strong young assistant wheel me out to find a pasture where I can while away my final days in a dementia-glazed bliss."

"Cute." There were dark bags under Chait's eyes. "We need to talk."

"Just a minute, I'll go find my teeth."

Ignoring his gibe, Chait drummed her fingers on her desk. "Another EMD lost electromagnetic balance, and I'm afraid that NASA is ready to pull the plug on the *Magellan II* program if this can't be remedied, and soon."

"Are you still using fusion reactors for generating the electronic signature?" he asked.

"Yes, Hikaru," she admitted. "NASA feels that this provides the most efficient means to produce the needed power."

"What you're actually saying is that they want more bang for their buck, right?" Before she could respond he answered his own question. "Of course they do, but as I've told you before, two lighter atomic nuclei are good for forming stars, not so much for controlling a much smaller energy source. If the power supply doesn't maintain precise calibration with the EMD, especially during braking, then there's a potential for pushback from the plasma. This alone is enough to cause the instability that ruptures the balance." He paused a moment as he studied the expression on Chait's face. "The balance is critical, Dr. Chait, as your recent accidents have proved."

"So that's your prognosis, Dr. Mizushima, but what's your remedy?" she asked, staring straight into her monitor.

"Return to the original fission design, Dr. Chait, and your instability issues will go away." Then with more intensity he said, "If you don't, then the *Magellan II* is dead in the water, and mankind is destined to die along with this dying planet. The key word here is *death*."

She visibly slumped. "I'll do what I can, Hikaru, but you do realize that I have a boss too, and he believes that the fusion power system can be tweaked until we get it right."

"Maybe he's right, but *you* have to ask yourself, as well as your boss, is there enough time to correct the problem? The clock is ticking, Bayla, and time is running out."

She silently nodded as her screen went dark.

Riku waited a moment while Hikaru stared at his dark monitor. "Do you think she'll do it?"

"Of course. She's a brilliant scientist. She wouldn't have called if there wasn't doubt in her mind but," he gave Riku a look of resignation, "she works for a political entity, and like all forms of politics, money talks."

Dr. Chait walked into NASA's director's office and tossed a report on his desk.

"What's this?" General Manuel asked as he began flipping through the pages. "You could've just emailed it to me."

"Not this time. I wanted to look in your eyes as you read it." With an arched brow he opened the report as she went on. "That's the answer we've been looking for."

"Good," he said, and began reading the report. After finishing the first page he disdainfully pushed it away. "This calls for a return to fission," he said sourly, "and you know that we're committed to the new fusion system."

"Take a look at the last page," she told him forcefully. An irritated frown creased his brow, but he complied with her request. Chait studied her boss's face as he read, and when his frown deepened she continued, "As you can see, that's my resignation letter if you don't return to Dr. Mizushima's original design."

"Are you blackmailing me, Bayla?"

"Yes."

"Fine," he groused, "I'll take this under advisement. That's the best I can do."

"Good to hear, Cleavon, because a brilliant man recently told me 'the clock is ticking.'"

CHAPTER TWENTY-THREE

THE PERFECT MATCH
CAMBRIDGE, ENGLAND

B y the time Nadya reached twenty-six years old, she'd spent three years in Cambridge with her head either stuck in a Petri dish or a microscope. Her long blond hair, striking green eyes, and slender figure meant that she had no end of willing suitors, but the young woman from Siberia ignored them all. Biological science was her only passion, and her time in Cambridge the most fulfilling time of her life. Her professors were astounded at her extraordinary progress, and it soon became apparent to the faculty that she was not just their top student, she was the best student in the long history of Cambridge.

A month before graduation Nadya was asked to meet with the dean of the science school. She arrived for her appointment at the Old School wearing a grey cashmere sweater over a blue knee-length skirt and flat heels. She was surprised to see the vice chancellor and all nineteen members of the University Council waiting for her. As Nadya entered the well-lit council room, everyone around the large circular table stood up and applauded. Nadya blushed as her eyes sought out the dean of science who stood next to the vice chancellor. After a moment everyone but Nadya and the dean sat.

Dean Sondra Singh, a tiny middle-aged woman, smiled thoughtfully at Nadya and told her, "I apologize for this ambush, but the council wanted to meet the doctor who has changed the curriculum here at Cambridge forever."

Nadya adopted a crooked grin. "Thank you, Dean, but I have no idea what you mean."

"What I mean," her arms swept the entire room, "what we mean, is that your doctoral dissertation on evolutionary genetics is so advanced that it will become a doctorate program all on its own." She brought her hands closer together, palms up in an imploring manner. "And we want you to chair it."

"That's…" placing two fingers over her mouth, Nadya sought the right word. "Nice." With a small shrug, she added, "But I can't accept your offer."

The vice chancellor's smile disappeared and Dean Singh's mouth fell agape. She stared at Nadya for a moment before asking, "Could you please at least consider the offer for more than a few seconds before turning it down?"

Looking down at the floor, Nadya shook her head. "Thank you all for this tremendous opportunity—honor," she turned her eyes toward the group, resolve firmly reflected in them, "but I have a commitment to return home after graduation, and that's what I must do."

Two days before she was scheduled to return home, Nadya walked through her favorite place at the university, the Botanic Gardens. It was one of the last healthy woods left in Britain, and to Nadya, it was a slice of heaven.

As Nadya wandered through the 200-year-old trees, she didn't notice the finely groomed woman sitting on a shady bench wearing a pink cotton dress, fashionable sunglasses and a large English lady's hat.

"Dr. Nadezhda Yanbeyeva," called a cheerful voice, "you have no idea how wonderful it is too see you and revel in your accomplishments."

"Mother Olga!" exclaimed Nadya. "What're you doing here?"

"Why, I came to see my favorite grandniece graduate summa cum laude from the world's most prestigious university," she said proudly, then kissed Nadya on both cheeks. "And I've always wanted to see London. In the flesh, I mean."

"You do realize that I graduated two days ago," Nadya said flatly.

"Ah yes, that," Olga fussed, "unfortunately I was stuck in that nasty blizzard that shut down all air traffic in Moscow for a week, but I *was* here, my dear. Standing right next to you."

Nadya narrowed her eyes ever so slightly. "So," she needled Olga, "you were spying on me."

"Oh, don't act so offended." Olga pushed her sunglasses down in order to look Nadya eye to eye. "I spy on everybody. It's what I do, and if it's any consolation, when I got back to my body in that dreadful Moscow hotel room, there were tears in my eyes. These eyes!" The glasses went back into place, and she gave Nadya an affectionate hug. "I'm so proud of you, I can't even begin to find the words."

"Mother Olga at a loss for words," teased Nadya, "that must be a first." Then in mock terror she asked, "Is that a good thing, or a bad thing?"

"Foo, my dear," scolded Olga, "let's go see London, and we'll talk all about it." She locked elbows with Nadya and allowed the young woman to lead her down the garden path.

They took the train to London, watching the once-lush English countryside flash past them. It was now parched, dead. The rising Thames was not due to excessive rain. London had built a ten-meter-high concrete wall in an attempt to hold back the rising water, but it was a losing battle.

A half-hour into the trip Olga shifted her attention from the window and studied the beautiful face of the accomplished young woman. After a moment she cleared her throat, took a deep breath, and revealed her true purpose for coming to London.

"You want me to what?" the new graduate exclaimed five minutes later. "I've been away from my family for three years, doing exactly what you told me to do, and now you say that I'm to leave permanently?"

"Nadya," the matriarch told her, "you are an extraordinary evolutionary leap forward, and would be destined to take my place as head of the family."

"But, why the *Magellan II* project?" Nadya demanded.

Olga looked over at her with sympathetic but unrelenting eyes and reminded her of her own predictions. "You've already answered that, my dear."

"My visions," whimpered a crestfallen Nadya.

"Exactly," Olga said. "What you've seen doesn't exist on this planet, so that could only mean that it exists," she pointed at the sky, "up there."

"But you've always said that I'd take your place as the family matriarch."

"Oh, but you shall, Nadya." Olga reached across the bench in the private car and took Nadya's hands in hers. "There will soon be two branches of the Yanbeyeva family tree. One here, and the one that you'll start once you get to your dragon world." Olga ignored Nadya's frown as she continued to paint the picture. "You must understand that life as we know it here on Earth is rapidly coming to an end, and if you stay, then you'll spend the rest of your life in that dreary old hole in the ground." Nadya frowned as Olga elucidated. "The mines, my dear."

Nadya fought back tears. "What about my parents, my sister?"

"Like myself, they will end their days living in the confines of the underground bunker, but we, the family, will survive, and the family you start on your new planet will survive as well. Surely your visions have shown you that?"

Nadya pulled her hands away, looked out the window, and saw only the faces of her family back in Koryak. "My visions are vague," she confessed. "I'll grant you that although I've seen this starship up close, and I guess I always knew that I would be aboard, it's not what I want." The tears flowed freely now. "My visions become darkness with only fleeting glimpses of what lies beyond the starship."

Olga sat back and crossed her arms. "My dear, you'll know all by the time you reach your new home, and the family you start there will have an impact on both worlds." A forlorn smile crossed her lips. "It's already in your stars."

Nadya finally caught on. "What do you mean by 'my family'? I don't even have a boyfriend, much less a husband."

A sly smile quickly replaced the previous one. "Oh that," she let the words linger, "I guess I forgot to tell you."

"Tell me what?" Nadya wrung her hands, holding them tightly against her stomach.

"There's someone I want you to meet, and wouldn't you just know it?"

"Know what?" Nadya had seen a man's face in her visions, a pleasant face with kind eyes.

"He's meeting us in London."

The young man's image evaporated, and Nadya rounded on her matriarch. "Really, Mother Olga," she snapped, "you're my matchmaker now?"

"Oh, don't act so flustered." Olga dismissed Nadya's ire with a wave of her silk-gloved hand. "You've always known that you were to be matched. This has always been the way of our bloodline."

"Everyone but you," Nadya accused her elder. "You never married. Why is that, and why am I expected to?"

Olga looked pained and stared at the city passing by. Her own eyes began to glisten. "Because, my young mistress," she said as her damp eyes wandered back to Nadya. A small sniffle helped stop the tears. "I'm as barren as a winter rain. My side of the bloodline dies with me." Nadya started to say something, but Olga held her hand up to silence her. "It's your progeny that's destined to rule this family, not mine."

"How can that be if you're sending me to another planet?"

"You'll leave a seed here on Earth." Nadya's jaw dropped as Olga went on. "And that seed will become our family's strength for scores of generations. It will produce the most powerful Yanbeyev in the history of the family."

"Stop!" begged Nadya. "I don't want to hear any more."

"Fine, have it your way," Olga relented, "for now."

The wedding was a casual affair held in matriarch's large home. Olga had wanted a lavish spectacle, but after a bitter battle with Lena over everything, it was not to be. Exasperated with both women, Nadya threatened to elope, but compromised when the combatants buried their hatchet.

Wearing a white birdcage veil and her mother's high-collared flared wedding gown, Nadya affectionately locked arms with her father as he escorted her down the aisle. Waiting at the other end was the young man chosen to be her husband.

Sasha fidgeted his trim 179-centimeter frame in his black tuxedo until Yevgeni offered him Nadya's white-gloved hand. Even though his black wavy hair had been trimmed for the wedding, a mop of bangs fell across his high forehead, partially obscuring one of his dark brown eyes as he smiled down at his beautiful bride.

Ever since their first meeting in London, Nadya had been taken with the young man from Vladivostok. Sasha was intelligent and kind and to Nadya, he was the most handsome man she had ever seen. Irina, his great-grandmother, had been old Tadeas's younger sister, and since that side of the family had not solely concentrated in Koryak, the Path wasn't strong in them. Because of this, Olga had reservations about this pairing, but the book of bloodlines had been clear, and she'd made her choice.

Any misgivings the matriarch might have had about value of this match dissolved as she watched the young couple say their vows. Both Olga and Lena cried when the new groom lifted the wedding veil and tenderly kissed his bride. It was obvious they were in love.

One of the family's stipulations for their marriage was that Nadya's maiden name would remain, and they were now Mr. and Mrs. Yanbeyev. The groom couldn't have cared less. As far as he was concerned, he had the world's best catch.

Sasha was the perfect match.

CHAPTER TWENTY-FOUR

TIGHTEN THE NOOSE
BAKU, AZERBAIJAN

The Caspian Sea was once the largest inland sea on Earth, with its crown jewel the glass-towered metropolis of Baku. Oil money had transformed the once-drab Soviet stronghold into a sparkling show city free of Russian rule. But then the sea began to shrink. Unlike the oceans of the world, that were continually rising, five major rivers flowed into and filled the Caspian. Now, with global precipitation all but gone, only the Ural and the once-mighty Volga flowed into this vast central Asian lake, and the Volga had slowed to a trickle. The Caspian was now only half the size it had been fifty years before.

The massive western oil platforms, once far out at sea, were giant rusting steel structures towering over a dusty plain. They were monuments to man's quest for energy and his greater need for profit. These towers had created fabulous wealth from the reservoirs found deep beneath the dry bed of the Caspian Desert.

Now they were a stark testament to a dying planet.

The waterfront in Baku had once been a lush seaside park several kilometers long. A meticulously planned and well-maintained playground where parents could take their children and lovers walked hand in hand. It was a place where intellectuals sat at seaside cafés discussing events of the day while enjoying a refreshing sea breeze.

Lately it had become an almost deserted haunt for conspirators.

A pair of attractive young ladies strolled past two men wearing cheap suits and smoking cheaper cigarettes at an open-air café in the park. Deep in conversation, the women paid no attention to the men. As they sauntered past one of the ladies dropped something into a dead bush next to the men's table. The suits waited until the women were well past before one of the men reached into the dry brown leaves and retrieved the item. He turned it on and scrolled through its menu.

"Eldar," the man reported after reading the memo. "President Aliyov's plane will be leaving Astana in two hours." He tossed his cigarette on the ground and stood up.

"As much as I like birds, Akif," quipped Eldar, his eyes glued to the young women walking away, "it's time to send the text."

"We should probably head to the airport ourselves," Akif mumbled as he dug in his pocket for taxi money. "We're done here."

"Pity," replied Eldar, still watching the ladies. He got his disposable mobile phone out, hit an international number, and typed *The bird's nest has two broken eggs*. Both men quickly left the café, dumped their phones in separate trashcans, and hailed a taxi on Neftcilar Prospekt.

Deep inside the large grey building at Arbatskaya Square, a beehive of activity was taking place. It was not business as usual. The inaugural use of the VOLK proton cannon against a hostile target was about to take place.

"General Skumin," reported the operation's second-in-command, Colonel Trusov, "we've received word from Baku, and the sparrow will soon be in flight."

For two hours the general from Tajikistan watched the satellite imagery screen. Finally, its scanner picked up a small metallic sliver still well inside Kazakhstan. "Zoom in on this," he ordered the technician. Instantly the sliver became the unmistakable image of an Airbus 400 with President Aliyov's official insignia on its side. It was on a southwest heading near a massive dust cloud that had once been the Aral Sea. "Colonel Trusov, the sparrow is now in play," Skumin informed him. "Please make final target acquisition and stand by."

"Da, General." The colonel sat at his console and made slight plot adjustments. Two thousand sixty-three kilometers above the Mediterranean Sea, the six-meter-long satellite made thruster adjustments and centered its main weapons array toward the coordinates the colonel had plotted. It instantly locked onto the Airbus, and as the VOLK approached the Black Sea, the plane flew ever closer to Baku.

The moment the plane reached the Caspian's former shore and left Kazakhstani airspace, the general gave the order. "Colonel, if you please, engage the target." The colonel nodded once and pressed the fire code sequence. After receiving the ground transmission, a port slid open on the satellite's energy projector and made a final adjustment. A millisecond later the VOLK fired a two-second burst down through the atmosphere.

The energy beam cut through the plane's fuselage and half the right wing. The Airbus blew up in a powerful fireball and broke apart as it spun out of the sky. A scorched three-meter crater in the Caspian Basin marked where it impacted. Five generations of unbroken dictatorship ended when Aliyov slammed into the dry seabed.

A call was quickly made to the Kremlin, where the news was relayed to another long-standing dictator. Volkov's assistant tapped on the President's door and then walked in on the old man, who was watching an old Russian sitcom on television. "President Volkov," he interrupted.

The old man gave him a scornful look, and snarled, "What the fuck do you want this time, Petrov? Lose your way to the bathroom again?"

Without the slightest reaction Petrov stated, "Sir, the hawk has caught the sparrow."

"When?" demanded Volkov.

"About four minutes ago, sir."

For the first time in Petrov's presence, the old man smiled. "Ha!" He clapped his hands. "Now that the head is off the snake we can strangle the body." The smile faded when he looked at Petrov. "Don't just stand there like there's shit in your mouth," he barked, "get my cabinet together right now."

An hour later, the six members of the inner council were seated inside a secure Kremlin conference room. Petrov wheeled the President in and placed him at the head of the table.

Volkov waved Petrov away, and then turned his attention to the other men sitting at the table. The dictator studied the face of each council member.

Volkov cleared his throat and addressed the group. "The criminal who ruled Azerbaijan has had a most unfortunate accident. It seems as though his shiny new Airbus has crashed, and everyone aboard is dead." He looked around the table, gauging their reactions while allowing his words to sink in. No one uttered a word. "Reports are coming in that

Baku is now under martial law due to unrest. In short, Azerbaijan is about to slide into chaos. Armenia has alerted its troops and is massing them at Nagorno-Karabakh. I believe that we need to intervene and support our little brother in his hour of need." He didn't wait for anyone to say anything, and no one seemed inclined to do so. Volkov pushed a button, and the broad Asiatic face of General Skumin came on screen.

"General, I'm with the ruling council now, and we've decided that our good friends in Azerbaijan are in desperate need of help." Volkov looked around again. No one had moved a muscle. "Do you have any troops that we can send in as humanitarian aid?"

"Da, sir," reported Skumin. "We have four mobile armored divisions south of Derbent, and two more south of Vladikavkov. The Derbent divisions are less than 200 kilometers from Baku and can be there within ten hours. The divisions on the western front will need to go through the mountains surrounding Tbilisi and will take twenty-four hours to reach the Azeri western frontier. They'll create a pincer on Baku."

"Good to hear, General," said Volkov, "and can you please send a few brigades of airborne to take and hold Heydar airport, so none of those pesky terrorists get away?"

"They're already in the air, Mr. President," came the response.

"Thank you, General, that will be all for now." Volkov switched off the monitor and turned to the rest of the group. "Well done, gentlemen. All of you can go home secure in the knowledge that everyone has done their part to help protect the innocent Azeris from hostile elements. Thanks to your humanitarian efforts they will once again be under the protective embrace of Mother Russia."

CHAPTER TWENTY-FIVE

COINCIDENTAL
HOUSTON, TEXAS

Work on the *Magellan II* was two years behind schedule and dangerously close to slowing further. NASA was barely able to keep it alive with money stripped from the American defense budget. The Russian space agency, Roscosmos, had stopped all funding but continued to be part of the planning, and many on Capitol Hill were calling for an end to the project altogether. In the wake of the Pytheas disaster, and Russia's controversial annexation of Azerbaijan, support in Congress was drying up. During his campaign, candidate Mario Puentes had pledged his full support to the ark ship, but President Puentes had been backed into a corner, and if he couldn't get funding out of his Russian counterpart, the entire *Magellan II* project was dead.

During a tour of NASA's Houston complex with a group of senators, President Puentes decided it was the perfect time to call that cagey old bear in the Kremlin. He was with the head of the Armed Services Committee, who was hard on his back about losing defense allocations when Russian support, or lack thereof, was at zero.

Sitting in General Manuel's office, Puentes had his assistant place the secure call, and a moment later Volkov's gruff voice came on the line. "What's the meaning of this?"

"Oh, hello, Yuri," came Puentes's chipper greeting. "How're you today?"

"Sleeping! It's the middle of the fucking night."

A crinkle found its way to Puentes's eyes as he flashed thumbs-up at his entourage. "I just wanted to call and compliment you on the 'humanitarian' operation to save Azerbaijan from the chaos caused by the sudden death of their President."

"Yes," rumbled the old man, "it was most fortunate that we had the resources to step in and keep the peace."

"Fortunate is a good word. Some might even say coincidental, if not convenient. I have a report that says that one of your VOLK systems fired at the exact moment that Aliyov crashed. Also a convenient coincidence, wouldn't you say?"

"What are you trying to say, Mr. President? The VOLK missile defensive system was simply test-fired and had nothing to do with the tragic crash of Aliyov's plane."

"I completely understand," Puentes said, "but my understanding has a price."

"And what price would that be, Mario?"

"Well, considering that you've just removed—"

"We had nothing to do with that plane crash!"

"Of course not, Yuri, a poor choice of words on my part. What I meant to say was now that a major competitor has been removed from the oil market, the price per barrel has skyrocketed."

"A coincidental consequence, I assure you."

"No doubt. However," Puentes's voice dropped to a conspiratorial tone, "now that you've gained this financial boon, I believe that Russia can start living up to her *Magellan II* commitments."

"And that's the price of your 'understanding'?"

"In a word, yes. It is, and that price is now 996 billion rubles," Puentes told him. "Do you need that converted into dollars? If so, then

I'll go find someone with a calculator. There's about a million of them here at NASA."

"All right, Mr. President. I'll have the money wired tomorrow."

"Today would be better," pressed Puentes. "I've got half of congress breathing down my neck over here."

"It's fucking night over here, or did you forget?" hissed Volkov. "It'll be in the NASA account in the morning."

"In that case, Yuri—Yuri?" He turned to an aide and shrugged his shoulders. "I do believe he hung up on me."

The next morning half the money in arrears was wired into the *Magellan II* account.

With the large infusion of Russian cash the *Magellan II* project accelerated, and by the time the crew complement was agreed on the project was more than two-thirds finished. It took much wrangling between the two principal partners before an agreement was hammered out. NASA would provide the ship's captain and the majority of principal officers, while Japan would provide the drive system engineers. The security department would be commanded and staffed by Russians.

A top priority was steelworkers, and they came from all over the world. It was considered crucial that the new colonists should be able to find, extract, and smelt their own metal. The most advanced smelters ever made were placed on board.

A key point of contention was who would be the top physician on board. A heated debate took place with NASA holding her ground on this important position.

Among the many responsibilities Dr. Chait held in the *Magellan II* project, one of the most important was chairing the crew selection committee, and when presented with the Russian choice for head physician her initial response was a swift and emphatic no. Chait wanted someone with experience and impeccable qualifications, and said so in her denial of the Russian candidate. But Dr. Gemma Kuznets, her Roscosmos counterpart, was relentless, and forty-eight hours after Chait had denied the Russian candidate Kuznets unexpectedly arrived in Houston.

Chait was sitting at her cluttered desk poring over alternative candidates when her assistant buzzed her. "I really didn't want to be disturbed this afternoon," Chait said curtly. "I thought I made that clear."

"Understood, Doctor," came the subdued response, "but there's someone standing in front of my desk who I believe you'll want to see."

"Who is it?"

"Dr. Gemma Kuznets."

Crap, crap, crap. Chait glanced at the list of physician candidates on her screen, sighed, and minimized it. "Fine, send her in."

Wearing a wrinkled olive pantsuit and orthopedic shoes, a tall heavyset middle-aged woman with more grey in her hair than brown walked into Chait's office. "Please excuse my appearance, Bayla, but I came straight here from the airport."

"It's your appearance *here* that concerns me, Gemma," Chait said with all the politeness she could muster. "Why exactly are you in Houston?"

"To give you these." Kuznets dropped a file on the other woman's desk. "And to tell you personally that you've made a mistake in your denial."

"Really," muttered Chait. She rubbed her eyes, and then glanced down at the thick manila envelope now adding to the clutter on her desk. *Double crap.* "And just what is all this?"

Dr. Kuznets plopped heavily down in a chair, pulled off a thick-soled shoe, and began massaging her foot. "Those are copies of the attachments I sent to you when I submitted my proposal." Her eyes narrowed when she saw Chait open the folder. "I was sure that with your busy schedule you simply didn't have time to look it over, so I decided to hand them to you personally."

"Don't blow smoke up my ass, Gemma." Chait then admitted, "But you are right, I didn't read the attachments. But I did read her résumé, and she's not even twenty-seven years old."

"Please read the first letter." Kuznets pointed with her chin. "I came a long way just to ask you to do that."

Chait closed her eyes and took a deep breath. When they opened she looked back down, picked up the top sheet, and read for a moment. "This is from the vice chancellor of Cambridge," she finally remarked.

"Yes, it is," confirmed Kuznets, "and as you can see, it's signed by the entire University Council. Please take note of the reference in the second paragraph where he writes—"

"I see it," interrupted Chait. She kept reading. After a minute she glanced up at the other woman. All her previous irritation had evaporated. "He writes," Chait tapped the document, "that your candidate is the most advanced geneticist in the world, and I quote, 'of unprecedented qualification' which, if I'm reading this right, means he called her the most advanced in the history of the world."

"That was my understanding as well." Kuznets pulled off the second shoe. "Which is why my feet are now stinking up your office."

"But she's so young," Chait said.

"With the criteria you set for this candidate, you won't find anyone but old farts, who will probably die within a decade of landing on the new planet," Kuznets said. "So, I think you should ask yourself what's really needed: old, qualified, and die soon, or young, qualified, and last for generations."

"You do make a compelling argument, Gemma," acknowledged Chait as she closed the manilla envelope and handed it to the other woman.

Taking it back, Kuznets casually waved the file beside her head. "So, was my trip worth it?"

Chait switched her computer off. "It would seem so."

Kuznets blew a sigh of relief. "For what it's worth, Bayla, I too felt the same about her youth, but all my research to produce a viable candidate kept pointing in only one direction." She twisted her lips into a crooked smile and gave a little shrug. "It was the oddest thing, but her name cropped up in every single search request."

"Doesn't that seem strangely coincidental to you?

"Actually, it seemed fortuitous."

CHAPTER TWENTY-SIX

BANISHED BROKE FROM EDEN
SYDNEY, AUSTRALIA

The young man pushed the wheelchair on stage and up to the podium. The youth was tall, thin, with the same serious scowl worn by the old man. As they got to the podium, the younger man adjusted the microphone so the lecturer could speak without standing up. As soon as the microphone was positioned, the old man covered it with his hand and said, "Thank you, Robert. I can take it from here."

"You sure you don't want me to stand by?" the young man quietly asked. "You know, Grandpa, just in case?"

A smile lit the old man's face as he looked fondly at his grandson. "No, no, I'm an old hand at these things." He patted the young man's hand, still holding onto the wheelchair handle. "I'll be fine. Just watch and see." His grandson let go and backed away, leaving Dr. Randall Burt alone on stage.

As soon as Burt was ready, he pushed a button on his remote, and the hall filled with background music. It was an ancient rock and roll song from another era. Another world. "Ninety-seven years ago, a rather popular rock and roll band from Rotterdam sang a song about the state of the planet." Burt spoke to the audience in between the song's lines.

On the long walk back from Eden,
"Even back then, it was obvious that we were in trouble."
The path was paved with gold,
"But it was fool's gold, and we were blind to the sham."
But we been banished broke and bleed'n,
"That banishment is self-inflicted."
Our souls had all been sold,
"And the bill for that is about to be paid in full."
Cuz there's no go'n back, back, back, can't go back,
"Because we've lost our way."
Once banished broke from Eden,

"There's no going back, folks." Burt's head slumped forward and his next words were barely a whisper. "Not now. Not ever." It took a moment, but soon his lapse passed, and when it did, he maneuvered his wheelchair to the edge of the stage. He looked out at the climate conference members, and for the first time ever he saw only agreement, concern, and outright fear. The hostility that he'd engendered in these conferences for the past fifty years was gone. All his dire predictions had proved accurate, and the calamity that he'd warned against so many times was now a stark reality. "Even this city, one of the most progressive, well-planned, and beautiful in the history of the world, is under severe threat. All the sea walls in the world can't hold back the curse of our path.

"Much of the Earth is already dead, and the majority of the rest of it is dying," he said without the fervor he once used during these conferences. "Eleven billion human beings are now living on parched waterless landmasses, and are starving to death at about 10,000 a week." He stopped speaking and drummed his fingers in time to the music.

Burt rocked along in his wheelchair singing as the song wound down. It was as if he was alone in that giant concert hall, and not in front of 500 scientists watching his every move.

Cuz we can't go back, back, back, can't go back,
Once banished broke from Eden—

The concert hall went deathly quiet when the song finished. Burt looked up and in a subdued voice addressed the convention again. "We've had our chances, in Rio, Kyoto, Bonn, Paris, Los Angeles, Munich, and now here in Sydney, and we've squandered every single one of them." There was a sad finality in his voice that he'd never used before. "While the world literally burns, dies of thirst, and starves to death, we are still fighting wars. Fighting over the few remaining scraps that are left, and folks," his voice rose as he spread his hands out wide, "there's almost nothing left." He motioned for his grandson to come get him. Before he was wheeled away for the last time, he looked out at the convention. "God help us all, because we haven't the fortitude to do it ourselves. Goodbye and good luck to you all."

As the old man was wheeled away he hung his head. *I'm so damn tired,* he thought, *soon I can finally end the pain.* He looked up at the young man and said, "At least I can die knowing that my grandson will accomplish things that I wasn't able to."

"Nonsense, Grandpa," scolded Robert, "your predictions are the cornerstone on which the decision to build *Magellan II* was based. Without your unwavering warnings, mankind would die out here on Earth."

This brought a grim smile to the old man's face. "So, Robert," he asked as they left the conference center, "can you come spend some time with me in Boulder before you have to go?"

"Sure, I have a couple weeks before I'm due back in Houston, but after I get there, I won't be able to leave again. So, I'll try to come before." He gently laid his hand on his grandfather's shoulder. "I know that you're almost completely alone now."

The old man smiled, reached back, and gripped the young man's hand. "I'll never be alone knowing that you've escaped what's coming."

"Thanks." His grandson patted his hand. "I'm going to bring Sharon. I want you to meet her before we leave. She wants to meet you too."

"When's the wedding?"

"Grandpa, we were married last month."

"I see." A little disappointment crept into the old man's voice. "But I see the logic of that." He perked up a little and asked, "So, is there a little Burt on the way?"

"No, not yet, everyone is supposed to hold off until after we reach the new planet. They don't want pregnancies during the hibernation period."

"Good, that's good thinking." The two Dr. Burts went silent as they made their way back to the hotel.

The view of the iconic opera house was partially obscured by the giant sea wall built to protect it. In spite of the obstruction, it was still one of the grandest sights left on Earth.

CHAPTER TWENTY-SEVEN

EGG CONTRIBUTION
KORYAK, RUSSIA

The late-night council meeting was held in Mother Olga's lush backyard garden. It had been scheduled for ten in the evening so the attendees could enjoy sunshine until well after midnight. Summer at this latitude meant that the sun would only dim four hours before light filtered back into the heavily wooded landscape. It was one of the last places on Earth that still had precipitation, and the surrounding forest was a healthy green.

It was like another planet altogether.

"Thank you all for coming to this late meeting," Olga greeted her guests. "I just didn't want to miss out on all the beautiful weather, because it looks like rain again tomorrow." Groans echoed throughout the garden. "First order of business, Yevgeni, how are the bunker accommodations coming along?"

Everyone turned to the normally recalcitrant family council member as he gave his report. "The living quarters are almost finished, and soon we'll have enough bed space to accommodate 3,300 people."

Olga glanced around the council, knowing full well that all of them were included in that number. Koryak had a population of 40,000, and not even 10 percent would be able to escape into the survival bunker. "And the reactor?"

"We've finished plumbing the water purifier and are now bringing topsoil down to the farm," said Yevgeni. "And yes, the small reactor is almost ready."

"Time is crucial, Yevgeni," Olga stressed. "Because without energy, we can't survive for long."

"I understand, Mother Olga, but the enclave's survival is solely dependent on this one reactor, and we can't store the fuel rods inside the main bunker. If something happens to them the enclave dies."

Olga knew Yevgeni had just ripped the scab off a wound that would fester if she didn't staunch it here and now. "Then we'll have to send out a team to fix the problem."

"You do realize that anyone who leaves the bunker will probably die." A collective gasp swept the room with most family shooting concerned glances at one another. "It'll be a suicide mission."

"But," her voice was even and steady, "the rest of the enclave will survive, and besides, they'll be wearing radiation suits."

"Which will only prolong their eventual death," he countered.

"True, but not until they've rectified the problem, and again—the enclave survives. That is what's truly important." Olga felt like throttling Yevgeni but kept her face an impassive mask.

"Exactly how long will we be forced to live underground, Mother Olga?" asked one of the other council members.

Olga sighed. *Thanks, cousin.* "I thought everyone knew what the future held, but that seems not to be the case. So, allow me to expound on what life, our lives, will be like in the very near future." She looked at the family member who'd asked the question, and in a very casual voice told them all, "We will never see the light of day again. The rest of our lives will be spent underground, but we will survive. And in a few generations, our descendants will emerge into a new world." She studied everyone's reaction. "A world much different from the one we have now."

Most of the group had heard this before, but until now it had just been a vague concept. This latest discourse had darkened their mood.

"Well, not *all* of us are going to spend the rest of our days in a mole hole," Olga continued, smiling over at Nadya, who was attending her first council meeting. "Someone very special has been chosen to head the medical department aboard the *Magellan II*, and will lead the family on another planet." She clapped her hands together, and with a bright sparkle in her eye said, "Our little Nadya, excuse me, Dr. Nadezhda Yanbeyeva, has made us all so very proud. Of all the medical staffs in the entire world, we—she has been chosen. Isn't that just the most exciting thing you've ever heard?"

There were a few half-hearted congratulations from the group with a few casting accusing glares at the young doctor. The rest wouldn't even look at her. Nadya squirmed in her seat and pulled at a loose thread on her sleeve.

"I just knew you'd all be as thrilled as I am," gushed Olga. "However, since Nadya is leaving us, I've decided that she must leave her genetic code here on Earth."

Both Nadya and Yevgeni instantly went alert. "What do you mean by that?" asked Yevgeni. Nadya sucked in a breath.

"What I mean," Olga informed him, "is that she needs to leave direct descendants here on Earth."

Nadya flushed. "I can't get pregnant before the voyage. NASA rules."

"I'm well aware of that, Nadya, but your sister can."

"What the hell are you talking about?" stormed Yevgeni.

Ignoring the angry father, Mother Olga continued speaking to the young woman. "I need you to contribute two eggs, so Leka can carry your child—hopefully children." Nadya jumped to her feet and started to speak, but Olga cut her off. "And you need to do this right away." Nadya backed up a few steps and turned to leave, but Olga's next words stopped her cold in her tracks. "Your genetics are the most important in the history of this family, and without them here on Earth, our family's evolution will not make the advances we need to survive. Nadya, *you* are responsible for the family's survival on two planets, which means the fate of the human race rests in your ovaries."

Nadya fled the garden without saying another word.

An hour later Olga was alone in her kitchen drinking a cup of chai. The waning sun cast a dark purple hue on the world outside when the small knock sounded at her kitchen door. She looked through the screen door, hesitating a moment before opening it. Her visitor had stepped back in the lengthening shadow, and though Olga couldn't see the face, she did see the clenched fists, and felt the fury radiating off her visitor. "I didn't think I'd see you again for a while," she told Nadya, "and I do regret the way I broke the news to the council."

"If that's an apology—it sucks."

"I've never been very good at the repentance thing."

"Which may explain why mankind used to burn *our* kind at the stake."

"And now we're returning the favor," Olga shot back.

The two most powerful members in the history of the family just glared at each other for a moment before Nadya broke the silence. "Whatever. I have just one question for you." Nadya took an aggressive step forward. "And I'm not leaving until I get an answer."

Olga shuffled back. "Come in and have a cup of chai," she said cordially, "and we'll talk."

"Then you'll answer my question truthfully?"

"Of course. It's time you and I bare our souls to each other." Nadya stepped into the kitchen and Olga poured her cup. "Sit, and we'll begin the baring."

The teacup rattled in its saucer when Nadya picked it up. "How do you know that it's my bloodline that's going to do all those things you said—save mankind in particular?"

"Your visions."

"But I've never told you all of them, and never what you talked about tonight."

"True," Olga's eyes darted away, "but I've seen them nonetheless."

"What do you mean, you've 'seen them?'"

"You know that I can astral project at will," Nadya's eyes narrowed, "and that I can go anywhere in this projected state?" A deep frown creased the younger woman's face. "What you don't know is that I can project into other people's subconscious, their memories, and see what they've seen."

Nadya's nostrils flared as she hissed, "You mean to tell me that you've been rooting around in my memories, my mind, without telling me?" She gripped the teacup almost to the point of breaking it. "That's so—so—"

"I believe the word you're looking for is invasive."

"Fucking right it's invasive, and it's wrong. Don't you ever do that to me again!" Nadya raged. "Do you understand what I'm saying? Never again!"

"I don't have to," Olga confessed. "I've already seen all I need to."

"Yeah, and what's that?"

"Haven't you been listening? Your visions. They've shown me the future. Did you mean to keep everything to yourself?" She wagged her finger. "You know what's at stake."

"My visions aren't always clear. Often, I don't even know what they really mean."

"Oh, but I do, and your bloodline must remain on Earth here once you've left."

CHAPTER TWENTY-EIGHT

TIES THAT BIND US
EDWARDS AIR FORCE BASE, CALIFORNIA

N ASA's launch facility had long since departed from the submerged cosmodrome at Cape Canaveral. The high Mojave Desert had become the world's biggest spaceport, launching shuttles that rendezvoused with the starship. The Mojave had always been hot, but the excessive heat in the late twenty-first century was too much for most life to exist outside the air-conditioned buildings at Edwards Air Force base.

Nadya and Sasha were to be some of the first to board the *Magellan II*. They'd just donned their light blue body-hugging flight suits and were preparing to enter the launch safety briefing when Nadya looked up and saw Mother Olga approaching. To see them off, the matriarch wore a stylish mustard floral print dress and yellow heels. "Please forgive my intrusion, Nadya," she told her grand-niece, "but I just felt compelled to be here."

"There's nothing to forgive, Mother Olga. I'm not surprised that you wanted to be here on the day we leave," Nadya said, looking askance at her matriarch, "and never return. However, I can't help but feel that you have an ulterior motive. I mean, you always do."

"Ah, daughter, you do know this meddling old woman too well, but in point of fact, there is that teensy tiny ulterior reason." With crossed arms, Nadya turned her head to the side and tapped a foot.

"I guess we could have done all this back in Koryak, but I just didn't want to burden you with it."

"You mean more burdensome than following me halfway around the world to have a family chat on the day that I'm to leave Earth forever?"

"See, I knew you'd understand."

"I was being sarcastic."

"Of course you were, my dear, but be that as it may, I need to know what your latest visions are, and more to the point, what you see for Earth's immediate future."

"Why don't you just go rooting around in my head to find out?"

"Because, dearest child," said Olga, "I promised you I wouldn't do that anymore. Remember?" Nadya barely nodded. "And, in spite of what you must think of me, I do keep my promises. Especially to my favorite."

Nadya stopped tapping her foot. She gave one nod and turned to face her matriarch. "All right, then, just what is it that you want to know?"

"Just what I asked you—what have your latest visions shown you?"

Nadya glanced at Sasha, and with her eyes silently asked him to leave the two women alone for a while. He shrugged nonchalantly, mumbling, "I'll just, um," and strolled away.

Olga watched Sasha leave. Once he was out of hearing range she said, "He seems like a fine young man, and totally devoted to you."

"And virile too," added Nadya.

"Oh my."

"Now, can we get back to your ulterior motive?"

"Your visions," Olga reminded her.

"Right. It's like I've told you: my visions aren't defined. I only see glimpses and then try to interpret them."

"I need to know what these glimpses are," Olga pressed, "because, in spite of what you believe my motives are, your visions are the ties that bind us, and I need to know how next to proceed."

"As if you don't already."

"Truly, I don't know the exact Path right now, and only your visions can help guide me. See? You still have a role, however brief, to help me. I need you, Nadya, and it's now or never."

Nadya took a deep breath, eyes slightly glazed, and recounted her latest vision. "There's still fire and water," she told Olga, "but now something is else brewing. Something political that will quickly spiral out of control soon after I'm gone."

Olga leaned in close and whispered, "Go on."

"What have you been up to in Baku?" she asked bitterly.

"What must be done, and now you've just confirmed that it's working."

Nadya's emotional state went up by a factor of ten, and she barely managed to keep it in check. "I know that Leka won't get pregnant until after I've left." Olga nodded. "I need you to promise me that everyone will be safe."

Olga's shudder was almost imperceptible. "Yes, Nadya, all is prepared in the bunker, and the family will eventually thrive, and all because of those twin babies of yours that Leka will soon carry."

At the mention of the children she would never see, Nadya's emotional control evaporated and her face contorted into a mask of revulsion. At that moment she hated her matriarch, wanted to tear clumps out of that perfect hair and curse her. Instead she hissed through a clenched jaw, "You've manipulated me all my life, and now, here at the end, it's my children who'll pay the price."

Olga glanced away, visibly shaken. It took a moment, but she composed herself and whimpered, "It's actually the beginning." Olga paused briefly and seemed to deflate before going on. "How you must despise me, but please, sweet child, understand I've always worked in the best interest of the family."

"I've never been good with any of this, Olga."

"You are definitely your father's daughter." Olga smiled weakly and without explanation took one of Nadya's hands in both of hers, kissed it, and slipped a small jewelry box in it. "One day, Mother Nadezhda, when the fate of all those you love is your cross to bear, you'll be forced to make soul-stealing choices. Choices that will determine who lives, and who dies." Olga sniffed back a sob. "When that day comes, and it will, my dearest child, then I pray you'll remember this old lady with less venom in your heart than you have right now." She kissed Nadya on the cheek and walked away.

Nadya watched as Olga disappeared into the crowd. Taking even breaths, she placed a hand on her chest and felt her pulse begin to slow. Finally glancing down at her other hand, she opened the box. Inside was a medallion with a green dragon eye in the center.

CHAPTER TWENTY-NINE

JIGSAW PUZZLE
EARTH ORBIT

Three years and nine months behind schedule, at a cost of $898 billion, the *Magellan II* was only six months away from her launch date. The twenty-second century was only two months away, and the crew complement had been finalized for almost a year.

Engineering and construction staffs had been living on board for over two years. The giant magnetic accelerator was having the final calibration tests conducted by Riku Sumida and his Mizushima staff. The elderly scientist had been living on the giant craft for the past eighteen months, but his time there was soon coming to an end. Riku would eventually return to Earth before launch, and his son, Isami, would take over as the chief EMD engineer once his father had disembarked.

Every department head spent months on board setting up their respective departments. They had to make sure that there were enough supplies to last not only the first ten-year leg of the journey, but the expected twenty-two years it would take to return to Earth.

Nadya and Sasha had been living on board for almost a year. The young couple was responsible for setting up the ship's infirmary and readying the thousands of suspended animation pods that the bulk of the crew would use for their ten-year sleep. It was a mammoth task, and the husband-and-wife team, plus an additional twenty-seven medical staff, spent months preparing for the rest of the crew.

As each crew member arrived, they were given close-fitting light blue jumper suits emblazoned with their name and department, and most wore them on or off duty. And they came in dribs and drabs, a dozen from one department, and then a couple hundred from another. The criterion for arrival was as per the need during the construction phase, and if the ship needed a score of welders, then that's what the medical staff prepared for. Even when there weren't any new crew members coming aboard, there was never any rest for the medical staff. The Yanbeyevas often worked twenty-hour days, and it still seemed as though there wasn't enough time.

———

Easily seen in its orbital path around Earth, the huge craft slowly took shape. The white metallic skin of the command module was dotted with hundreds of viewports concentrated in the upper levels, and as the ship slowly filled with crew these windows lit up until the twinkle of lights flickered like a city in space. Built on Earth, each modular section was shuttled into orbit and fitted to the massive craft. It was like putting together a giant jigsaw puzzle; everything had to not only fit, but interface with all the other pieces. It was a complicated task, and like the medical team, the engineering department was never idle.

The crew module was the first structure built but was closely followed by the engineering module housing the drive system that would propel them across the galaxy. Like the command module, this rectangular-shaped structure was a kilometer in length. The two segments were built separately while orbiting in close proximity to each other and would not be linked together until the end of the construction period.

A narrow nine-kilometer-long causeway holding all essential bulk supplies eventually connected these two separate modules. The causeway also housed all the equipment that the crew would need to build their colony once they arrived at their new home. This included two shuttle crafts needed to ferry equipment to the new planet's surface.

The bridge, life support, and crew quarters were housed in the same module, a sphere over a kilometer in circumference. Workstations like the bridge and infirmary were utilitarian in nature with only a deep blue-green color scheme to break the monotony of endless steel, plastic, and electronics. But much of the ship was dedicated to off time leisure, and these areas used well-developed aesthetics to make life bearable for extended periods of time. A team of horticulturists not only raised all manner of vegetation in the massive hothouse taking up two full floors of the crew module, but also took care of hundreds of large potted plants found in all common areas. Fresh fruit and vegetables were always available in the galley. Several crew members were artists, and within months corridors and living areas filled with original sketches and paintings.

An extensive DNA library was housed in a large vault next to the infirmary. Nadya had worked tirelessly to collect every known biological specimen on Earth, including many that had gone extinct, and as a result of her efforts the *Magellan II* had the most extensive collection in existence. She considered it a key element of assimilating to life on the alien planet, and with a tinge of remorse she was thankful for the skills Mother Olga insisted she learn.

Communication with the home world was considered essential, but existing technology would never work within the time frame needed.

The solution was fifty EMD-equipped drones. These drones were to be stored in the causeway next to the shuttle bay and could be flung out into space using a novel approach that Isami Sumida had invented, the EMD catapult. Without the catapult, their tiny EMD would take an unacceptable 100 years to reach Earth. Utilizing it, the drones would take ten years, the same amount of time it took the *Magellan II* to make its own journey.

All the components were finally put together, and the most expensive, most ambitious project in human history was ready to make her maiden voyage. Mankind was finally leaving Mother Earth to establish a permanent colony in another star system. A planet that was almost 1,200 light years away from the one they were fleeing. The launch date for *Magellan II* was set for the early months of the next century.

It seemed the race against time had been won.

CHAPTER THIRTY

FREEDOM AT ANY COST
BAKU, AZERBAIJAN

Maya leaned against the tiny linoleum kitchen counter in her 120-year-old Soviet-era apartment, one of thousands still housing most of the Azeri population. Russia had occupied the Caucasus oil state since the coup that had followed their president's plane crash, but it was an uneasy relationship. After 100 years of autonomy, Azerbaijan had been forced to become a vassal state again, and tension between master and slave was simmering to the boiling point.

The attractive thirty-two-year-old petroleum engineer worked for the giant firm that had taken over the rich oil reserves that once belonged to her country. Russia had kept the old Azeri name, SOCAR, to help with the pretense, but it was a lie. As Maya saw it, she worked for the enemy, but her position was valuable to the resistance.

Her dark, almost black Persian eyes took the measure of each cell member now crammed inside her sweltering one-room apartment. Everyone smelled like the unwashed bodies they were, but they weren't judged on odor.

Only loyalty mattered.

Maya was about to disclose an operation that would deal a hard blow to their Russian masters, and she had to know for certain whom she could trust. The coming operation would likely have severe consequences for Azerbaijan, but was calculated to garner sympathy from the West. She knew it was a dangerous gamble, but the independence movement had stalled as of late, and it was time to do something drastic. Now was the time for freedom at any cost.

Like all their meetings, no names were used.

"Thank you all for coming on such short notice," she greeted the group, "and please forgive the heat. They've cut off the electricity again. The bastards barely give us enough to run our televisions so we can watch their slick propaganda bullshit." Her cell members all nodded, but no one spoke, so she continued. "As some of you may know, I have access to information about the company that's been raping our reservoirs, and something has just come to light, which is why I called this meeting."

"It must be something really important for you to take the chance on exposing all of us like this," warned a male member of her group.

"We have an opportunity to strike back. Something that will rock them like nothing has before," Maya told them. "I've just learned that President Volkov is going to make an unannounced tour of their—our oil facilities sometime next year."

"Next year?" queried an elderly lady wearing a faded blue headscarf. "You know that his plans change abruptly. What's the window look like?"

Maya pushed a damp tendril of her autumn-toned hair off her forehead as she addressed the group. Exposing too much, even to her most trusted confidants, could be dangerous to them all. "The window will be around mid-year, and all indications point toward him actually making this trip."

"How can you be so sure about that?" asked the same lady. "He's made plans before and canceled them at the last minute."

"Let's just say that my confidence is high," Maya said, while her eyes darted to the street below making a well-practiced scan, "but for obvious reasons I can't divulge why."

"Is your source reliable?" asked the man leaning on the door.

"Extremely so." Maya cocked one meticulously trimmed eyebrow and gave him an encouraging smile. "The reason that I'm telling you all this is because when Volkov's trip takes place, then I'll need every one of you to help end Russian occupation."

With a grimace of doubt the man pushed off the door. "So, your plan is to assassinate him?"

"Let's just say, eliminate," she told them. "Volkov eliminated our President so they could eliminate our freedom, and now it's time to turn the table."

"We know all that," the man countered, "but won't that just bring more misery down on us?"

Just then the electricity came back on, and Maya's little television, sitting on a cheap table next to a vase of faded plastic flowers, flickered to life. The channel was tuned to a well-known Russian serial, and all talk in the room ceased the moment the volume blared. Everyone's attention was drawn to the show with its beautiful actors, dressed in beautiful clothes, living beautiful lives.

If Maya had been worried about her cell's resolve before today's meeting, their mocking sneers at the TV all but evaporated that concern. "In order to remove this shit," she wagged a finger at the television, "from our lives, then we must start by removing Volkov."

The meeting broke up and everyone left, everyone but one person. No one had even noticed her. No one ever noticed her.

Once Maya was alone, Olga watched her closely for several minutes. The young woman retrieved a cell phone from its hiding place inside the unused air conditioner, typed in a number, and sent a text.

Olga waited a few minutes to see if a response was forthcoming. It was.

Maya read the text, deleted it, and re-hid the phone. Peeking out her grimy window, she scanned the street for any loiterers, but a dust storm had blown up, filling the air with dirt, so she let the curtain drop. The only one who had been watching her was still in the apartment, and soon she too left.

Olga had seen all she'd come for and projected back to her body resting at home in Koryak. Standing up and stretching, she made herself a cup of hot chai and stood at a window watching a rainstorm pound her little remote corner of the world.

A world she knew had less than a year to live.

CHAPTER THIRTY-ONE

ESTABLISH A DEMOCRACY
EARTH ORBIT

Before any new group of passengers could assume their duties they were given a complete medical. The final group of civilians to arrive was the legal team headed by a young lawyer named Kurt Lawson from Minneapolis.

Sasha was just finishing up a lightly blanched asparagus salad when Lawson arrived for his medical. Dr. Yanbeyev quickly put the plate away, rinsed his mouth, and prepped his patient. He was curious about the need for lawyers among the colonists, and after the examination asked the counselor, "You and your wife are in very good shape, Mr. Lawson, and please forgive my asking, but why are lawyers included as part of the crew?"

Of medium height, and build, with brown eyes and brown hair, Lawson seemed to embody the typically average human male. But his mind was well above average, and he was ever quick with an answer. Lawson's tone bordered on condescension as he dumbed down his explanation for Sasha's benefit, "Doctor, once we become an established colony, we'll need laws. Civilian laws. Right now this ship is governed by a military system of protocols. All that must change on the new planet."

"I see, but won't the civilian laws we have on Earth be enough?"

"Which laws are those, Doctor?" queried Lawson. "Most countries have similar laws, but not exact. Laws tend to differ as per their country's special needs or cultural expectations. Are you getting it now?"

"I guess so," Sasha muttered as he puffed his cheeks, and blew out a sigh.

"Once we're settled," Lawson went on to explain, "we'll create laws that'll fit our own specific needs, and even though there are certain universal laws that we'll bring from Earth, there'll be site-specific considerations that we'll also have to take into account." He lowered his voice and moved closer. "Do you really want to live under the martial law system that military organizations use?"

"No, I guess not," Sasha admitted, "but I haven't given it much thought."

"Well, that's why legal is here," Lawson said; "we have given it a lot of thought. Hopefully there won't be a jurisdiction dispute with the present authorities when we decide the time is right to build a civilian government."

"Do you honestly think that there'll be issues?"

Lawson suddenly glanced around. "Out of a crew of 10,000, fully 15 percent are soldiers. That's 1,500 men and women under arms, and they now have complete control over every aspect of this ship's governance."

"The captain has complete control," Sasha asserted.

"And who backs him up?"

Sasha pursed his lips and gave his patient a hard look. "I've never seen even a single instance where the captain's used them to enforce a command."

"Yet," Lawson barely relented, "but look at it this way: the ship's flight crew consists of 636, mostly from NASA, but the remaining contingent of soldiers are basically from Russia. They have no real assigned duties aboard the ship, and each are armed with those new pulse rifles."

"I'm still not seeing where you're going with this, Mr. Lawson," Sasha countered. "We could very well need their protection once we reach the new planet."

"True, but with all the authority now in the captain's hands, how much of that power do you think he'll be willing to give up?" Lawson asked.

"I see. So you want to establish a democracy?"

"Eventually, probably, hopefully." The lawyer grinned guiltily, shrugged, and said, "We have no choice but to wait and see what our needs as a society will be."

Once the construction and systems integration phase was complete, the launch countdown was set. It still took weeks of running diagnostics to make sure everything was properly interfaced with the bridge. Working in conjunction with Bayla Chait, the ship's commander, Captain Trevor Troy, NASA's most experienced astronaut, had hand-picked almost all of the flight crew. He knew more than anyone else how dangerous space flight could be. There were a million things that could go wrong, and with a ship this size, there were a million things the starship captain had to make sure didn't go wrong. Born and raised in Penticton, British Columbia, his athletic frame topped out at eleven centimeters under two meters, and his icy-grey eyes missed nothing.

"While I agree with your contention about fission over fusion, Dr. Sumida," Troy stressed his point in an ongoing debate with the elderly scientist, "I'm still not convinced that it can remain a stable power source, especially during a jump sequence."

Riku and Troy had discussed this before with neither actually conceding to the other. The scientist made a slight bow and dipped his head. "Captain, Interstellar Mizushima Incorporated has produced stable drive systems for almost thirty years now using fission reactors and have never had the type of accident that began occurring when NASA switched to fusion." He made another bow to the officer after making his point.

Troy sat heavily into his captain's chair and absentmindedly scratched at the stubble of his closely cropped dark brown hair. It was a vexing subject, but one he couldn't back out of now. "Did you know that I was on the Pytheas investigation committee?"

"Yes, Captain, I did."

"Pytheas," Troy grumbled through gritted teeth, "was an unmitigated disaster."

"While I agree," acknowledged Dr. Sumida, "that keeping its existence a secret was perhaps unwise, I also believe that building the Olympus Mons base was ultimately a good idea. Look at the success it's had since the switch back to fission."

Troy eyed him coolly. "Thanks for putting a positive spin on the fiasco, Riku, but we were talking about the longevity of the EMD." He took a deep breath and went on. "And given my experience during the investigations, well, I just don't trust the damn thing."

"I understand your misgivings, Captain, but I assure you IMI has built an extremely safe drive system," insisted Riku. "There will be no accidents on board the *Magellan II*."

"But," countered Troy, "you have had accidents."

"Of course," admitted Riku, "but only during the early days."

"My point exactly, Doctor, because these are the early days for this particular system. There's never been an EMD this powerful, and never one that's made multiple jumps over a period of years. If there's a Pytheas-type accident—"

"There won't be."

"Nevertheless, I want you to remain on board as the head of the engineering."

Riku gave a subtle grunt. "Captain Troy, my son Isami is as familiar with the EMD as I am, and as you well know, only couples of child-bearing age are permitted to be part of the crew."

Troy looked askance at his engineering chief, and told Riku, "I *am* the final word on board this ship, Doctor. With a simple command I could ensure you a berth."

Shaking his head, Riku sighed. "I am well past the age of producing children, and the one that I did sire, Isami, is more than competent to take my place. Besides, if I were aboard that would eliminate someone who's needed far more than me."

"I respectfully disagree," said Troy, and then dolefully added, "However, I won't force the issue." Standing next to a view screen on the bridge, they both looked down at their planet. The last of the Amazon rainforests was burning, as were those in the Congo. They could clearly see dark smears of smoke, and, like serpentine ribbons of fire, the inevitable advance of the flames. "And by sending you back, Riku, I'm sentencing you to that."

The reality of Earth's condition was most evident looking down at it from orbit. But the starkest confirmation was the radioactive dead zone of the Far East. From space it looked like a malignant black cancer had infected eastern Asia.

As the two men somberly stared at their home world, Troy softened his tone. "Riku, there's not much time left down there." He looked compassionately at the older man. "I find it difficult to reconcile sending someone who I deeply respect back down to that." They were approaching the Japanese coastline, and the snowless peak of Mount Fuji could clearly be seen from the bridge.

Riku cringed at the sight of his homeland but shook his head. "Thank you for your concern, Captain Troy. However, there is much I must do to make ready for my departure from this life."

"What could be more pressing down there than a life here?"

Riku tried to explain. "Before his death, I made promises to my lifelong friend, Hikaru Mizushima, and I must return to fulfill these promises. I have to ensure that Mizushima Interstellar will survive until the *Magellan II* returns for the second group of colonists, and he had some very personal matters that can only be attended to by myself. So you see, Captain, I have no choice but to return."

"We all have a choice," insisted Troy. "What could be so important?"

Riku's voice became solemn. "Hikaru left a collection of extraordinary samurai swords at Fukuoka. I promised to preserve these. It'll be a last act of respect for my Shin'yū."

"Close friend," Troy repeated the word in English.

Riku made a slight bow. "Most important, there's a particular sword from the fifteenth century, unique in its construction. Legend says it was made from a star."

"I understand," Troy conceded, "about honoring promises."

"Yes, Captain, I must, especially for the Hoshi Katana."

CHAPTER THIRTY-TWO

INVITATION
MOSCOW, RUSSIA

V olkov's sixty-sixth presidential anniversary was a national gala that went on for three straight days. In spite of the rainstorms that pounded Moscow, hundreds of thousands attended the parades and speeches praising Volkov for returning Russia to world prominence. He couldn't have cared less.

Borya would have found a way to get him out of this repugnant waste of time. But he was gone, and to Volkov, his present aide was as much use as an asshole with taste buds.

The first day Volkov spent less than an hour watching the mind-numbing parade roll past his sheltered seat above Red Square. The next day he suffered ten whole minutes. On the third day, when Petrov came to wheel him out to Lenin's tomb, he snarled, "Fuck off, Petrov, and don't waste any time about it."

"Very good, sir," responded the now-greying, much-abused personal assistant, "but please keep in mind that the new American President is scheduled to call at noon."

"Wonderful," bitched the old man, "just what I need today—to talk to, what's this now, six American Presidents I've had to deal with?"

"She's the eighth, sir."

"And another fucking Hollywood actor to boot. How original."

"Actress, sir."

"What, are you going to correct my every word, you witless sycophant?"

Petrov, ever the modicum of patience, simply said, "Of course not, sir. I'm just trying to help maintain your image as the strong, resolute leader you actually are."

"You're just trying to get a taste of my boots." It was his usual insult of late. "Now, leave me the fuck alone until what's-her-name calls."

"President Crissy Caryn, sir."

"I know that, you moron, now what part of fuck off aren't you getting?" he shouted just as the door clicked shut. Sitting alone at his desk, Volkov watched raindrops on his window sparkle from another flash of lightning.

Two hours later Petrov stuck his head in the door and told the unattended Volkov, "Sir, President Caryn is on the line."

"Where the hell have you been, Petrov?"

"In the outer office, sir."

"Well, check in once in a while, you idiot, I might need you for something."

"Very good," Petrov said evenly. "Um, sir. The American President?"

"I know that, now leave me alone while I deal with this bimbo." Alone again, Volkov touched a button on his monitor. A beautiful bleach-blonde wearing a red low-cut blouse, pearl necklace, and a vibrant red-lipped smile came up on his screen. "Hello, Madame President, how're you today?" he asked, cordially for once.

"I'm good. Thank you for asking," came the well-practiced response, "and you?"

"Wondering why I have the honor of speaking with you." He trusted no American President, especially the female ones. The last one had regularly kicked his ass.

Caryn flashed him her brightest smile. "I'd like to extend an invitation to you. I'd be honored if you'd be my guest in Houston for the launch of the *Magellan II*."

"Madame President, I'm truly honored by your magnanimous invite, but I have a pressing engagement in Azerbaijan that cannot be put off any longer."

She gave him the pout made so famous in her movies. "Oh, Yuri, I'm so disappointed. I was so looking forward to standing next to our distinguished partner in the creation of this magnificent starship."

"I truly regret not being by your side at the launch, but I do have more earthly concerns at the moment."

She dropped her disappointment act and replaced it with a direct gaze. "Oh, you mean that growing separatist movement in Baku, and why their oil production has dropped by 43.7 percent in the last two quarters."

For a moment all he could do was stare at the woman on the screen. He shuddered momentarily and then, with a steady voice, said, "Yes, that and a few other matters that need my personal attention."

"Oh Yuri," the pout was back, "you'll be sorely missed. I'll make it a primary point to stress how we couldn't have accomplished this wondrous event without our Russian friend's help."

"I'm humbled that you feel so strongly about this, and I wish the crew, from both our nations, the best of luck, and God's speed."

"What a kind thing to say, and if you don't mind, I'd like to quote you on saying exactly tha—"

Volkov cut her off mid-sentence and hit his intercom. "Petrov! Get in here now," he yelled at his assistant who immediately appeared in his office. "Find out exactly how much we've spent on that giant space debacle and find out now!"

"Do you want to know in dollars or rubles, sir?"

"I'm surprised you don't ask me if you should wipe your ass after taking a shit." Volkov banged his hand on the wheelchair's armrest. "Of course in dollars."

"Yes, sir," Petrov replied without hesitation, "that would be $371 billion."

"You know that figure off the top of your head?"

"And the amount in rubles as well."

"Fuck off, Petrov."

CHAPTER THIRTY-THREE

LAST GOODBYE
EARTH ORBIT

The new century burned into history full of hope and promise for the crew of the *Magellan II*. The starship was finally finished, and almost ready to embark on its historic mission. The mammoth job of ensuring all nonessentials were put into suspended animation was almost finished. It had taken eighteen grueling months. The starship itself required a flight crew of 300 during its ten-year flight, but only half of these would remain awake at any one time.

Nadya and Sasha were the last crew members put to sleep. Everyone who remained awake would age normally for the duration of the flight, but those who were under suspended animation would barely age a few days. Nadya would remain the young woman who left Earth.

With a week to go the Yanbeyevas were worn out, especially the boss. "Nadya," bemoaned her husband with a mouth full of potato salad, "you're working too many long days and aren't getting enough sleep. Let me take over here so you can eat some kartoshka and get some rest?"

"I'm not hungry, Moozh. You have enough duties already, and besides," she said, wanting this to be the last time he brought this up, "I'll be asleep for ten years."

"But you won't be sleeping with me." His arm slipped around her slim waist.

"Don't talk with your mouth full, horny man." She nudged him away. "We'll have plenty of time to start a family once we get to the new colony."

"But ten years—"

"You still have to finish the blood work on the core crew," she said, ignoring his entreaty. "Now scoot, and let me finish up here."

"Fine, I'll just be going now," he said, wiping his mouth on his sleeve.

Nadya had bigger concerns than her husband's needs. She tried focusing on the job at hand, but the closer it got to the launch date, the more relentless her nightly visions had become. For the past year her endless days of working provided Nadya with her only means of escape, but as the workload declined, access to rest increased. It was the last thing she wanted. Only when surrounded by the antiseptic smell of her sanctuary did she feel protected from what awaited her every time she gave in to sleep.

She rarely left the infirmary.

With only a handful of days left, Nadya found herself sitting at her desk trying to ignore the fatigue that threatened to overwhelm her. It was quiet in the clinic when she dimmed the lights, mentally preparing for the hardest conversation of her life. With only the soft sound of electronic chirps disturbing the silence, she made the call that would sever all ties with Earth.

Her heart heavy, her fingers tapped in the commlink. Within seconds Leka's full face appeared on the screen. Nadya felt a twang of both regret and pride when she saw her younger sister, the woman who would become the mother of the children she would never know. "How is everyone?" Nadya asked.

Leka's eyes grew pained. "Mom and Dad have disappeared."

"When?" asked Nadya, and then a moment later demanded, "What did Olga do?"

"A week ago, but I don't think Mother Olga did anything," replied Leka, and then paused a moment before asking, "You didn't see?"

"No," Nadya admitted, "I haven't seen anything." Confusion replaced suspicion as she whispered, "Why didn't I see?"

"You're asking me? Look, Dad's been really depressed since he finished preparing the bunker, and now I'm worried that he can't face going into it."

"But, why haven't I seen anything?" Nadya asked again. Then it hit her: "My visions are blocked."

"If you still mean Mother Olga," Leka said, "I don't see how that's possible. All she can do is astral project."

"Oh, she can do much more than that, believe me." Nadya didn't want to believe it either, but no other explanation made sense.

Leka frowned and looked away. "If you say so. You know her much better than I do." Leka twisted a strand of hair around a finger and continued in a subdued tone. "After all, *you* were her life's work."

"Don't go there, sister," warned Nadya. "Make no mistake: her life's work is much bigger than me. You and I are just the latest pawns in our family's evil legacy." Nadya's visions had fueled a growing revulsion about Mother Olga's culpability and soured her devotion to the family. "Be careful you don't get caught up in her vile web."

"She says you're the family's only hope," Leka said forcefully, "and affectionately refers to you as our beautiful dragon queen."

"What's that supposed to mean?"

"You figure it out."

Nadya crumbled. The conversation wasn't going well, and she didn't want her final words with Leka to end like this. Nadya took a deep breath, swallowed her anger, and asked, "Are all the preparations finished for you?"

"Yes, sister." Leka sounded indifferent, but the blush betrayed her. "Thanks to you, I've been given preferential treatment." Her eyes softened as she leaned in and placed a hand on the monitor screen. "Nadya, please be assured that the children are a blessed event and will be treated as such."

"I know. Leka, it's just that—"

"Mother Olga has made our—their comfort her personal priority."

Nadya's eyes narrowed. "It seems as though she has many priorities these days."

"She does," agreed Leka. Her eyes darted away for a moment, and when they found Nadya's again they were swollen with tears. "I hope Mom and Dad return soon."

"Me too. I'm sure they'll want to see their grandchildren." As soon as those words were out both sisters gulped in a sob; the children would belong to them both. "Goodbye, dearest sister. My heart is with you. Now and forever." Nadya cut the commlink and stared at the dark screen for several minutes.

Of the non-passengers who finally disembarked, Riku was the last to return to Earth. He'd spent as much time as he could with Isami, going over every detail of the massive engine that would propel mankind's first interstellar starship. "You need to ramp up the fission no less than one week before the launch," he told his son, "so that there'll be enough power for an immediate hyper jump to the next electro-magnetic field."

"I know, Papa-san," said the short balding engineer. He looked just like his father.

"And you need to make absolutely sure that the power balance between the inner and outer core is perfectly aligned."

"I know," Isami said patiently. "I helped design the system."

"Of course you did, son." The old man grew pensive, struggling for something to say. "It's just that I'm leaving within the hour, and I may never see you again."

"I'll be back in twenty years, and you'll be here to greet me when I come back," said Isami. "Hopefully I can bring your grandchildren back for you to meet."

"I'm sixty-seven years old, Son. We both know I won't be here when you return."

Isami shook his head. "Please don't say that."

"As for my grandchildren," pleaded Riku, "you'll tell them about me, and Earth?"

They both looked out a porthole at the fires raging all over the world, the world that Riku was going back to, the world that Isami had to find some way to tell his children about. "Of course, Papa-san. Come, let me walk you to the shuttle bay."

As they made their final walk together, Captain Troy met them in the departure lounge. "Dr. Sumida, Riku, it's been my honor to have worked with you and come to know you personally. Be well, my friend." He shook the man's hand, held it tightly for a moment before releasing it, turned, and left the father and son alone for the last time.

Isami helped his father into his space suit, and once ready, Riku threw his arms around his son. Then, embarrassed, he stood back, bowed, and told him, "I've never been prouder about anything in my life as I am of you this minute. You will carry on both the family name and the Mizushima tradition." Bowing again, he turned and stepped into the airlock.

After the airlock whooshed shut, Isami said in a very low voice, "I will, Papa-san, and I'll never let the family forget the dedicated hero who really saved mankind."

Isami had the fission drive up to full power, enhancing the magnetic effect by millions of percentage points. He also had the reverse gravitational balance in perfect sync for the interior of the giant ship. Once all the power parameters were ready for launch, Captain Troy opened communication with Houston. After a few minutes of technical dialog between Command Actual and ground control, he was put in contact with President Caryn. As soon as she came on, Troy motioned over the highest-ranking Russian officer. "So good of you to see us off, Madame President."

"I wouldn't have missed this for the world, Captain Troy." The President was on world television and looked every bit the Hollywood icon she used to be. "I'd just like to say how utterly proud we all are of you and your crew on this the first step of your historic journey."

"Thank you, Madame President," said Troy in as neutral a voice as was possible. "Allow me to introduce Major Sergei Moroz." He turned and motioned the major forward. "He's the commander of our security forces and has been of the utmost help in preparing for this mission."

The President opened her mouth slightly, revealing perfect teeth. "It's so very good to meet you, Major Moroz. And where do you call home?"

One dark brow slightly rose above the major's intense brown eyes. His snug-fitted jumpsuit revealed a narrow-waisted, tall, muscular man with a powerful chest. "I am originally from Donetsk, Ukraine, Madame President."

"It's very nice to meet you, and I'm sure everyone back in Donbas are as proud of you as I am."

"Thank you, ma'am," muttered Moroz.

"And I'd just like to say, on behalf of all mankind, how happy we all are to share this moment with our Russian partners." Adopting her best pout, she added, "Unfortunately President Volkov couldn't be here, but I spoke with him, and he sends his best wishes as well. We're all so very grateful for his cooperation in building this magnificent ship, and it couldn't have been done without him and your wonderful country."

The major stood at parade rest. When he recognized that she was finished, he quickly spoke the few words that were scripted for him to say. "Thank you again, Madame President. It is my great honor to be part of this mission and will fulfill all expectations." He bowed slightly and went quiet.

The President didn't miss her cue when Moroz had finished his brief speech. "God's speed, gentlemen, and you have the assurance of the entire planet when I say that the hope of all mankind goes with you." She flashed her brightest Hollywood smile at the camera as she finished her scene. "Oh, and Captain Troy?"

"Yes, Madame President?"

"Although I won't be in office when you return, I so look forward to personally meeting you in twenty years. Until then, a fond farewell."

"Thank you, Madame President, as do I," Troy replied, and cut the commlink.

Three hours after the President's call *Magellan II* was ready for initial thrust. Troy had gone over all the EMD initialization protocols with Isami multiple times, and when it came time to leave Earth orbit Troy called him again. "Dr. Sumida, do we have the precise fission power for the first leg to Jupiter?"

Isami got nods from his entire engineering department, and answered, "Roger that, Captain. Our gravitational balance is 100 percent, and we have 21 percent fission power ready to engage the drive."

Troy then called the infirmary. "Dr. Yanbeyeva, strap in for the initial launch."

"I'm strapped in now, sir," replied the medical chief of staff.

The captain turned and made the initial launch command. "Helm, the general order is given; launch when the Jupiter intercept window is set."

The helm chief held up her fist and said, "Corridor window arriving in thirty seconds, sir." She counted down with her console clock. Half the Earth, smoke shrouding its atmosphere, was on the bridge view screen. The instant the EMD engaged, the dirty blue planet quickly shrunk until less than a minute later it was nothing more than another point of light in space. No one on the ship felt so much as a single G-force increase as the ship accelerated. Isami had the gravitational balance synced perfectly.

Using only a fraction of its power, it took the *Magellan II* almost three hours to reach her first objective and its massive electromagnetic field. As they approached, Isami called the bridge. "Captain, I've achieved lock on the Jovian EMF and have full fission power available for our first jump."

"Roger that, Doctor," the captain said and, turning to the helm, gave the command, "The moment we have our trajectory lock, engage full EMD, and let's be on our way."

In an instant, Jupiter disappeared as the giant starship made its first gravitational warp jump. The *Magellan II* was now hurtling toward its next jump point. That rendezvous would take almost a year to reach, but once she hit the powerful rivers of electromagnetism that flow throughout the galaxy, the starship would make multiple jumps for the next nine years.

CHAPTER THIRTY-FOUR

HOLES IN THEIR HEADS
BAKU, AZERBAIJAN

Seven weeks after the historic launch of the *Magellan II*, President Volkov made his trip to Baku. He wore his favorite dark blue suit, but lately it fit loose, sagging on his gaunt frame.

As his presidential Ilyushin Il-99 flew over the Caspian Basin, he smiled grimly at the leverage he would have over those infernal separatists. "Petrov! How long until we land at Baku?" he demanded.

The answer was immediate and accurate. "Thirty-two minutes, sir. Then we'll take a convoy from the airport to the SOCAR Tower, where you'll meet with the head of their state oil company."

"I need more than smoke blown up my ass, Petrov," warned Volkov, "so it would be in his best interest to have some of his top engineers available to explain this mess." Volkov turned and stared out the plane's window. "That jumped-up bureaucrat better have some hard facts and viable solutions."

"It's already been arranged, sir," his assistant informed him.

"That's good, Petrov."

It took more than an hour before Volkov's flying palace managed to land. A huge dust storm had kicked up, creating severe turbulence, making visibility and a safe landing all but impossible. Once the dust had blown past, the presidential plane made a rough landing. Dressed in a perfectly tailored grey silk suit, Petrov stood holding the President's wheelchair steady during the final descent.

After landing, Volkov was met by Russian-only security. Lowered out the bottom of the Ilyushin by a specially designed elevator, the President was whisked away in an armored limousine and taken directly to SOCAR's modern glass tower.

The convoy set up a perimeter around the entrance to the underground parking structure and, surrounded by heavily armed security, the President was escorted to a secure elevator. With only Petrov and Volkov inside, it stopped at the forty-second floor, the top floor of the tallest building in Baku. It housed the plush office of the managing director who, in spite of being Russian, Volkov suspected of gross incompetence at best and collusion at worst. Either way, the director was on thin ice.

Petrov pushed Volkov out the elevator and wheeled him through a deserted outer office. "Sir, I had the security team remove all unnecessary employees for this meeting. The MD is in his office with his top petroleum engineer."

"Why isn't the security team here now?" demanded Volkov. His head anxiously whipped back and forth.

"They'll be here as soon as the building is clear, sir."

"Get them the hell up here right now, Petrov!" Volkov ordered, just as they entered the office. There was only one other person in the office.

"Right away, sir, but first I'd like to introduce you to SOCAR's top petroleum engineer, Maya Kazinova," Petrov said as he shut the door and locked it.

The attractive young woman wore a white lab coat and smiled at Volkov. "It's my supreme honor to meet you at last, President Volkov." She moved out from behind the desk and stood directly in front of Volkov, who grew alarmed at this breach of security protocol. "Especially on your last day in office." She reached inside her lab coat. "My father was with Aliyov when you shot his plane down."

Volkov swiveled his head toward his smug-looking assistant. "I thought I told you to get the security team, you shit-for-brains!" he yelled at Petrov but went rigid when he realized what was really happening. "You traitorous bastard, you'll never get away with this!" He turned back to the woman and flinched when he saw the silenced pistol pointed at his head and snarled his final words. "Petrov, you ungrateful shit-for-brai—."

Pop! Fired at point-blank range, the 9mm bullet punched a hole through Volkov's forehead and blew the back of his skull off. Bloody bits of hair and brain splattered Petrov's suit; he casually pulled out a handkerchief, wiped his jacket, and told Kazinova, "Put the gun down."

Staring at the man she'd just executed, Maya's face grew pallid and she started breathing in a series of shallow pants. After a moment her eyes wandered from Volkov's ruptured head and found Petrov studying her. She dropped the gun, took an unsteady step back, and vomited.

Looking at the ashen-faced woman, Petrov coolly told her, "You'll be all right in a moment, but we must move quickly." He used the handkerchief to take a cell phone out of his jacket and handed both to her. "Here, clean your face, and then turn this on. Call the first number on the contact list."

Maya wiped her mouth and peered oddly at Petrov. "You want me to make the call now?" she asked hesitantly.

"Yes, do it now," Petrov told her non-threateningly, "and then leave at once. I'll deal with everything here."

She picked up the phone, turned it on, found the contact list, and punched the first name. As the number came up she looked at Petrov again. "The country code is American, why am I—" The phone exploded, blowing her hand and part of her face off. The force of the explosion threw her body over the desk where it hit the chair and slid to the floor. Her face was unrecognizable.

Petrov got out his own pistol, walked over to where Maya lay groaning, and shot her several times in the head, mangling it even more. He pulled out his own cell phone and called the Presidential head of security. "The President has been assassinated in the SOCAR director's office. I killed the assassin. She was trying to call someone when I shot her. Find out who she was calling," Petrov insisted. "Also, she was one of their top petroleum engineers, so I want your men to arrest the managing director on sight and kill him." He listened impatiently for a moment, then barked, "Yes, of course, get your ass up here right away, you imbecile. I'm standing next to two dead people with holes in their heads. Oh, and call the Kremlin. Tell them that I'm calling an emergency inner council meeting for this evening. Once everyone has arrived, arrest them all."

He hung up the phone without a trace of emotion. Looking down at his former boss slumped over in his wheelchair, still leaking gore onto the plush rug, Petrov bent over the body and casually said, "If you want my opinion, it's your brains that look like shit now." Turning away from the fresh corpses, he calmly left the office.

Mother Olga stayed for a moment looking down at the bloody mess in the office: two murdered people, ultimately her handiwork. She wasn't aware that Petrov was going to kill his accomplice so fast, but now that she thought about it, it made sense from his perspective. He was a cool customer, that one, she thought as she left the office and astral projected back to her body lying in bed.

Witnessing the murders actually shook her, but she knew that these were just the first shots fired. Seeing it vividly and so close was a shock she wasn't emotionally prepared for. She'd seen death before, even killed before, but never messy like this. She knew that she'd have to get used to it, because before this was over, it was going to be magnified billions of times over. Squeamishness was a weakness she had to get a grip on. Pity about the young woman, though.

CHAPTER THIRTY-FIVE

TRAGIC SECRET
MAGELLAN II, INTERSTELLAR SPACE

Seven weeks after launch the *Magellan II* had become quiet as a tomb. There were few people left to admire the corridors filled with art or gather in the inviting cafeteria. The once noisy off-duty gathering spots became hushed and subdued. Except for the few core crew still awake, the entire ship was in deep sleep. On the final day of active duty before she too was to be put into suspended animation, Nadya went to bed for her last normal sleep period.

It was a night of terror.

They came in vivid waves of fire and destruction. Nadya tore at the sheets and screamed herself awake. Lying next to her, Sasha felt helpless, but he wouldn't give up. Finally, after he wrapped his arms around her, she sobbed herself back to sleep. It didn't last. Within an hour she'd thrashed the bedding from her legs and gasped in fright. "What is it, Nadya?" Sasha asked, dreading the answer.

"Something's happened," she whimpered, "and it's going to destroy Earth."

He gently wiped the tears from her eyes and drew her head to his chest. It took a few minutes, but her rapid breathing slowed to normal. Her visions had caused distress before, but never like this. All he could think to say was, "Mother Olga is moving quickly, isn't she?"

Nadya clutched the sheets under her chin, as if to hide from what she knew, but there was no hiding from this. "President Volkov has been assassinated, and his personal assistant has had the inner council imprisoned or executed." She pressed her face back against Sasha's chest and mumbled the rest of what she knew. "He's now the President and is ruthlessly cunning."

"But how does this endanger the rest of Earth?" Sasha asked.

The images she'd seen were frighteningly clear and unmistakable. "He's convinced the Russian intelligence service that it was actually the Americans who killed Volkov." Her breathing became ragged again as the words spilled out, one on top of another. "They're preparing for a first strike." She looked at her husband, gripped his chin, and sobbed. "A nuclear first strike."

"That's insane," he whispered, "it can't be possible. America is well prepared and will quickly retaliate." Wide-eyed, he placed a hand to his forehead. "War between Russia and the West will destroy all life on the planet surface."

"Exactly, Sasha." Nadya again buried her head in his chest. "It was Olga's plan all along, but I had hoped against all hope that it would never happen."

"And now it has?"

"No, not yet, but the two sides have turned openly hostile, and they've already exchanged ultimatums. Accusations that can't be unsaid."

"How long until this happens?"

"I'm not sure. Days, weeks maybe, but events are quickly spiraling out of control." She began crying again. "Oh, Sasha," she blubbered. "There won't be an Earth left for the *Magellan II* to return to."

As the implications of what his wife just said sunk in, Sasha put his arms back around her. "Tell me what you saw exactly."

"I—I saw fire," she stammered, "so much fire."

"What does that mean, exactly? Describe it to me."

"Do you really want to know? I mean it's devastating, hell on Earth."

He gently stroked the side of her face. "Yes, my love. I can't allow you to carry this burden alone. We must share everything, and hopefully together we'll find the strength to—to, oh shit, I don't know. Maybe it means that we were meant to survive."

"That's what Mother Olga always said, you, me and our descendants were to start another branch of the family on this new planet."

"So, she waited to implement her plan until after we were away and safe from what was to happen," he said, shaking his head. "It was all so hard to believe before."

"Yes, Moozh, that's exactly what I'm saying, and I really didn't want to believe it either," she admitted. "I've never had visions this clear before. They were always vague, and my interpretations were just conjecture, but now—"

"Now?" He asked again, "What exactly did you see?"

"I saw hundreds, thousands of nuclear strikes. Every major city, every one, Sasha, took multiple hits. Even non-combatants."

"Maybe we should tell the captain. Maybe he can do something?" Sasha suggested.

"What are you saying?" she asked, gripping both his hands. Her voice turned desperate. "Half this ship is Russian, and the rest are from the West, mostly America. What do you think the reaction of the crew will be if they find out that their countries have fought a war that destroyed our home world?"

His answer was barely audible. "A war here on this ship."

"Exactly. We must keep this to ourselves, then find a way to make sure this ship never returns to Earth."

Her logic was irrefutable. And as unpalatable as it was, Sasha knew this ship was now the only chance humanity had. If what happened on

Earth and the national interests behind its destruction were known, those same divisions could take root on board, and mankind's only hope of survival would be destroyed. "It'll be our tragic secret."

It was with a heavy heart the next day that Nadya was put into suspended animation. By the time she awoke Earth would be long dead. Mother Olga had promised the family would survive. Her own children would survive. That was Nadya's last thought before she succumbed to a decade of sleep.

CHAPTER THIRTY-SIX

POSTURING
WASHINGTON, D.C., AMERICA

An emergency meeting of the National Command Authority was called just after midnight. Held in the high-tech conference room on the second floor of the Pentagon, the room's two-story wood-paneled walls were covered with large screens from floor to ceiling. The eighteen chairs surrounding a seven-meter T-shaped table were filled with the highest authority, both military and civilian, in the United States. President Caryn sat at the center of the T-bar looking like she'd just arrived for a movie premiere. Wearing a dark red pantsuit and matching lipstick, she was elegant, impeccably groomed, and mad as hell.

The President bored a hole through the Director of Central Intelligence with a glare that could melt iron. She leaned forward in her chair so she could better see him sitting two seats to her left and, in a departure from her Hollywood persona, hissed unabashed annoyance at the man. "Just how the hell did an assistant, who couldn't find his ass with both hands, get a secure, and direct I might add, line to your office?"

The DCI shrunk back in his seat and stared at the table. Finally, mustering the courage to meet the fire in his commander-in-chief's icy blue eyes, he looked up and told her, "I don't know, ma'am, but we're looking into it."

"Imagine my relief, Director." She scanned the others at the table and found few of the most powerful men and women in the world had the fortitude to look at her. "Because without knowing, then we have no plausible deniability." She turned back to the DCI. "And we are not responsible, *are* we, Director?"

"No, ma'am," he quickly answered. "Volkov was a contrary old bastard, but we had zero ops against him."

Settling back in the chair, her glower softened ever so slightly. "Then this has to be a setup, which means that one, we've seriously underestimated Viktor Petrov, and two," she leaned forward once again, her hands folded tightly in front of her, "we need to prepare for the worst."

"I couldn't agree more," said Admiral Emily Johnson. Seated at the top of the T, Johnson was the chairman of the Joint Chiefs Staff. "I fully recommend that we move to DEFCON two at once."

"Is that really necessary?" asked Robert Macmillan, the Secretary of State. "Wouldn't the Russians see that as nefarious intent?" Sitting just to the right of Caryn, Macmillan locked eyes with Johnson.

"Nefarious intent is painting every one of our THOR units," countered Johnson, not giving the secretary any ground, "and moving their boomers into blind positions." She turned to face the President. "If we don't respond in kind, then we are grossly derelict in our duty to protect not only this country but our NATO allies as well."

"I'm with the admiral on this, Bob," said William Sanderhaust, the President's closest advisor and longtime friend. He rarely left her side. "Now is not the time to let down our guard."

"Derelict or not," stressed Macmillan, "DEFCON two is putting a twitchy finger on the hair trigger of the gun pointed at our own head!"

"That's a gross simplification," snapped Johnson, "and an insult to the successful protocols that we've—"

"Enough!" flared Caryn. "I need advice, not bickering. If anyone gets to bitch it's me. Am I clear?" No one uttered a word. "Good. Now then, Admiral Johnson, other than a heightened military readiness and diplomatic posturing," she glanced at her NSA to gauge his reaction, "just what exactly does DEFCON two entail?"

"It means that all our strategic weapons systems are placed on a moment's-notice attack profile," Johnson told Caryn.

The President's perfectly manicured fingernails began an impatient beat on the tabletop. "I know that, hell, everyone in this room knows that. I want specifics." The drumming increased in intensity. "I may be blond, but I'm not *a* blonde. Am I getting through here, Admiral?"

"Yes, ma'am," Johnson contritely affirmed. She sat up rigidly, tapped her tablet, and then gazed up at main screen. A giant map lit up. It detailed orbital paths across the globe. Tapping her finger, the admiral focused everyone's attention to specific objects on the screen. "The yellow triangles are THOR units. DEFCON two means we continually reposition them, never remaining in the same orbital apogee for two consecutive orbits. We'll also have one-third of our B-4B space bombers aloft at all times," she tapped on clusters of orange arrowhead shapes, "armed with both nuclear-tipped rail gun darts and EMP missiles."

"And the navy, Admiral, how does this affect them?" Caryn asked. The finger drumming slowed to a death march.

A few more taps and two other screens lit up. Each depicted a hemispheric map of the oceans. "Every yellow circle is a Kona II," Johnson explained, "and the red, a Russian Kosatka. As you can see, our attack subs are shadowing all their boomers, even in the blinds: six in the Pacific, four in the Atlantic, two in the Arctic, and one in the Gulf of Mexico.

"We'll move every carrier battle group to within zero fuel dock strike distance, swarm their border with Predator IV drones, and set up a defensive umbrella of F-47s. We'll also move the bulk of our armor units in Europe and central Asia to strategic strike positions. No one will be able to fart in Russia without us knowing about it, ma'am."

The President set her custom Hermès bag on the table, patted it daintily, and informed the group, "In that case, ladies and gentlemen, the football is now in play. Please make no mistake: if pressed, I will not hesitate to throw the Hail Mary. Having said all that," she interjected a little light into the gloom that had gripped the war room, "I think it's time we try a little diplomacy." She flashed those famously white teeth at Sanderhaust. "Don't you, hmm?"

I don't think it'll do you any good, Madame President, thought Olga as she left the Pentagon and appeared in the Kremlin. *I believe my dupe in Moscow is pushing for an overwhelming first strike, and he now has the political muscle to do it.*

A nostalgic feeling began to seep into her thoughts as she floated through these halls she knew so well. She'd never actually been to the Kremlin in her physical body, but her astral-projected one had been here many times and probably knew more than anyone exactly where all the bodies were buried. Olga made her way to the new President's office, now devoid of any sign that an old man had once held the reins of power in Russia. President Petrov had redecorated the office. His new assistant was a tall slender young redhead with vibrant green eyes and wore her dresses a size too small. Her name was Zula, and her mind was easy for Olga to penetrate. All Yanbeyeva minds were easy for her to penetrate.

Since Zula was sleeping with her boss, this made Olga's job much easier. Much easier than it had been when Petrov was the assistant. She'd often penetrated his mind, but controlling it took effort. With Zula's help, controlling one of the most powerful humans to ever live was as easy as opening a zipper.

CHAPTER THIRTY-SEVEN

A DANGEROUS GAME
MOSCOW, RUSSIA

Russia had a new President. The introverted former assistant was far more conniving than anyone had ever suspected, especially the late President. Viktor Petrov wasted no time replacing Volkov's inner council with those he could control. He'd promised the Russian people a free election within a year, the first free election in two-thirds of a century. It was a promise he had zero intention of keeping. Petrov fully understood that the way he'd gained the presidency raised serious questions, and the chances of him winning a fair election was the same as his intention of allowing it to happen.

Gaining the presidency required a cunning no one had expected of the man. Keeping the presidency required a plan so risky that he was willing to gamble the fate of the entire planet. Petrov knew the only way he could keep his new job was to create a crisis situation that was foolproof. Only a tried and true method for rallying the country around him would work. It was brilliant in its simplicity.

First, blame the enemy for an unforgivable act, and then go to the brink of war with them. Nothing stirred patriotism stronger than indignant fury.

Built in the sixteenth century, the Kremlin palace had been renovated many times over the centuries, but one room had remained virtually untouched. Hanging from its ornately curved ceiling was one of the world's most lavish crystal chandeliers. Its forty-six lights illuminated the President's plushily furnished council chamber where seven men sat at an oval table waiting for him to speak. Surrounding himself with sycophants, Petrov had called his first inner council meeting to gauge just how tractable each one was. They were there simply to nod their heads and lick his boots, exactly like his predecessor had taught him.

He'd learned his lessons well.

Zula stood directly behind the President's chair wearing a tight Versace grey print dress, black heels, and her usual disapproving frown.

With the setting exactly as she'd scripted it, Petrov addressed the council. "Gentlemen, the Azeri assassin was calling her puppet masters when she died," the lie garnered no response, "when I killed her. Fortunately, our efficient intelligence service was able to trace her call." Everyone in the room nodded at the superiority of Russian investigators. "Which was placed to the director of the CIA." The group looked aghast. "Directly to his office!" Petrov shouted.

No one questioned the ludicrousness of this scenario. They were all prepared to follow his lead, and it wasn't long in coming. "The sovereign state of Russia cannot let this travesty, a flagrant violation to the international rule of law, pass without retribution." There were murmurs of agreement throughout the room. He stopped speaking for a moment as Zula bent down and whispered in his ear. He then continued with barely controlled rage, "We will respond in kind, and since America has already heightened their defense level to DEFCON two, we have no choice but to raise our defense status accordingly." Louder exclamations of assent greeted this.

"The Russian people deserve no less from us, so I have instructed our military command to counter every threat now thrust upon us by American hegemony—" Again Zula whispered something in his ear, and he bellowed out, "No unprovoked hostility!" Petrov's voice rose with each passing word. "America believes that she has the right to rule this planet, murder whomever she believes is in her way, but we will not be bullied into submission. We will not become subordinate to America and her warped view of the world order." He looked around the room and took in every face now hanging on his every word. Satisfied, he lowered his voice to an almost inaudible level. "This government will see to it that the opposite is true. America will be forced to submit. We alone have the excess water to feed the world." A rare smile made its way to Zula's perfectly formed mouth. The rest of the council noticed this and smiled their approval as well. "America cannot even feed herself any longer." This was a blatant lie, but no one dared to correct him. "They need our water. And just like the Chinese, America will feel the righteous wrath of the Motherland, and they will feel it soon. On that I give you my word!" Petrov swept the room with an angry glare, and then stalked out followed by his assistant.

Olga waited until all the council members had left the room before she returned to her body. *Never underestimate the power of the fairer sex,* she thought. *Men may hold most of the important titles, but they're putty in the hands of a size two with a beautiful face and long legs. Now, if all women were as influential as my little helper in Moscow, then none of these titled men would stand a chance in hell, which is soon to be the case.*

She called her own council and got yet another update on the status of the bunker. Yevgeni was a no-show. Olga knew what had happened to him but decided against saying anything to Leka. She didn't want to needlessly upset the young woman.

Besides, Olga needed to start moving the family underground as soon as possible. Even though she had a direct inroad to the events unfolding in Moscow and Washington, something could happen. Something even she didn't have control over. The Earth was sitting on a powder keg and the slightest spark could ignite it. Her people needed to be ready now. There was no time to spare.

As usual, Zula walked into the President's office unannounced, something Petrov almost never dared to do when he held her position, and casually sat down in the heavily cushioned chair next to the President's desk. Her chair. "Viktor, I've just got off the phone with the American ambassador, and he's informed me that President Caryn is wanting to speak with you right away."

"So, she's going to try diplomacy," he said confidently. "It only makes sense, but I don't believe that's possible."

"Be strong, Viktor," Zula encouraged, "and don't give in to any of her protestations."

"Believe me," his smirk was grim, calculated, "she won't have her way with this conversation." Zula got up from her chair, moved behind her boss, and gently massaged his shoulders. "When will she call?" he asked as the tension in his neck eased but increased below his belt.

Zula leaned over so that her lips were touching his ear and whispered, "She's on hold now, Viktor."

"Ha! Then let her cool her heels a little longer," he said as his heart rate increased. "Don't move for a minute."

"I have no intention of doing so, my President."

Ten minutes later Petrov took the call. When President Caryn's angry face came up on his screen, he said, "Good afternoon, Madame President. What can I do for you?"

The American President wasted no time with pleasantries. "Let's get right to the point, Petrov, shall we?" Her voice was hard as nails.

"If that's the way you want it, then fine by me," he curtly responded. "What's on your mind?"

"We've been set up, and you damn well know it."

"What I know is that I witnessed President Volkov's assassination, and that his killer called your CIA within seconds."

If he thought that Crissy Caryn was an easy mark, he had her figured all wrong. "The assassination and the subsequent phone call were so ludicrously amateurish that it boggles the imagination with its simplicity."

"What are you implying, Madame President?" he demanded.

"Three people were in that room. Two died there, and the third is now President of Russian. You do the math."

Petrov's nostrils flared in anger. "How dare you—"

"Oh, I dare, Petrov, and now you are falsely accusing us of killing President Volkov, our partner and friend. Let me be frank: America had nothing to do with his murder, and this setup is pathetic."

"And yet the evidence, Madame President, says otherwise," he responded, "so, if you don't mind? Do get to your point."

"Fine. My point is this: you've target acquired all of our THOR units, placed your boomers in blind spots, and are flying your fighters irresponsibly close to our aircraft."

"Only in response to your escalation to DEFCON two, and since all your THOR systems orbit above Russia, what choice did we have but to respond in kind?"

Caryn's voice dropped to a menacing tone. "I'm not going to sit here and listen to this bullshit, so listen well, Petrov: back off or things will ratchet out of control. If that happens, know this: we are fully prepared to go the distance, and will not hesitate to react accordingly."

"Meaning what exactly, Madame President?" he asked curtly.

"Meaning that if one of your hotshot pilots shadowing any of our aircraft steps on his dick we *will* cut it off, and we all know where it goes from there. Don't we?"

"Are you threatening war, Madame President?"

"I am promising swift reaction to any provocation, Petrov."

No one, especially a woman, could talk to the President of the Russian Empire like that. "You're playing a dangerous game, Caryn."

"This is no game," she shot back. "What this is—was your one and only warning."

"I don't believe you're capable of understanding the—" He scowled at the screen when Caryn's image disappeared. "That bitch just hung up on me."

"Well, the diplomacy thing went well, Crissy," said Robert Macmillan. Her young, handsome Secretary of State's voice sounded typically unflappable. "Shall I have our ambassador call on Petrov and offer to patch up some of the claw marks you just left on his face?"

Caryn was still fuming. "How the hell can you be diplomatic when you're being bold-faced lied to?" she demanded of her chief diplomat. "That bastard has an agenda based on bullshit, and I'll be damned if I'm going to cater to those lies."

"That's why they call it diplomacy, Crissy," he gently informed her, "and what we pay the diplomats to do."

"What!" she exclaimed indignantly. "You seriously want to send in our ambassador just to sit there, act like Petrov's bullshit smells like roses, and make nice to—to that lying murderer?"

"Exactly."

"I just don't know if I can do that."

"Which is why we pay those diplomats so well."

She gave his smug look an icy glare. "You know what I mean. If we make a conciliatory gesture, then we'll seem weak or, worse, guilty."

"Think of the alternative, Crissy."

"You mean war?"

"I mean total world destruction."

"Even Petrov isn't that stupid," she said with a flip of her wrist.

"Are you willing to risk everything that he isn't?"

As she considered the alternative, her anger subsided just enough for her to see Macmillan's point. It was a toehold, but maybe there was still some hope that diplomacy would have better success than she just did. "Fine, send in the diplomats. Do not, however, allow them to retract one word I said." She sat rigid in her chair. "But see if they can patch up a few of my claw marks."

"So, you want them to do the impossible?" he asked quirking his brows.

"Didn't you just tell me that's what we pay them for?"

"Exactly."

"Do not be so gloomy, Viktor," cooed Zula as she sat on his lap and stroked his cheek. "Caryn will soon send us her ambassador to smooth things over."

"Have I gone too far?" he asked his closest confidante.

"I'm not sure," she said, "but we'll find out soon enough."

CHAPTER THIRTY-EIGHT

TIME

MAGELLAN II

Time was a delirium. It had no beginning, no end, no substance. While her body lay in a state of dormancy, her mind was vividly active. The visions had returned, but they were different this time. Time.

Barefoot and naked, she stood in front of a weathered old door. A door she'd never seen before, but whose location seemed comfortably familiar. It wasn't in a room, nor was it even in a building. It was on the arboretum path at Cambridge, her favorite place on Earth.

But this wasn't Earth.

The door stood unattached, alone, inviting. Kissed by rays of golden sunlight filtering through those magnificent trees, the portal beckoned. Nadya stood at its threshold, compelled to enter, but there was no doorknob. No way to open it. She pushed with her hands, but it held fast. She then noticed something in her hand: the family medallion. How was this possible? It was securely packed with her few personal effects on the starship. And yet, here it was.

Reaching out, Nadya placed the medallion against the door's unpainted surface. The portal shuddered and then creaked open. Beyond its rough-hewn frame stood the Universe.

She stepped through.

Infinity stood before her. Everything was there, the past, the present, the future. She could go where she wanted, when she wanted. Time held no barriers. The only barrier was the limit of her will. Somehow she understood that beyond that door her Path and her will were irreversibly connected.

Her first inclination was to go back to Earth. She wanted to see her children, wanted to know they were safe. These were children whom she would never meet, but the maternal instinct was compelling, so very strong.

Her only boundary was fear. Did she really want to see everything, or was it better to leave some knowledge alone? She understood that seeing, knowing, would bring pain. But still, they were her children. She knew that they weren't even born yet, not in her time, but she needed to see them. What would they be like? How would she feel about never being able to hold them, nurture them?

She decided it would be best if she were to see them as when they were ten years old. Seeing them as vulnerable infants might create a longing she wasn't prepared for. A small room appeared. It was poorly lit, and the walls were made of cold stone. Understanding swept over her: they were underground and would spend the rest of their lives knowing nothing but this subterranean existence.

Nadya drifted slowly toward them, a boy and a girl. Together they were drawing something. And they were pale, so ghostly pale. The children took the drawing to a larger room and gave it to Leka. They called her Mama. It was all Nadya could take. She fled the mines and returned to space. She had no body, no substance, but somehow, she was weeping.

Nadya knew what had driven them underground, and again needed to see for herself. What she saw was more devastating than any vision had ever been. She wasn't prepared for the assault on her soul.

The stark reality of what had befallen Earth crushed her very being. Everywhere mushroom clouds blossomed. Powerful beams of destruction blasted down from the heavens, adding their fire to the burning planet. Seas boiled, cities vaporized as the atmosphere exploded in a white-hot conflagration, consuming everything. Nothing on the surface escaped the holocaust. Like a pack of rabid dogs, mankind had turned on itself.

Again she wept.

It was the raging fires that disturbed her most, because she'd seen them so many times. The planet-wide inferno would last months, and those small pockets of humanity, those who'd escaped the surface, would take hundreds of years to re-emerge. Her own children would never see the light of day. Billions of other children would never see another day. They'd turned to ash, and she'd done nothing.

She'd been given glimpses before, but never fully understood the absolute totality of it. Now she did. Did Mother Olga truly understand the violence she unleashed? Was this what generations of her family had worked so hard to achieve: wiping the slate clean, a new planet, a new human race? Nadya was sickened by it. This wasn't cleansing. This was speciocide.

It was evil incarnate.

As the images broke her heart, she wanted, needed to end the pain. But there was no leaving this state of consciousness. She tried to find the door again to lock it behind her, but it was nowhere to be found. She had to escape, but how?

Only one thing could counter fire.

Water.

She found herself floating over a watery world. An ocean covered everything, but that couldn't be. There had to be land, or this whole argosy would be for nothing, and now there was no home to return to.

She pictured land and was instantly hovering over a large bay at the end of a giant peninsula. It looked like paradise.

Hope began to filter out the despair that had earlier consumed her.

She followed the peninsula north for 2,000 kilometers until she reached the mainland. Here was a wild place, a river valley carpeted with an unbroken forest lying between a single mountain range. These towering mountains were topped with snow-encrusted crystal peaks that began as a ring around the north pole, and then coiled ever outward to the edge of the landmass. She'd seen these mountains since she was a little girl and sitting directly at the top of the planet was the largest mountain of all. A parabolic cone that towered above all the others.

She made a close inspection of the land and saw it was inhabited. Countless species of animals lived on this continent. Reptiles. Again, full understanding: these were like the dinosaurs that had populated the Earth for millions of years, long before the destructive nature of man arrived.

Mankind was about to arrive again.

Nadya explored the rest of this new planet. She found a second continent at the opposite pole. It was different from the northern one. This landmass was smaller, and even though it was heavily forested it had no mountains except for one: a second parabolic cone.

Other reptiles lived here as well, but these were much different. These were bipedal, lived in huge cities with populations of hundreds of millions, and it was obvious that they were intelligent. It suddenly dawned on her that she had just discovered the first sentient being other than humans ever encountered. But something was not quite right with these beings.

She spent weeks wandering their teeming cities, and what she learned convinced her that humans and these reptilians could never be compatible. These creatures were overtly violent and inherently cannibalistic. They bred at an alarming rate, but kept their population controlled by eating not only their elderly but most of their young as well.

An ocean would separate the two intelligent species on the planet, but would it be enough? Would the southern reptilians eventually find them?

The answer sent a chill down her celestial spine: war after war between the two species. She went forward in time and saw that two human colonies would eventually be established, one at that large bay, and one high up in the northern most mountains. The mountain colony was inside giant crystal cliffs, an impregnable fortress city. She was shocked to see that this northern colony could fly, but not in aircraft.

This human colony had become an army of dragon riders.

The more she explored the future of this planet, the more she realized how much influence she would have on its development. The knowledge gained by these visions would lead her to write a series of books.

Prophesy books.

The responsibility threatened to overwhelm her. How could her written words influence a civilization generations after her death? There was only one answer: she would have to become a leader. The type of leader subsequent generations would follow long after she was gone. But the question begged, how? She struggled with this dilemma for some time before deciding to will herself ahead and find the end game, the final point in time where her influence had run its course. What she found was a 1,000-year gap between the first human arrival—her arrival—and some sort of final conflict.

It was so shocking that at first she wasn't sure if this could possibly be. She saw a man, a descendant from the children she left on Earth.

Her bloodline had survived.

Somehow he'd arrive on this planet and lead the humans in the final battle with the reptiles. A war that would decide the fate of humanity on this planet; but he had help, another being, a giant dragon. This dragon had watched for his arrival for 1,000 years. After observing them, her shock became more unsettled, because she realized that this dragon was the same one from her visions. She'd seen it since she was a little girl. Nadya now understood the inscription on the medallion: Mea Drakon, *I Dragon.*

She was the dragon.

Nadya didn't know how long she had spent in this visionary state. By the time her freedom to roam was at an end she knew exactly what she must do. But would she have enough time to do it? Her moment in time felt like centuries. Time was a fickle destination, infinity without boundaries and a universe without end.

CHAPTER THIRTY-NINE

WORLD WAR EXTINCTION EARTH

Wearing a short lapis skirt and matching jacket, Zula strolled into President Petrov's office with the latest news concerning their not-so-subtle military mobilization. "Viktor, the Americans have shifted orbits of all their THOR systems. Every time we reacquire them, they move out of the target window." Her usual pout took on a more serious expression. "Not only that, but all of our newest Kosatka subs stationed in blind spots received a single sonar ping at exactly the same time an hour ago."

"So, the Americans have found all our boomers," he said while punching up the latest report on his computer.

"And they've let us know it." Zula tossed the paper report on his desk. "They are playing with you, Viktor," she goaded him.

Ignoring her taunt, he glanced at the report and matched it with what his computer said. "What's this about them targeting our VOLK units?" he asked as an uneasy feeling swept through his mind. "Their targeting of our missile defense shield could be a sign of a first strike."

Zula plunked down in her chair, crossed her long legs, and impatiently tapped an armrest with one bright blue nail. "They're doing exactly what we're doing," she said dryly. "The only difference is that their latest THOR units are all equipped with EMD engines and can easily shift orbit. The rocket thrusters on our VOLK systems have limited capacity to alter their trajectory." Delicate creases formed in the perfect skin beside her eyes. "If they launch a first strike against VOLK, there's nothing we can do about it."

Petrov ran his fingers through his fast-thinning hair. "If that bitch thinks intimidation will work, then she's a fool," he swore. "She's leaving me only one option."

The finger tapping stopped. "Actually, this leaves you two options, Viktor." She paused for a moment, giving him time to digest this. "Give up," the words came out as if they tasted of something vile, "or take them out with a first strike." She held a hand up, admired her nails and, satisfied at what she saw, placed it on her exposed thigh.

"Yeah, I get it," he said, "and I will not pull back. America will soon feel the teeth of an angry bear."

"Then it must be a first strike," she asserted, and pulled her hem up higher, "but we must be careful. You know that, right?"

"Of course," he mumbled, allowing his eyes to wander. "We pretend to pull back, relax the tension, and then strike once they've stood down as well."

"Blindman's bluff," she said, leaning over and placing both her hands on his knees.

Petrov had to tear his eyes away from the three undone buttons on her blouse. He'd already been thinking about life after America. "Water has become our most valuable export, and without American interference, our water-based foreign policy will rule the planet for 1,000 years."

Zula bit her lower lip, sucked in a shallow breath, and said, "Once America is eliminated, *you* will be the greatest leader in the history of the world."

President Crissy Caryn was back at the National Command center receiving the latest reports from her various intelligence services. Sitting next to her was the Secretary of State, Robert Macmillan. "It seems that our ambassador has had the desired effect on Petrov. The Russians have pulled back their forces and stopped harassing our flights."

At age fifty-five, the silver-haired William Sanderhaust looked precisely like the Boston aristocrat he really was. With his tailored suits, strong opinions, and a penchant for dropping the letter R, it was with some surprise to the rest of the cabinet that he wore the same suit three days running. What wasn't surprising was the National Security Advisor's take on what this Russian stand-down meant. "Crissy, I believe that this lessening of tensions is simply a ruse to lure us into relaxing from our present DEFCON position."

"While I concur," declared Caryn, "officially it behooves me to explore every option."

"Then I have a few suggestions," offered Macmillan.

"There's only one," insisted Sanderhaust.

"So, what are you suggesting, Bill?" asked Caryn. "That we stay at this alert status while they reduce tensions?"

"Absolutely," Sanderhaust told her. "We cannot allow ourselves to be drawn into Petrov's trap. He's too unstable to ever be trusted."

"President Caryn," Macmillan cut in, "I have assurances from my Russian counterpart that this lessening of tensions is legitimate. If we continue with DEFCON two, they'll have no choice but to resume their heightened state of readiness, and we're right back at the brink. We need to give diplomacy a chance."

"And leave ourselves wide open to a first strike?" Sanderhaust countered, staring down the Secretary of State. "That's irresponsible at best, and suicidal at worst."

"Gentlemen," cooed Caryn, "we can do both." The tension around the table barely mitigated as she went on. "Officially we'll ratchet down to DEFCON three and try to play nice with Petrov, but we'll keep our reaction forces on a tight leash. I have no intention of falling for any more of his subterfuge, but we can't be seen as the only aggressor if we're to have any influence in other theaters of foreign policy."

"Meaning what, Crissy?" asked Sanderhaust.

"Two can play at this game. We let them think we've reduced readiness, but I want your eyes to stay on everything. Don't even blink, Bill," she ordered him. "If they make the slightest move toward breaking the trust, we will instantly react."

"Does that mean first strike options?" Sanderhaust pressed.

"Nothing is off the table, gentlemen. But we need to give them an opportunity to prove that they're sincere."

Macmillan squirmed in his seat. "And if there's the slightest hint of a Russian first strike?"

"Then God help us all," answered the last President of the United States of America.

Within hours of the agreed-upon stand-down, the Russian submarines moved away from their perceived blind spots. The American carrier battle groups pulled back from the ring of iron they had clamped around the Russian empire. Whole squadrons of B-4Bs and the hypersonic F-47 fighters returned to base, but neither the THOR nor VOLK systems stood down.

The most obvious retraction of hostilities were the ones that the world's news organizations could detect and report on. They were happy to broadcast that all border incursions into each other's airspace had ceased, and that armored units across Europe and central Asia were being pulled back. The world breathed a sigh of relief as the two most destructive nations in the history of the planet seemed to back away from the brink.

A week after the stand-down, President Petrov sat at his big desk with his hand hovering over the phone. He knew what had to be done, but since his personal advisor and closest confidante had disappeared, he was no longer so sure of himself. He'd found no suitable replacement for her, and hadn't really tried, hoping she would return soon. But the time for hope was past. His hand wavered indecisively, but only for a moment; he'd made up his mind: it must be first strike. The Americans had pulled back their carrier battle groups and stood down the majority of their B-4B space bombers. There would be no better opportunity to do what must be done. As his resolve firmed, his hand steadied. He gripped the receiver and called the Russian command center. "General Skumin, initiate Operation Cherniy Glaz."

"Da, Mister President," responded the chief of Russia's military, "we will begin as planned."

"Very good, General. Call me once the missiles are away," ordered Petrov. "I'll be in my war bunker and will expect the call within the hour." His hand shook as he hung up the phone.

"Crissy," yelled Sanderhaust as he flew into her office. "The Russians have reversed their stand-down and have launched hypersonic missiles toward our airspace."

"That fucking lying little weasel," she hissed. "Is THOR in position to shoot them down?"

"We have complete target acquisition and are tracking their trajectory." The anxiety was clear in his voice. "But we need your authorization to commence the national defense initiative. They'll arrive in six minutes."

"Fuck yes!" she yelled, jumping up from her desk. "Do it! Do it now. No holds barred. We retaliate with the full throw weight of our entire defense network." She kicked off her high heels and began running toward the security elevator. It would only be a matter of minutes before someone's missiles detonated.

The worldwide news wires exploded with broadcasts of the impending Earth-shattering catastrophe. The airwaves quickly filled with panicked pleas to both nations, but it was too late. The planet-killing arsenals of the Russian empire and NATO had already launched en masse.

Carrying her high heels, Caryn stepped out of the pneumatic elevator and into a world of concrete and steel. The President had only visited the emergency bunker twice, and both times it was dank and deserted. Now it was a beehive of activity filled with Space Force uniforms and military chatter. After a few steps on the cold cement floor Caryn placed a hand on her advisor's shoulder and slipped her shoes back on. She jumped when several metallic impacts sounded from inside the inclined shaft. "It's just the blast doors sealing off the elevator," Sanderhaust told her; "we're safe now."

"Sealed off?" Caryn asked, glancing up. "And the rest of the cabinet?"

Sanderhaust shook his head. "Executive protocol, Crissy. The bunker is sealed once the POTUS has entered."

President Caryn gave him a haunted look, squared her shoulders, and walked into the war room where she approached the highest-ranking officer in the bunker. The man stood between two rows of officers manning an array of command and control workstations. He was talking to a junior officer when his commander-in-chief interrupted their conversation. "If you please, Enon, get me up to speed."

Her military liaison, Colonel Enon Midkaff, a tall middle-aged USSF officer from Lubbock, Texas, just nodded as he told the junior officer, "and I need that now." Midkaff then turned to Caryn, pointed at the Earth Observation Station, and with a hint of a Panhandle drawl began a running narrative. "Those yellow lights are incoming EMP weapons, ma'am."

"What happens when they reach target?" Caryn asked as she sat down.

"The ones that get through our defenses will disrupt the civilian power grid."

"Disrupt, Colonel?"

"Destroy, ma'am."

"And the defense grid?"

"We've been hardened and have a high probability of survival."

"I see," said Caryn. She tapped a finger on her lips. "How long until impact?"

"Seconds, ma'am." Midkaff touched his earpiece, glanced up at the EOS, and then back at his commander-in-chief. "We have inbound multiple entry warheads concentrated along the I-95 corridor from Boston to Baltimore. Detonation—now."

The yellow streaks on the screen suddenly blinked out as a series of powerful EMP bursts had an immediate effect. The resolution on the

Earth Observation Station screen scrambled and went dark. Colonel Midkaff screamed, ripped off his headset, and slumped over a console. Several officers began talking into their mics, trying to get someone—anyone—on their line. No one got a response. The American command and control was now deaf, dumb, and blind.

President Caryn went rigid, unable to tear her eyes away from the blank screen she demanded, "What the hell just happened, Colonel?"

Sanderhaust rushed over to help. "I don't think he can hear you, Crissy."

"I need answers," the President yelled. "Can anyone enlighten me?"

The colonel groaned and sat back up, eyes squinting in pain, and spoke too loudly. "That was more than just an EMP. We didn't know the Russians had anything this powerful."

"What else don't we know about?" shrieked Caryn. Her eyes darted back to the screen. "Can we get that back online?"

Midkaff rubbed his temple and shouted to an officer across the console, "Captain Treyhan! What's the status of the Earth Observation Station?"

Bent over a computer terminal, the Space Force captain turned his head to answer. "Colonel, systems analyst Ricci here has just reported that the entire GeoStar system is down." The analyst nodded at Midkaff. "But thinks she can tie into a THOR unit."

"You can do that?" asked Caryn.

"Get it done," ordered Midkaff.

The young woman turned and began furiously working at her console. After a few seconds she looked up and said, "I've got a link, sirs."

The screens suddenly flickered to life, but the former grid map was gone. In its place was a live feed of Earth.

"What're we looking at now, Colonel?" Sanderhaust asked.

"That's the North American Atlantic coast," said Midkaff. "Is all we've got, Ricci?"

"For now, Colonel," the analyst answered over her shoulder as she continued working her keyboard. "I'm searching for another live link."

Caryn jumped up from her seat and began pacing in front of the EOS. "So, without GeoStar there's no way for us to monitor our defense status, is there, Colonel?" The officer shook his head. "And you're telling me that all we can do is sit here," she jerked a thumb at the screen, "and watch?"

"Yes, ma'am."

The first nuclear blasts impacted north of Long Island. A tsunami of blinding mushroom deflagration clouds then swept southward toward Manhattan, consuming it in seconds. At that moment the camera zoomed in on New York City just as hundreds of bright flashes lit the screen. Caryn stopped pacing and placed a hand over her mouth. "Oh my God," she whispered through her fingers.

As she watched the carpet of detonations cascade toward Washington, President Caryn became frantic. "I thought THOR was supposed to shoot those damn things down!" she screamed at Midkaff.

"They must be, ma'am," he stammered out. "We just can't see it happening."

"What I see," she hissed, "is my country being destroyed. What makes you think THOR is even operational?"

Midkaff had been frantically trying to restore a comlink to NORAD. He stopped jabbing at the button and shouted his answer. "Because, ma'am, what we're seeing is hundreds of blasts, but a Russian first strike would have sent thousands of warheads at us. This is barely a fraction of what should be detonating."

"Are you saying this could have been worse?" she screeched while glaring at the screen.

At that moment a strong jolt shook them. Yelps of dismay filled the bunker as the shocked occupants first looked at each other, and then back at the screen. The nuclear storm had reached Washington, D.C.

"It just got worse, Crissy!" Sanderhaust yelled as the bunker jumped again. All eyes shot toward the elevator just as a deafening explosion blew the blast door across the war room where it crashed into the steel console, killing Ricci, and filling the bunker with searing heat. Sanderhaust leapt toward Caryn and threw his body over hers.

"Nooo—" she wept. "I've failed, Bill."

"We all did, Crissy," he said just as another blast ended their conversation.

———————————

"I'm scared, Yevgeni," cried Lena as he held her close. It was a sultry morning on Tverskaya Street and promised to be a sweltering day. They could see the Kremlin a few blocks away.

"I know," he told her. "I'm scared too." He kissed the top of her head and whispered, "Forgive me, my love."

"There's nothing to forgive, husband. We're where we should be this day."

The high-pitched scream of air raid sirens suddenly shattered the calm morning. Everyone else on the street stopped and looked up, but the couple from Koryak saw only each other. Yevgeni gently ran his fingers down his wife's cheek. "I meant about blocking Nadya from seeing us," he confessed.

With a muffled sob, Lena buried her face in his chest, just as a tall young woman wearing dark glasses approached them. A few strands of red hair dangled from underneath her blue headscarf. "Please forgive my intrusion. May I join you?" she politely asked.

"We were just waiting—it's not safe here," Yevgeni told the stranger.

"I see." The woman lowered her glasses. A sorrowful shadow was attached to her vibrant green eyes. "Then I'm right where I should be."

The small group looked up just as the sky above Moscow exploded.

North America and Europe were ravaged. The VOLK units fired their particle beam weapons into the massed American counter-strikes, but only 17 percent of the stealthy American ICBMs were hit. Moscow and every major Russian city disappeared in a sea of fire.

And the combatants were far from finished.

Once the initial missile attacks were over, the American space-based defense network continued to pound any Russian target. The VOLK units did the same until both sides of the conflict had been devastated beyond anything previously imaginable.

Once there weren't any more surface targets to destroy, THOR and VOLK turned on each other.

The war lasted almost twenty-four hours. At the beginning of hostilities the world's population was over 11 billion. The next day only 4 billion survived, and these would die within the next month as the radioactive fallout from tens of thousands of nuclear detonations blanketed the entire planet. Both the Russian and American governments were destroyed in the first hour. Within days no national government survived.

The era of nation-states was over.

Almost all life on the landmasses ceased to exist. The oceans fared little better. In less than a month the total surviving human population numbered less than a million souls. The day the Earth died was called World War Extinction, or, as it came to be known by later generations—WWX.

The war to end all wars did just that.

CHAPTER FORTY

A BETTER SLAVE RACE
OFOL'R, LOG'RFOLD

Hidden 3,000 meters below the ocean's vast surface and built directly on the equator of the planet that humans had named Kepler 3211a, sat Ofol'r, the domed underwater base of the Normad'r. This was not their home world. It was only one of thousands of planets they had colonized for the resources needed to give life to their highly advanced civilization. They called this outpost world Log'rfold, and it lay very close to the outer perimeter of their vast intergalactic empire. Only one other planet in their empire was more remote than Log'rfold. This too was a watery planet and inhabited by a race of beings prone to self-destruction. That planet had been visited, bio-engineered, and cultivated many times over millions of years. The inhabitants of that world called it Earth.

The base was manned by several hundred Normad'r, who used the extreme depth to protect any knowledge of their presence and the work they did there. Protection of this base and the planet it controlled was vital to them. There were better postings throughout their empire, on more advanced planets, but none carried the importance of Log'rfold. Their empire's very existence depended on the riches this lone planet held in abundance.

Log'rfold's powerful electromagnetic field was a byproduct of an immense energy source that powered the Normad'r Empire, and for that reason a three-stage defensive network protected their interests here. It had never failed them.

They'd placed 1,000 dormant attack drones in orbit around the planet that would be activated by any ship, other than Normad'r, that landed on Log'rfold's surface. They also placed a seemingly benign but deadly cloud system over both continents. These clouds could disassemble anything molecular, be it metallic, electronic, or biological. Everything that entered these clouds didn't survive. The Normad'r tolerated no interference with the slave race they had bio-engineered to provide the labor force needed to extract the precious resource.

The Normad'r were large, almost three meters tall, but with a low physical density. Their cardiovascular system was not liquid, but a lighter-than-air gas, which gave them a translucent blue skin that glowed when emotionally stimulated. They had fine white hair and golden eyes. Except for the fact that they had no feet, having no use for them, the Normad'r also looked remarkably like many other races of beings that they'd engineered throughout the galaxy. This included Earth. But they looked almost nothing like the bipedal reptilians they'd used as slave labor for hundreds of thousands of years. The Normad'r gave these beings, known as the Thith, limited capacity for creating technology, ensuring that the hundreds of millions of them would never be a threat to the few hundred masters living beneath the waves. Masters that only a select few of the Thith elite ever had contact with. The Normad'r were worshiped as gods.

Humans were engineered for a different purpose. They were given an almost limitless capacity to create, evolve, and destroy. Having a self-destructive yet intelligent slave race had its merits and its drawbacks. The Normad'r had bio-engineered hundreds of sentient races throughout the galaxy, and except for one species, the Normad'r remained absolute masters.

A patrol ship arrived from Earth, dropped out of the cloudless sky, and plunged into the ocean where it dove to the underwater base. Within minutes, Kanend'ra, the Administrator of Genetics, sought out her leader. His name was Erland'r, and he carried the title of Mab'r, the Superior Being on Log'rfold.

She found him floating in his dwelling near a floating orb that could project holographic images of any scene within the red dwarf solar system.

Erland'r feigned indifference as she approached him. "A starship has just returned from Earth," Kanend'ra reported. "The Homo sapiens have finally destroyed themselves."

The Mab'r looked at his subordinate with an interest he hadn't shown before. "So, the self-destructive gene you placed in their genetic code has finally paid off," he mused. "It only took 100,000 years."

"Yes, Mab'r," responded the geneticist, "most of the planet's surface will be unlivable for hundreds of years. Some areas will take thousands."

Erland'r floated away from the orb to a cabinet and took out a crystal decanter filled with a lighter-than-air gas. He poured himself a glass without offering any to Kanend'ra. She was not of sufficient rank to share a drink with. "Did the bloodline we instilled with advanced evolutionary abilities survive?" he asked as he took a sip.

"Yes, Mab'r. Of the five thousandths of 1 percent who survived the planet's destruction, that bloodline was among them." Kanend'ra could have cared less about the lack of an offer for the drink; she was completely inured to the privilege of rank. "There's more, Mab'r." She watched as the Superior Being glided back to the orb, his drink floating beside him.

"More?"

"A member from this bloodline is aboard the starship the humans are presently sending here." Her voice dripped with respectful indifference. "A powerful member," she clarified. "A female."

"It only makes sense that it would be a female, considering that you implanted the strongest genes into that gender," the Mab'r remarked, meeting the geneticist's eyes for the first time. "What ability does she master, and will she survive the trip?"

"I believe all the humans will survive, Mab'r," opined Kanend'ra. "They've invented a crude but effective magnetic drive system." Erland'r's internal gases glowed yellow in amused silence. "She is part of the ship's crew, and her abilities are those of a Spak'rna. Her visions of future events prove entirely accurate."

"Interesting development. Make sure that we remain invisible to her," Erland'r said decisively. "It would be counterproductive if she suspected our presence." Then he more thoughtfully added, "I must have the planetary defenses reduced in power. We don't want them destroyed by the Rond'r." He studied the orb's holographic image of the defense network. "We simply need to make sure that they never leave Log'rfold."

Kanend'ra didn't quite understand. She knew her place, but curiosity overcame her penchant for discretion. "Mab'r, why would we allow them to even land, much less establish a colony? Wouldn't they become a threat in the future?"

"We will keep them from becoming a threat to us but will allow them to build a low-tech civilization. I believe war with the Thith is inevitable, but it's always been the view of the Council of Drott'r that humans will eventually become an active warrior race."

"Will we use the humans to extract the Ramm'r?"

Erland'r rotated so that his back was to Kanend'ra. "No, of course not. Humans are much too fragile to survive the heat of the mines," he said dispassionately, "but we have other uses for their specific talents."

Kanend'ra knew that she'd already pushed the Mab'r farther than she should, but this human question was far too intriguing. "What use could we possibly have for them, Mab'r?"

The Superior must have been in an unusually tolerant mood, because after a moment of reflection he explained. "The Ulfen Empire is expanding at the far edge of the galaxy. Given this minor annoyance, the Council of Drott'r considers the humans' genetically engineered propensity for war as an asset."

It took a moment for her to understand before it became clear. "You mean we'll use them as soldiers against the Ulfen?"

"Of course," he acknowledged, "we've always used the dominant species we've engineered as warriors. We Normad'r are too few and live far too long to waste our lives on fighting wars."

"They are to fight the Thith?"

"Of course."

Kanend'ra was still confused, knowing the history of humans. She had, after all, helped engineer them. "But, Mab'r, humans have already proved dominant, on Earth."

"That was against your other not so successful experiments," Erland'r pointed out. "This will be the first opportunity to see them fight for dominance on an alien planet. A most important attribute, given our plans."

Kanend'ra still had one last question for her Mab'r. "How long will we give them to prove their superiority, and what happens if they exterminate the Thith?"

Erland'r ran a three-fingered hand through his gossamer hair. "Give or take 1,000 years, and we will never allow the Thith to die out. You of course will ensure their continuation as a species. We need them too."

"So, just a short period of time, then," mused Kanend'ra. "I hope that I'm still assigned here to view their conflict. It should be interesting."

"They always are," replied Erland'r as he rotated away from the geneticist.

CHAPTER FORTY-ONE

AQUEOUS
MAGELLAN II

I t first appeared like a distant star, no more than a twinkling point of light in the fabric of space. Unable to help herself, Nadya gravitated toward it, and out of the darkness she heard the echo of her name. The dim light became brighter as the voice grew stronger. "She's coming around." A sudden yearning gripped Nadya, compelling her toward the voice. It was Sasha. Her eyes opened for the first time in ten years. Everything was blurry when she felt the prick of an IV going into her arm. She tried to sit up, but a gentle hand held her down. "No, Nadushka, lie still. It'll take a few hours before you can sit up, and a few more before you can stand." The affection in her husband's voice and the tenderness of his touch was more comforting than anything she could remember, and she remembered eternity.

A month later the *Magellan II* had established full orbit around the watery world of Kepler 3211a, now being called Aqueous by the crew. No one remembered how the name originated, but shortly after achieving orbit the bridge began using it. Soon the whole ship called it that.

Nadya and Sasha worked around the clock waking up the rest of the crew. In what little down time they had together Nadya tried explaining to Sasha what had happened to her during the ten-year voyage. "These visions were much different than anything I'd ever experienced before."

"How so?"

Nadya closed her eyes as she recalled the centuries of memories. "For the first time I had complete control," she explained to him, "and could go anywhere, at any time. All I had to do was think about a destination and it appeared. It's never been like that before. All my life the visions have just been images that flashed by, some clearer than others, and I had to interpret what they meant. No clarification was needed this time."

"Is it possible that these were, oh, I don't know, dreams?"

"Did you dream, Sasha?" she asked, irritated that he of all people would question her.

"Well, not that I can remember," he muttered.

"Really? What a coincidence, because no one else did either." She turned her back to him. "And neither did I. This was something else. It was a ten-year vision of what is to come, and you must listen carefully, because we haven't much time."

Sasha sat in shock as she explained as much as time allowed. When she finished, Nadya knew that her husband no longer doubted her. More importantly, what she said involved him as well. They had to send a message back to Earth, and they had to do it soon, within the next few weeks at most.

CHAPTER FORTY-TWO

LAST WORDS
KORYAK, EARTH

Her room, like the entire bunker, was a dank grey. The few paintings did little to brighten its décor. Color had been washed from everyone's life. Grey dominated everything: the walls, the ceilings, and their spirits. All their former lives, everything they had ever known on the surface was gone. It was a despondent adjustment for the 3,300 souls buried deep underground. For the survivors, a new culture had to replace the old. The former norms had irreversibly died with the past.

Mother Olga faced several dilemmas. Keeping her people safe from the radioactive destruction on the surface had been accomplished, but now she had to deal with the day-to-day issues that thousands of unhappy people presented her with. It was like trying to bail water out of a leaky canoe during a hurricane.

Olga had never envisioned that mass emotional trauma would manifest itself so fast, or so strong. The constant barrage of petty problems tried her ability to come up with solutions. It was a never-ending parade of discontent, but one dilemma stood out more than any other: Olga was dying. She'd astral projected to watch the nuclear consumption of Earth and thought that she'd be immune to the radiation while in her astral-projected state, but she was wrong. Within days of returning to her body Olga began coughing up blood. She'd developed acute leukemia, and its advanced state meant her time left would not only be limited, but painful.

Olga knew the end was near. Her health declined rapidly after the internment, and she used every minute of what little time there was to ensure the enclave's survival. But most important of all, the matriarch had to name her successor. That was paramount.

For generations the matriarch had never visibly aged. She was always a striking beauty. But in the past few months the decades caught up with her. Dark purple bags formed under her eyes, and her once-vibrant bearing was now twisted in pain.

Six months after WWX she painfully got out of bed. All her joints screamed in agony as she shuffled her way to the council chambers and found Leka already waiting for her. Olga limped over to the Matriarch's chair and collapsed in it. It was the last time she would sit there. "Thank you for meeting me today, Leka." She managed a smile as she looked at the other woman's swollen belly. "I know how difficult it is for you to move around these days."

"Mother Olga," Leka said sympathetically, "we could have met in your room. There was no need for you to leave the comfort of your bed to talk to me."

"There's little comfort anywhere, child," Olga confessed. Her words were clipped and strained. "So, this is as good a place as any to say what must be said, and besides, the pain's not too bad today," she lied, "and I need to discuss my choice of successor. Aahh—" she groaned painfully. "Since this chair is the seat of power, then it's only fitting that I make my decision known from it."

"Please, Mother Olga," begged Leka, "let's not talk about this now. You've been the family's matriarch since before I was born. You're all I've ever known."

Olga's smile was more of a painful grimace. "But now the end is near, and I can't put this off any longer." She covered her mouth and coughed. Her hand came away speckled with red spittle. "As you can see," she said, wiping her hand on her thigh, "my time is growing short, as is my ability to talk for very long, so please, Leka, just listen, and accept my deepest apology."

"You have nothing to apologize for," Leka said.

"Oh, but I do, child." Her voice was raspy but businesslike as she continued. "You see, being matriarch is not easy. It requires several attributes, the first of which is the strongest of resolve to make even unpleasant decisions. The second is having the strongest bloodline lineage flowing through their veins, or in this case, growing in their womb."

Leka recoiled at these words but mutely waited for Olga to continue. "So, you see, Leka," Olga's voice went from all business to cold calculation, "I have no choice but one to name my successor."

"W-who?" Leka stammered.

"You."

At that instant Leka felt two strong kicks. She absentmindedly placed a hand on her bulging belly. "But, I'm not strong like you," Leka protested. "How can I ever live up to your standards?"

Olga smiled as a small drip of red drool escaped down her chin, her voice sympathetically indulgent. "You're stronger than you think, Leka." The young woman shook her head and stared at the table. "You accepted to carry your sister's children, and that took strength." Tears began streaming down Leka's cheeks. "You accepted the marriage that I arranged for you, and that took strength."

"I would say the opposite," Leka barely squeaked out.

"Then you'd be wrong." Olga reached out and patted the distraught woman's hand. "Your sacrifices took an immense amount of strength." She glanced down at the younger woman's belly. "And your ensuring the family's bloodline continuation is the strongest selfless act I've ever witnessed. That, my dear, is why you will lead the enclave for the next generation."

The magnitude of this conversation was overwhelming. "If I accept this—"

"You will."

Olga slipped the medallion off and handed it to Leka, who stared limply at it for several moments before slowly closing her fingers around it. "Fine, but I have reservations, and questions."

"That's only natural," Olga croaked out. "Ask me anything."

Leka didn't hesitate this time. "When the time comes, who will I name as successor?"

"Why, one of those two babies in your womb, of course." Olga's small chuckle elicited another bloody cough. The strength of this one wracked her whole body.

"But, which one?" Leka asked, suddenly oblivious to Olga's pain. "How do *I* choose?"

Olga's face had gone pale. She hung her head and spat a handful of bloody mucus into her lap, and then painfully looked up. "You'll know when the times comes." She gasped for breath; her words difficult to understand. "You'll have years to evaluate which of your children is best suited."

"My sister's children," Leka quietly corrected.

"Technically, but you'll be the only mother they'll ever know, the mother who raises them, teaches them the values that they'll need, that the enclave needs to survive." Olga attempted to stand up, signaling an end to the meeting. Her strength failed, and she barely managed to hold onto the table without falling to the floor. Leka rushed to her side and placed Olga's arm over her shoulder. A woman in the eighth month of pregnancy practically carried a dying one down the grey corridors that would house the next several generations entombed inside them.

An hour later Leka had helped the dying woman into bed. Olga gripped her arm with surprising strength. "There's something that'll help you guide the family." She weakly pointed to a leather-bound book on her desk. "Over there."

In her first command as matriarch, Leka whispered, "Hush, we can talk about that later. When you're feeling better."

"Th-there won't be a later." A coarse rattle was evident in Olga's voice. "It must be now. Please indulge this old woman just a few moments longer."

Using a towel, Leka wiped the blood weeping out of Olga's mouth as the older woman tried to talk. "That's the book of succession—with a family tree of bloodline mixes—it was written long before I was born." Another painful cough, more of a burp, filled Olga's mouth with blood. She spat it out and painfully went on. "To c-continue to strengthen the family."

"Mother Olga, please rest now," begged Leka.

Another coughing fit wracked Olga's body, doubling her into a fetal position. The blood flowed nonstop, but her hand still held Leka's arm. The new matriarch turned to get help, but Olga's grip was too strong to let her go. "Th-the children. They're everything. The future of the fami—" she released Leka's arm, "and the future of the human race depends on th-them."

"Olga," Leka begged again, "please stop!"

"Education, Leka," she barely croaked, "is key. Enhance—improve it. Th-that is to be your legacy—the dynamic that accelerates the evolution of—" a powerful cough blew bloody particles onto the stained sheets, "the f-family. It's n-now yours, Mother Leka." She gagged on these last words before the coughing ran its course, and her life ended.

CHAPTER FORTY-THREE

THE MESSAGE
MAGELLAN II

Weeks of waking the crew had taken its toll. Nadya spent twenty-hour days in the infirmary making sure every crew member was handled with precise care.

The strain was relentless, and it had become difficult for Sasha to continually watch his wife beaten down like this. One morning he came into the infirmary, saw the disheveled hair and the haggard look, and couldn't stay silent any longer. "Nadushka, enough," he gently chastised her. "Look at yourself. You must get some rest."

He walked over to where she was conducting yet another blood test, placed his hands on her shoulders, and lightly rubbed them. She pushed them away, glared at the collection of blood samples on the counter, and took one more look in the microscope. "There's no time for sleep, Moozh," she said curtly. "The entire crew must be awake before we send the message." She gave him a hard look. "Or did you forget?" she asked accusingly.

"I've forgotten nothing," he said defensively. "While you've been killing yourself here, I've been studying how to launch a communication drone from a remote station, but all my work, how to breach command protocol, will come to nothing if you're not at peak efficiency, and that means sleep."

"I know, Sasha," she whispered, "but sleep is not my friend these days."

"Neither is working yourself to death," he declared, "and what do you mean by 'not your friend'?"

A nurse entered the lab, sensed the tension, and quickly backed out. As soon as the door shut Nadya whispered, "The visions."

"So, you're still having them?"

She nodded. "Every time sleep overtakes me."

"But this is a good thing, yes?" he asked, cautiously hopeful. "I mean, the visions are giving you more information, right?"

"These are vague," admitted Nadya. "They're only glimpses now, and once again they're unclear and confusing." She looked back at the microscope.

Sasha absentmindedly scratched an ear unsure of how his wife was really feeling. "So, does this mean that you're having second thoughts about sending this drone back to Earth?"

"Of course not," she reassured him. "I know what, when, and who I saw." She looked at him with total conviction. "I know that this message must be sent as planned. There is no alternative."

"So, what's troubling you now?"

Sagging against the counter, she sounded as haggard as she looked. "Now, when I try to visit the planet surface, all I see are clouds, and in those clouds," she gasped at the memory, "all I see is death."

"So, you believe the clouds are deadly?"

"I-I'm just not sure," she admitted. "I just don't know."

Wary of pushing too hard, Sasha still pressed. "Then give me your best guess."

"Guess?" she asked incredulously. "This isn't a game, Moozh."

"That's not what I mean." He sat down on a lab bed. "I just meant that incomplete or not, in the absence of hard facts we could use an educated guess." She nodded as he went on. "That's the best information we have."

"Shit! I hate having all this responsibility on my shoulders," she swore, then closed her eyes, allowing the vent to pass. "Okay, fine, to answer your question, yes, I believe that the clouds mean death."

"So, we avoid the clouds."

"Oh Moozh." The edges of her mouth bent upward. "The rocket scientist in you never fails to amaze."

Ten days later the entire crew was awake and recovering, and the medical team was finally able to stand down. Nadya knew it was time to talk to the captain. She rehearsed for an hour before approaching him in the galley and found him at the salad bar plunking fresh radishes on his plate. "Captain," she said timidly, "I need to talk to you about something important."

Troy looked down at his meal and sighed, then back up at his medical chief of staff. "Follow me," he motioned with his head, and walked to his seat. "So, Doctor, what's brought you to my table?" He sat down, salted a radish, and raised it to his mouth.

"We're going to crash-land on the planet."

The radish froze in place before he could take a bite. "Is that some kind of sick joke? If so, it isn't the least bit funny." He took a bite and glared at her while chewing it.

"It's no joke, Captain," insisted Nadya. "*The Magellan II* is never leaving this planet; we're going to be stranded—"

Troy threw his palms up and growled, "Just stop!" Blinking twice at her, he got up and walked away, leaving his plate unfinished.

Knowing it was futile to go after him, Nadya returned to her cabin defeated and depressed in the knowledge that she handled that all wrong. She had squandered her only opportunity with the captain, and now he would be suspect of her every move from this day forward.

Drained of energy, she finally had a chance to get some real sleep for the first time in weeks, but the thought of this tormented her even more than failing to get through to the captain. Giving in to exhaustion, she crawled in next to Sasha and laid her head against his chest.

The moment she fell asleep the visions hit her with the force of a cyclone. Images swirled around her with ever-increasing force, and those seemingly benign clouds she'd been seeing lately had turned into a violent storm. One vision stood out more than any other. She saw a small spaceship buffeted by high winds and hammered by lightning.

The next thing she saw was the young man she'd seen so many times during her ten-year journey through the universe. He was critically wounded, hanging on some surf-pounded rocks with a sword run through his upper torso. He finally lost grip and fell into the killing surf, but then something surreal happened. The golden dragon from her visions plucked him out of the water an instant before he sank beneath the powerful waves and placed him on a quiet beach beyond the reach of the pounding surf. It opened its mouth, engulfing the man, and discharged a viscous red liquid from glands in its mouth, drenching him. Then the dragon gently picked up the unconscious man and did something so unexpected, so unsettling, that it shook Nadya to her core. It looked straight into her eyes as a powerful voice entered her mind. *You need to hurry, Mother. Everything depends on your message.*

Never before had anyone, anything from a vision acknowledged her. How could they? These were not communication, but this being, this dragon, whom she'd seen many times throughout her life, not only communicated with her, but it did so in a voice that she knew intimately well.

Because it was her own.

Nadya abruptly woke, breathing hard. The sheets were soaked and her mind was in turmoil. She kicked off the clammy sheets, scrambled into her rumpled jumpsuit, and reached over and shook Sasha. "Get up!" she practically screamed. "We've no time to waste."

Sasha woke groggily, blinking his eyes. "Nadya, what's happened, what's the matter?" he asked, yawning. "Is it the visions again?"

Nadya ignored his question. "Get dressed and come with me." His eyes went wide at her command. "Because it's time."

"Time for what? To send the message?" he asked as he slipped into his jumpsuit.

"Of course," she said, impatiently waiting for him to get ready, "what else?"

It took them almost an hour to get from their cabin to the drone bay housed in the nine-kilometer causeway. Sasha had been down here several times lately and knew exactly what he was able to do, and more importantly, what he couldn't do. "You must realize," he explained to Nadya, "that I can't access the catapult from here. It's not a redundant system, and there's not enough time for me to access it before the bridge discover there's an issue and shuts us down."

"I don't care," Nadya told him as she began accessing the computer she needed to upload the message. "All that matters is that we make this launch irretrievable."

"Okay, but do you understand that without the catapult it'll take this small EMD 100 years to reach the Oort cloud?"

"That's why I had you program the 900-year power-down," she reminded him.

"Of course it is," Sasha mumbled and began the launch sequence. "You're the boss." He seemed not to notice her withering glower. "Okay, it's now or never."

"Then launch already!" Nadya implored him.

"But you haven't uploaded the message yet," Sasha protested, but hit the launch button anyway. They heard an electric whoosh as the three-meter craft floated into space on its 1,000-year mission. "Ladna, it's away. I hope we don't end up in the brig."

"Hush, Moozh, while I finish." She typed as fast as she could. "I'll send in a moment." Nadya finished, hit the upload button, and then swore. "Shit!"

"Nadya, the bridge has cut off the message." He looked at his wife, worry etched across his face. "I don't think all of it made it."

"I know, but hopefully it was enough. God help them all if it wasn't."

CHAPTER FORTY-FOUR

BRING THEM DOWN
OFOL'R, LOG'RFOLD

A different color light illuminated each of the stacked domes that made up the Normad'r undersea base. Its top dome emitted a soft green hue and was called the chamber of interposition. From it Kanend'ra studied everything taking place on the human starship. She listened to their conversations, observed personnel movement, and knew exactly what the humans planned to do.

The Earth ship had been orbiting for weeks now, and as soon as their Spak'rna had uploaded her message to the drone, Kanend'ra reported it to the Prime Leader. "Mab'r, the humans have launched a communication drone back to Earth."

"When was it sent, and who sent it?" asked Erland'r.

Kanend'ra held out her hand, and an image appeared in her palm. "It was sent seven minutes ago, and the message was created by the Spak'rna."

"What did she communicate?" Erland'r wanted to make sure that their plan was coming to fruition, and this message was the key.

"She reported that they've already established a colony on Log'rfold, have observed a green nebula, and that they expect an invasion," replied Kanend'ra. The smooth skin of her flawless face emanated a light hue. "There is no nebula, Mab'r, not to mention that they haven't even landed yet, and we have no need to invade once they do."

Erland'r opened his palm, allowing his orb to float free. Within seconds it projected a holograph of the starship. "It seems this Spak'rna has had a vision and knows what even we haven't foreseen." He fluttered his fingers at his orb, and the holograph vanished. He turned to Kanend'ra and asked, "What's their next planned operation?"

"They plan to disembark by sending down shuttles. Once that operation is complete, the starship will return to Earth and return with more colonists," she explained to her Mab'r. "They must not realize their home world has been destroyed."

"How can this be?"

Kanend'ra considered her options before answering, "This drone is the first communication sent by the ship, and they've received nothing from Earth."

This interested the Mab'r more than anything else she'd reported, and instantly made his decision. "We need to bring them down before they begin disembarking. Their ship must not return to Earth, but they are not to be destroyed, and we must not allow any type of radio communication once they are on the ground. See to it."

"As you command, Mab'r," responded Kanend'ra. She reflected a moment before updating him with the present status of the Spak'rna. "It seems as though the woman is to be incarcerated for sending this message. Shall I destroy the drone?"

"No, her message is essential," Erland'r explained, "but not the return of their colonial ship. That would complicate things."

"They plan to begin disembarking within the next planetary rotation, Mab'r," she informed him. "I'll have the Rond'r orbs powered up."

CHAPTER FORTY-FIVE

BRACE FOR IMPACT
MAGELLAN II

"**C**aptain Troy," came the ship-wide hail, "report to the bridge at once. Condition red!"

Troy heard the hail in his bunk, scrambled into his jumpsuit, and hurried to the bridge. "What's happened?" he asked the officer of the watch, Commander Aapo Afua.

"Sir," the science officer answered in his heavy West African accent, "something dramatic is happening at both poles on the planet surface."

"Dramatic enough to disturb my sleep period, Commander?" Troy wasn't angry, but he was never pleasant upon waking. "Show me what's got you so worked up."

Afua worked the controls, and as the main screens flickered to life he reported in an even voice, "I'm bringing an image of the planet up now. As you know, we've observed an unusual cloud cover over both landmasses."

Troy took a sip of coffee, trying to clear the cobwebs as he looked at the screen. "Yes, I know about these, but they're just clouds. What's happening now?"

"The clouds are changing." The science officer pointed at the screen. "Both poles are experiencing some sort of storm, and what had seemed to be benign cloud systems have now become roiling hurricane-force storms."

Troy rubbed his eyes. "You woke me up because there's a storm on the planet?"

"I woke you because two storms, one forming around each pole, began at exactly the same instant," Afua patiently explained. "These seem to be more than just a storm, Captain, and there's something else." Troy's eyebrows slightly rose. "The storms have created eyes at their center, and we can now finally see below the clouds."

"What's below them?" asked Troy, his interest now fully engaged.

"The eye of each storm has revealed two strange-looking mountains exactly at the planet's axis points. They're a perfect 180 degrees apart."

"That's odd, I admit, Commander, but what else is so strange about them?"

Afua tapped the control panel and adjusted his joystick. Two shocking images split the view screen. "As you can see, sir, the mountains are perfect parabolic cones, and exactly 9,006 meters high. That's taller than Mount Everest."

The bridge went dead quiet as the implications sunk in. The silence broke when Afua continued, "Captain, there's an extreme thermal increase building up inside each mountain. They're now at 230 degrees Celsius, but the temperature is rising so fast that it's hard for our sensors to keep up."

Troy was staggered. Nothing in his experience came close to what they were witnessing now, and he needed answers to questions that had never even occurred to him before. "Are they volcanoes?" he asked and then saw that everyone on the bridge was waiting for him to give them guidance.

"I'm not sure, but those things look like jet nozzles," answered Afua. At that instant huge lightning bolts erupted from their peaks, spreading out for hundreds of kilometers. "Oh shitty wahala," muttered the science officer.

"While I concur," Troy's voice was taut, "I need something more technical."

Afua studied his console, then looked up at Troy. "Giant resonant transformers with alternating current."

"Tesla coils, Commander?"

Afua turned back to his screen. "Well, yeah, for lack of a better term."

The lightning suddenly stopped arcing downward and began rising, closing like giant glowing flower petals until all the lightning shot straight up. Within moments the individual bolts coalesced into a single massive beam of energy blasting into space, one at each end of the planet.

"Sir," exclaimed Afua, "that thing's hit something."

"What's up here besides us?" Troy demanded.

"I'm zooming in now." Afua focused the long-range telescope. Once he got an accurate focus it took his breath away. "Captain, the beam has targeted a satellite—no, wait, there's more than one. Oh double shit wahala, there are hundreds of them." The targeted satellite began transferring the energy out toward another, and then another. Within two minutes 1,000 satellites that they hadn't even known were there had powered up.

Troy and Afua looked at each other as the ramifications sank in. "Captain, the satellites are drones, and they've begun moving."

"Moving?" Troy whispered his question. "Moving where?"

"Toward us."

The hair on Troy's neck stood up. "Then we are being attacked?"

"I-I don't know," stammered Afua, "but I think—maybe."

As the drones closed in, several fired beams of light, but none struck the starship.

"Those seem like shots across the bow, sir," Afua practically shouted, "warning shots."

"A warning?" Troy made his decision. "Well, let's not stick around for their warning to get real." Troy looked at the helm and ordered, "Get the EMD online."

"And go where?" queried Afua.

"Anywhere but here!" yelled Troy, as the helm spooled up the fission reactors. The giant starship couldn't leave orbit for several minutes.

They didn't have that much time. A few drones fired more energy beams directly at the ship, blowing chunks out of the EMD module. Hundreds more of the attackers fired and hit the ship from aft to fore, but instead of damaging the *Magellan II* the beams wrapped it in a tight cocoon of energy.

And began pushing it toward the planet surface.

"Helm, get that EMD online now!" ordered the captain, never taking his eyes off the screen. The planet slowly grew in size as they moved inexorably closer. Troy remembered Dr. Yanbeyeva's warning. She'd told him that the ship would crash, and never return to Earth. At the time he'd thought she was suffering from some sort of dementia, but now—

"Sir!" The voice of the helm officer, Lieutenant Paige Nikolasos, snapped him back to the present. "I've got partial power, but the EMD isn't responding." The lieutenant frantically worked her controls, but there wasn't any throttle response. She quickly hailed the engineering department. "Dr. Isami, my remote access is disabled, and we're on a collision course with the planet."

Dr. Isami's response gave little hope for the stricken ship. "The EMD has taken a direct hit by some kind of energy weapon and is inoperable," he reported. "I can give you fission power for the thrusters, but not enough to break free of whatever is forcing us down to the surface."

The next thing Isami heard was Captain Troy's voice, and it was frantic. "So, what are you saying, Isami?" He was beyond distraught at the thought of crashing. The chance of survival was zero.

Isami gave him a small glimmer of hope, but it wasn't what the captain wanted to hear. "Sir, we have enough thrust to slow our rate of descent, but unless something changes, we will impact the planet."

Troy went rigid as he stared at the view screen. For a moment he didn't blink, didn't move a muscle. When he finally spoke it was with a low even tone. "Can you give me enough thrust to at least dictate where we crash-land?

"I'll try, Captain," said Isami, "and coordinate with the helm." He contacted Nikolasos. "The thrusters now have all available power. You'll have to use them to guide the ship to whatever landing spot you pick. I'm sorry, but that's all I can do."

"Roger that," replied Nikolasos. Calling over her shoulder, she told the captain, "I'm aiming for that big bay at the end of the peninsula on the northern continent."

"Just get us down in one piece," urged Troy. He opened up the ship-wide intercom and told the crew, "We're being forced out of orbit. The EMD is damaged and we can't break the lock on us." He closed his eyes and said the words no captain ever wanted to say. "I order everyone into their bunks, strap down, and brace for impact."

Perspiring heavily, Nikolasos used the soft fabric of her sleeve to wipe sweat from her eyes. "Sir, I've got thruster response, but they were never designed to land a starship."

As the gigantic ship entered the atmosphere, the planet's gravitational pull took over from the drones. Unknown to the humans, the traction beams that had been pushing now reversed their energy flow and pulled at it, keeping the starship from terminal velocity. Between the ship's thrusters and the energy beams, the *Magellan II* slowed to a survivable rate of descent.

Troy had been trained on what the ship was capable of and, just as important, what was impossible. Every conceivable law of physics dictated that the thrusters didn't have a fraction of the power needed to guide them down safely, but physics be damned, somehow they did.

CHAPTER FORTY-SIX

PAROLE
AQUEOUS

The giant craft's bow missed the strange clouds, but the EMD module passed directly through them. Screeching metal and human screams wailed from the ship-wide intercom. Many vital systems disappeared, and the stern thrusters lost all power.

Distress alarms blared throughout the ship.

Severely damaged, the now powerless EMD module plunged toward the planet surface. Stripped of power, its balance gyro ceased functioning. The effect was immediate. Violent shockwaves oscillated out from the stern, sending a debilitating vibration throughout the craft.

Simple tasks turned arduous.

Secured to her station, Nikolasos could barely make control adjustments. Many crew members that weren't strapped in properly broke free of their restraints and were hurled against bulkheads. Dozens suffered broken bones, including two broken necks. The ship and her crew were ebbing toward annihilation.

"Captain, the EMD module is falling at terminal velocity," reported Nikolasos, "but command is still on a slight trajectory." All her attempts to regain trim had failed, and the stern continued to pick up speed.

"What *is* the status of engineering?" Troy demanded.

"It's swinging down. We—the ship's become a pendulum." Nikolasos's words were coming fast. "It'll impact first."

The planet's surface came up quickly. Right before impact, Captain Troy hit the ship-wide intercom, shouting, "Brace! Brace! Brace!" The *Magellan II* had reached an almost vertical stem-to-stern pitch when the EMD module slammed into the planet surface with such force that it was torn off the causeway. Without the weight of the EMD dragging it down, and the bow thrusters at full power, the vital command module began to slow even more.

Forty-seven seconds after the stern smashed into the planet, the bow made a hard landing. It impacted in a heavily forested region and bounced once before settling down into a rough slide. The fragile nine-kilometer causeway flogged the ground, twisting and buckling like a whip. With an ear-splitting screech, the causeway violently tore loose from the command module and broke into thousands of fragments.

After the initial bounce, the command module slid more than three kilometers through rugged terrain. It broke giant trees and tossed aside huge boulders. Pieces of it ripped off before it finally ground to a halt, listing hard to port. The deep impact furrow was scattered with the debris torn off during the wild slide. Though the crew compartment was battered, it remained intact.

The bridge filled with smoke and the relentless blare of alarms and the screams of crew members. Electrical fires ignited as many of the ship's systems failed and short-circuited. Trying to be heard over the cacophony on the bridge, Captain Troy shouted orders the moment the ship came to rest. "Get extinguishers on those fires right away!" He unstrapped from his chair yelling, "Comms! Do we have communication to any other part of the ship?"

The dazed communications officer had a gash on her forehead, but immediately responded, "I'm trying right now, sir." She frantically tried to raise a hail with the rest of the ship, but her console was a mass of blinking or, worse, dark lights. She quickly reported back to Troy, who was manning a fire extinguisher. "I've got nothing but static here, Captain."

All power suddenly went out. Except for the groans of the injured, the ship went deathly quiet as it plunged into darkness. Within seconds the emergency lights came on, but the smoke made visibility almost impossible.

The bridge crew began to move around the darkened cabin trying to deal with a situation that no one had ever prepared for: a crash landing. Troy knew that what the crew needed most right now was strength of leadership, *his* leadership. "We need to find out the status of the rest of the ship." He looked around and saw Major Moroz painfully limp into the bridge, holding a hurt arm. "Major, do you have any security people unhurt and able to fan out across the ship?"

Moroz grimaced and gave him an uncertain nod. "I'm not sure what the status of my department is," he reported, wincing in pain, "but I'm about to go find out."

"Do that," ordered the captain, "and while you're at it, tell your command I need them to make their reports in English, especially when they're using a radio. I need to understand what's being said."

"I'll issue the order, Captain," said Moroz, "but can't guarantee complete compliance."

"Insist on it, Major, and get me that status report." Troy ran his fingers through his short hair, finding a sore bump at the back of his skull. He looked around the destroyed bridge and muttered to himself, "I need to know what's become of my ship." He looked up at Moroz with desperation written on his face. "And I need your Russian speakers to do it."

He turned back to his communication officer and relayed his greatest fear. "Do you have any contact with the EMD module?"

"No, Captain," came the stressed answer. "I've been trying to hail them, but so far, nothing."

"Keep trying and report to me the moment you make contact." He turned to Moroz; his voice wrought with tension. "Major, I need to know the worst hit departments. They'll have the greatest need."

Moroz left the bridge and went directly to his office two floors up. All the elevators were out of operation, so he made the painful climb up the emergency access ladders with a shattered knee and a sprained arm. When he limped through the hatch he saw that his security personnel were already responding to the ship-wide catastrophe.

They stopped what they were doing and waited for their injured commanding officer to give them direction. "We've been ordered to inspect the ship, and the bridge wants a status report right away," he told them in a strained voice, "and we've been ordered to speak English during all communications." Moroz hesitated a moment and then said, "First things first. Send a team to the infirmary. Check their status." Then a thought hit him. "And for God's sake, release Dr. Yanbeyeva and her husband from the brig."

"Do we have the authority to do that, Major?" asked one of his officers.

"Authority is now a fluid situation," Moroz growled, "and I'm granting them parole."

"Sasha!" yelled Nadya, as she ran her hands over her husband's unconscious body. He groaned and his eyes fluttered open. "Can you hear me?" She had some bruises but had been ready for the crash. Both she and Sasha knew it was coming and had strapped themselves in the best they could, but the brig didn't offer much protection. He'd thrown his body over hers and bounced badly, hitting his head against the upper bunk.

Nadya heard her keypad chime, and stood up as two security men came in. "The ship's crashed on the planet," one of the uniformed men said, "and we need everyone, especially doctors, right now."

"Does that mean prisoners as well?" she asked him.

"You've been released," he told her, "by Major Moroz."

"In that case," Nadya ordered him, "help me get my husband to the infirmary, and I'll start getting things organized for the injured who'll soon be filling it up."

The security men lifted Sasha and made the difficult trek down five floors to the ship's hospital. When they got there, it was already full of injured crew members. Her staff was barely able to cope. With no power, the most they could do was administer antibiotics, apply splints, and stitch up wounds.

Nadya immediately took charge and was organizing when Major Moroz limped in. She saw him and rushed over. "Thank you for letting us out, Major," she said while examining his swollen knee. "You've got to stay off this."

"I don't have that luxury, Doctor." The major winced as she felt the extent of his injury. "This ship is in serious trouble, and I need to be front and center."

Nadya pursed her lips. "You need to delegate, Major, because this knee is shattered, and if you don't stay off it, you could be crippled for life."

Moroz started to argue, but the disapproving scowl on Nadya's face stopped any more protests. He relented. "Fine, Doctor. I'll follow your advice, but I need to be able to at least work in my office, so if you can give me something for pain and splint this thing up, then I'll do as you advise, and delegate."

She arched a suspicious brow. "Fair enough, Major, but you do realize that sooner rather than later, I will have to operate on that knee."

"I understand," he told her, "but I'm pretty sure that your scalpel will be very busy for the next few weeks, and if I've got to delegate, then you'll have to prioritize."

Major Moroz's prediction proved accurate. All the uninjured doctors spent days on end in the emergency ward attending the injured crew. Three days after the crash they were finally able to get a small amount of electricity, and most of it was given to the greatest need: the hospital. Once power had been restored the medical team was able to do more than just rudimentary first aid. They began operating in earnest with Nadya choosing her priorities. Moroz was the first patient who went under the knife, and it was obvious to Nadya that it would never be the same.

Captain Troy was initially perturbed that his prisoners had been released, but soon realized that having his medical chief of staff behind bars was not in his best interest. He was under tremendous stress, and their conversation was as strained as their jobs.

The moment Nadya entered the bridge Troy cornered her. "The only reason I've dropped all charges is that this ship needs your medical skills more than it needs two hungry prisoners, but make no mistake, Dr. Yanbeyeva," he warned her, "any further infractions and you *will* land back in the brig."

Nadya maintained a neutral expression. "Captain Troy, I warned you, but you ignored me."

"How could you possibly have known this would happen?" he snapped at her. "And what possible difference would it have made?"

"The ship would have been better prepared, and I would now have far fewer patients in my hospital."

"Be that as it may, how could you have possibly known beforehand, unless you had a hand in it?"

"Are you accusing me of complicity? Why would I warn you if I was responsible?"

"Then how the hell did you know it would happen?" he demanded.

"Because, Captain, I see things." He gave a disbelieving grimace, but she kept talking. "Things that will happen. I've seen other things that'll happen to this ship and her crew. Things you need to know about."

He smirked at her. "This is just crazy, Doctor. What are you, some kind of seer?"

"Exactly," she told him. "I've been one all my life."

The smirk was replaced by incredulity. "A seer on my crew. Who knew?" he said sarcastically. "What fantastical visions do you have for me now, Doctor?"

"Earth is gone," she informed him, "and if this ship had gone back it would have found a smoldering radioactive ruin."

"I don't believe it." He waved his hand in dismissal.

"You didn't believe the *Magellan II* would crash either," she countered, watching his eyes blaze, "and believe it or not, there'll be no follow-up missions for 1,000 years." His face went pale, but she wasn't done. "We're on our own, Trevor."

Troy walked over and slumped in his chair. Placing his head in both hands, he stared at the floor for a moment before looking back up. The strain was evident when he finally ventured a glance at his medical chief. "Look, Nadya, I'm not saying I believe you, but if what you say is somehow true, then we'll have to build a colony with what we now have aboard this ship."

"Well, it is what I'm saying. We have to make this planet our home without help from Earth."

The captain's back straightened. Whatever lapse had occurred a moment ago was gone and Troy used his best commander's voice to tell her, "However much that now seems likely, no one's leaving this ship until I'm satisfied it's safe to do so."

"I'm glad that you're finally accepting the truth of our situation, because I know more, a lot more, but this is all I have time for today. I still have a hospital full of injured patients." She stood up, but before leaving the bridge she turned and told him, "We'll talk more, Captain. Our survival as a species depends on it."

CHAPTER FORTY-SEVEN

I WANNA GO OUTSIDE
KORYAK, EARTH

Being the mother to the enclave as well as two children was far more than a full-time job, it was a crushing undertaking. There wasn't enough time in the day to raise her children, much less the childlike issues that confronted her daily. It seemed the more she groomed the twins into becoming respectful responsible people, the more she had to deal with the exact opposite in the adults who lived under her watch.

When Mother Leka first took over the enclave, her shoulder-length caramel-brown hair was thick and full-bodied. A decade later it was straggly, mostly grey, and fell limply across her dull grey eyes whenever she worked at her desk. Lately, Leka spent a lot of time there sitting with her head in her hands hoping for a miracle.

At the beginning of her tenure she'd thought that the book given to her the day she took up her position would be a manifesto to help her lead the enclave.

It wasn't.

It was simply a guideline for carrying on the family's bloodline. It listed the pairings for generations. There was nothing in it to help her deal with the myriad complaints about everything from the lack of light to the ever-unpleasant task of dealing with waste. The daily litany of complaints marched into her office unrelentingly.

"There's not enough light to read by." A typical complaint.

"We need grow lights for food," Leka would answer.

"That crappy smell from the waste is overwhelming."

"We need it for fertilizer."

"Our children are suffering from lack of sunlight."

"Send them to help in the gardens where there's enough light."

"But the stench—"

"I can't solve all your problems!"

"But you're Mother Leka!"

"I know, I know—"

And so it went.

Almost everything required electrical power to operate, and the small reactor that had once been adequate proved anything but as the years wore on. Another power source had to be found. After almost eleven years below the surface, the population had grown to the point that these complaints not only had merit, but a crisis was brewing, and it all centered around too many people surviving on too little power.

Leka called an emergency meeting with her best engineers. They had to come up with a viable solution, or the enclave would eventually die out.

The meeting was held in her office, the same office where Leka had been given leadership of the enclave more than a decade before. The thought that her last days as head of the enclave might happen in this same room was never far from her mind.

She sat listening to all the different proposals from her engineers, but so far it was just rehashed ideas that offered no real solutions. She rejected idea after idea as the meeting became heated, and threats against her rule started to rear their ugly head.

Leka was almost to the point of not caring.

Quietly slipping into the room, her two blond-headed, green-eyed kids, Natasha and Albert, stood silently near the back. They'd brought something with them. After listening for a moment, Natasha walked over to her mom and tried to get her attention.

"Mama, Ally and I have something that might help."

"What are you doing in here?" demanded Leka. Her nerves were frayed and the last thing she needed was to have her children witness this ugly scene, her fall from grace.

"But, Mama, Ally and I have seen things—"

"You need to leave right now. This is no place for children."

"But we've seen things. We know how to help," pleaded Natasha.

"Mother Leka, you don't even have control over your own children," sneered one of her biggest detractors. "How can you expect to run this enclave?"

"You two, out now!" hissed Leka. Natasha turned to leave but stopped and dropped a piece of paper on Leka's desk, then together with her brother left as silently as they'd entered.

After a few more minutes of wrangling with the group in her office, Leka finally glanced down at the sheet her daughter had left on her desk. When the rest of the group saw that she was no longer paying attention to them, the chief engineer, Boris Utkin, got up. Once a heavy smoker, Boris had to quit when he entered the bunker, but his crooked yellow teeth still bore the stain of twenty years at two packs a day. Since quitting he'd gained fifteen kilograms on his 168-centimeter frame, and he waddled more than walked over to see what had totally absorbed the enclave's leader. He picked it up and read it. His eyes soon shot from the sheet to the door.

"Your children drew this?" he asked.

"Yes," whispered Leka.

"What're you looking at, Boris?" asked one of the other engineers.

"Come take a look, Ivan, and tell us what you see."

Wearing a scowl, the stoop-shouldered Ivan walked purposefully to the desk and studied what had caused all the fuss. After a moment the scowl disappeared and he told Leka, "Maybe we should ask your children to come back. I have a few questions for them."

Leka hurried to the door and opened it to call for her kids. They were standing next to it waiting for the summons they knew was coming. "Oh, here you are, can you come back inside, please?"

"Yes, Mama," they said in unison, and walked back to their mother's desk.

"Where did you get this?" asked Boris.

"Did you sketch it from a textbook?" questioned Ivan.

"No. We just drew it," answered Natasha.

"We did it together," said Albert. "We drew it from our mind."

"What do you mean *from your mind?*" Ivan demanded.

But Leka knew. Her sister had seen things too and drawn many pictures of her visions when she was a girl. Leka remembered it well, and now she was seeing it again. "Kids, did you both see this in your mind?"

"Yes, Mama," replied Natasha. "We saw and drew it together. We knew it could help you."

Boris bent over the paper and scratched his head. "This map. It's proportionally perfect." He looked over at the two children. "And these lines. What did you see as these lines you've drawn?"

The two kids looked at each other and shrugged their small shoulders. "They're just tubes," Albert told him. "Long tubes."

"They're pipelines." Boris turned and told the group, "Oil and gas pipelines, from Sakhalin Island to Vladivostok." He turned back to the kids and asked, "But what are these lines, here?"

Again the children didn't know, but someone else in the room did. "Those are water pipelines that run from here to Vladivostok," said Ingra, one of the other engineers who'd also approached the desk. "I know. I helped design and build them. They're large, and well-constructed."

The engineers studied the map. They couldn't believe the simplicity of what was in front of them. It was the answer to all their energy needs. Except for one thing. Someone had to go connect them.

Leka took each child by the hand and asked, "What did you see, children? Tell us everything."

Natasha looked at Albert, and by silent consent, the girl spoke for them both. "We saw them, Mama, just like we said. In our minds."

"Did you see any damage?" she asked anxiously.

"No, Mama. They'll work just like they always did."

Mother Leka gave the group of engineers a hard look. "Boris, can this be done?" she asked the chief engineer. "Can you link these two pipelines, and bring gas to Koryak?"

"Conceivably," Boris answered cautiously. He glanced over at the other engineers. "But, it's still hot out there. In a survival suit someone can live a few weeks, but the dose will be chronic, and whoever does the job won't live very long. The job can be done, but who's willing to forfeit his or her life to do it?"

"I will," volunteered Ivan. "I'll find a small team. Everyone either slowly dies here, or a few can die knowing the enclave will survive."

"Gentlemen." Leka was shocked. "I can't ask you to do this."

"You're not," Boris told her. "It has to be done, and we're the only ones who know how."

"Not true, Boris," protested Ingra. "I too am an expert and will be part of this team. Besides," she grimly told the group, "I wanna go outside."

Leka realized two things that day—her enclave had a chance at survival, and her children traveled the same Path as their mother.

CHAPTER FORTY-EIGHT

TAKE A NUMBER
AQUEOUS

Nadya spent weeks operating on the injured. Aside from two fatalities, the front module had suffered several major injuries and hundreds of relatively minor ones, but there'd been no word about the sixty-seven crew members that had been in the rear engine compartment. It was dozens of kilometers away, and the causeway that had once connected the two ends was now just torn and twisted metal. No one on the command module knew its status, and none of their radio transmissions had been answered.

Five days after the crash, a search and rescue team was sent to investigate, but after thirty minutes all communication was lost and never re-established. The six-member team disappeared without a trace.

It would be months before anyone else left the ship again.

Almost everyone had some kind of injury. They either had a few bumps and bruises, or broken limbs like the indispensable Major Moroz. In spite of her insistence that he stay bedridden, it was not to be. Two weeks after she reconstructed his knee, she found him up, against doctor's orders, and ranging through the ship trying to reorganize what had turned out to be an organizational nightmare. Security on a starship was one thing. Security on a crashed, marooned starship was altogether different.

"Major Moroz—" she scolded.

He quickly cut her off. "It's Sergei, please, Nadya." With a shrug of his broad shoulders he told her, "I know what you're going to say, but you must understand my position. I simply cannot let things lapse anymore."

She crossed her arms across her chest, squinted at him, and said in her best schoolmarm voice, "Fine, Sergei, but you really don't want your baby boy outrunning his father. Do you?"

"What baby boy?" he asked, narrowing his eyes. "You've examined my wife—"

Nadya touched his arm and whispered, "Not yet, but she needs to come see me right away. Today would be good."

"How do you know such things?" He looked at her with amazement. "I've heard the talk around the ship, but," he had to ask, "can you really see things, know things?"

"Yes," she said, and then steered away from that subject. "Have her come by at two this afternoon. Oh, and get off that knee. We need the real Major Moroz, not the one who can barely walk."

Petya Moroz was indeed pregnant, and as the weeks went by, so were a growing number of women.

A baby boom was on the way.

Wearing the same uniform four days running, unshaven, with bags under his eyes, Captain Troy sat in his chair concentrating on the water maker diagnostic when he heard the bridge crew give the popular Dr. Nadya a cheerful greeting. His shoulders tensed as he took a deep breath and turned to face yet another department head coming to vent their frustrations right where the buck stopped. "Yes, Doctor?"

"We need to talk."

"Take a number."

She gave him a sympathetic smile and tried to sound the same. "I understand you're stretched thin—"

"You have no idea."

"Actually, Trevor, I do." She reached over and switched off the diagnostic monitor. He glowered momentarily, then relented and waited for her to continue. "And since we're bound to have this conversation sometime soon, it might as well be now."

"And since I've obviously finished trying to figure out the problem with that," he glanced at the blank monitor, "we might as well have the conversation I knew was coming."

"So, you're willing to hear me out?"

"Like I have a choice?" he muttered.

She dove straight to the heart of the matter. "We need to create stability."

"Look, I know we're listing 11 degrees to port, but there's no way to right the ship," he patiently told her, "and I'm fully aware that the bilge system on that side of the ship has problems—"

"It doesn't work at all."

He hung his head. "I know."

"That smell," she sniffed the air, "is shit, and it's become a biohazard."

"I know."

"And now we have another growing burden on the sanitation system."

"More than shit?" he glumly asked.

"We have 361 pregnant women on board."

His face practically drained of blood. "Babies—figures." He sounded defeated. "What do you propose?"

"It's been three months since we landed."

"Crashed."

"My point exactly. This ship will never fly again."

Troy let out an exasperated groan. "You're telling me?"

"Yes, Trevor, I am," Nadya said, "and we need to get off this ship, rescue the survivors on the EMD module, and start building accommodations."

"Survivors?" he asked.

"Of course survivors." She locked onto him with a head-on stare. "We need room to grow as a civilization." She placed both hands on his chair's armrest and leaned in close, speaking in sotto voice. "Because that's what we've become—a human civilization, who cannot stay on this wreck of a starship much longer."

"Do you know what's waiting for us out there?" He pointed at the view screen. "Have you seen what's just outside the ship? There's dinosaurs out there." Her brows raised. "Okay, alien reptiles, but big hungry-looking reptiles. Some are fifteen meters tall with meter-long teeth."

"Do you know what'll be waiting for us here in about seven to eight months?" she countered. "Hundreds of hungry little babies, with no teeth, and all needing room to grow."

"You'd want to raise children on an alien planet full of predators?" His voice rose for the first time.

"Of course not, but that's the hand we've been dealt."

"Dare I ask? Where are you going with this??"

"We have to eliminate the danger."

"Eliminate—you mean you want to kill the local fauna?" He frowned at the screen.

"Want, no. Need, yes. Look Trevor, there's a new predator in town, and this one has a security force with ray guns and stuff. We can do this.

We must do this. We're out of options, and soon we'll be out of room." She pushed off his chair and said, "Oh, and one more thing."

He tensed as a small groan escaped his throat. "It's never just one—what now?"

"We need those reactors from the EMD module, and we need them soon."

He hung his head in resignation. "We'll have to fight our way there, won't we?"

She already knew the cost of the coming battle for species supremacy. She'd seen it and knew that it would take years before the human civilization would ever be completely safe. A thousand years, in fact, but a city had to be built first, and before that, all danger to the colony had to be eliminated. There was no alternative. "Yes," she said.

CHAPTER FORTY-NINE

GONE
AQUEOUS

"Vinmany!" barked the hugely muscled Sergeant Orlov when his commanding officer limped into the staging area. The bustling of soldiers snapping to attention filled the small room.

"English, you lunkhead," grumbled Moroz as he picked his way through the soldiers. "As you were."

"Govno," muttered a soldier under his breath.

The major was instantly in the soldier's face. "Care to share more of your opinions, Private Gulin?"

Saying nothing, the young soldier rammed to attention and barely shook his head, but the soldier next to him said quietly, "It's unfair, sir."

"So," Moroz turned to the speaker, "tell me, Lobov, just what part of a soldier's life do you find fair?"

The private dropped his eyes to the floor and shrugged.

"Exactly," Moroz said. He then raised his voice for the whole group to hear. "I get it. You think speaking English is unfair to you but stow your pride for a fucking second and give it some thought. You might find that having a single working language is in everyone's best interest." His eyes darted to each soldier, read their silent reaction, and told them, "Now let this be the end of it. Carry on."

The squad resumed their preparations. Armed with powerful pulse rifles the team members continued donning their flexible body armor while making the small talk soldiers make before a mission, but their eyes followed every move the major made as he limped over to their squad leader.

His recently reconstructed knee prevented Moroz from making the strenuous climb down the side of the ship, so the squad leader he chose was one of the top officers in his department: a short brown-eyed dynamo of an officer, Commander Vera Askakova.

Moroz approached as the squad commander made ready to open the hatch. Struggling to find the right words, he inspected her harness, snugging it tighter. "Look, I know we covered most of this at the briefing, but—"

"What more do I need to know, Major?" Askakova asked as she patted her pulse rifle. "These plasma rounds can burn through metal."

"Yeah, and hopefully that's enough, but we've all seen the video feeds. These creatures are massive." Moroz glanced up and saw that the rest of the team had stopped their preparations and were watching them. "You lot get ready," he said, harsher than he intended, then turned back to Askakova. "Vera, we just don't know what you're gonna find or what's gonna find you, so I want you to keep it tight down there."

"Meaning, sir?" Her brows knitted under her helmet.

Moroz leaned in closer and spoke in a low tone. "The ship only has three operable surveillance cameras and zero recon drones, so our ability to follow your movement is limited, to say the least."

"I understand, sir."

"Good," he told her, and then added, "just keep your squad close. No stragglers, and make a rapid withdraw if you feel at risk." He stepped back, allowing the rest of the squad to form up, then noticed the newcomer. "What're you doing here?"

"I just came to make sure that *you* are not going to abseil down the side of the ship."

"Of course you did." Moroz turned away from the ship's doctor and reiterated his earlier order. "Any risk, Commander. Got it?"

"Any risk," Askakova's head barely bobbed as she repeated his order, "and I order retreat."

"Withdraw, Commander," he corrected.

"Right, that too," she said. A small smirk split her chiseled face.

Moroz grunted and turned to leave. "Just be careful," he called over his shoulder as he left the staging area. "I need my best commander."

"Thanks, sir. We will," Askakova assured him, and turned to her team. "Make ready the fast line and prepare to rappel. I want a clean insertion." She hit the latch, and the airlock whooshed open, allowing the outside atmosphere to wash over her team. A thick pungent odor of foul water and rotting plants filled the chamber. Several team members wrinkled their noses. "Get used to it, people," warned Askakova. "It'll be stronger on the ground." She grabbed the rope, backed up to the coaming, looked over her shoulder and said, "There's a low-lying mist covering the ground. Soft landings, people, I don't want any sprained ankles." She jumped out the hatch.

Landing in thick mud, Askakova's boots sank past her ankles. The mist shrouded the ground and she couldn't see below her knees, but she felt the sucking pull of muck on her boots as she splashed aside to give access to the landing area.

"Ain't this a bitch," griped Sergeant Orlov, splashing down next to and towering over Askakova. Her head barely reached his shoulder.

Within five minutes the entire team had formed up in the muddy swamp surrounding the ship.

It was deathly quiet outside the starship. The squad glanced uneasily at each other until something chirped close by. All eyes shot toward the shadows. Whatever chirped did it several more times, followed by the rustle of wings. A feral grunt came from deeper in the forest and was punctuated by the crack of a breaking branch.

The forest had come back to life.

Askakova engaged her helmet scanner to reconnoiter the area and got nothing but distortion. She switched it off. Her naked eye did little better as the tall tree canopy restricted what little light managed to filter through the omnipresent clouds. There was nothing to see but shadows and mist. "Helmet lights, people," she commanded, and ten beams of light stabbed into the gloom. "We're not alone out here."

Keeping her eyes fixed on the forest, Askakova told Orlov, "Looks like this mud is only in the debris field underneath the ship." She pointed at the trees. "Once we enter the forest, we should find solid ground. Prepare the squad, Sergeant. I want tight spacing and a full periphery defense. Move out."

The forest went silent again as the soldiers slogged away from the ship.

The swamp only extended a few meters before giving way to the hard ground of the forest. The terrain was uneven, and the squad had to climb over rocks and fallen trees and push their way past the leafy ground foliage that severely restricted visibility. Within thirty meters the forest had completely swallowed them. They couldn't even see the ship. Once they had penetrated fifty meters, Orlov stopped and keyed his intercom. "Commander, check our eleven. There's something lying behind that tree up there." A creature was partially hidden by a large tree trunk.

Askakova's eyes shot to what Orlov's light focused on. "Point, lock onto whatever that is. Sentinels, look sharp."

The squad moved closer. Four red dots locked on the target, but the creature didn't move. Orlov inched his brawny frame toward the huge quadruped and reported, "It's dead, ma'am. Looks like major trauma to its neck and torso."

"Those are bite marks," Askakova said, walking up to Orlov. "Something fed here recently; the blood is fresh." She quickly swept their surroundings with her light, and within seconds illuminated a pair of yellow eyes staring down at them from ten meters off the ground and as many away. She sucked in a breath, took a step back, and ordered, "Company, prepare to fire." The glowing eyes blinked out just as a deafening roar shattered the stillness of the forest.

The squad tensed as a nearby tree violently shook, raining leaves down. A sharp splintery crack split the air, and the tree trunk seemed to explode. It crashed directly on top of the squad, who scattered, but three men didn't get out of the way fast enough and were pinned to the ground. Their painful screams mixed with a snarl of something massive.

An eleven-meter-tall bipedal reptile suddenly charged out of the mist and leapt on top of the downed tree. Using its smaller upper arms, the creature tore through the branches to get at the screaming humans and bit down through the leaves, silencing one.

Orlov brought his rifle to bear. "What the hell is that thing?" he asked no one in particular as he pulled his trigger, yelling, "Fire!"

All seven remaining soldiers swung their pulse rifles into position and fired point blank at their attacker, blowing the monster off its feet. It spun around and fell in the midst of the soldiers. Screeching in fury, the huge creature writhed violently on the ground, causing them to dive for cover again. More plasma rounds tore bloody chunks off its armored hide but didn't kill it.

The beast lashed out with its upper arms. Large curved talons skewered a soldier through his shoulder and yanked him to its face. The creature sniffed Private Lobov for a moment, and then bit down on his head with a sickening crunch. Its thrashing three-meter-long tail caught another soldier in his torso and flung him into a tree.

In seconds half the squad was either injured or dead.

From the opposite direction another angry roar sounded as a second monster charged into the rapidly shrinking group of soldiers. Before anyone could turn to face this new threat, a soldier was crushed under the creature's massive hind foot and Private Gulin had the top half of his torso bitten off.

"Fall back to the ship!" shouted Askakova as she tried to drag an injured soldier from under the fallen tree. The wounded monster was now unsteadily back on its feet, and whipped its powerful tail, catching the commander below the knees, flipping her into the air. The other beast caught her leg in its mouth and bit down. Askakova fell four meters to the forest floor, breaking an arm. A bright red plume jetted out of the femoral artery where her leg had been severed above the knee.

In the blink of an eye Askakova was yanked off the ground by her backpack. At first her leg felt numb, but that quickly changed as excruciating pain flooded all her senses.

She began screaming.

Orlov ran several meters through the forest dragging his commander before slinging her small frame over his shoulder. Her screaming drowned out all other sound, and he ran faster, not daring to turn around. As he splashed across the thick mud surrounding the ship Orlov heard the whump whump of pulse rifles being fired overhead. The instant he grabbed the rope someone began pulling him up.

When Orlov reached the bottom of the airlock, helping hands reached out and grabbed the now-silent Askakova. The sergeant hung onto the rope until his unconscious commander was pulled into the open hatch, and once free of her weight he scrambled into the ship. He heard the commanding voice of Major Moroz yell out just as hands grabbed for him, but sharp teeth sunk into his legs first, ripping him out of their grasp. By the time any pulse rifles were brought to bear, the creature was ten meters away with Orlov dangling from its mouth.

Nadya knelt in Askakova's arterial blood, working furiously to save her. She glanced up at Major Moroz, who handed her a defibrillator.

Moments later Commander Vera Askakova's eyes fluttered open, her breathing shallow and ragged. Unsteadily, she grabbed her commanding officer's pant leg. "My t-team?" she cried.

Moroz swallowed hard and managed only one word: "Gone."

CHAPTER FIFTY

ALL THE VISIONS
AQUEOUS

In a fury, Captain Troy ordered Nadya and Major Moroz to the bridge. "You're the one with all the visions," Troy accused her. "I've got one maimed survivor from an entire fire team!" Jabbing his finger at the view screen, he seethed, "Didn't you see this coming?"

"Yes," she admitted, hanging her head, "and there'll be more deaths before we've established a safe habitat on the surface." Raising only her eyes, she finally met Troy's angry glare. "You know we have no choice but to continue."

"We're safe aboard this ship!" he shouted. "This," his chin jutted angrily, "is unacceptable. I'm sending people to their deaths out there."

"Nadya," agreed Moroz, "I have a sizable security force, but these losses cannot be sustained."

Pushing her hands as deep as they'd go in the pockets of her smock, Nadya said softly, "I know, gentlemen, and we will eventually create a safe region for our colony."

"Eventually!" Troy fumed. "How many have to die until that's accomplished?" He glared at both of them. "How many more do I have to watch die before you're satisfied?"

Snapping her head back up, she declared without hesitation, "Dozens more, and there's no satisfaction in this for me, Captain! The teams need to change their tactics, or these types of slaughter will continue."

"No shit?" Troy spat back. "Ya think?"

Moroz set his jaw and admitted, "We were unprepared for the speed and ferocity of this beast." Troy just glowered at Nadya as Moroz continued. "Not to mention the density of the forest. From now on we'll send three teams at a time. One to hunt the animals, and two to watch each flank."

"Yeah, and who'll protect the watchers?" Troy shook his head, still not willing to consider taking more losses. Every loss was irreplaceable.

"We'll cut the forest back," Moroz suggested, "at least 100 meters from the ship and create a defensible perimeter. I'll also place fire teams in airlocks higher up who can maintain ground surveillance from an elevated position."

The captain still wasn't convinced. "That's fine for the immediate area surrounding the ship, but you know damn good and well that whole blasted forest will have to come down for it to be effective."

"I know, but it's a start, Captain," Moroz told him. "We'll cut down the upper canopy trees and then burn the dense lower growth."

"We'll see," growled Troy, "but if this happens again, I'll put a stop to it."

The new tactics began to show results in the immediate area around the ship, but Troy's concern about venturing farther out proved correct. More soldiers were lost, but not another team. The security crews quickly learned how to anticipate the Terror Rex movements and set traps for them.

It was a battle where both sides inflicted casualties on the other, but slowly the humans gained the upper hand, and the safe zone spread far beyond the ship.

The Terror Rex was the most formidable threat, and there were a lot of them. Killing these behemoths required the humans to retreat, regroup, and rethink.

It was survival of the fittest, and humanity couldn't afford to lose this battle.

It took weeks, but a perimeter of several thousand meters was eventually cut from the ship to the large river that flowed into the bay. This meant that platoons of ten or more could scout the area and return, seeing nothing more than a few small flying reptiles. The battle for the area around the command module was won, but nothing had been heard from the EMD module, and it was at least two days' journey away.

Nadya vehemently protested when she found Major Moroz at the airlock preparing to lead the expedition to the EMD module. "You're not fully healed," she said, "and you'll not only be vulnerable out there," she pointed at the airlock, "but a liability as well."

Moroz grunted and kept tightening his battery pack. Standing right next to him he couldn't avoid her, so after checking every piece of kit twice, he finally turned to face his doctor. "I can no longer watch from the safety of this ship while my department engages the enemy day after day."

"What if you fall?" she countered.

"Twenty-three of my department have already fallen," he told her as he slipped his helmet in place and adjusted the intercom. "It's time their commander takes his place, and this mission is the most important of all."

She slumped against the cold steel bulkhead and groaned in resignation. "If we lose you we lose our best chance at defending ourselves in any future conflict."

He dropped his visor into place and turned to face her. "No, Nadya, you and your visions are the best chance we have. I'm just a soldier whose present job description includes going into harm's way. Besides, like you pointed out, we need those reactors." He turned to the rest of the expedition's officers and gave the order. "Once on the ground, form up in squads, and wait until everyone is ready. My squad will take point. We'll fan out on both sides of the trench and follow it to the target area. All right, let's move out." Right before entering the airlock he turned back toward Nadya, nodded, and then rappelled to the ground.

The trek to the EMD module took two days. Moroz ordered the squads to hug the sides of the water- and debris-filled trench, but after a few hours the trench abruptly ended. They were able to continue by following pieces of the causeway's twisted metal, but visibility was reduced to just a few meters in the dense underbrush. The small expedition fell into a single-file trek as they were forced to pick their way forward through the forest. Few creatures were found, and all either ran away or were destroyed. When a steep escarpment blocked their way, Moroz made the group swear not to tell the good doctor, took a handful of painkillers, and toughed out the ascent.

As the light began to fade the terrain turned hilly. Moroz set up camp at the top of the ridgeline where they bedded down for the night. The next morning he sent the youngest member up the tallest tree. When she'd climbed as far as she could, Moroz waited a couple minutes and yelled up, "Well?"

"I think see it, sir. About five or six kilometers away."

The expedition set out with renewed hope, but when they got within a kilometer it was apparent the rectangular EMD module had suffered far more damage than had the command module.

When they were only a few hundred meters away from the wreckage, they came across the remains of several humans. It was difficult to tell how many had died in the kill zone because only partially eaten pieces remained. The expedition spent little time there and pushed ahead to the module. It was thrashed.

When Moroz approached the side of the module he heard a shout from above him. "Hey, up here!" The head of a bearded man appeared in a jagged tear on the side of the module ten meters off the ground. "We have twenty-one people left, but most are injured."

"Where can we enter?" shouted up Moroz.

"There's a large crack in the hull about ten meters off the ground." The man pointed. "You'll have to climb up, but I'll throw a rope down and meet you inside." The man's head disappeared, and as Moroz waited for the rope to come down he tried to contact the command module. He got nothing but dead air. "Lieutenant," Moroz called over to one of his squad leaders. "Try to raise the bridge."

After several attempts the lieutenant reported that he had the same problem. "There seems to be interference, Major. I can't get through."

"That's odd," Moroz commented as he turned to grab the rope. Even with his exoskeleton power assist armor, the climb proved difficult. He groaned as pain flared in his knee while climbing up.

The moment he entered the wreck, the stench hit him. A tall, malnourished specter wearing a tattered uniform slid past a twisted piece of bulkhead and limped over to shake his hand. "Am I ever glad to see you," he said. "My name's Peter Bulanski. I thought we were the only ones left and were gonna die here."

"We'll take your survivors back to the command module," Moroz told the relieved man. He got another whiff of death and wrinkled his nose. "You have dead in here as well?"

"Yeah." The man hung his head as he explained. "We tried burying them at first but were attacked and more of us were killed by those monsters." He nervously glanced out a rip in the module's superstructure. "We've been storing the dead in another area, but the smell seems to find its way everywhere. It's been attracting a lot of unwanted attention as well. You're lucky none were around when you arrived."

"You mean the Terror Rex," said Moroz.

"Yeah, that's a good name for the bastards." Bulanski's eyes were sunken pockets in his head. "We're unarmed here, and our small infirmary was all but destroyed. We have power, but little food or water." His grimy hands covered misted eyes. "I'm afraid if you hadn't come when you did, we would've been forced t-to—"

"There's no need to think about that now," Moroz tried to comfort Bulanski. "We'll take you back with us and get you back to rights. What about Dr. Isami?"

The gaunt man looked down and mumbled, "He stayed at his post during the descent." His voice quivered. "He knew the bridge needed all the power he had to give and wouldn't leave." He finally looked up at the major and his eyes began to glisten. "The engineering control room was completely destroyed. We never even found his body."

"I understand," Moroz said quietly. "Do you have any reactor engineers left?" He looked around at the devastation.

"Yeah," Bulanski said. "Me, and a couple others. We'll be able to salvage a few of them. You must have power on the command module?"

"Of a sort, Peter. We've used up our batteries and are using solar panels now, but this damn cloud cover makes that difficult."

"These fucking clouds never go away," Bulanski muttered with a grim look. "I haven't seen blue sky since we left Earth."

CHAPTER FIFTY-ONE

THE CRYSTAL CITY
CAMBRIA, AQUEOUS

A baby boom was underway, and that new life needed a safe place to grow. On Paleozoic Earth the first explosion of life happened during the Cambrian period, and one of the first new mothers was a geologist from Belle Fourche, South Dakota. After giving birth to a healthy little boy, she offhandedly used that reference for the new colony, and the name stuck.

She had called it Cambria.

Once it was finally considered safe enough to leave the ship en masse, the command authority quickly realized that life outside the ship needed two things: a city plan, and a robust building material. That material was crystal. It was strong, and its cleavage structure made it the perfect material for quarrying. It was also found everywhere.

Now they needed a plan.

One day the captain found himself in the practically deserted hulk of the starship, and for the first time ever he was purposely seeking out Nadya's advice. He wasn't completely convinced about her ability to know everything in the future, but he figured a few questions couldn't hurt. Troy found her dismantling the infirmary. "Hello, Doctor," he cordially greeted her.

"Grab that end of the cot," she ordered him, "and help me put it in the hallway."

Twenty-two cots later the hallway was full. Troy wiped the sweat off his forehead and got to the point of his visit. "Look, Nadya, the reason—"

"It's on the desk," she informed him.

"What is?"

"The reason why you're here."

"How do you—I just came in to—oh crap," he sputtered. Troy stared at the desk for a moment before picking up several large sheets of paper. After flipping through them, he glanced up and caught her blank look.

"That is what you came for, isn't it?" Nadya asked matter-of-factly.

"Well, yeah," he admitted, "but why didn't you just tell me about it?"

Leaning against a counter, her heavy sigh blew a blond straggler out of her face. "Because, Trevor, I barely had time to draw them, much less hunt you down, and besides, I knew you'd come for it."

"Of course you did," he murmured, and turned to leave. Then he stopped and pointed to the odd blue lines. "What're all these?"

"Canals," she explained. "The Crystal River will flow right through the city on its way to the bay, and the smaller lines are the canals that'll provide water."

"Hmm, sounds feasible, and you're sure all this is accurate?"

"Really?"

"Right," he chuckled, and left with a street grid for a major city.

Even though much of the dense forest still had to be cleared, Nadya made sure that thousands of trees and shrubs were left alone, and when the major boulevards, streets, canals, and parks were laid out, most were already lined with beautiful greenery. Radiating out from a huge central hub like spokes on a wheel, the new city began to resemble a large oval with the cross streets giving it a web-like appearance. Once the sewerage, water, and powerline trenches were dug, the city building began in earnest.

Within weeks the first single-family dwellings sprouted up. These were followed by a school, and after some hard lobbying by Nadya, the first hospital. It was the first multi-story building and in the early days it dominated the skyline. But larger buildings soon followed and within a year several new buildings dwarfed even the hospital. Tall circular observation towers were added to many of the largest buildings with the tallest a twenty-three-story spire built near the urban center.

Hundreds of kilometers of piping salvaged from the causeway were used to plumb the city. The five small reactors salvaged from the EMD module, along with repaired solar panels, gave the colonists a working power grid that provided abundant light for every building. Polished crystal enhanced even modest light, and at night Cambria was bathed with an effervescent glow.

The gleaming new city built entirely out of crystal was dazzling. Early on the young medical chief had argued that aesthetics were crucial, and as the city took shape the effect of its beauty on the colony's morale was enormous.

Soon Cambria became known as the crystal city.

One night a meeting was held in the almost finished town hall. Surrounded by fluted columns, the three-story structure resembled a classic Greek temple, and as the group gathered inside someone wisecracked that Cambria should be renamed Oz.

"But the crystal's not green," quipped another.

"So?"

"And where's the wizard?" someone else joked, and all eyes turned to Nadya.

———

One of the few items recovered intact was the all-important steel smelter. The geologists used advanced instruments to analyze the local lithology but found no ore. This was considered odd, but not insurmountable. The colony was determined to keep looking until they found something, and explored the entire region including the snow-capped mountain range towering above the young colony. Massive crystal spikes stuck out of the summits like a giant spinal column, giving the mountain range its name: the Spine.

———

The absence of ore required an alternative plan for building the colony. It was assumed that metal would eventually be found, but in the meantime the only available metal came from the starship. The smelters were put to work transforming metal scraps drug out from the debris trench and cannibalized from the huge ship to provide for their needs.

Only one person knew that it would be barely enough to ensure their survival, and after watching the smelters using it up at an extraordinary rate Nadya decided she had to say something. One day she found the captain standing next to two large pumps at the new sewage treatment plant and interrupted him. "Trevor, we need to have one of our talks."

"Oh goody," he groaned, "and as much as I'd like to do it right this minute, I'm up to my ass trying to figure out a way to keep thousands of daily bowel movements from fouling the river, and as you can see, it's a shitty job."

Nadya crossed her arms and glared at him.

"Fine," he relented, "what is it this time?"

"The ship's metal, Trevor," she said. "We need to prioritize and conserve. Especially the titanium."

He scratched behind his ear, took a deep breath. "You said we needed to build a colony. Dozens died accomplishing that, but here it is, and as you can see at the moment, poop has priority. Can we please build our city first, and then worry about the future?"

"No, we can't."

"Really? Look, I just don't have time to get into a pissing contest with you over what *you* so urgently advised me to do."

He started to turn and walk away, but she grabbed his arm and held firm. "It's the future I'm concerned about."

"So am I, Nadya."

"I need to explain—"

His eyes flicked down to the hand on his arm. "Explain then."

She let go. "The metal from this ship has got to last long after we're dead."

"I realize that. What're you driving at?"

"It's got to last forty generations," she said emphatically, "long after all our high-tech weaponry is gone."

His eyes narrowed. "Just what is it you know?"

"I know that in less than five years you'll send a sailing expedition across the ocean, and they'll find the other intelligent species who inhabits this planet."

"What are you talking about?" he demanded.

"The first Thith war," she told him, and watched as his head jerked back at the word *war*. "After which, the new government will create a metal guild."

"What war, what new government?" Troy spluttered.

"The civilian one that'll eventually replace the military one now led by you," she explained, "but that's not the point."

"And just what *is* your point?" His voice rose.

"My point is that the expedition will be captured by this race of beings, and they'll learn of us."

"So, what's wrong with that?"

"They're reptilian, Trevor. Warlike, and they'll see us as the invaders."

"We'll make them see that we're no threat," he offered.

"It won't do any good," Nadya countered. "They'll attack us over and over and keep attacking us for 1,000 years. The colony will need to defend itself. Arrowheads. Millions of them—tens of millions of them."

"Arrowheads," he scoffed. "And just when will we be attacked?"

"In less than six years," she answered, "and though we'll still have our high-tech weapons, there are no replacement parts, and no way to build more."

"Which means?"

"It means that after the first attack not only will we return to an older weapons technology, we'll need to create a cavalry corps. You do understand that horses will become our only real mode of transportation."

"What horses are you talking about?"

"The ones I'm going to bio-engineer from our DNA library."

Troy sucked in a deep breath, threw his head back, and stared at the sky. "Do you really expect me to ride a horse? Seriously? I'm a starship captain."

"Were a starship captain," she told him, ignoring his glower. "Now you're the leader of a colony that has to walk everywhere it goes. But there's more, Trevor."

"More," he mumbled. "I'm still listening, but I don't think I'm going to like this next part. Am I?"

"Probably not," she admitted, "but nevertheless, we still need that metal to build armor, swords, and arrow tips. Metal that only comes from the *Magellan II*."

"Are you fucking serious?" swore Troy, pointing at the hull. "That starship is our home—"

"Was."

"Was. Outstanding."

"Cambria is our home now," she insisted. "You need to accept that."

"That I accept, Doctor," he fumed, "but now you want to use all our metal to build bows and arrows."

"Not all, Trevor, but we need to conserve it, and build walls. While our buildings are strong, they're not enough. We need to surround Cambria with high fortress walls."

"We can only build so fast," he muttered and began walking away, "and right now castle walls aren't a priority, building a shit factory is." He stopped a short distance away, turned and threw his hands up. "All this is your doing. Now you want a fortress too? When does it end, Nadya?" he bellowed, and left her standing alone.

As she watched him walk away she knew her influence was eroding. With a lump in her throat she whispered, "It ends 1,000 years from now." But he was already too far away to hear.

CHAPTER FIFTY-TWO

THEY ADAPT
OFOL'R, LOG'RFOLD

K anend'ra used a variety of sensors to keep track of the humans, but her most reliable was a gaseous membrane only a few molecules thick. It floated in the ever-present cloudbank and kept track of every living organism on the landmass. Kanend'ra had studied the Earthlings' every movement since they crash-landed and recorded everything about the planet's newest residents. It was her sole task, and her reports went only to the Mab'r. He too kept watch, but only because these humans intrigued him.

They were an interesting species.

The filmy material of the light dress Kanend'ra wore wisped behind her as she floated through the air. "I have new data, Mab'r," she told him as she entered his dwelling. Her long white hair reached the middle of her back and gently fluttered as she moved. Kanend'ra opened her thin hand, and a holographic image of the wrecked starship appeared.

"I've been watching," Erland'r told her, "and see they've finally left the protection of their ship and have built a city to cluster in."

"As individuals they are weak, but as a whole they are quite strong," she observed. "I believe the dominance on their home planet was not an anomaly."

"True," said the Mab'r, "but you did program them to be dominant, as well as self-destructive. Have they shown any tendency toward that?"

"Only in the way they sacrifice their lives in order to assert that dominance."

"Like true soldiers," Erland'r mused, "their few die to benefit the species."

This wasn't really said to her, but she addressed it anyway. "Yes, Mab'r, in order to create a safe habitat beyond the confines of their ship, they've destroyed all threats."

The Mab'r brought up a recorded scene from one of the battles and watched the deadly fight. "Impressive. They destroyed the dominant species we seeded here."

Kanend'ra made a slight hand movement, and the hologram of the battle became more detailed. "As you can see, Mab'r, even though we've disrupted their communication devices, and after their first disastrous encounter with the top predator, they changed tactics and began to win, despite the fact that they are so fragile and only a fraction the size of their adversary."

"Their weapons are powerful for a species so young," commented Erland'r.

"As is their resolve, and penchant toward self-sacrifice," she ruminated. "They learn quickly, and most interesting of all," the aquiline eyes of the Mab'r narrowed ever so slightly at her assessment, "they adapt."

CHAPTER FIFTY-THREE

INEVITABLE
CAMBRIA, AQUEOUS

Three years after the colonists abandoned their wrecked starship, the human colony was well underway toward perpetual self-sufficiency. Every piece of equipment that could be salvaged was used to help the colonists build what they needed to create a semi-advanced society. A lot of the equipment had sustained some damage during the crash, but much of it was repaired and put to use.

Most of what the colonists needed had been brought with them, but their food supplies wouldn't last more than a decade. The population was growing rapidly; hundreds of babies were born during those first few years, and the birth rate showed no signs of slowing.

The surrounding forests were logged and used to fill thousands of homes and buildings with wooden artifacts, like roof beams, doors, and furniture. Crops were planted in the cleared land next to the city. A concerted effort was also made to replace the local trees around the river plain with a species better suited for building. The strength and density of oak trees made it the best candidate, and whole forests were planted from seeds brought from Earth.

Even though she was now with child, Nadya spent long days using her expertise in genetics developing grains, fruits, and vegetables that were compatible with the planet's ecosystem. Her pregnancy was no barrier to the research, and she spent a tremendous amount of time engineering livestock that would soon become the colony's mainstay for food, clothing, and transportation. And as Nadya had predicted, the colony became an equestrian society.

The *Magellan II* had been filled with every conceivable job description needed to create a self-sufficient colony. No matter the vocation, each needed its own set of workers, and these needed department heads. Guilds were created for each new department, and each guild became an entity unto itself.

The establishment of these guilds eventually created conflict with the military command structure that still governed the colony. The long-envisioned democratically elected government was now a topic on everyone's mind. As that mindset took hold, discontent with Captain Troy grew until it had reached a boiling point.

Nadya tried her best to stay out of the growing political turmoil, but the colony sought her opinion for so many things that she was reluctantly drawn in. One day Major Moroz, accompanied by the lawyer Kurt Lawson, found her speaking with a group of horticulturists. They waited until she had finished before approaching her.

Still a young man, Lawson was tall, and looked every bit the court warrior he had been on Earth. "Dr. Yanbeyeva," he cordially said, "it's been too long since we talked."

"I'm not hard to find," she told him. "What's so important now?"

"We need a new government," he declared. "The colonists are getting fed up with the military having the last word on everything."

She pursed her lips and eyed the two men. "And how exactly does this involve me?"

"Come now, Nadya," Moroz said with a crooked grin, "you know that everyone looks to you for guidance."

"Taken to exaggeration, have we, Sergei?" she mocked.

He shrugged. "You haven't heard the way people talk about you. Even my security men, and especially their wives, see you as the de facto leader of the colony."

Nadya glanced down at her swollen belly and insisted, "Captain Troy is our leader. I'm just another pregnant woman trying to help us survive."

"Oh, you're much more than that, Nadya," Lawson diplomatically pointed out, "and we need your help to remove the military from power."

Nadya crossed her arms and glowered at the major. "I won't be part of some kind of coup, gentlemen," she snapped at her visitors. "You should know me well enough by now, Sergei."

"I do, Nadya," he said defensively, "but there's growing discontent with the captain." Moroz moved closer as he made his case. "Troy listens to you—"

"I'd hardly say that," she countered. "He sees me as a thorn in his side."

"But a thorn he ultimately listens to," interjected Lawson, "and one he can't ignore."

Clenching her jaw, she demanded, "Just what exactly are you asking of me?"

"You're the reason we have all this," Moroz gestured at the garden, "and the reason why we're not dying out. We're not only surviving but thriving."

"You're dancing around your point, gentlemen. Again, exactly what is it you want me to do?"

Lawson handed her a sheet of paper. "We want you to give him this."

She took the letter, read it, and then exclaimed, "Really? This is an ultimatum, and you're asking me to be the sacrificial lamb who delivers it."

"I wouldn't put it exactly like that," protested Lawson.

"Of course you wouldn't," she shot back. "You're not the one who'll deliver this."

"Then you'll take this to him?" Moroz asked.

"What choice do I have—no, what choice have you given me?" she grumped.

"You're our best hope for a peaceful change, Nadya," Lawson said.

She took the paper, and told them both, "Fine, but like I've said: I won't be part of a coup." Both men nodded. She continued, "I'll do this for the good of the colony, but after that my part is done. It's up to you to make this government work. Am I clear?" Even as she said this she knew the falsehood of her statement, because Dr. Nadezhda Yanbeyeva would eventually lead the human colony, and she was fully aware of it.

But that was years in the future.

Nadya procrastinated on delivering the document to Captain Troy. The thought of removing him as the colony's ultimate authority was distasteful to her. She had a tremendous amount of respect for him and put it off as long as she could.

During her eighth month Troy came to see her in the lab. With an eye glued to a microscope, she was trying to take some weight off her strained back when she heard someone approach from behind and heard the captain's familiar voice. "Good morning, Doctor," he said congenially. "You spend far too much time in here when you should be home resting."

She sat up and turned to her visitor. "Bitching at patients is my job, Trevor. And besides, I still need to ensure our growing number of hungry mouths get fed." She patted her distended belly. "Is there something

I can do for you?" She was wary about conversations with him. The last one about metal conservation was still fresh in her memory.

"Well, I guess we better get straight to it, then." He kept his voice neutral, but his eyes told a different story. "I know you've been given a list of demands from both the civilian element of the colony and the head of my security force." She nodded. "And at the top of the list is a demand for me to step down as the governing authority."

"Yes, this is true."

"Then why haven't you come to see me about this?"

"This is difficult for me, Trevor," she explained. "In spite of what you must think, I have a lot of respect for you, and know you've done all you can."

"But, do you agree with them?" he pressed.

"It's not that I agree with *them*, but I do believe in the tenets of the demand."

He slumped back into the lab chair and sighed. "As do I, but I think that it's just too soon to change to civilian rule."

"Then we agree," she said, and watched his head jerk up. "We're going to be attacked within the month, and we'll need a strong defense when this happens."

"What? Attacked?" he asked sharply, leapt to his feet, and headed for the door.

"Don't go!"

"Why shouldn't I, Nadya?" he asked, flustered. "You should've told me before now."

She gave him a look of mock surprise. "I did tell you. Don't you remember? That day at the water treatment plant, I told you that the sailing expedition you sent would meet the indigenous species that dominates the southern continent. It's happened." He sat back down. "One of the boats has escaped, but the other was captured." He opened his mouth to speak, but she pushed on, "and now that they know we're here, they'll come to eliminate us."

"So, based on your theory—"

"It's not a theory, Trevor."

"Based on your suspicion, then." He saw her scowl. "Fine, based on your vision, you think the military should stay in power until after this attack, and then what?"

"Then," the scowl disappeared, but her intensity didn't, "you'll need to be ready to relinquish command authority to a civilian government."

"But if the military wins this coming war—"

"You will."

"So what case will they have for replacing me?" he demanded.

"Before we ever left Earth it had been decided that a democratically elected government would eventually rule here," she reminded him. "You already know this."

The captain closed his eyes in resignation. "So, do you have this list of demands?"

"In the drawer behind you." She leaned back and placed both hands on her belly. He found the document, and then spent the next few minutes reading it, shaking his head as he did. "Trevor, this is not an indictment of your command."

"From this side of the paper it certainly seems like it is," he muttered. "So, how do *you* feel about this?"

"It's like I said, Trevor: as with this coming attack, it's inevitable." Both babies kicked much harder than ever before.

CHAPTER FIFTY-FOUR

A ONE-WAY MISSION
KORYAK, EARTH

Prior to WWX, Mother Olga worked hard to ensure that Koryak's bunker complex had the protection it needed to survive. At the main entrance she placed an immense blast shield covered by several meters of dirt. But there were two mine entrances, and inside the other one she'd placed two large all-terrain vehicles behind their own blast door.

Each ATV could carry a dozen people, a large amount of equipment, and had towable diesel tanks. It was in these heavily tracked vehicles that the team of eighteen engineers, led by Boris, left for Vladivostok. The journey of almost 2,800 kilometers would take them more than two weeks and cover some of the roughest terrain imaginable. Most of the road network had been destroyed by the war, but these transports didn't need roads. They could travel anywhere and were especially efficient over snow.

The tranquil image of fresh white powder belied the fact that this snow was deadly. Even though it had been years since WWX and the radioactive fallout had diminished, there was still much of it left in the atmosphere. It would take decades to dissipate.

The two teams were greeted by a frozen landscape buried under several meters of snow and ice as they left the safety of the mine.

The snowfall in this region wasn't as radioactive as they had expected, so the teams took off their bulky HAZMAT suits. While this increased morale, Boris knew that as soon as they left the mountains surrounding Koryak the suits would be all that kept them alive for any length of time. He also knew that the closer they got to Vladivostok, the more radioactive it would be, and few, if any, would live long enough to make it back home. The only question was: could they live long enough to tie the two pipelines together and deliver natural gas to the enclave?

The trip had been meticulously calculated so that they could maximize fuel efficiency. Even so, they had no idea what they'd run into, or more importantly, what they would have to go around once they left the relative safety of the Koryak Mountains.

On the fifth day the expedition came to a sudden halt. "Boris!" Ingra shouted. "There's movement behind us."

Boris ordered one ATV to stay put while the other investigated. "Keep your eyes peeled. We need to be careful," Boris told his team. "Movement means life, and movement behind us means something could be stalking us."

"I'll get the guns," Ivan said as he dug into the baggage.

"Is this the place?" Boris asked Ingra as he slowed down.

"Yes," she pointed, "look, by that rock. Are those tracks?"

Boris maneuvered the ATV as close as he could, grabbed an AK-18 assault rifle, and told the team, "Ivan and I are going to take a look. Everyone else stay put."

A minute later the two engineers were staring down at a set of fresh tracks. "What the hell made those, a wolf?" Ivan exclaimed. "They're huge."

"Cat," answered Boris while scanning the horizon. "A fucking big cat."

"How can that be?" Ivan wondered. "Even if it survived, what would it eat?"

"Us," said Boris, "if we don't get out of here."

For the next few days most discussion centered on the possibility that life still existed on the surface. "If a Siberian tiger survived, then maybe humans did too," Ingra said.

"Highly unlikely," Ivan argued, "that cat probably hid in some deep cave. How many folks do you know who hang around in caves?"

"You mean other than us?" asked Boris.

After leaving the rugged Anadyr Mountains it became so hot that the HAZMAT suits went back on. The teams drove into a lethal landscape, and the closer they got to Vladivostok the hotter it became. As soon as they passed Lake Artem the devastation turned horrific. It was like crossing through an alien landscape. They began weaving around the region's ruined infrastructure. Every bridge they encountered was either destroyed or on the verge of collapse. This added precious kilometers to their trip, and their fuel consumption almost doubled.

It was a somber ride through what was once their motherland. Within fifty kilometers of Vladivostok there was nothing left except a few twisted ice-encrusted skeletons of buildings and a succession of blast craters. In one building a mangled rail car was jammed into the naked girders three stories up.

As the group approached the outskirts of the city, they came across several oddly shaped objects covered with snow. Boris forbade anyone to get out to investigate but did allow his ATV to nudge up one and knock the snow off. Underneath was a strange sculpture of wrecked cars and trucks fused together. They pushed on.

Some members sobbed quietly when they passed the remnants of Dynamo stadium near the waterfront; most were stunned to silence. Ivan approached the team leader with an ominous status report. "Boris, there's nothing left, and we've used over half our fuel and won't have enough to get back home."

Boris solemnly nodded, and quietly told his friend, "I know, but this was always a one-way mission for us."

"Of course." Ivan acknowledged. "So, do we even try to get back, or just die out here?"

"I'm not sure, we just have to complete the mission," Boris said confessed. "I have no idea what we'll find once we get to the pipeline."

"Or even if it's still there," Ivan added.

"It is, Ivan," countered Boris, "or the children wouldn't have seen it in their visions."

"Bah, you put a lot of stock in the stories of children, my friend."

"As did you, when you volunteered for this mission," Boris reminded him. "As did everyone who came with us."

Ivan screwed up his face and grumbled, "I wonder if we didn't make a mistake listening to those kids. We'll become martyrs for nothing if those pipelines aren't intact."

By some miracle, the pipelines were intact. In spite of the destruction all around them, the pipelines themselves weren't damaged, but they were empty. While this was good news for the water pipeline, it was crushing for the one that carried natural gas. It meant someone would take an unplanned trip over water to Sakhalin Island, and into even more atomic carnage.

It was understood that whoever made the trip would not come back, but since everyone assumed that their lives were already forfeit, it made little difference. The trip to turn the gas back on would just be a quicker death. Boris decided it best if he led this new group.

After looking for over a day, they finally found a boat seaworthy enough to make the voyage and filled it with only enough diesel for a one-way trip. Just before setting off he told the other team leaders his plans. "Ivan, you and Ingra finish up tying in the two pipelines. It should take us a couple days to make the trip, and hopefully no more than a couple more to get the gas flowing."

"How will we know when you've turned it back on?" asked Ingra.

"Keep the gas line valve shut on this end," Boris answered, "and watch the pressure gauge. If the pressure rises, then we've been successful." He left the alternative unsaid.

"I don't see why you have to be the one who goes," Ivan said. "You're our leader."

"My friend," Boris gently told him, "everyone here knows what must be done, and since this is my area of expertise, then who else is best suited to go?"

Ivan took the other man's hand in his. "Then it looks as if this is goodbye, Boris."

"We'll all say our goodbyes soon enough." With that said, the small group boarded the boat, waved at those left behind, and sailed toward the unknown.

The small boat took two days to make the 1,200-kilometer trip through the Sea of Othotsk. The closer they got to the island, the higher the absorbed radiation became. The crew stayed inside the boat's small cabin trying to ward off the effects of radiation sickness, but it was a lost cause.

Within sight of Port Nogliki, Boris helplessly shit a bloody mess inside his suit. He gagged at the stench, and barely managed to yank his hood off before vomiting. A rotten yellow tooth was disgorged with the bile. Everyone had been vomiting for days, but not like this. It was the first sign of how bad they really were.

Boris knew he had little time left.

As they approached the docks, they were forced to sail their way through the detritus left behind by huge oil tankers that lay scattered and half sunk around the harbor. After making landfall, the small group picked their way through the destroyed city to the pipeline pumping station. The building that once housed the pumps had been blown apart, but the pumps were still intact. The crew would be dead in days, they still had to figure out a way to start them, and there was no electricity. Boris staggered off in search of a generator.

———

"Ingra," Ivan struggled to say, "Boris has been gone ten days now, and the pressure is still zero. We're all dying. What are we going to do?" Red spittle dribbled down from his bleeding gums.

"I know all that, Ivan," Ingra said as she wiped pink drool from her own mouth, "and we wait."

"Wait! Wait for what?" he demanded. "We've finished linking the two pipelines."

"Until the pain becomes too much." Her voice cracked as blood ran freely out of a nostril. "Then we take the cyanide capsule that each of us is carrying and wait another twenty seconds."

———

"Mother Leka!" cried the enclave's new chief engineer as she ran down the set of stairs leading to the enclave leader's office.

It had been two months since the teams had left the safety of the bunker, and one month over what had been planned for the operation to complete. Mother Leka had been living in despair for weeks. She was convinced that the teams had failed, and in their failure lay her own.

"Mother Leka!" the call came again as the engineer burst into her office.

"What is it, Taya? What's wrong?"

Taya fell to her knees, then slowly lifted her head toward the enclave's leader. Her eyes were brimming with tears. "The pipeline pressure—it's risen to almost sixteen bar."

CHAPTER FIFTY-FIVE

THE FIRST THITH WAR
CAMBRIA, AQUEOUS

The town hall was no longer the largest building in Cambria, but it was the most beautiful. Its fluted columns held up the heavy wooden beams that supported the high wooden roof. Over 500 colonists sat inside waiting for the meeting to begin. Snow had dusted the ground outside, and the hall's interior was cold.

The temperature wasn't the only thing that was cool as Captain Troy made his way to the podium. The reception he got from the audience was just as chilly. He knew this would happen when he called this meeting, but there was no putting off the inevitable. The crowd was still buzzing when he held the list of demands up and waved it above his head. This had the desired effect, and the room went silent.

Troy glanced over at Nadya, who was seated close to the podium. She looked pale, and sat with her feet spread apart, holding her bulging belly. As their eyes met, she barely managed a smile and nodded. He turned back to the crowd, trying to take in as many faces as he could before finally speaking. "This," he said, bringing the paper down and holding it in front of him as if he were going to read it, "is the natural progression of any free-thinking society."

Murmurs of surprise emanated from the crowd. No one had expected him to acquiesce so quickly. No one but Nadya. "And this," his hands spread to encompass everyone in the room, "*is* a free-thinking society. Our colony is full of doctors, academics, and engineers. You—we are a rather clever lot. Wouldn't you say?" Many in the audience leaned forward, whispering to those close to them.

"Of course clever people want to have a say in their future," he went on, "and not be ruled by a military command, such as now exists." The murmurs grew into exclamations of agreement. "I too agree with this sentiment." He held his hand up for quiet as many began to clap and cheer.

"I will yield the command authority to a majority rule—a free election," Troy shouted over the clamor, "but not right now." The crowd went instantly quiet. "Because we face an imminent invasion, and my command must stay in place to face this threat."

Most were too stunned to speak, but a few shouted out, "By who?"

"What are you talking about?"

"This is just a stalling tactic!"

"No, it's not," yelled Troy. "Listen to me! Some of you may already know that two weeks ago one of our boats returned from the expedition I sent to explore the oceans." His voice went back to normal as the crowd became quiet once again. "At eight degrees south of the equator they met an indigenous species, an intelligent species, albeit one with a low level of technology. This species, like the rest of the planet, is reptilian.

"These reptiles captured one of our boats, but the other managed to escape, and when they approached the alien ship, the reptiles held knives to the throats of the captured crew. The free crew had no choice but to leave them, and report back to Cambria."

"But how do you know that they'll attack us here?" demanded Kurt Lawson.

Troy glanced over at Nadya, whose cheeks were puffed out, blowing deep exhalations. "Nadya, can you please tell them what you know?"

Perspiring heavily, Nadya sucked in a huge breath of air, gripped her abdomen, and gasped, "My water just broke."

Marta and David were born thirty hours later after an intense labor. Not including Natasha and Albert back on Earth, they were the first of seven children Nadya would have in her life.

She was resting in her own hospital bed when she heard a light tapping on the door. Sasha got up from the chair next to her bed and cracked it open to see both the captain and Kurt Lawson standing there. "How is she?" asked Troy.

Sasha opened the door a little wider as a tired voice called out from the room's interior, "*She* is doing fine, Trevor," answered the new mother. "As are Cambria's newest residents." Her voice sounded weak. "What can we do for you?"

"Just stay as you are, Nadya." Troy and Lawson exchanged an uneasy glance. "Because we all need you."

"May we come in?" asked Lawson. Troy glared at the lawyer and shook his head.

"She's just given birth to twins," Sasha interjected, "and it was a long labor."

"I can see you for a few minutes," broke in Nadya, and then, giving Sasha a crooked smile, added, "but only a few."

The two guests stepped inside and stood awkwardly silent for a moment before Troy began, "I sincerely apologize about this, Nadya," she gave him a weak hand wave, "but we'd like to know if you've had any visions of late."

"She's been giving birth as of late!" snapped Sasha.

The two men hung their heads and turned to leave, but Nadya stopped them. "Sasha, their need to know is for the good of the entire colony."

"But you've just been through two exhausting days," he exclaimed. "Can't this wait?"

"Yes, it can," Troy said as he turned and pushed on the door.

"Stay," implored Nadya, and gripped her protective husband's hand as proof of her strength. "You want to know about the coming attack, right?"

Troy stopped and turned back around. Both nodded. "These lizard people—"

"The Thith, Trevor," she told him. "They're called the Thith." Troy blinked in amazement as she went on, "and they'll be here in about a week."

Lawson scoffed. "How could you possibly know that?"

"It's like I told you, Counselor, she's seen everything," Troy explained to the younger man. "You'll just have to take my word for it."

Nadya sighed and shut her eyes as fatigue began to take over. After a moment she opened them back up and weakly said to Lawson, "Kurt, when the Thith attack, my children are newborns. I've had this vision before. Yesterday, during labor, I saw it again."

"Enough," Sasha broke in. "You've answered their questions, and a week is enough time to discuss it further. You'll be able to prepare."

The first Thith war started six days and ten hours after that conversation. The human security force had just finished preparations when a fleet of fifty-two crude sailing ships suddenly appeared at the mouth of

Crystal Bay. The ships were large oar-powered wooden vessels holding almost 1,000 lizard soldiers each.

Led by Major Moroz, the human defense force had no idea of what they would be facing but assumed that this threat would be no match for their pulse rifle weaponry. In this they were correct, but the Cambrians weren't prepared to face 50,000 enemy soldiers. Not even Nadya had foreseen this large a force.

The human command only had 616 men under arms. They were ensconced behind a wooden palisade that had been built 200 meters from the waterfront and across a 500-meter-wide defile that separated the city from the bay. The human force made no attempt to stop the ships as they lumbered toward the beachhead.

Two hours after they'd appeared at the mouth of the bay, the first ships ran aground on the beach. Within an hour all the warships had made landfall, and not a shot had been fired. The decks soon became a seething mass of reptiles as Thith soldiers boiled up from the holds and clamored over the sides of their ships.

Moroz and Troy exchanged anxious glances as the loose mass of troops gathered in front of their ships. For several moments neither side made a move. Troy leaned toward the major. "They don't seem very organized."

"Be that as it may, they still outnumber us by about 100 to one, and regardless of how organized they are, or how superior our weapons, those are overwhelming odds," Moroz told the captain.

"You're saying that they might win?"

"No, I'm saying that this will be a bitter fight," Moroz answered. He called out to his unit commanders and began issuing orders.

"Major," Troy cut in, "if you could, please speak English. I need to understand too."

Moroz rounded on Troy. "Captain, this is war, and my troops need to fully grasp the intent of their orders."

"As do I, Major. Speak English."

"Yes, sir," Moroz growled, and turned to his officers. "I want ten squads each to reposition themselves at the far ends of the wall and stay low. The remaining seven squads will remain in the center with me."

Troy frowned at this decision. "What are you doing, Major? You've seriously weakened our center and put our defenses in jeopardy."

Moroz didn't answer the captain directly but directed his next words to the platoon commanders. "Crossfire, gentlemen." He shot Troy a hardened look as he kept explaining to his men. "You are to remain hidden and hold your fire until I give the signal. We can't rely on radio communications past a few meters, so watch for my signal."

Troy went rigid as he listened to Moroz, and finally, fuming at the major, said, "When they see our weak center they will attack in force here and overwhelm us."

"You're partially correct, Captain, but they will never reach the wall." He turned his attention back to the platoon commanders. "They'll get close, and overconfident—massing here in the center. Look for my signal, then stand up and engage with enfilading fire into the sides of their lines. Maintain heavy crossfire until I order a cease fire."

Troy huffed, and turned his back and took a few steps. He immediately pivoted back around and stalked over to Moroz. "Do you seriously believe that seven squads can hold this center?"

"We must break their morale, Captain," the major answered while staring out at the mass of reptilian soldiers forming up for what looked like a charge, "and we can only accomplish that by doing something totally unexpected, like crossfire from forces they didn't know about using stand-off weapons that are decimating their interior lines. Maybe we can hold them with all our forces in one spot, but if they flank us, it's over." He locked eyes with the captain. "This is too large a force, and I cannot take that chance."

"So, dividing our forces is your answer?" Troy's voice became shrill as the clamor across the beach became an ear-piercing hissing sound.

"Captain, once we break their morale, their ability to fight breaks with it, and the only way to do that is with a surprise initiative." Moroz stepped up close to the captain so that only he could hear his next words. "You need to let me handle this. It's my job, and your questioning me in front of the troops may have the same effect on our own side." Moroz turned his attention back to his squad commanders and gave the order, "Deploy."

In seconds over two-thirds of the human defenders left the center, ran hunkered down to their respective ends of the wall, and hid. Moroz gave his next order: "Center group, bear arms. Hold your fire until ordered, but make sure you're visible."

A bench had been built behind the two-meter-tall fence, and the defense force now stood up on this and took aim over the wall. The massive Thith attack force now saw only a handful of human defenders holding the center. To their eyes there were only a couple hundred facing them. This was going to be a quick slaughter. The order to attack came as a series of vicious-sounding hisses, and half the invasion force charged across the sand.

The olive-skinned and lightly armored Thith were only a meter and a half tall, bipedal, and, like birds, they had rear-facing knee joints. They were also fast. Moroz was shocked when they covered half the distance in less than three seconds, and he gave the order, "Fire!" The first human volley blasted gaping holes in the Thith front line.

Every second scores of the attackers were torn to shreds by the pulse rifles, but there were hundreds more to take each fallen soldier's place, and the charge kept coming. Fountains of red mist sprayed up as the plasma rounds eviscerated the tightly packed formations. Fine red droplets wafted over the human line, coating skin, goggles, and weapons. The stench was nauseating, and more than a few human soldiers stopped firing to vomit.

"Maintain fire!" Moroz screamed. "Puke later." The centerline began a defilading fire as fast as they could. In spite of heavy losses, the Thith didn't slow down until the leading edge had almost reached the wall. Moroz yelled out, "Flank fire, commence!" Each end of the human line stood up and began laying down a concentrated suppression fire into each flank of the attackers. Volley after volley disintegrated hundreds of the enemy in a flash of sparks and blood. Within seconds, thousands of the highly charged plasma rounds had torn grisly chunks out of the exposed Thith flank.

And still they came.

The first attackers had reached the wall, massed and jabbed at the defenders with crude crystal-tipped spears. The human center fired point blank into the swarm of reptiles, killing dozens every second, and barely managed to keep them at bay. It seemed to Moroz that it took an eternity, but the heavy fire ripping into the Thith flank finally had an effect. The frontline faltered as new soldiers were no longer replacing those killed, and within seconds the attackers began a panicked retreat back to their ships. "Cease fire!" Moroz ordered. The first assault evaporated as quickly as it had launched. At least a third of the attackers littered the killing ground between the two sides, and most of these were unrecognizable. Body parts were strewn across the battlefield. Almost without warning, the roar of battle turned deathly quiet as the attackers fled the slaughter.

Captain Troy looked dumbfounded but relieved. "That went well, Major. We didn't lose a single soldier."

Moroz was less than enthused. "Captain, we're still greatly outnumbered, and now the element of surprise is gone. If they change their tactics, then we need to change ours as well." He motioned for his platoon leaders to come get their new orders. The speed with which the enemy could move made every second count.

The ten platoon leaders ran up to him. "Listen up, this is a fluid engagement." His eyes raked across each officer. "If they deploy as they did in the first attack, then we stay in our original positions, but if they fan out, as I expect they will, then I want you to spread your men across the wall and link up with the center. After the first volley, stop firing straightforward, and then walk your fire in until you've achieved a full crossfire effect. Do I make myself clear?" All his commanders nodded.

"Lieutenant Svoboda." Moroz turned to the officer closest to him. "I want your platoon to form up as reserve squads and haul ass to any point of need."

"But Major," she protested, "that'll keep us out of the fight."

"That's an order, Katina," Moroz growled. "I need you to plug holes. If they get through our lines we've lost. Now move it, people!"

The officers shot furtive glances at each other and then raced back to their platoons.

Angry hissing reached the wall as the Thith began another attack. Like the first charge, it only took a few seconds for them to cross the distance, but unlike the first time Moroz didn't wait for them to reach halfway. The instant they began charging he ordered all units to fire and maintain fire.

This time the Thith made ready to throw their spears, but as thousands of reptilian arms cocked back, plasma fire destroyed their front ranks. Hundreds of spears, many still attached to severed arms, flew harmlessly away from incinerated bodies. But thousands of the deadly projectiles were launched and slammed into the Cambrian defenses, killing dozens and wounding a score more.

Fire from the human center evaporated.

The lizard attack surged forward in a brutal attempt to exploit the breach. Moroz raced to the weakened center, shouting for reinforcements. "Reserve—to me!"

He was quickly joined by Troy, and for an agonizing few heartbeats the two overall commanders of the human defense force were all that stood between survival and annihilation. "Captain!" Moroz yelled. "Stand down. What if both of us fall?"

"What does it matter if the center collapses?" the captain thundered back. Moroz lunged at Troy violently shoving him aside just as a spear sliced past Troy's throat and punched through the forehead of the fast-approaching Lieutenant Svoboda. Several of her squad stumbled over her body as she crumpled to the sand.

The first lizard into the breach scrambled up, dove for the supine Troy, and grabbed the captain's leg, sinking its claws into the meat of his calf. "Arrgh!" Troy screamed, and hammered at it with his free leg. The kick flung the little reptile back into a swarm of advancing Thith, blocking them for an instant, but they quickly recovered and lunged at Troy just as several pulse rifles opened up.

Reinforcements had arrived.

The rate of fire picked back up, but hundreds of Thith had already made it to the wall, and thousands more were rushing in. The fighting turned hand-to-hand in dozens of individual engagements and was so close the combatants could smell the stench of each other's fear. More human reserves reinforced the center and fired hundreds of rounds point blank into the enemy, decimating their front ranks, but there was no let up in the attack.

As the seething mass of lizards clambered over the growing pile of their own dead to get at the humans, blood and body parts rained down on both sides. Life expectancy at the front was measured in seconds as the rival species tore at each other for survival.

Troy and Moroz gave one another a grim nod, and then dove into the heaviest fighting, firing their plasma rifles as fast as they could. Within seconds Moroz took a spear thrust to his shoulder, dropped his rifle, and fell off the firing platform dragging his assailant down with him. The lizard squirmed to its feet and twisted the spear deeper into the yelling man. It yanked the spear out to make another stab just as its head vaporized. Troy lowered his weapon, pulled the lower half of the enemy soldier off the wounded major, and then swung around, emptying his clip into the carnage.

The pulse rifles finally gained the upper hand as thousands of ionized rounds burnt through the reptilian horde with pyrophoric explosions, but scores of Cambrians were also killed, and just as the last of the human reserves made it to the front, the Thith attack faltered. Almost undetectable at first, and then all of a sudden it was over.

Panic gripped the reptilian front ranks as they tried to get away from those deadly rifles. Hundreds of Thith whipped around and began clawing, ripping at anything to escape the slaughter at the front. They fought each other just for a chance to run away. Moroz saw what was happening, lurched to his feet, and ordered a cease-fire.

The disorganized retreat was almost as quick as the charge. The attackers didn't regroup this time but scrambled aboard their ships to get away. Soon their oars began frantically pushing the ships away from the beachhead.

Most of their army lay ripped to pieces on that bloody beach.

The first Thith war had lasted less than three hours. In its aftermath two things became clear to Captain Troy: they almost lost, and they needed a bigger wall. It needed to be massive.

Troy remembered something else Nadya had told him: humanity would be forced fight future conflicts on horseback and with low-tech weaponry. A thought struck him like a hammer blow, and he ran to where Moroz was receiving first aid. "Sergei, how much ammunition do we have left?"

With a grave look, the major gave him the alarming stats. "In this one battle we expended half of what we had."

CHAPTER FIFTY-SIX

A COLONY DIVIDED
CAMBRIA, AQUEOUS

Ten years after the first Thith war, the colony's population had grown by thousands, and the furious building program that Cambria had engaged in over the past decade was all but complete. Not only were the buildings bigger and more sophisticated, but a massive fortress wall had been erected around their city.

It was the wall that would stand for a millennium.

Whatever doubts that might have existed before the Thith war evaporated. The entire colony now believed Nadya's every utterance, especially the new democratically elected government envisioned long before the *Magellan II* ever left Earth.

As she had told Captain Troy, an election was held less than six months after the Thith attack. His rule over the colony was finished, and he couldn't have been happier. But there were those who weren't so enamored with their newly elected officials. Discontent reached the breaking point soon after the new government severely cut back on defense and enacted the single language reform act. The new authorities felt that devoting precious resources to maintain a large military was no longer a priority. Especially since Nadya had assured them that another attack wouldn't happen for another eight generations.

Since the bulk of the security forces were Russian, their influence in Cambria diminished proportionally. The first crack in the colony's common interest occurred on election day. Very few Russians were elected, and none to the top posts. In spite of the colony's reverence toward Nadya, the Russian contingent was being systematically pushed aside, and the law promoting English only reinforced this perception.

Nadya knew this wouldn't end well.

As the colony's medical chief of staff, Nadya not only dealt with everyone, but she treated everyone equally, and did her best to stay out of politics. She already knew what the future held and saw no need to compete with the present. In spite of her aversion toward anything political, she was continually sought out for advice and guidance. It took away precious time from her four children.

Time, she knew, was short for all of them.

The baby kicked again as Nadya sat in her garden pulling purple carrots out of the soil. Nearby, the foundation was just being poured for one of the last buildings to be built. It would become the center of life in the crystal city and be the grandest building ever built in Cambria.

They called it the Citadel.

Sitting in the dirt, she could hear the grinding of huge crystal blocks as they were dragged into place. The tranquility of her little garden had become a noisy construction zone, but the unhurried clip-clop of unshod hooves still got her attention. Turning, she saw the former captain leading a golden dun Andalusian stallion toward her. With a smudged face and splayed legs, Nadya tried, and failed, to stand up to greet him. She gave up and just sat in the dirt. "Hello, Trevor, it's nice to see you again. How're you and Arrogante?"

Once Troy was no longer the governing authority, he'd moved over 100 kilometers away, to the edge of the frontier, and started a ranch with animals that Nadya had bio-engineered from the DNA bank. Other colonists followed him, and soon they called their growing little community Troytown. "His name fits better than it should, and my butt's sore," he said, and extended her a hand.

Gratefully taking his offered hand, she struggled to her feet. "So, what brings you to my patch of weeds?"

The two old friends were now only one meter apart, and he made no move to widen the distance. "I've had visitors, Nadya," he confided, "and they're concerned."

"Why did Moroz send *you* to come talk to me?"

His brows knit. "I suppose he didn't want to disturb a pregnant woman." He smiled indulgently. "I, on the other hand, felt two years was long enough to not see one of my oldest and dearest friends." Her eyes twinkled at his words, and he took a step back and nodded approval at her soiled smock and swollen belly. "Hence, my presence here today."

"So, you decided to take time out from your ranch just to see me?"

"In a manner of speaking," he explained. "Sergei asked me to come."

"I know that, Trevor."

"Of course you do."

Nadya wiped her hands on the smock's apron and began walking toward the new park that would surround the Citadel. Troy tied Arrogante to a shrub that the horse immediately began to eat, and then followed the pregnant woman to a nearby bench where they sat down.

"Why didn't he come himself?"

"You tell me, Nadya, you seem to know everything."

She made herself as comfortable as possible and tried to find the words to dig out what he seemed reluctant to say. "Not everything, Trevor. I have no idea why you're here and not Sergei."

"Because he knows that you and I have had years of these types of conversations."

"So, you're going to start swearing at me?" She punched his arm.

A blush tinted his cheeks. "No, of course not."

Grinning at his discomfort, she asked, "Then just what is this conversation, Trevor? You're having some difficulty milking the cow here."

He finally relaxed. "Yeah, as usual, you're right." He gave her a sad frown. "The colony's ready to split. Sergei told me that the Russians have had enough and are ready to leave Cambria to start their own colony."

"Yes, I know," she admitted, "and I agree."

"Y-you do?"

"Yes, and like the election, it's inevitable, but not now."

It took a moment for the shock of what she said to register, but when it did he found his voice. "Then when? They're ready to leave now, as in the next couple days."

Nadya awkwardly pushed off the bench, brushed the dirt off her smock, and gave Troy a penetrating gaze. "Trevor, have Sergei come see me. He won't bother me, and we really need to talk this through."

Three days later there was a knock at Nadya's laboratory door. She'd been working on a project of the utmost importance and had everything she needed except the two most important items. "Please come in, Sergei, we need to talk." Moroz was visibly upset, and what troubled him troubled her as well. "How're you doing these days?"

He came into her lab, sat down, and ran his fingers through his ever-lengthening grey hair. "I swear, Nadya, you never seem to age. I've known you for, what, twenty years now, and you look the same as the day we met back on Earth."

She gave him a guarded smile. "Thank you, Sergei. It's all the vegetables I eat. But I don't think you came here just to compliment me, did you?"

"I came because you asked to see me."

"I did," she confessed, "because we need to discuss this secession movement now afoot."

He nodded. "There's a tremendous amount of dissatisfaction on our side." He tried and failed to keep the exasperation out of his voice. "We're ready to begin our own colony. Away from Cambria."

"Our side," she dolefully repeated. "And to be honest, I agree."

"You do?" Moroz squirmed in his seat.

"Yes, of course, but this needs to wait a while longer."

"Wait, why, and for how long, Nadya? We're ready to leave now."

"And you shall," she told him, "but you'll need to return before we can all leave to build the new colony."

"We? So, you're coming too?"

"I must."

"All right, but what exactly is your timeline?" he pressed.

"In about three years the Russian contingent will go to the site of the new colony."

"Three years! We can't wait that long, and you know it." He jumped up from the chair and began pacing. "This is unacceptable."

"No, Sergei, it's not. You need to accept our priorities."

"*Our* priorities?" he blurted out. "Don't you mean your priorities?"

"It affects everyone here, and everyone who'll ever be born on this planet." She saw his scowl and tried to explain. "I need to do something first, and before that happens, I need two items that your expedition to the site of the new colony will bring back with you."

"My expedition?" Moroz stopped pacing and folded his big arms across his chest. "This keeps getting better and better. Where will this new colony be located, and what exactly do you need?"

"The new colony will be very near the north pole, and as for my needs? Two eggs, one from the flying creatures who live on a mountain there, and the other from a Terror Rex."

CHAPTER FIFTY-SEVEN

FAMILY LINEAGE
KORYAK, EARTH

Twenty-eight years of keeping the enclave alive had taken its toll on Mother Leka. She looked far older than her fifty years and seemed to weaken daily. She knew the time for succession was near, but who would be her choice? She'd always thought that Albert would take over, but her son, her sister's son, had no inclination to lead. Natasha, on the other hand, was more prone to take control of just about any situation. Leka knew that they both possessed abilities far beyond those of any family members to date. Except, of course, for their long-gone mother.

They were still young, but almost the same age as she was when the family medallion was thrust upon her.

The enclave had prospered since the inclusion of natural gas fifteen years before. They had all the energy they would need for hundreds of years, and the only threat they now faced was the overwhelming desire to leave the safety of the mines.

It was a constant source of discontent.

Leka knew that whoever took over leadership would not face the same problems that had plagued her early days, but keeping thousands of people content to live underground was a daily grind, one that dominated her every decision. It crushed her emotionally and physically. She wasn't Mother Olga, who'd thrived on the trappings of power. Leka was the opposite; this duty was a millstone around her neck choking the life from her.

After spending three straight days confined to her bed, she finally got up and went to her office. Leka sent for her two children, now young adults, to inform them of her decision.

Standing at the same height, Natasha and Albert whispered to each other as they approached the door to their mother's office but went quiet the moment they saw her. "Come in, kids," said Leka, motioning toward the bench seat in front of her desk. "We need to talk."

The twins' bright green eyes exchanged a worried glance as they sat down. Natasha spoke first. "Mama. Why did you want to meet here? We could have met in your room."

A wan smile found Leka's pale lips. "I asked that very same question a lifetime ago."

Their faces were masks of concern. What she said next concerned them even more. "It's time I step aside and name my successor." The twins automatically turned to each other as Leka continued, "and I've made up my mind who it will be."

Both kids recoiled at her words, but said nothing as she went on. "You both will lead the enclave. Equally."

That ended the silence. "But, Mama," protested Natasha, "I'd rather teach and raise a family. Can't Albert do it?" Ignoring her brother's frown, she went on, "What if we disagree on something? Wouldn't that be counterproductive?"

"When have you two ever disagreed on anything?" Leka asked. As one, the twins shrugged their shoulders. "See what I mean? That makes a dual leadership all the more plausible. The enclave needs both your strengths. Together you will rule stronger than only one of you.

Stronger than I ever did." Mother Leka removed the medallion and set it on the desk in front of them.

"Not so, Mama," protested Albert, "you've been the strength that our people needed to survive." He placed a hand on the bench beside him and found Natasha's already there.

Leka smiled knowingly. "It is as it should be."

"But why us?" Natasha appealed. "I want a normal life, Mama, not this." Her chin jutted at her mama's desk, piled high with documents.

"There is no such a thing as a 'normal life' in our family," Leka told them, "and that's why I've decided you both will take over."

"You want to split the responsibility, so that we're not over-whelmed," Albert surmised, "don't you?"

"Yes, but there's more you need to know." Leka gulped nervously. "Something of equal, maybe even greater importance than my naming you as successors." She cleared her throat and tightly folded her hands. "You both have abilities far greater than I. Have you ever wondered why this is so?" They nodded.

"You never met your Aunt Nadya. She left Earth before you were born." Leka took a deep breath to steel her nerves. "She too had strong abilities, the strongest in the family's history."

"We know all this, Mama," Natasha said. "What's this got to do with us?"

"She's not your aunt."

For a moment the weight of the statement silenced the small family. Finally finding her courage, Leka's voice dropped to an almost imperceptible tone. "She's your real mother."

"Our *real* mother?" both siblings blurted out at the same time.

"What do you mean?" Natasha demanded. "You're our mother," her voice became less assured as she asked, "aren't you?"

"Yes, and no." Leka felt like she was stumbling around in the dark. "What I mean to say is that after my sister left Earth, we implanted her eggs into me." She looked down as tears welled up, afraid to see their reaction. "I gave birth to you, that much is true, but you came from her. You inherited her abilities, not mine," Leka confessed. "I have none to speak of."

The two siblings jumped up, walked around the desk, and threw their arms around her. "You *are* our mother," Natasha whispered.

"The only one we've ever known, or ever will know," Albert confirmed.

"And we'll always love you as such," they both said.

After a moment Natasha stood back and asked, "But why did you carry her eggs?"

Leka sniffled and casually wiped a tear from her cheek. "Because of her extreme abilities. It was deemed imperative that she leave direct descendants here on Earth."

"But why?" Albert pressed. "Why did she decide to have children she would never meet?"

Leka tried to swallow the growing lump in her throat. "It wasn't her decision. She simply followed orders. As did I."

"Mother Olga," Natasha said sardonically.

"Yes, Natushka, we, everyone complied with her wishes. There really wasn't a choice. There's something else, something important that you need to know."

"More important than who our mother really is?" Albert had sat back down.

Leka reached inside a desk drawer, pulled out an old book, and set it on the table. "Look at page three. It'll explain what I find I cannot."

Natasha picked up the book and held it so both she and Albert could read it together. She opened it to the designated page, and after a moment both their mouths dropped. "This isn't your hand-writing, Mama."

Leka dropped her eyes and shook her head.

Both twins sucked air through their teeth. "So according to this we don't even have a choice in mates? What gave her the right to arrange marriages so far into the future?" Albert demanded. "Not only is that blatantly unfair, it's unnatural."

Leka reached out and took each of her children's hands as she told them, "Our entire family is unnatural, and this," she gave the book a scornful look, "ensures the continuation of that unnatural family lineage."

CHAPTER FIFTY-EIGHT

SEVEN
CAMBRIA, AQUEOUS

Moroz spent a month organizing the expedition that Nadya had thrust upon him. He still retained the rank of major, but since the election he commanded a much a smaller force, and it was from these soldiers that he handpicked his twenty-five best men and women. He knew it was going to be a dangerous trip—everyone did—and the whole enterprise rankled him.

He felt like a pawn in a fixed game.

The small rafts that they'd spend the next year in were provisioned with as much equipment as they could carry. Most important of all were the pulse rifles and the 4,000 plasma rounds they'd need once they left the colony. Beyond that point every step was unexplored.

He knew that Nadya had chosen the route they would take, and that she'd known for years exactly where their final destination was—the top of the world. He also knew the expedition would take over a year to complete, and that there would be casualties

Less than a week before departure the expedition leader met with Nadya. Moroz had never seen her look so haggard but gave it little thought. He had bigger concerns.

The major had the map he would use, but not the final mission parameters. He knew they were to gather some biological specimens, but not exactly how. "We're almost set to go, Nadya," he told her while looking over the map she'd drawn up for them. "We'll take the schooner and sail up the other side of the peninsula." He looked up and pointed to a spot on the map. "You're sure we can find the river estuary here?"

"Yes, that's the continent's main river, and its headwaters are very close to your final destination." She tapped the point he questioned about, and added, "It's there, Sergei, you must believe me."

The scowl turned grim as his feelings spilled out. "I always believe you, it's just that this is uncharted territory." Nadya arched her brows. "But I guess it's about to be charted?" She nodded. "I thought so."

"You'll paddle up the river, and once you get to the headwaters you'll continue on foot to the base of the tallest crystal cliff on the planet," she told him as she pointed to their location. "It's there that we'll eventually build our colony."

"We're going to live in cliff dwellings?"

She traced her finger along the ridge of the mountains as she explained. "There are giant caverns inside the cliff, and a thermal vent that that'll keep us warm. It's almost inaccessible isolation will ensure our safety forever."

Hovering at a nearby sink sterilizing test tubes, Sasha wiped his hands dry and turned to explain, "One of the specimens we'll get is very near the polar mountain itself."

"We?" exclaimed Moroz, turning his attention to Sasha. "I wasn't aware that *you* were going."

A short silence followed before Nadya explained, "I need an egg from the creatures that live on the mountain." Moroz shrugged as if this was a given as she went on. "A female egg."

"How will we know which is female?"

"That's why I'm going," Sasha told him, "to make the determination."

Taking a civilian wasn't in Moroz's plan, and he had no compunction telling them both. "He'll be a liability to my team," the major said, "and has had no training in weapons handling."

Sasha stood across the table from his wife and folded his arms. "Don't worry about me, Major, I'll carry my own weight, every step of the way."

"I have to worry about you, and everyone else on this expedition," Moroz snapped back. "It's my job, and having someone, anyone who puts my team in danger is an unacceptable risk."

Nadya waded in. "The whole purpose of this expedition is to get me what I need." She locked eyes with the major. "There are only two people qualified to do that. Sasha is one. Would you prefer I went instead?"

As he always did, Moroz wilted under her gaze. "No, of course not, but I can't guarantee his safety, or anyone else's, for that matter. You've seen everything, so tell me, do we suffer any casualties?"

The husband and wife shared an anguished moment before she answered, "Yes."

"That so?" Moroz shot back. "Care to enlighten me?"

"I'd rather not," she said softly.

"Well, this expedition doesn't make a move unless I know what you know," he warned her, "and now would be the perfect time to tell me. How many?"

She slumped forward, and her unkempt hair fell across her face. "Seven."

Shocked, Moroz's tone turned blistering. "I'll lose seven of my team?"

"No, Sergei," Nadya barely choked out the next words. Her eyes began to glisten. "Seven will make it back." Sasha reached across the table and placed his hands on hers.

"I'm to lose three-quarters of my team protecting him and your blasted eggs!"

"I won't be one of the seven, Major." The room closed in on Sasha's words.

Moroz grew cold. His next words were impervious to the tears now streaming down Nadya's face. "You mean to tell me that you're sending your husband, the father of your children, out to die?"

"It was my choice, Sergei," Sasha defended Nadya, who'd jumped up, and hurried out of the room. The two men watched her leave in silence. As soon as the door shut, Sasha gave the major a steadfast gaze. "Considering the alternative, no sacrifice is too great."

CHAPTER FIFTY-NINE

HUMAN EXPANSION
OFOL'R, LOG'RFOLD

The Normad'r Prime Being closely tracked the human expedition. It was of extreme interest to him that this fragile species was willing to venture far from the safety of their walled city. This willingness to endanger their lives intrigued Erland'r.

Few warrior races ever took such risks.

In spite of his interest, no one understood humans better than Kanend'ra. Only she could penetrate their thought matrix, and it was for this reason he made sure she made regular reports. "What can you tell me about this group?" Erland'r asked her as she floated into his dwelling. "What mission could so modest a complement accomplish? Why will they explore so far from their colony?"

"Their expedition has an explicit intent, Mab'r," answered Kanend'ra.

"Elaborate."

"It is an exploration of sort, but they have a specific mission objective in mind."

This intrigued Erland'r even more. How could they know enough about the interior of the continent to have a definitive purpose so far from their isolated colony? "What are they seeking?"

Kanend'ra floated to the image and pointed to a specific human. "That one is the mate of the Spak'rna. He is one of their top scientists. All the others are soldiers, presumably to protect him. The female has sent him to gather certain specimens that she requires to carry out her program."

Erland'r turned his attention away from the holographic orb and directed it at Kanend'ra. "What exactly are they seeking, and where shall they find it?"

"She has sent them to retrieve two eggs. One from the O'rmsliki and one from the Ovaett'r."

He rotated back to the image and scrutinized the group more closely. This was an extraordinary concept. These eggs were from vicious creatures; one lived only on the Rond'r Mountain, while the other roamed the northern continent as the dominant species. "What possible motive could she have?"

"To be specific, Mab'r, she has requested female eggs from both species," Kanend'ra told him. "Her motivation is genetic engineering. A crude form, to be sure."

These humans were proving to be an unpredictable species. A faint blue glow emanated from Erland'r as he commented, "In order to achieve that goal, they must go to the Rond'r Mountain itself." This was logic, and now another concern troubled Erland'r. "Does this expedition pose a threat to the defensive system?"

"Yes, it most certainly does," said Dreng'r, newly arrived to the conversation. The thin green tunic he wore couldn't hide his emotional state as his internal gases glowed a bright red. Dreng'r was the Administrator of Mines, and he took any threat to the Rond'r seriously.

Rotating toward the newcomer, Kanend'ra said, "They have a dangerous journey ahead of them, and may not even reach the Rond'r. Even if they do, the O'rmsliki will probably destroy them."

"And if they achieve their goal," Dreng'r countered, "they will have discovered the Rond'r, which could lead to discovery of the Ramm'r Crystal. That is unacceptable."

CHAPTER SIXTY

THE EXPEDITION AQUEOUS

A steady wind blew up from the river plain as the expedition set out on the largest of the colony's ships. It was the twelve-meter schooner that had escaped capture by the Thith and had been kept in good condition. Under full trim, the graceful little ship made good time escaping the confines of the bay. It was an auspicious start to their journey.

On the open water, the team was finally out from under the oppressive cloud cover and basked in the unobstructed glow of the red star. It was rare to feel the warmth of the sun, and they spent most of their time on deck soaking up all they could get. The ship's crew of ten brought the initial complement up to thirty-five human souls, and it took them five days to reach their disembarkation point on the continent's main landmass.

As the expedition approached the mouth of the river, they encountered a massive alluvial fan extending out from the estuary. A pressurized depth finder helped guide them as far as they could go aboard ship, but 100 meters was as close as they could get to shore. The ship's captain was wary of going any further. A sand bar could ground his boat, and after conferring with Major Moroz, they decided that the away team would transit to shore in the rubber rafts.

The plan was to paddle up all the way up the river until they reached its headwaters near the north pole. This was going to be a physically demanding trip, rowing against a current for thousands of kilometers. They also knew the river would have many impassable points where the team would be forced to leave the safety of the river and portage everything until they found calm water again.

"Get those rafts in water," Moroz ordered from the ship's bow. The four-meter-long rubber rafts were launched, and the crews rowed toward the shore. Once there, the rafts were dragged onto a beach. The first portage began as soon as the crews had rested.

The major well remembered battling the deadly predators when the colonists first ventured off their crashed starship, and as far as he was concerned the beasts on the main continent were welcome to it. His command just needed to pass through, and evasion was their best chance to survive.

They spent an uneventful night on a small grassy island close to where the river met the sea and set out at dawn. The estuary had a wide mouth and a weak current with dozens of channels meandering around scores of grass-covered islands. Small red flying reptiles squawked as they dove into the water all around the rafts.

The company made good time all morning, but once they reached the main channel the current became stronger and progress slowed to a crawl. It soon became apparent that the continent was full of wildlife. They passed hundreds of creatures that first day, mostly large quadruped herbivores, and only caught a glimpse of one Terror Rex in the dense forest. The beast snarled at them but made no move to come any closer.

Everyone knew that monsters lived on land.

Gigantic crystal cliffs towered hundreds of meters over each side of the river valley that was up to ten kilometers wide at some points and narrowed to less than one in others.

That first uneventful week saw the explorers traveling less than 100 kilometers when they came upon their first set of rapids. The river dropped through a narrow gorge, filling their encampment with the roar of white water. They were worn out and decided to take a couple days to recuperate. Moroz decided that after the rest, they would portage past the white water.

The two days respite was welcome after all the hard rowing, but carrying all their equipment through the trees proved even more difficult. The terrain was uneven, and often they had to stray away from the river itself. On the second night of portaging they bivouacked on a high rocky ledge overlooking the rapids. Sentries were set, and a large fire was built in the center of the camp. The exhausted group fell asleep as soon as they lay down.

One of the sentries, the youngest member of the company, was bone-weary. The eighteen-year-old had slept a scant three hours before his watch began and fought to stay awake, but days of physical exertion had taken their toll. Four hours into his watch, and just before dawn, his dozing body was savagely ripped off the ground. The shocked youth gasped awake to find his face being smothered by something wet and putrid. He couldn't breathe. Terror quickly replaced confusion when it hit him that he was being eaten alive. A muffled shriek wailed out from the young man's throat as huge teeth bit through his body. In a panic he squirmed uncontrollably, but his dark wet tomb began constricting once the masticating began. The crunch of compounded bones and the warmth of his blood stimulated the monster to chew faster, and as boy's mind spiraled into agonized dementia, his ruptured body began convulsing and his fingers curled.

Moroz bolted awake and brought his weapon to bear just as the monster's head exploded in a flash. Its massive body crashed to the ground just outside the camp.

The major immediately threw up a defensive perimeter. They could hear more of the monsters prowling just outside the camp, but only got fleeting glimpses of shadows moving in the dark. The expedition waited until first light, reluctantly left their dead comrade, and hurriedly carried their equipment down the bank. The current was still strong, but the adrenaline-charged team powered away from the bank.

Their first casualty taught them a hard lesson, one that dictated how they made landfall from now on. More sentries were posted, and no more camps would be made more than a few meters from the water.

A few days after the attack, the major approached Sasha. The scientist was eating a hybrid nutrition bar he'd fashioned out of fruits and grains his wife had bioengineered. As usual, he ate alone. "How the hell are we going to find and take an egg from those fucking things?" Moroz demanded.

Sasha chewed a moment while he contemplated his answer. "A diversion will allow me to sneak into their nest and examine the eggs. Once I've found the right one, the other team members will move in and take it."

"Oh really?" Moroz was beyond skepticism. "Just like that, my team is going to waltz in and get your trophy?"

"It's not a trophy, Sergei. It'll ensure humanity's survival." Sasha solemnly went on, "And they won't exactly 'waltz in'. The female will be close by."

"So, how do you propose to steal the egg with her present?"

"I'll lead her away."

Moroz clenched his fists, glaring at Sasha. "This was never going to be a simple snatch-and-grab, was it? And just when exactly do you plan on carrying this operation out?"

Sasha mumbled his reply. "On the way back from the north pole."

The anger fled Moroz's eyes as he caught Sasha's meaning, and reluctantly asked the question that had been plaguing him since that last meeting with Nadya. "Is this where—"

"Yes, Sergei. It is."

"Oh," mumbled Moroz, and silently walked away.

CHAPTER SIXTY-ONE

HOLLOW MOUNTAIN
AQUEOUS

Two months of hard rowing brought the expedition to a strange landscape. No one had even imagined terrain like this. The river valley widened to more than twenty kilometers with the river splitting into dozens of small channels that wove between hundreds of giant crystal towers. At first this made for easy rowing through the gentle currents, but after fifty kilometers they encountered punishing elevation changes and impassable white water.

Portage was the only way around these rapids, and in most cases, close access to the riverbank was impossible. At times, the crews had to tote their provisions hundreds of meters away from the safety of the river over rough terrain, and progress slowed to a crawl. More often than not, the only way they could navigate anywhere close to the river was the sound of water crashing in the distance.

There were several minor encounters with roaming reptiles, but these ended with a few well-placed plasma rounds. Their luck ran out on the third morning.

Sasha's raft group was late leaving that night's camp, and in the dense forest they became separated from the rest of the group. They tried to catch up, but in their haste took a wrong turn in the thick undergrowth. An hour later they were lost.

"I hear water." Corporal Willa Chernova swiveled her head toward the sound. "Over there, below the tree line." The tall young woman with closely shorn black hair pointed downhill and moved off in that direction. "Grab the raft and follow me."

The trail she led them down quickly became overgrown with tall ferns and, unable to see any further, Chernova ordered a halt. "This damn thicket is too dense to go through. We need to backtrack."

"Say, Corporal," suggested one of the privates carrying the raft over his head, "can we please go in the wrong direction some more, cuz me and Max here think it's a hoot."

"Shut the fuck up, Usov," hissed Chernova, "and move your—what was that?"

A hair-raising roar sounded only meters away. "Where did that come from?" Sasha squeaked, and frantically unslung his rifle. "There!" He pointed his rifle and squeezed the trigger, but nothing happened.

"Your safety's on," yelled Usov from under the raft.

Suddenly, from the opposite direction of the roar something huge crashed through the foliage. A Terror Rex leapt on top of the raft, crushing Max to death and trapping Usov. The animal's talons tore through the rubber, grabbed the screaming private as he tried to crawl away, and ripped him in half.

Sasha fumbled with the safety, brought his rifle up, and fired at point-blank range. His shot exploded in the soft hide under its jaw, killing it. Sasha dropped his rifle and ran to the bloody raft.

"What are you doing?" Chernova shouted. "You know these fuckers always travel in pairs. We've got to go!" Her wide eyes darted back toward where more heavy footfalls were rapidly approaching.

"They might need help," Sasha yelled back just as a second Terror Rex charged into the carnage.

"You fucking idiot!" Chernova swore in panic. "They're already dead." Her voice turned shrill as she spun around and fired, wounding the charging animal in the leg. The monster screeched in pain and lunged at the hysterical woman, snatched her up, and shook her like a rag doll. The glade filled with the sound of animal grunts, breaking bones, and Chernova's painful scream. "Help meee—" Her agony abruptly ended when the creature bit down.

Sasha dove for his rifle. The Terror Rex stopped chewing and dropped the dead corporal. Turning its bloody maw toward Sasha, the creature growled at the puny human, who'd managed to grab his weapon and swung it around just as the creature attacked.

Weeks later something that had been eating at Moroz finally bubbled to the surface. The major had been studying his crew wondering who would make it back, and one day he found Sasha sitting alone at a campfire. "You know who lives and who doesn't, don't you?"

Sasha's back stiffened as his gaze never left the fire. "I only know the fate of two crew members, Major."

"And?"

Sasha stood up and began walking away.

"As your commander, I order you to tell me."

Sasha stopped, turned to Moroz, and told him, "Fine. Here's what I know." He moved closer and dropped his voice. "You make it back. Do you really need to know any more?"

Moroz shook his head.

It took six more months of endless rowing and fending off deadly creatures before the expedition finally reached the river's headwater. Instead of being elated at seeing the end of their rowing, morale was the lowest it had ever been. They'd lost eight more of the expedition: five more to attacks, two drownings, and one crew member who went to take a piss and simply vanished. They were now in a sweeping forested valley that dead-ended into the tallest mountains they'd seen yet. On one side was a sheer cliff over 1,000 meters high. Ten kilometers away and slashed all the way through the opposite mountain was gigantic V-shaped split. Seemingly, there was nowhere for them to go.

Moroz approached the scientist. "Now what, where do we go from here?"

Sasha studied the cliff face. "There, that's where we'll make our city."

"You expect us to climb that?" asked Moroz. "We don't have enough rope."

"We have enough, Sergei. There's a cave near the bottom that leads to a series of caverns, and once inside, it'll be an easy climb." He pointed at the cliff. "That mountain's hollow and is where we'll build our new home." He hesitated a moment, and added, "Your new home."

CHAPTER SIXTY-TWO

EGG THIEVES
AQUEOUS

With only helmet lamps to guide them, climbing in the pitch-black of the caverns was anything but easy. It took six harrowing days before the expedition's last eleven members reached the top of the hollow mountain. Once there, Sasha led them out the cavern's north face, and onto a rocky precipice. Stretched out below them lay the circular valley that capped the top of the world. They'd been climbing in near darkness, and when they stepped into the light of day their vision failed them.

"We rest here until our photopigments regenerate," Sasha instructed the group.

Moroz massaged his eyelids. "Our photowhat?"

"Until our eyes adjust," explained the scientist, "and stop rubbing them."

Ten guilty hands dropped.

An hour later everyone could see, but what they now focused on was hard to believe. Rising up from the center of a fifty-kilometer-wide valley was the tallest, strangest mountain any human had ever laid eyes on. The top of it disappeared into the omnipresent clouds, but the size of the peak wasn't what was so unusual about it.

It seemed to be alive.

Everyone stared. No one dared move a muscle until Moroz, looking through high-powered binoculars, asked Sasha, "Is that the mountain we saw from orbit?"

"Yeah," replied Sasha, "it is."

"It looks unnatural, and dangerous," Moroz commented, never once lowering the field glasses from the seething mass of red. "Is that where we're going?"

"No, what we need is on this side of the valley," Sasha explained. He trained his own binoculars on the jagged ring of mountains that encircled the valley.

"But the dragons are over there," Moroz said. Large flying reptiles could be seen swarming all around the mountain, both in the air and covering every square meter of its perfectly cone-shaped surface.

"True," Sasha agreed as he scanned the mountain base they were standing on, "but their rookery is on this side of the valley." He pointed to a canyon that gashed the ring of mountains. "Down there, about twenty-five kilometers from here."

"And that's where we'll become egg thieves?" Moroz noticed the scientist's frown, sighed, and said, "Fine, where we'll acquire egg number one?"

"Yeah."

"Then let's get to it."

"It'll take us three days to get there," Sasha informed him.

"We can make that distance in a day."

"Under normal circumstances," Sasha pointed out, "but we can only move at night, and even then we'll need to stay concealed in those foothills." He pointed at the forest-covered hills far below. "Those creatures are fast, and won't take kindly to us invading their nests."

"Like I said," grumbled Moroz, "egg thieves."

It was an arduous climb down the steep cliffs in the pitch-black dead of night. Once the sun dipped behind the giant mountains, the temperature dropped below freezing. Feeling uneasy about the night trek, Moroz groped along the ledge until he found Sasha. "Someone could get hurt, or worse. That's a helluva long way down." He hissed at the scientist, "I'd rather face those creatures in daylight than wonder if my next footfall is going to send me plummeting to my death."

"No, you wouldn't," Sasha said firmly. "If even one of those things sees us, then we're all dead. You just need to trust me."

"Trust you? I can't even see you."

By the time they reached the relative safety of the forested hills, the sky had brightened and they could see again. Sasha approached the major as he was inspecting the rest of the group. "The next couple days will be a lot easier, now that we're off those cliffs."

"What a frigg'n relief," Moroz groused.

Sasha turned to walk away, but the major's next words stopped him in his tracks. "What's your plan to steal the egg?"

Sasha stopped and offered a single word: "Diversion."

Late afternoon, two days later, the group was hiding in some boulders near the rookery. Sasha pulled Moroz aside. "The rookery has the least activity at this time of day." He pointed at the last creature in the area. "We move in when that one leaves."

"And if another one arrives?" Moroz asked.

"Shoot it down. It'll be our diversion."

An hour later Sasha had crept as close as he dared and waited for the flying reptile to leave. The creature finally took off, but three more approached. When the animals were still over a kilometer away, three plasma rounds blew them out of the sky. But instead of solving the problem, it attracted more dragons.

It also provided the diversion.

Sasha raced out to inspect the eggs. Each nest had only one dark green twenty-five-centimeter egg, and the first one he inspected was female. He grabbed it and hurried back to Moroz, who asked, "Did you get it?"

"Yeah, but we need to get the hell out of here." Sasha looked nervously over his shoulder and saw a scorch of dragons heading straight for them.

"You don't have to tell me twice," said Moroz, and motioned to his troops. "Maintain an active rear guard and move out!"

The scorch had spotted them and swarmed their position. Protected by large rocks, the expedition began blasting the creatures out of the air, but more dragons arrived, and soon their ammunition began to run low. Three soldiers ran out they were dragged into the air and torn to shreds. For another two hours the remainder of the humans fought off the angry reptiles, killing hundreds.

The attack ended a few minutes after dusk. A livid Moroz found Sasha weeping in a crevice, huddled over his egg. "So much for your fucking diversion," Moroz seethed while punching an empty magazine out of his rifle, "and just so you know, we've have three dead, and we're out of ammo."

"I know."

"What the hell do you mean by that?" Moroz exploded at the scientist. "You mean you know that we're out, or that you knew we would run out?"

"Both."

"Great, that's just fucking great," the major ranted. "I should never have let your wife talk me into this debacle, and just how the hell are I and the six soldiers I have left supposed to protect you the next fucking time?"

"You don't."

Three days later, the expedition had returned to the rear entrance of the crystal caverns. They used a hard plastic container to carry the egg, but it was only half full. Their next objective would fill the other half.

The expedition's first leg had been an exhausting nine-month ordeal. The trip back would take less than a quarter of that length of time.

Weeks later, the expedition found itself sailing back through the valley of towers. They were making good time through a section of the river that had proved so deadly on the outbound leg. Fewer portages were needed this time, and the crew was surprised when Moroz ordered an early camp in the shadow of a particularly short, squat tower.

Only two rafts remained, and these were beached on the riverbank. Moroz approached the scientist. "You're sure this is the spot?" Sasha just nodded. He'd been more quiet than usual lately, and up until now, the expedition's commander had left him to his thoughts. "Understood. What do you need?"

"Just my bio-diagnostic kit, and the two fastest crew members."

Moroz scratched underneath his scraggly beard before asking, "Is there no other way, Sasha?" He moved in close and said in a low tone, "Nadya could've been wrong. Have you ever considered that?"

Sasha placed a comforting hand on the major's shoulder. "No, Sergei, I haven't." Moroz closed his eyes. "Nadya doesn't create these events." Moroz tried pulling away, but Sasha tightened his grip. "She has no control over what the visions show her."

Moroz's eyes flew open as he spat out, "And yet she uses them to further her agenda!"

Sasha limply dropped his hand. "Come on, it's time."

An hour later the extraction team was creeping through dense foliage. When Sasha spotted the clutch ten meters away, they stopped. It held three dappled brown and white eggs, and no adult. Leaving his two companions hidden, Sasha crept forward until he was an arm's length away from the nest. He reached out and placed the diagnostic instrument on the closest fifty-centimeter-long egg and studied the readout: male.

Sasha tried to control his breathing, but it was no use. He began hyperventilating and jammed a hand over his mouth to stifle the wheezing. This took precious seconds, but there was nothing he could do, so he waited it out.

A minute later Sasha scooted closer and diagnosed the next egg. It too was male. He ground his teeth and scrunched closer to inspect the last one. That was when his wife's vision manifested itself. His pounding heart stopped cold when he heard the unmistakable sound of something crashing through the forest.

He tried calming his nerves, but a metallic taste filled his mouth, and he had to swallow back the bile that burped up. A trembling hand placed the instrument's sensor on the last egg and pressed the button. It took a moment for the diagnosis to make its determination. During that time, an ear-splitting roar sounded just as a massive reptile hurtled out of the forest.

It was the mother, and he was touching one of her eggs.

Sasha's eyes darted to the readout: female. "This one!" he yelled and, dropping the instrument, scrambled for the cover of the forest in the opposite direction from the team. The Terror Rex screeched in fury and launched itself after the fleeing man.

As soon as the two other team members saw the vacant nest they rushed over, grabbed the egg, placed it in the container, and sprinted away.

Sasha knew running was futile, but terror has its own agenda. Feeling hot breath on the back of his neck, the panic-stricken man darted around a tree, trying to out-maneuver his attacker, but the tree crashed down, pinning him to the ground. He tried wriggling out from under the sharp limbs, but a giant clawed foot stomped a jagged branch into his chest and through a lung. Sasha cried out in agony, and then gagged as his mouth filled with blood. He quit squirming, trying to ease the pain, and for the briefest moment neither predator nor prey moved as they locked eyes with each other. The beast's yellow eyes soon narrowed. It snorted and ground its foot back and forth, shoving the branch deeper into Sasha's body. Coughing blood out of his mouth, he started screaming. A second later a filthy talon drove deeply through his open mouth.

The screaming stopped.

A faint sound, like a human in agony, reached the other two members just as they ran into camp. Turning, they cast a wary glance back the way they'd come, but no one, nothing had followed them out of the forest.

Moroz had heard it too, and frantically scanned the forest for any sign of the scientist. There was none. He turned back to the hard-breathing team members. "Sasha?" But he already knew the answer. The two men looked down and shook their heads. Moroz spotted the container. "Is that it?" One of the men nodded. "Right, then let's get the hell away from this fucking place."

The expedition had suffered its last casualty.

CHAPTER SIXTY-THREE

THE HATCHLING
CAMBRIA, AQUEOUS

For months, depression had plagued her every waking hour. Nadya couldn't eat and slept only when exhaustion drove her down. Sometimes, in her darkest despair, she'd remember her last conversation with Mother Olga. The matriarch's final words were forever etched on her soul like an epitaph on a tombstone. Nadya would recall those words and curse the woman.

Nadya knew what she had to do the moment the expedition returned to Cambria, and to that end, she worked tirelessly in her lab day and night. Her eldest children, Marta and David, had just turned twelve, but they were the only ones she could stand to be around for any length of time, and became her only lab assistants.

Since the day she and Sasha said their goodbyes, Nadya labored on the most important project of her life—the most important project that would ever take place in the human colony. It was the only thing that kept the depression from debilitating her completely. After months spent sequestered in her lab, she finally had everything she needed except what the expedition brought back with them.

Twelve months and fourteen days after the twenty-six members of the expedition left Cambria, seven disembarked from the schooner that had waited for them at the mouth of the Spiral River. Heading straight from the dock, Major Moroz found Nadya weeping at her desk in the lab. Without even looking up she knew who it was, what he'd brought, and who wasn't with him. "Did you find the caverns to your liking, Sergei?" she asked softly, wiping her swollen eyes.

"It will serve us well," he answered solemnly, and then asked with barely restrained fury. "Do you want to know the details of our return trip?"

"No," she cried, and sunk her face in her hands. "But I n-need to," she said, raising her head, "so please tell me about it."

He pulled up a chair next to hers and gave her the briefest of accounts. "The plan to retrieve the dragon egg from the mountain was a fucking disaster, and I lost three more of my team. We also expended all our ammunition, and oh, I almost forgot, we got your precious egg. The last operation didn't go too well either. We only lost one person in that shit storm, but I guess you already knew that." She sniffled and nodded her head.

"Just so you know, I think Sasha is—was a noble man." Moroz clenched his hands into fists and tried and failed to keep the stern look from his eyes. "He sacrificed his life for these." Jabbing a finger at the container, the major demanded, "Was it worth it?" Nadya said nothing—could say nothing, so Moroz stood up. "I don't need an answer." His visage grew even harsher. "I just needed to ask the question." He walked out, leaving the widow alone with her eggs.

Crushed by guilt, Nadya worked without rest. She now had what was needed to engineer a hybrid species unique anywhere in the galaxy. It was to be a one-of-a-kind being, and her criterion was long and exacting. From the Terror Rex she gave it size and strength; from the mountain dragons she gave it aerodynamics. A genome from Earth's Naja cobra gave it the ability to spew a powerful stream of an ignitable fluid from a gland in its throat. The mountain dragons already had these glands beneath their talons, but Nadya placed them in her creation's throat.

While all these features were vital to the being's biology, its most important attribute would be intelligence. For this Nadya infused her own DNA.

It took endless weeks of work, but eventually she developed an egg with what she fervently hoped would be exactly what she needed, what humanity needed to survive.

Given the time frame, this creature had to live a very long time. This was the hardest part to engineer, but by altering the genomes of Earth's giant Seychelles tortoise, the end result was a being that could potentially live for thousands of years. The project was almost complete. All she had to do was wait for the egg to hatch.

Once the yolk settled to the bottom of the amniotic fluid, Nadya left it untouched in the incubator. She and two her young lab assistants took turns monitoring the temperature and humidity around the clock as the yolk rested on a bed of vermiculite. It took seven weeks before any sign of life took place within the clear synthetic shell, but on the fiftieth day there was a flicker of movement.

The embryo was alive.

Nadya was sitting at her desk five weeks later when a chirping sound suddenly entered her head. It wasn't an audible sound. It was something else, something telepathic, and it came from the egg. For the first time in almost two years, Nadya smiled.

Within twenty-four hours the egg began to vibrate. Slowly at first, then with far more intensity, and five minutes later a crack appeared in the shell. A tiny screech entered her head. Seconds later the shell cracked wide open, and a gooey thirty-centimeter baby dragon emerged. Within minutes the infant moved unsteadily around inside the incubator.

Nadya gently picked up the hatchling, cleaned it, and placed a Petri dish with a couple grams of raw horsemeat in front of it. The infant sniffed its first meal, looked at the human, and attempted its first growl. It was more of a squeak, but a tiny puff of smoke wafted out of its mouth. A second squeak produced a tiny flame that it pointed at the dish. It only lasted a couple seconds, but the smell of cooked meat filled the lab. The little dragon buried its mouth in the dish, devoured the contents, and belched.

A small tear slid down Nadya's cheek as she picked up the little dragon and held it to her breast. The teardrop landed on the newborn, and it made a tiny purring sound. Nadya whispered, "I will teach you everything." The creature nuzzled its head under her throat. "My little Rodinya."

A small chirp entered Nadya's mind, and it surprised her that she understood the word. "*Rodinya*," it had mimicked.

CHAPTER SIXTY-FOUR

HOME LESS WANTED
CAMBRIA, AQUEOUS

Rodinya grew fast. In two months she was over a meter long. The only things that grew faster than her body were her mind and her obsession to fly. The young dragon was becoming impatient to use her wings, and it became a source of frustration for both Nadya, who forbade it inside the lab, and Rodinya, who constantly pushed the boundaries.

Nadya was reluctant to reveal her creation too soon. She already knew what the colony's reaction was going to be. Rodinya had yet to go outside, remaining sequestered in the lab, but her size and curiosity about what lay beyond its door made keeping her secret from the rest of the colony impossible for much longer.

David was working in the lab one morning. Except for his green eyes, he'd grown into an almost exact copy of Sasha, but had little of his father's patience, and had been sullen and distant for months. Wanting to play, Rodinya jumped on his shoulder. He jerked back, knocked her to the floor, and swore, "Get the hell away from me!" Rodinya squawked and scurried under a counter.

"What's the matter with you?" Nadya snapped at her teenage son. "Why would you do such a thing?"

"Thing?" he cried, pointing at Rodinya. "We sacrificed everything for that—that thing."

Nadya coaxed the frightened dragon out and picked her up. "You know how important she is—"

"So you keep telling us," he ranted, "but all she does is eat, shit, and remind me my father is gone."

"I miss him too," Nadya said sternly, "but your father understood—"

"Well, I don't," David fumed and stalked to the door. "I've heard it all before, Mother, and I really don't want to hear it again. All right?" After the door slammed, Rodinya cocked her head and mewed.

Nadya knew it was time for a change.

Rodinya was beginning to resemble the sleek golden-scaled creature she would eventually become. Her viper-shaped head was smooth with only small winglets on either side of her throat to break the unblemished lines. Muscular arms, somewhat resembling a human's, hung down from powerful shoulders just below where graceful wings merged with her broad back. An expansive rib cage narrowed to a slender waist where two powerful hind legs could propel her into the air three times her body length. Her long smooth tail had small winglets identical to the ones on her throat. The little dragon had become an aerodynamic beauty, but she had yet to fly.

One morning Rodinya was playing, flapping her wings and jumping around, when she accidently broke a counter-full of glass beakers. The shattering glass scared her, and she reacted by burning a portion of the lab. Nadya put out the fire and opened the door to air out the lab. "Come on, you," she scolded the young dragon. "Go outside. Scoot."

Rodinya looked at her mother and cocked her head. She then bolted out the door, squawked with joy, leapt into the air, and clumsily flew for the first time. Tears filled Nadya's eyes when she heard the gleeful cries as the young dragon quickly mastered the use of her wings. Rodinya flew for hours that first day.

Soon everyone in Cambria knew about the little golden dragon.

In between nurturing Rodinya and her other duties, Nadya spent weeks writing three books to be left in the care of her eldest daughter. Marta was to become the first member of the Final Order, as well as the first head librarian. The books entrusted to her care would become the cornerstone of human culture on Aqueous.

Because of their DNA link, Nadya and her children were the only humans who could hear the young dragon. To the rest of humanity she was just another strange animal on an alien planet.

Rodinya learned speech quickly, and any word she was taught she never forgot. Nadya taught her to read, and once the dragon had mastered that, her vocabulary knew no bounds. Her wandering also began to push boundaries, and more than one rancher complained about missing livestock. Especially horses. The young dragon was healthy, intelligent, and mischievous. She was also sensitive to David, who made no effort to hide his feelings. She spent less time at home, more time away from Cambria.

But Rodinya wasn't the only large animal roaming the frontier. Occasionally a rogue Terror Rex raided the frontier, creating panic, and sometimes a colonist was killed. The authorities always reacted quickly, but finding a lone animal was difficult and highly dangerous. A permanent solution had to be found.

Civilian Troy had come to Cambria to deliver livestock and visit the Yanbeyeva family to help celebrate Rodinya's first birthday. He was there when the new governor, Kurt Lawson, and the paleontologist, Dr. Burt, arrived with a proposal for Nadya.

It was the beginning of the end.

Nadya knew what they wanted and that the long-awaited colonial split was at hand.

"Good morning, Dr. Yanbeyeva, David, Captain Troy," Lawson greeted them, but the look on Nadya's face told him this wasn't going to go well. "I guess you already know why we're here."

Nadya answer was stony silence.

"Right, well, we've come to ask your assistance in an important matter."

She found her voice. "You want me to genetically engineer a mammalian top tier predator to counter to the Terror Rex, and I won't do it."

Leaning against a counter eating a blue apple, David arched a brow.

"Perhaps you could wait until we present our proposal before making a decision," Lawson countered.

Nadya tapped her computer, and the image of exactly what they wanted filled the monitor. She ignored Troy's clumsy attempt to hide his grin as she told them, "You want me to resurrect an animal that's been extinct on Earth for thousands of years." She pointed to the screen. "You think the short-faced bear can be that counter, and maybe it can, but it's also the most dangerous mammal to ever walk the face of Earth. The extreme peril it poses to humanity will be far greater than any benefit."

"But, you can engineer control measures into them," Burt argued. "Just like you've attempted to do with your dragon."

David coughed, and took another bite.

"Attempted?" Nadya growled at the other doctor.

"It's well known that this," Burt shot a glance at Rodinya, who belched something foul in his direction, "thing has been raiding ranches. Irreplaceable livestock has gone missing."

Nadya gave Troy an accusing glare. The former star ship captain jumped up, waving his hands, and approached Rodinya's accuser. "No, no, you've got your information all wrong," he told Burt. "It's true that she's come to the frontier a few times, and it's true that she feeds on livestock." Burt adopted a smirk. "But she only eats what we ranchers give her. You do realize that we need to occasionally cull herds?"

"Be that as it may, Captain," Lawson reiterated, "we need the doctor to engineer a defense for the colony."

"I'm not a captain anymore," Troy told no one in particular.

Nadya huffed at the two men. "It can't be done the way you want. With Rodinya I used live eggs, and splicing techniques to mesh reptiles from Earth and Aqueous." She pointed at the image of the giant bear. "There are no indigenous mammals on Aqueous to do that with. All I can do is reproduce the animal. I can't change its instincts. It'll be uncontrollable."

David tossed the apple core in the trash, pushed off the counter, walked over and opened the door. "Gentlemen, as much as it pains me to say this, it looks like you have your answer."

"If you won't help us, Dr. Yanbeyeva," retorted Lawson, "then we'll do it ourselves, and I think it would be prudent to ban your creation from Cambria as well."

"That went well," David said and followed the delegation out the door.

Later that evening another meeting was held. But it was a different group that met with Nadya this time, and they couldn't have agreed more with the first group's ban.

It was what they'd been waiting for.

"It's time we left Cambria," insisted Moroz. "Those pompous self-important assholes have done us a favor," he grumped at Nadya.

"We've given you the time you asked for, and now it's time you lead us away from this, place. It's time we built our own colony."

"And what about Rodinya?" Nadya asked the group.

"We're not going anywhere without her," said Troy.

A warm smile brightened Nadya's face. "Trevor, thank you for defending her today, but I know she's has eaten some of your livestock." Her young dragon suddenly found something interesting to study on the ceiling. "And yet, you still want her to come?"

"We need her as much as we need you," Troy answered. Nadya gave him a mock frown, and he amended, "Well, maybe not as much as we need you, but how will we make this dragon army without her?"

"You can't, gentlemen, or without me."

"It's settled then," Moroz declared harshly. "Soon we'll leave this home less wanted, and found a second human colony." His voice lost most of its venom as he asked, "What will it be called?"

"A suitable name," Nadya told the group. "A name that will inspire our people and command respect from all those who hear it. We will be known as Drakon Rus."

CHAPTER SIXTY-FIVE

A BARE MOUNTAIN
OFOL'R, LOG'RFOLD

Erland'r watched with growing concern as the humans built a second colony high in the crystal cliffs near the northern Rond'r Mountain. A small force had arrived seven years earlier and taken an O'rmsliki egg back to the colony at the southern tip of the continent's peninsula. This had once intrigued him, but what the humans were doing now was troubling: they were removing all the O'rmsliki eggs from the mountain and taking them back to their new cliff city.

Erland'r summoned his two top lieutenants to discuss this disturbing operation. "The mountain's protection is being systematically eliminated." He pointed at the holographic image. "What will be the ramifications if they succeed in this endeavor?"

Kanend'ra weighed in first. "It's true, Mab'r, that the end result will be the elimination of the mountain guardians, but ultimately it will have no impact on our dominance of Log'rfold."

"How can you say that?" demanded Dreng'r. "The O'rmsliki have protected the Rond'r since you engineered them thousands of years ago." He rotated toward his Mab'r and stated his case. "In all that time, nothing has ever threatened the Rond'r, but now we have a bare mountain."

"Dreng'r makes a valid point, Kanend'ra," Erland'r said.

She floated closer to the holographic orb and studied the northern continent. "Perhaps, Mab'r, but in all the time that the O'rmsliki have guarded the mountain, no threat has ever manifested itself."

"Which proves my point," insisted Dreng'r.

"It only proves that their presence is not needed," she countered.

Erland'r was curious about her lack of concern. "Why do you think this is not important, Kanend'ra?"

"The leader of the new human colony is from the enhanced family, Mab'r."

"Did she not engineer an O'rmsliki of her own?" asked Dreng'r.

"Yes, it's why they delivered its egg to her," Kanend'ra explained. "She created a one-of-a-kind being to aid in their survival."

"And you don't see this as a threat?" Dreng'r asked accusingly. He began emitting a bright green glow.

Kanend'ra slowly rotated toward Dreng'r. "No, I see this as an essential element of their survival." She floated back toward Erland'r. "The Spak'rna has visions, and these divinations have led her to create this giant O'rmsliki, as well as establish this new colony."

"But to what end?" asked Erland'r.

"The eggs they've taken will become the nucleus of their survival. They will domesticate the hatchlings and use them to build an army— an army of O'rmsliki."

"You still haven't adequately addressed the question," accused Dreng'r.

Kanend'ra directed her answer to Erland'r. "To fight the Thith in future conflicts."

CHAPTER SIXTY-SIX

YOUR LINEAGE
KORYAK, EARTH

Leka died less than a year after passing leadership to her two grown children. The last few months were some of the happiest of her life, but years of ensuring the enclave's survival had eroded her health. She was weak and lethargic at the end, but she'd also made sure that the line of succession was in good hands.

While initially reluctant about the responsibility of leading Koryak, both Natasha and Albert accepted the importance of succession, and with some reservations also embraced the Book of Bloodlines as the family's legacy.

It covered the entirety of the next 40 generations.

Natasha married two weeks before her mother passed away. It was the last time Leka made a public appearance, and the former matriarch broke down and cried when she saw her daughter married in the same wedding dress Nadya had worn all those years before.

Leka retired to her bed that night and never got back up. Day and night her children remained in vigil by her side as she passed in and out of consciousness. At the end Leka opened her eyes for the last time and managed to say one final thing to them. "Please forgive your mothers." She exhaled her last breath and passed peacefully.

"There's nothing to forgive," whispered both children.

Like all of the enclave's dead, Leka was cremated, and her ashes were scattered in the underground crop caverns. Natasha and her new husband, Misha, along with Albert and his fiancée, Alla, watched solemnly as the only woman they'd ever known as mother became part of Koryak legend. As they left the ceremony Natasha approached her brother. "We'll become the twin pillars of strength that hold this enclave together."

"I'll do what I must, but you need to keep that," said Albert, pointing at the medallion around Natasha's neck.

"No way, Albert." She pulled him to one side. "I need you. Our enclave needs you. Mother made sure that we'd rule equally."

"I've never been your equal, Natushka," he admitted. "We both know that truth."

"Don't you dare abdicate your right to rule," Natasha whispered forcefully. "I didn't want this in the first place," she said as she took the medallion off, "and can't do this alone. Besides," she pointed her chin at his betrothed and handed him the dragon eye, "you and Alla need to keep this safe."

Albert sighed, glanced at Alla, and said, "We will."

"I hope so, brother, because if you haven't read the Book of Bloodlines through to the end, you really should."

"Why's that?"

"Because the seventh-generation male that follows our biological mother to the new planet comes from your lineage, not mine."

CHAPTER SIXTY-SEVEN

THE PROPHETESS
DRAKON RUS, AQUEOUS

Snow flurries spat down from the mountain towering over the sheer face of Drakon Rus. Having arrived fifteen years before, the colonists wasted no time carving out their cliff city. But it was a never-ending struggle to stay ahead of the growing population. As soon as a new apartment was chiseled out of the crystal, two more were needed.

Nadya tightened the warm cloak around her as she stood on her terrace and looked down at the blanket of snow-dusted forest 900 meters below. Rodinya lounged close by. The dragon had grown to over ten meters, half her eventual size, and Nadya knew that soon both she and her dragon daughter would leave the cliff city.

Nadya would never return.

Having led the colony since it left Cambria, Nadya knew it was time she abdicated her position and completed her life's work: writing the last of the prophecy books that would guide human civilization.

The dragon army grew slowly, and now stood at 500 strong. Stripping the flying creatures' rookery of its eggs had eventually eliminated this species from the mountain. Drakon Rus was now harvesting all the eggs, and all new hatchlings were born in domesticity. But taming these wild animals proved difficult. Once again, Nadya used her genetic engineering abilities to breed out much of the dragons' instinctive aggressiveness, but not all. The army wouldn't be effective if their mounts were too tame. She'd found a tolerable compromise between vicious predator and docile herd animal.

Her work here was done.

Now that Moroz's son had married her third daughter, she knew her bloodline would not only last but become the dynasty that ruled far into the future. She also knew that maintaining blood ties with Cambria was essential. The bloodline she'd left there would strengthen the bond between the two colonies. It was also crucial for implementing the prophecy that she had only partially finished.

She turned to the adolescent and asked, "Are you ready to leave this place to make another home, daughter?"

The young dragon raised her golden head and cocked it to one side. *"Are you sure it's time, Mother?"*

"Yes, Rodinya." Nadya affectionately stroked a spot above the dragon's eye. "I've accomplished all I can do here, and there's just one more thing that needs to be done before—"

"I understand, but I don't want you to leave me."

"I'll never leave you, daughter," lied Nadya.

"Please, we both know that once you've finished writing the prophecies, you disappear forever." Rodinya was barely able to get out those last words.

"We both know that this is my Path." Nadya hugged the dragon's large head. "But let's not think about that now. There's still much to do, and we have a long journey ahead of us."

This seemed to soothe the dragon. *"What's left to do?"*

Nadya walked back a few paces, taking in the full measure of her creation—a creation so much like her creator, but with a mind of her own. "We've got to build the Sanctuary of the Final Order, and staff it with members of our bloodline."

"Once you're gone," Rodinya choked up again, *"who will keep the sanctuary manned?"*

"You will."

"You place much faith in me, Mother."

"Faith that's well founded," Nadya reassured her. "Your responsibilities will be tremendous, and everything depends on you carrying them out."

"I won't fail you, Mother."

"I know. You're all I'd ever hoped for." The dragon purred at these words. "And much more. Sometimes, I wonder if humanity deserves you, but it's both our Paths."

Sergei Moroz had aged much since first arriving on Aqueous. What little hair he had left had turned completely white, and the deep lines around his eyes made his scowl seem permanent. The limp was constant now, and his stooped body ached in this high cold climate, but he worked tirelessly to complete the task set before him. Drakon Rus wouldn't be finished for another 200 years, but he'd given it a good start. It was well thought out and flawlessly executed. Moroz had few friends left from the old days, but one he did have had been like a brother to him since the day they'd saved each other's lives during the battle on the beach. Trevor Troy never had much use for the Cambrian authorities, and gladly gave up his ranch to come help build the new colony.

"Of course I wasn't too keen about my son marrying a Yanbeyeva, but what choice did I have?" Moroz grumped to his old friend.

"None," Troy pointed out, "you grouchy old fart. They seem happy, which is more than I can say for you."

The scowl deepened. "It's just that I don't trust that old witch." The mere thought of the misery caused by her machinations left Moroz bitter and resentful.

He and Troy were working with mining engineers building the massive stockade that would house the dragon army. It would be the largest single room on the planet.

While measuring a portion of the cavern, the two old men were approached by a young officer. "Major, Mother Nadya has come to see you."

"I'm not a major anymore," Moroz grumbled, "just an old man with nothing better to do." He brushed dust off his work clothes and motioned for his old friend to come with him. "I wonder what she wants this time?" he grunted at Troy.

"Never can tell with her, but one thing's for sure," observed Troy.

"Yeah, what's that?"

"She'll get her way."

"Isn't that the truth of it," Moroz grumbled, and then shouted at the young man leading them, "Hey, slow down, boy, we're old back here."

The young officer acted like he didn't hear him. Nobody seemed to listen to him anymore—nobody but Trevor and Nadya, and lately Sergei couldn't have cared less what she thought.

"Hello, Sergei, Trevor," Nadya greeted them. "You're both looking well."

Sergei frowned. "No, we look like old men, which is exactly how we should look." He squinted at her. "You, on the other hand, look as young as you did the day we met in Houston all those decades ago."

"You always did know how to flatter a girl, Sergei."

"Girl, yes. Flatter? It wasn't my intent," he told her caustically. "How is it that you never seem to age?"

"Sergei," scolded Troy, "is this how old friends talk to each other?"

"I age, Sergei." Nadya crossed her arms and glanced away. "And soon it will catch up to me."

"I doubt that. You're the prophetess, our divine oracle whose every utterance is accepted as sacred doctrine."

"Old man," Troy snapped, "enough!" He tried to move between the two.

Moroz ignored the plea. "Oh no, Nadya, time may catch up with you, but age will not." He glared at her for a moment, then took a deep breath. "So, why was I summoned today?"

Keeping her arms crossed, she turned to face him, but found it difficult to meet his harsh eyes. "I need your help, Sergei. I need a squadron of dragon riders to follow me to a specific destination."

"That so?" grumped Moroz.

"Give her a break." Troy finally managed to step between them. "You must forgive him, Nadya, he's been in an evil mood lately."

"It's not me who's evil," snapped Moroz, giving them both a dark look.

Nadya avoided looking at the bitter man as she made her request. "I need a few engineers as well."

Without giving her any sign of support, Moroz turned and yelled at someone close by. "Korzhev, front and center."

A tall redheaded young man with muscles like tree trunks jogged up, made a slight bow to Nadya, and said, "Yes, Major, what can I do for you?"

"It's not me who needs you." He curtly nodded toward the colony's leader. "Mother Nadya does. For what, I can only venture to guess." Moroz turned and limped away.

The small group watched in silence as the old major left. Troy gave the distraught woman a sympathetic smile, kissed her on the cheek, saw the tear in her eye, and left to tear a chunk out of Moroz's ass.

Embarrassed, Pavel Korzhev shuffled his feet. "I'll do whatever you need, Mother."

"Thank you," Nadya barely whispered. She brushed the tear away. "I need a team of engineers to help build a small set of dwellings and a gathering room."

The young man looked around him at all the work being done, furrowed his brow, and asked, "Where do you want this built?"

"Not here." She'd regained her composure. "In fact, far from here on a remote tower. We're going to build and staff a sanctuary on its summit."

"Who's going to build and staff this, what'd you call it, a sanctuary?"

"You are, Pavel. And my son David, Rodinya, and a few others."

He scratched behind an ear. "How long will this take, Mother?"

"The rest of your lives."

CHAPTER SIXTY-EIGHT

SECLUSION
SANCTUARY OF THE FINAL ORDER, AQUEOUS

Fifteen hundred kilometers south of Drakon Rus sits the valley of towers. For 200 kilometers these giant crystal towers span the breadth of the valley floor, creating soaring islands in the sky. Most were over 1,000 meters tall, but one in particular was only half that height. It was short, squat, and had a small forest growing on its wide summit. It was here that Nadya, riding Rodinya, led the group.

The tower was difficult to find, hidden as it was between its much taller neighbors. The remoteness of the location was one reason Nadya had chosen this particular tower, but there was another reason, one that had nothing to do with pragmatism, and one that would always tear at her heart.

Sasha had died in its shadow.

Crucial to her plan was the width of its top. Its 40-meter-wide summit was much wider than every other tower and its uneven peak had a cave that the members of the Order could carve out to live in. It also had a small spring bubbling up on its crest, providing water for the few dedicated humans who would live out their lives protecting humanity's most precious artifacts: the last two books of the Hope Prophecy.

Upon arrival, the first thing the engineers built was a cistern around the spring. They took on the cave next. Three rooms were carved out of its interior, wooden doors attached to give privacy. It was to one of these rooms that Nadya sequestered herself with all her writing tools. The room held only a small bed, desk, and a crudely built chair.

Before entering the room, Nadya had a private chat with Rodinya, who'd been pensive ever since arriving at the tower. "You need to calm yourself, daughter," the prophetess told the young dragon. "Your mood is having an effect on the engineers, and we need them to complete the task of making this a livable habitat."

"You mean for after you're gone," Rodinya fussed, *"don't you?"*

"Yes, dear one."

The dragon huffed as a low growl rumbled in her throat. *"And what of me?"* she challenged. *"This place is too small for me to live, and besides, David hates me."*

"He doesn't hate you, child."

"Yes, he does, and we both know I'm not welcome at Cambria or Drakon Rus."

"Why would you think you're not welcome back at Drakon Rus?"

"The old major," Rodinya lamented. *"It's not just you he blames."* The growl grew deeper, and smoke wafted out of her nose.

"I didn't know," Nadya confessed, but when Rodinya huffed more smoke Nadya took note. "Truly, I didn't." She gently stroked Rodinya's neck. "Once I'm finished here, there's somewhere else we need to go. Just you and I."

Rodinya sucked the smoke back in. *"What are you talking about, Mother?"*

"A home for you," Nadya whispered, "and only you."

At first Rodinya was excited about this news, but then she understood what her mother was really telling her. *"Only me, and what of you?"*

"I'll be with you—"

"We're going to live together, then?"

"In a manner of speaking." Nadya laid her cheek against the soft scales on the underside of Rodinya's throat. "I'll always be with you, but this place is special. Only we will know of its existence."

Rodinya became pensive again. She was the only one of her kind, and humans would always shun her. *"Who will I talk to, Mother? I'll be all alone once you—you—"* She couldn't bring herself to say it.

"You'll have these to talk to," Nadya said, and spread her arms out, "the members of the Final Order." Rodinya gave her another suspicious glance as Nadya explained. "Once I'm gone, then it'll fall to you to pick the new members until the prophecy coalesces."

"But, how will I do that? I can't talk to humans."

"You can if they're of our bloodline, and that's who you'll have to choose from, in both Drakon Rus and Cambria."

"But they won't be you," the dragon whimpered.

Nadya tried to reassure her. "It's like I said, I'll always be with you."

"Those are just words you're saying to make me feel better."

"No, it's true. I won't be there in physical form, but I'll be there nevertheless."

"But, I won't be able to see you," Rodinya huffed. *"I won't be able to talk to you, so in point of fact, you won't be there, and I'll still be all alone."* With that said, the pouting dragon leapt off the tower and flew away.

———————————

Three days after Nadya had entered the room, David was helping Pavel Korzhev build stairs near the edge of the tower top. These would eventually lead all the way to the ground, and had to be hammered out with a chisel, and muscle. They attached a canvas lanyard to a nearby tree to secure the man hanging over the ledge wielding the hammer, but the lanyard was old. It had been an original piece of equipment from the *Magellan II*, and should have been taken out of service long ago.

Nadya's son took the first turn with the hammer. He backed out over the edge, gave the lifeline a tug, and then swung with all his might.

"David!" Korzhev shouted when the lanyard came apart. Pavel lunged toward the falling man and caught the frayed end just as it was about to whip over the edge. The rough strap ripped the flesh off Pavel's palm down to the bone, but he didn't let go. "I got you," he yelled, wincing in pain.

But David's weight was dragging them both over the ledge. Pavel used his free hand to grab at something, but as his fingers tried to find purchase on the hard crystal, several fingernails ripped off. "Pavel," David hollered, "you've got let go, or we both die."

"No," Pavel grunted out, but the lanyard began slipping through his blood-slicked palm. "Shit! Try to find a handhold, David, and take some weight off."

Suspended hundreds of meters above the ground, David snapped his head around looking for something, anything to grab hold of. "There's nothing. Save yourself. Let go."

"I'm. Not. Letting. Go—" was all he managed to say before David jerked backward, yanking the lanyard from Pavel's grip. "Nooo—" bellowed Pavel as David hurtled toward the ground.

David shrieked in terror as he plummeted hundreds of meters down the steeply angled side of the tower. He was still screaming when he stopped falling. His panic quickly subsided when he saw what had snatched him out of the air. "Rodinya," he wailed, "oh my God! Rodinya."

"Be still, David," the dragon told him. *"Your moving is making it difficult to fly."* She'd grabbed him by a leg, and when they reached the tower top she hovered just above the deck and let go.

After landing close by, the young dragon watched as her brother collected himself. *"David,"* she cautiously asked, *"are you all right?"*

Weak-kneed, David unsteadily stood up, stared at her for a moment, and hung his head. The gratitude he felt was only overshadowed by the shame. He shuffled over to Rodinya and finally looked up. "Thank you, sister," he said in a low tone.

"Sister," she echoed, and cocked her head to one side as a slight mewing sound filled the space between them.

David's voice betrayed him so he just threw his arms around her neck. After a moment he regained enough composure to utter, "Forgive me."

Nadya used her visions to write the prophecy books. She already knew what needed to be said, but still, she often lapsed into extended periods of a trancelike state to make sure that her memory stayed true to the visions.

Cloistered for weeks, hardly eating or sleeping, she wrote night and day. Finally after everything was complete, she re-emerged to find work on the tower almost complete. The only thing left to do was finish the set of stairs down the treacherous side of the tower.

Nadya wanted to inspect everything, make sure the sanctuary was as it should be, but the absence of her two children worried her. Curious, she approached Pavel. "Where are David and Rodinya?"

"You didn't see?" Pavel asked, grinning from ear to ear.

"See what?"

"They've been inseparable for weeks now," he told her, "and fly off all the time."

"Really?"

"Oh yeah, and there's something else you should see." He led her through a door carved out of solid rock, and into a six-meter-wide circular great room. The single skylight set in the center of the low ceiling concentrated a beam of light directly on a round wooden altar. "Look inside, it's the receptacle for your books. I built that," Pavel said proudly. "And there's more."

"It's all so overwhelming," she gushed. "What more could there be?"

He reached behind the altar and set a meter-high object on the alter top. "And David made this."

"Oh my goodness," Nadya whispered. "It's the most beautiful thing I've ever seen." Her son had carved an exact replica of Rodinya out of crystal. Illuminated by the skylight, the statue's glow filled the room with refracted light. Nadya slowly approached the altar, ran her fingers across the dark wood, and then looked up at the skylight. "How?"

Pavel's bandaged hand pointed at the skylight's pane. "David made that too. He used the same piece of crystal as the statue, shaped and polished it into a lens. The effect is, well, ethereal."

David and Rodinya returned an hour later, landing next to the cistern. David jumped off his sister's back and ran over to his mom. "You look gaunt," he observed. "We need to get some food in you."

"And that," Nadya gestured at Rodinya, "looks dangerous. You should be using my riding harness."

"Aw Mom, she's gotten really good at catching me."

"What?"

Rodinya groaned and looked away.

"So, what happens now?" David asked quickly.

"Now, you stay here and become the first Keeper of the Order," she told her son, "and Rodinya comes with me."

"Are the books finished?" He sounded disappointed.

Nadya studied her kids for a moment, smiled, and said, "Yes, and now it's time for Rodinya and I to leave."

"Where are we going, Mother?"

"I've told you, someplace special, someplace for only you."

"Well, since you're leaving us, then I want to stay here with my brother."

"Yeah, Mom, why can't she stay here?"

Nadya placed her hands on her hips. "You have no idea how gratifying it is to see you two like this, but Rodinya must have a place of her own, and your place is here, David. Besides, Rodinya will come here often." The two siblings shared a glance. "It'll be her second home."

CHAPTER SIXTY-NINE

SPYING
KORYAK, EARTH

After the war, whole generations lived and died underground, never feeling the sun on their faces. Never hearing the song of a thrush in springtime. Never knowing anything but the close walls of a subterranean existence. Children grew up learning to speak softly, and tread even softer. Respect for their elders was absolute, and rebelliousness was rarely tolerated. Everyone had to pull their share of the workload, and for children, this meant education.

Mother Olga's last instruction to Leka ensured that education would not be neglected. Mother Leka took this several steps further and passed this on to her own children. It became a fixation that the family's legacy would be the advancement of medical knowledge. Students from other families became the engineers and teachers, but the Yanbeyeva children were all taught the healing arts.

Koryak had no way of knowing that their enclave was the most medically advanced on the planet. At the beginning no one even knew if other enclaves existed. For all they knew, they could be the last survivors on a dead planet, and survival became an obsession. Natasha and Albert fully understood that disease could quickly wipe them out, especially in the closed confines of an underground city.

It was in the third-generation underground that it became apparent to the two rulers that something extraordinary was happening to the girls in the family. Abilities that had before been confined to a select few were now becoming widespread. Astral projection was now the rule among the Yanbeyeva women. These abilities not only helped advance their medical prowess, but for the first time there was knowledge of other surviving enclaves.

Koryak was not alone.

Natasha went to find her brother. He'd begun losing hair in his mid-thirties and by the time he reached fifty, it was completely gone. His bald pate was as pale as everything else. It had never seen sun. Albert had just finished up grading tests when his sister approached. "We need to talk."

"About?"

"The girls' abilities are becoming stronger every day. Soon they'll be too advanced for us to teach."

Albert set down his pen. "I've noticed the same thing, and couldn't agree more," he confided. "We're at the end of what we can actually teach them about their abilities, but they still need academic skills."

"True, but keeping their minds focused is growing more difficult."

Albert studied his sister's face for a moment. "I have an idea but haven't tried it yet. It's a bit over the top."

"Uh-huh."

He hesitated a moment, allowing her to digest this, before outlining his idea. "I'm going to allow them to astral project as a group. This should give them a sense of unity."

Natasha frowned. "But, how will you control where they go, and more importantly, how will this impact their studies?"

"I'll have them look for other enclaves," he explained, "and study their skills."

"So, you want to turn them into spies?" she challenged him.

He winced. "In a sense, Natasha, but I believe this will both benefit their expanding minds, and channel them in a constructive manner."

"But spying, Albert, seriously? They're kids."

"Kids who're accelerating this family's abilities much faster than ever before," Albert said resolutely. "It's my opinion that we're one of the most advanced enclaves. But, are there others more advanced than us, and could we learn from them?"

"All right, Albert, I'll concede your point that allowing the girls to keep an eye on life outside this hole in the ground would be in our best interests, but I have a proviso. We must not neglect their studies, because if they don't know what they're seeing, how can they convey the knowledge we need?"

"So, you agree with my methods?"

"To a degree," she replied. "Now we must come up with a curriculum that incorporates both academics and spying."

"Can we not call it that?" Albert implored. "That's what nation-states did to each other before the war—they stole secrets to gain superiority—but in the end, no one had an advantage." He noticed Natasha's blank stare. "Fine, let's just call it clandestine studies." One of her eyebrows rose. "Have it your way then, but even you have to admit that it'll give us the best tools to survive."

"Right, spying," she said playfully. "Like I said."

The students embraced this program with a gusto that Albert hadn't foreseen. They could finally escape the drudgery of life underground. It was new and exciting.

Natasha and Albert listened to their reports with keen interest, and one thing was painfully obvious: mankind wasn't doing very well.

Many of the enclaves they visited had already died out, and several more were on the verge of doing so. Anarchy, for the most part, was what the sick enclaves had in common. As resources dwindled, the strong inevitably conquered the weak. It was as if they'd learned nothing from their planet's destruction. Likewise, healthy enclaves also had commonalities, like an advanced educational system and equal rights for women.

Attributes that the Koryak enclave already exemplified.

CHAPTER SEVENTY

THE LAIR
THE SPINE, AQUEOUS

After leaving the sanctuary, mother and daughter flew down the Spiral River valley for weeks. They spent a night at the estuary where Sasha and the expedition had stayed so long ago. Another lifetime, it seemed to Nadya, but the proof of its importance was the companion she now rode. So much sacrifice, so much heartache, but there was more to come, and this sentient creature was the catalyst to see it all through.

A pair of Terror Rex were hunting in the marshes, but a blast of Rodinya's fire sent them scurrying off to the protection of the forest. They roared in fury but didn't return.

The next morning a cool sea breeze met them as they left the mainland. After a few hours of flying over open water they spotted land, and soon the towering peaks of the peninsula's spine dominated the horizon. *"Mother, you're taking me back to Cambria?"* Rodinya asked anxiously. *"I thought I wasn't welcome there anymore."*

"No, daughter, we're headed to the tallest peak on the Spine. And while it'll be relatively close to Cambria, you'll still be far enough away that you won't be disturbed, and they won't be frightened."

"But, why so close? Isn't there somewhere else that would suit me better?"

"There's no place on the planet where you'll have as much privacy as here."

"It must be well hidden then."

"You have no idea."

They flew along the mountains for several hours until at last Rodinya spotted the highest peak she'd ever seen. *"Are we there yet?"*

Nadya smiled. "Almost." She pointed to a cluster of massive crystal columns that dominated the horizon. "That's your new home."

"I'm going to live on top of that mountain? How will that give me privacy?"

"No, silly, not on top, but inside," Nadya explained. "You'll see. No one will ever find you there."

As they topped the giant columns, Rodinya saw that there was actually a ring of them surrounding a deep shaft that dropped into the mountain farther than she could see. *"Down there?"* the dragon asked as they circled overhead.

Tightening her harness, Nadya said, "Yes. Glide into the opening and circle to the bottom. It's not far."

Rodinya adjusted her trajectory and began a sweeping glide inside the shaft. Once below the summit, she saw a red glow at the bottom. She'd never seen anything like it before. *"What's that strange light?"*

Nadya patted her daughter's neck and reverently whispered, "That, child, is the heart of the planet."

"I don't know what you mean, Mother," said Rodinya, landing next to a five-meter-tall crystal stalagmite jutting up in the center of the floor. The glow from the crystal bathed the bottom of the shaft in red light. *"It's warm down here. Is that because the heart is warm?"*

Nadya slid off her back, stretched, and walked over to the stalagmite. Her memory flashed back to the decade she spent roaming the galaxy, and the uncountable times she'd had visions of Rodinya in this very place. "Yes, child, warmth is where the heart is, and mine will always be here."

The young dragon huffed, *"I'm not a child, and that's just your sticky-sweet way of saying you're leaving me."* Rodinya crossed her arms and turned to stare at the wall.

Nadya placed her head against the dragon's throat and closed her eyes. "Please don't pout." The dragon twisted her head around to look down at the tiny human. "Be assured that I will never leave this place of power."

"This place of what?"

"This shaft, your lair, is a powerful gateway."

"To what?"

"Energy," Nadya explained. "The womb of this planet holds tremendous energy, enough to power an entire galaxy."

"And that's why you picked it for me?"

"Yes, this place will only make you stronger."

"Stronger than what?"

"Stronger than anything to have ever lived on this planet," she explained to her creation. "Strong enough to survive and ensure the survival of our bloodline."

Rodinya lowered her large forehead and gently touched Nadya's. *"I'll make sure our family is safe."*

"But there's more you should know." The dragon lifted her head, blinked once, but said nothing. "The survival of the galaxy is tied to the survival of our family."

The lair's black glassy walls were pure obsidian that extended all the way to the top, but the red glow gave them enough light to see by, and they spent the next week making the lair comfortable for Rodinya. Working together had drawn them closer than ever before. It made what would come next much harder. Leaving Rodinya was almost as hard as saying goodbye to Sasha and Leka.

It occurred to Nadya that her whole life was a series of final farewells, first on Earth, and now here. She also knew that this wasn't the last one.

Eventually all the dragon's food ran out and Rodinya left to go hunt. Nadya made a small wave goodbye. As she watched her young dragon fly out of the lair, she knew that it was the last time she would ever see her. A tear appeared at the corner of her eye as she made yet another final farewell.

Nadya steeled herself for the next part. Even though her visions had shown this scene many times, she wasn't sure she was ready, but there was no going back now. She stepped up to the red crystal, touched it, and said, "Show yourself, Kanend'ra. I know you're listening."

The glow emanating out of the stalagmite became effulgent. It turned so bright that Nadya shielded her eyes with her arm. It became hotter, and she took several involuntary steps back, sweat dripping from her brow. Within seconds the light dimmed back to its former state, and Nadya dropped her arm.

Standing between her and the stalagmite stood a being of surprising stature, with long white hair and smooth blue skin. The being floated about a meter off the floor, and though it had substance, it was translucent.

It was also obviously a female.

The being floated close to Nadya and studied her with yellow emotionless eyes. She stopped less than a meter away. The being spoke in an alien language, but somehow, Nadya understood every word. "How is it that you know of me?"

"I've seen you many times," Nadya told her. "I have visions, and you've appeared in several of them. I know you live here on this planet, and that your name is Kanend'ra."

At the mention of her name a dull red light emanated from the being's body. It glowed for a few seconds and then disappeared. "All of which is correct," noted Kanend'ra, "but this shouldn't be possible. Long before your conception I engineered your family's evolutionary enhancements and instilled a gene that disallowed your ability to sense us."

"And yet, I can." As a geneticist, Nadya appreciated the dilemma that Kanend'ra found herself in. "You also implanted an evolutionary gene, did you not?"

"Yes, I did."

"Then maybe we've evolved much more than you had intended." Nadya's words caused Kanend'ra to drift away as if in deep thought. Her glow turned from red to blue.

After a moment the being reversed direction, floated back toward Nadya, and asked, "Why did you call out to me?"

"Because I need you," Nadya confessed, "and you need me."

"You speak of needs," Kanend'ra ruminated, "but I cannot think of what these could possibly be." The glow went out.

Nadya was ready for this. "In 1,000 years there'll be the final Thith-Human war." Almost imperceptibly, Kanend'ra nodded. "Two generations after that another will be fought, only this war will be with a different species, and its outcome determines your survival."

The flash of bright red light seemed to propel Kanend'ra backward. "What war is it that you speak of?"

"The one with a species that, like humans, you engineered to be a warrior race, but who rebelled against you. They know about that," Nadya pointed at the luminous red crystal behind the blue being, "and they know whoever controls that, controls the entire galaxy."

Kanend'ra said nothing for a moment, and when she finally spoke her glow become a meager pink hue. "But I can't fathom—how can we possibly help each other?"

"I need to be here when this war takes place," Nadya told her, "but as we both know, you engineered us to be a short-lived species."

"Yes, I did, but how do you think that I can reverse your biology?"

Nadya walked over to the stalagmite and said over her shoulder, "In there." She made fists to keep her hands from trembling. "You can place me inside, and I'll return when the time of the Ulfen war is upon us."

Kanend'ra was completely taken aback and momentarily flashed red again before the light went out completely. "Your request is to be entombed inside the Ramm'r crystal for 1,000 years. You do realize that this is special crystal? It contains infinite energy. The galaxy's biggest supply is here on Log'rfold."

"Ah yes, the name you've given this planet," stated Nadya.

"It is. I know your species calls it Aqueous," Kanend'ra explained, "but we've been here for hundreds of thousands of years."

Nadya decided it was time to reveal more of her knowledge. "And your race is called Normad'r."

"We are, and this galaxy is our empire."

"Except where this rebellious species has gained control."

Kanend'ra made a slight bow. "The Ulfen, and you are quite correct, but why do you feel they're a threat here on Log'rfold?"

"Because I've seen the war," answered the prophetess, "and like yourselves, I know they're coming." Nadya again pointed at the crystal. "For that. You need humans to fight them. Otherwise you'll lose this planet. If you lose this planet, you lose your empire. If you lose your empire, you'll—"

"Go extinct." The Normad'r finished the human's thought.

"And therein lies the basis for our mutual need."

"While I can't confirm or deny your supposition," commented Kanend'ra, "I will take it under advisement. And this why you believe we need you?"

"Not believe. Know. Without me, your chance of garnering Earth's help is zero."

"And you will guarantee their help? Will they listen to you?"

"Not me, but another member of my family is the key to both the survival of humanity on Aqueous," she spread her arms and made the correction, "Log'rfold, and the key to saving your galactic empire."

"Who is this family member?" asked the Normad'r.

"A seventh-generation male from Earth."

"Earth?" Kanend'ra questioned. "Earth has been destroyed."

"Not completely. My family, my progeny, survived and will produce a direct descendant more powerful than any human before him." Nadya felt a trace of satisfaction as she noted Kanend'ra's blue flash of surprise. "It seems as though the evolutionary gene you instilled in my family isn't finished yet. He'll arrive in 1,000 years, and I need to be here when he does."

"Very well, Spak'rna of Earth, I will help in your return."

"In there?" Nadya asked, pointing at the red stalagmite.

"Yes, it will keep your consciousness alive for the required time."

"And my body?"

"I cannot say," answered Kanend'ra. "I have no data on which to base such a conclusion. Do you still want to proceed?"

"Yes, I'm ready," Nadya said with more confidence than she felt.

The Normad'r nodded, and slowly waved her delicate hand toward the stalagmite. "Embrace the crystal and allow it to consume you. You must accept it with every aspect of your being. Hold nothing back."

Nadya stepped forward and placed her hands on the warm crystal. Within seconds its light and heat increased. It burned her flesh, her blood, her soul, but still she hung on. The hard crystal grew soft, pliable. Nadya felt her body being absorbed—every facet of her being becoming one with its matrix.

She became entombed. She became enabled. All the visions of her life flooded back into her consciousness, but they seemed minuscule, almost nonexistent by comparison to what she saw now. The universe, multiple universes opened up to her. She suddenly became aware of the entire spectrum of life everywhere it existed. Life was infinite.

Nadya was now irreversibly linked with the Ramm'r crystal, and the crystal was linked to infinity.

Kanend'ra waited until Nadya's meld into the Ramm'r was complete, and then she too disappeared.

A shadow appeared above the shaft. Rodinya gracefully glided down to where her mother waited, but when she landed no one was there. The lair was empty. But it was warmer than before, and that warmth came from the red pillar. The dragon cautiously approached it and looked inside, trying to see something, anything, but there was nothing. She lay down, curling her body around the crystal, and squeezed tight.

Sadness washed over the young dragon as she lay next to the pillar. Rodinya tucked her head under a wing and softly cried, *"I'll be a good girl, Mother. I'll earn the faith you placed in me. I listened, I learned, and from this moment on, I'll watch the stars for his arrival, and if I must—I'll watch forever."*

End

PROLOGUE: ENDEAVOR'S RUN

MESSAGE SENT
MAGELLAN II—AQUEOUS—ORBIT DAY 11
AD 2110

There were no victors, nor vanquished, in the eternal war between land and sea. It was a bloodless conflict that had never produced a casualty until today.

For millennia, a wall of giant crystal shards stood an unyielding vigil at the battle line: a small stretch of coastline on the watery world of Aqueous. Century after century these sentinels had held firm against the ocean's relentless assault. Murderous waves broke against the jagged columns, and died in a frothy spray, giving life to the warm swash that gently caressed the unconscious man bleeding out at the waters edge. Crimson rivulets of his blood turned pink as they diluted and soaked into the wet sand.

Though the Earthling had only moments to live, fate decreed that he would not die alone. A giant dragon towered over him spewing a white-hot jet of flame that blasted a dozen meters in the air. After a few seconds the flame died out and the dragon craned its long muscular neck downward so that its open mouth hovered a mere meter over the unmoving man. Steam rose off the viscous red liquid that dripped from the dragon's carnassial teeth and bathed the man's body just as its jaws were about to engulf him. But there was a third being present as well, someone who had watched this perpetual spectacle uncountable times throughout her life.

The constant witness.

Looking down from her disembodied state, the woman was unable to tear her eyes away from what the dragon was doing to the man. This was a reoccurring scene, one she'd seen many times in her life, more than any other vision. But it had never been like this before—never this vivid nor palpable.

She watched transfixed as the dragon suddenly tensed, flicking tiny droplets of water off its golden hide, and lifted its gaping red drenched maw away from the dying man. The creature seemed to sense her presence, and slowly turned its reptilian head until it faced her. Its eyes; green with red viper pupils narrowed with recognition as they bore directly into hers. The woman was shocked beyond comprehension; how could it possibly know she was there?

This too had never happened before.

A voice—she was certain it came from the dragon—strong and resolute, suddenly entered her head, *'Please, Mother. You must hurry. Everything depends on your message.'* Its fierce unblinking gaze lingered a moment before turning back to the blood stained sand, and then, with unexpected gentleness, the dragon picked up the mortally wounded man, leapt into the air, and flew towards the human colony.

'Mother?' Why did it call her that? What could that possibly mean? The dragon's words—especially its tone, sounded literal, but that was impossible. The bond between mother and child was the strongest among all life forms in the universe, and, like the injured man, the woman was a human born on Earth.

But this was not Earth.

Even more disturbing than the dragon's words was the voice it used to speak them, a voice she found hauntingly familiar.

Because it was her own.

Doctor Nadezhda Yanbeyeva gasped for breath as she bolted awake, heart pounding, and kicked off the damp sheets that clung to her legs. The nightly vision had hit her hard again, but it was much different than ever before; this time it interacted with her. Nadya gripped the edge of her bunk, and shook her head to clear it from the fog of sleep. How could she possibly interpret this? How was it that an entity from a vision so far in the future could acknowledge her?

It took a moment, but as her mind became focused an unsettling clarity slowly replaced her confusion, and the dragon's words began to make sense. If taken at face value they could only mean one thing; a warning; 'You must hurry'. Nadya groaned with understanding, pushed the sweat-darkened blonde tendrils away from her face, and scrambled out of bed. In her rush to don her uniform, a slight groan of frustration escaped her throat, because she knew the dragon's warning meant that there was little time left to carry out the most important moment of her life; the event she had been born to do. She hurried to begin the process that would result in a man of her bloodline leading humanity during their most desperate hour.

A thousand years in the future.

An hour later she and her husband, Sasha, were in the launch bay preparing a drone for its return mission to Earth. The Earth she alone knew no longer existed.

While Sasha retrieved the override program he'd buried deep in the starships database, he glanced at his wife. "Tell me more about this dream," he asked, and then dropped his voice. "Sorry, you know I meant 'vision.'"

Ignoring his entreaty she pushed hard to complete her task. "I'll explain later, Sasha, but we must launch now!"

"Alright Nadya, but I still can't access the catapult system. My override is limited," he told her as he finalized the drone's flight plan. "You do realize that without the catapult the drone's small EMD will take almost one hundred years to reach Earth," he explained while initiating the launch sequence, "and besides, your message isn't uploaded yet."

"It doesn't matter. I'll upload it after it's too late to retrieve. Now launch!"

He tapped on the Nav-Screen. An electronic alarm sounded just as the airlock doors opened, and the drone was flung into space. "It's away, Nadya," said the worried man. "I hope we don't end up in the brig."

"Hush, Moozh, while I send the message."

"Captain Troy," yelled the star ships navigation officer from across the arkship's bridge, "a communication drone has just launched."

"What? I haven't authorized this!" The captain jumped out of his control chair and ran over to the navigation console. "How was it accessed?"

"Sir, there seems to be a remote override installed from the launch bay itself."

"Retrieve it now!"

The navigation officer frantically tapped his keyboard for a few seconds, then stopped, turned and told his captain, "I can't, Sir. The override has locked out this console."

"Damn it to hell," growled the captain of the Magellan II. "Can you at least access the message it's carrying?"

"Yes, Sir. I still have telemetry function." A slight frown creased the officer's brow. "That's odd. There's no message aboard—wait! A message is being uploaded now."

"Cut it off. Cut it the hell off now!

———————————————

"Nadya, the bridge cut off your feed." Sasha looked over at his wife even more worried than before. "I don't think all of it made it."

"I know, but hopefully it was enough. God help them all if it wasn't."

ABOUT THE AUTHOR

Author Tobin Marks has masterfully created an alien watery world called Aqueous. Orbiting a Red Dwarf 1187 light years from Earth, Aqueous is teeming with dangerous reptilian life...and one long forgotten human colony.

Marks is a world traveler who grew up in a household of rocket scientists. As a boy he had a front row seat observing many NASA and NOAA projects. Now from his home in north west Baja he has written the trilogy: The Hope Prophecy. Book one: Endeavors Run, is a blend of real science, science fiction, and fantasy. Book two: Katana Red, and book three: Drakon Rus, are exciting continuations of the series.

He has released the action packed prequel: Ark of the Apocalypse published by Boyle & Dalton, and is now working on the second trilogy: The Hope Progression.

www.ingramcontent.com/pod-product-compliance
Lightning Source LLC
Chambersburg PA
CBHW051933240626
47153CB00005B/1476